D0030047

# Lawrence Sanders

# Love Songs

BERKLEY BOOKS, NEW YORK

This Berkley book contains the complete
text of the original hardcover edition.
It has been completely reset in a typeface
designed for easy reading and was printed
from new film.

LOVE SONGS

A Berkley Book/published by arrangement with
the author

PRINTING HISTORY
G. P. Putnam's edition published 1972
Dell edition/July 1973
Berkley edition/January 1989

ISBN: 0-425-11273-X

A BERKLEY BOOK ® TM 757,375
Berkley Books are published by The Berkley Publishing Group,
200 Madison Avenue, New York, NY 10016.
The name "BERKLEY" and the "B" logo
are trademarks belonging to Berkley Publishing Corporation.

PRINTED IN THE UNITED STATES OF AMERICA

10  9  8  7  6  5  4  3  2  1

# LOVE SONGS

---

# 1

There were two blasts of a horn; the bus from the airport came down Main Street and rolled to a stop in front of the post office. Peas of rain trembled on the bus roof and wrinkled down the sides: tears on dusty cheeks. The single streetlight, orange and dim, reflected back from fogged windows.

The bus door slammed open. He came slowly down the steps: a dreamer. He looked around, mouth slack and eyeballs rolling. The colored driver followed, went to the side of the bus and unlocked the luggage space. He pulled out two suitcases, and two suitcases, and two suitcases. He stacked them neatly on the wet sidewalk.

"My baby don' care for clothes," the dreamer crooned softly. A soiled raincoat hung armless on his shoulders.

She followed, finally; something silvery and bright about her. She glimmered in the mist.

She moved her head toward the driver.

"Catch Rastus," she growled.

The dreamer handed over a bill. The Negro slid it into his pocket without looking at it. His eyes fed on the woman.

"Will you sing for me again?" he asked.

"Loser," she jeered.

The two, man and woman, stood quietly alongside their luggage. The driver stepped back into the bus and closed the door. The engine coughed to life; the bus pulled away. They watched red taillights dwindle down the darkened street. There was a single horn blast, echoing and mournful.

Then the exhaust fumes thinned away; they could smell the sea.

"Snakes in Paradise," she said.

"Vipers in Eden," he said.

"You've been reading books again," she accused. "Harvard freak," she scoffed.

They stood there calmly, waiting, secure in their isolation.

A heavy figure came around the corner of the post office. They watched him approach.

"Welcome home," he said to the woman.

She looked at him a long moment. He saw pearls of drizzle on her false eyelashes.

"Hello, Len," she said finally. "I've missed you."

"Ben."

"Hello, Ben," she said. "I've missed you."

He moved his head back in a silent laugh. He picked up three suitcases, tucking the smallest under one thick arm.

"This way. I've got a station wagon."

The windshield wipers went "Woosh-*wheesh,* woosh-*wheesh.*"

"Nice tempo," the dreamer said. He began to sing in a high, papery voice: "Don't you woosh the worst for me when I wheesh the best for you."

"No cigar," the silver woman said. "Ben, this ghost is Hapgood Graves. He's my accompanist and arranger. You can call him Hap, but he hates to be called Happy. Isn't that right, Happy?"

"That's right, mom," he said agreeably.

"Hap, this is Benjamin Todd. Old-friend-of-the-family type. He's a doctor."

"Listen, doc," Graves muttered, staring straight ahead, "I've been suffering from these hemidemisemiquavers."

Her name was Roberta Vanderhorst, but she used the professional name of Bobbie Vander. She had silver-blond-white hair, very fine and cut short. It was a Boy Scout's haircut, parted on the left, plastered flat to her skull.

They turned off the paved highway, headed toward the sea on a graveled road.

"How's the Patroon?" she asked.

"As well as can be expected."

"And mother's condition is 'satisfactory'?" she mocked.

"Yes."

"Thank you, doctor. Your bedside manner is underwhelming."

He slowed coming up the driveway, then stopped the car under the portico of a white gingerbread house. A porch light was on, misty in the rain. A monument was planted there, leaning on a cane.

"That old son of a bitch," Bobbie said admiringly.

Pieter Vanderhorst had been hacked out of flint, quartz, granite; chiseled from a mountain. But there had been a rumbling deep in the earth, a shift along a vertical fault.

From forehead, face, chest, torso, to leg and foot, the stroke had displaced the mountain half an inch. The left side hung: bulging eye, drooping lip, cramped arm, useless leg.

She flung out of the car, leaped up the steps, clasped him in her arms.

"Patroon," she said, kissing that wet, limp left side of his mouth. "Marry me."

He clamped her close with his good right arm. Slowly his eyes hooded; heavy shutters came grinding down.

"Daughter," he said thickly.

They gave Hapgood Graves a bedroom on the third floor, below the eaves. Tom Drinkwater carried the single suitcase. He switched on the light. The first thing Graves saw was an old-fashioned four-bladed electric fan hanging from the center of the ceiling.

"Bathroom?" he asked the boy.

"End of the hall. South end."

"To the left?"

"No. To the right."

"Anyone else on this floor?"

"My mother's room. North end. She's the housekeeper here. I got a room across the hall from you. Sam Lees—he's the caretaker—he's down the hall. The other rooms are empty. I mean they got furniture, but there's no one in them."

Graves stared at him. The boy returned his look steadily.

"You an Indian?" Graves asked finally.

"Yes."

"What tribe?"

"Ikantos."

"Ikantos? Never heard of them."

"We used to own all this land. All along here. As far south as Massachusetts and as far north as New Brunswick. We were part of the Iroquois Nation."

"Ikantos," Graves repeated. "Many of you left?"

"No," the boy said. "Not many."

When he was gone, Graves saw a handsome brass bolt on the inside of the door. He moved it slowly into its socket. Then he tried the door. It was solid.

The walls were white, the iron bedstead painted white. The bed was covered with a white quilt. There was a small wicker desk, a wicker straight chair, a wicker armchair: all painted white. An oval mirror with a white frame.

The floor was pegged hardwood in random widths,

waxed to a high gloss. The room smelled faintly of must and lemon. Graves held his right hand out in front of him, fingers spread. It was beginning to tremble.

There was a white dresser, a white drysink lined with copper. In the sink was a white porcelain pitcher and a bowl. They were crackled. The pitcher was filled with water. A dead mosquito floated on the surface.

"Hello, me," Graves said aloud.

He opened the window, pushed it creaking up. A morbid wind blew in from the sea; the long white curtains signaled. He could hear the smash of surf and smell the salt. It was still raining, but clouds were shredding. There was a moon.

He undressed slowly, sitting on the bed to pull off socks and shoes. He opened his suitcase and dug under clothes to find a little silver filagree pillbox. He put it on the wicker bedside table.

He switched off the light and moved naked to the open window. The night reached for his skin and touched him.

He leaned forward to stare out. He saw a specter float from the house down to the sea. Silver hair shone in the moonlight. Bobbie Vander was wearing a white robe. It was silk with streamers, all waving out behind her.

"Snakes and vipers," he murmured.

He watched as she drifted across the lawn, through a copse of scraggly trees, over the dunes, onto a narrow beach. She flew in moonglow, all of her glinting.

She waded into the sea until surf licked her smooth legs. She bent to scoop up milk froth and let it tinkle from her fingertips. She moved back and forth in the surf; then staggered as a wave hurled to embrace her. The thin gown plastered flesh, and she spread her legs wide and looked down. The sea lapped up.

Graves shut his eyes. He stood a moment, then turned away from the open window. He found towels in the

cupboard beneath the drysink and took a small handtowel.
He peeled quilt and comforter off the bed.

Lying naked on the rough sheet, he propped pillows
behind his head so he could look down at his ravaged body.
It gleamed pale in nightlight. It was all bone, tendon,
swollen blue veins: a waste of a body.

He took a pinch of white powder from the filagree
pillbox. He took a sniff for each nostril, then lay back on the
doubled pillows. He smiled to see his stiff straining for the
moon.

He stared at himself for five minutes. Or was it an hour?
He stroked his shiny shaft lightly—only twice. Then he was
sea and surf, surging. He was pounding up between
Bobbie's hairless thighs.

Sighing . . . Sighing . . .

Until he could sleep.

---2---

When Pieter Vanderhorst was brought home from the
hospital in South Canaan, recovering from the stroke Dr.
Benjamin Todd was certain would have shattered a lesser
man, Todd said to him: "Patroon, you will be chained to a
wheelchair for the rest of your life."

He knew Vanderhorst was knotty enough to take such a
harsh assessment.

The Patroon described exactly the kind of wheelchair he
wanted. Not one of those aluminum, steel, and plastic
things. He demanded a chair in bentwood, infinitely

adjustable. With a cane seat and wood handwheels mounted outside the rubber tires.

They found a chair like that in an antique shop in New Hampshire. Grace Vanderhorst spent a month making a nice cushion for him. The Patroon tried it once, then threw it across the room. He sat on the cane seat.

But it made no difference. He was harder than even Todd had judged. Within a month he was on his feet and moving about with a heavy blackthorn cane, sent for by mail to a store in New York City called Uncle Sam's Umbrella Shop. But he still used the bentwood wheelchair as an easy chair. He liked it: to rest in and to read in. It fitted him. And he had conquered it.

Julie Vanderhorst, the older daughter, suggested they convert the downstairs sitting room of their summer home into a bedroom for her father. She had worked it out logically.

"Patroon," she said, "there's no point in your climbing stairs a dozen times a day. We can move the sitting-room furniture up to the third floor and bring down a bed and enough furniture to make you comfortable. The sitting room faces the sea, and you'll have the sun. It's closer to the kitchen, and Mrs. Rebecca will have an easier time in case you want a late snack or breakfast in bed or something like that. You'll be by yourself, and away from the noise upstairs. The French doors open onto the porch and you can sit out there when you like. I think you should move downstairs."

"No," he said.

So he slept on the second floor in the master bedroom. He slept with his wife, as a man should. He dragged himself up and down the wide staircase, scorning the banister.

It was a suite: big bedroom, bathroom, a smaller attached room where his wife sewed. It was on the sea side, and the rooms were clean and spare. There were chintz curtains and seat cushions, and on the wall was the original Vanderhorst grant. It was faint now and stained; signed by George III.

On the mantel over the fireplace were a few handcarved bird decoys, pitted and elegant. And over the mantel was an oil portrait of Theodore Roosevelt in Army uniform. He was wearing steel-rimmed spectacles and a campaign hat pinned up on one side.

Grace Vanderhorst was a sparrow. A month after their marriage the Patroon realized he had wed a silly woman. But he was willing to endure the consequences of his bad judgment.

He learned that physical contact was distasteful to her. She kissed him on the cheek. Occasionally she picked up his hand and kissed it. But he had insisted on two children, convinced he could beget only sons. She bore him two daughters. He hid his disappointment.

Still, there was the one big bed. He gave not a damn what she thought of his great, shifted body. It was all hairy: hard and firm on one side, soft and slack on the other. He was two men.

Grace had thin, frizzy white hair. It was covered, sometimes, with wigs, blue, pink, gray, strawberry. She called them transformations. She was immaculately clean and wore frilly things. She chirped incessantly. . . .

". . . think it is right? I, for one, Mister Vanderhorst, do not. She travels all over the nation with him, exhibiting herself in public. They stay at the same hotel and . . . do you think the pink thread would be best for the trim on this guest towel, or the blue?"

He raised his massive head.

"The blue."

"I am sure Roberta has never done a wrong thing in her life—but still . . . appearances. They mean so much. What did you think of him?"

"Roberta says he writes poetry."

"Mrs. Rebecca found some beautiful strawberries today. Did I tell you? She is soaking them in wine and brandy, and they should be just right for breakfast. Just the two of them, traveling all over the country. I realize she is very popular, although, in all honesty, I must tell you I prefer Galli-Curci. So thin. Isn't she thin, Mister Vanderhorst?"

"Galli-Curci?"

"But I'll put weight on her. I'll fatten her up. Did you have the piano tuned, dear?"

"I told you. Last week. Isaac Beemis came over from Gresham. He says the instrument is warped. The sea air. But he did what he could."

"He seems such a nice boy. So innocent. Do you think he'll like French toast?"

"Why not? He writes poetry, doesn't he?"

"I'll tell Mrs. Rebecca. French toast and perhaps some of those little pork sausages. How is your leg tonight?"

"How is your wrist?"

"Swollen and throbbing. You really must speak to her."

"She goes her own way."

"Or perhaps pancakes. What do you think, dear? Love songs? Isn't that what she said?"

"Yes. His poems set to music which he will write and she will sing. It will be a phonograph record."

"No, I think French toast. Benjamin's daughter doesn't want to go to college. Did I tell you?"

"Yes."

"She wants to take a year off. To think things over, she said. Are you listening?"

"I am listening."

"I do hope this rain doesn't finish the Herbert Hoovers completely. Susan is a dear, sweet girl, and I love her as my own daughters, but she is a willful girl. Although when you consider that her mother simply signed her away, you can . . . Perhaps bacon instead of the pork sausages. What do you think, Mister Vanderhorst?"

Having patience where she was concerned, he let her prattle on. He grunted when required. Finally she put her sewing aside, turned out the lights. She undressed in the darkness.

She put on her light flannel nightgown. She climbed into bed alongside him. She kissed him on his good cheek.

"Good night, father," she said. "Sleep well."

But he did not.

------ **3** ------

Julie Vanderhorst's bedroom was on the second floor, on the land side. It was an enormous room of doors; to hall, bathroom, closets, porch. There were two brass bedsteads and a Victorian loveseat in faded rose velvet. The wood was cherry.

Roberta Vanderhorst came in, dripping, laughing, and exalted.

"My God"—Julie looked at her admiringly—"you're soaked. Wasn't it cold?"

"The greatest douche in the world." Bobbie laughed. "The whole Atlantic."

"I'll get you some hot tea."

"Forget it. I feel great. Oh, was that great! I haven't been in the sea in years. I'll just towel off."

She went into the bathroom. Julie continued to lay out her

game of solitaire. When Bobbie came out of the bathroom, naked, her sister didn't look at her. She pulled on a faded cotton robe. Julie sat back, lighted a cigarette.

The older Vanderhorst daughter was a plump woman. She had wide hips and heavy thighs with patches of brown up near the crotch. Her breasts were large and veined. Her beautiful hair was sheer. It was cut to her shoulders and curled under: a burnished casque.

Bobbie came over to brush cheeks with her sister.

"Good, good, good," she said. "So good. Sweetie, you're fat."

"I know, I know," Julie said sorrowfully. "How the hell do you do it?"

"Almost two hundred and fifty one-night stands and concerts last year. Who had time to eat? We kept going on pills and yogurt. Made a lot of money. But we're drained. Both of us. We really need this."

"But you're going to work?"

"Fun work. We've got this contract for an album. Hap's love poems set to music. Me singing. He's got most of them done. A lot of nice stuff. We'll need about fifteen songs. Rehearse up here, then go back to New York to record. Meanwhile we'll eat and swim and soak up some sun. God bless the Patroon."

She sat down opposite her sister and crossed her legs. The robe fell open. She began to file her nails.

"What about the doctor? Anything doing?"

"I wish, I wish," Julie said, laying out her cards. "Sometimes I think and sometimes I don't. He's been divorced over a year now."

"Make it with him yet?"

"No."

"Like him?"

"Yes."

"*Why*, for Chrissakes? The man's a lump. On the drive in he hardly said word one."

"Well, I like him. He's very—he reminds me of the Patroon."

"The Patroon?"

"In a lot of ways. The ways he moves. He's quiet and—you know, solid. Very masculine."

"No one's like the Patroon."

"Ben is. You'll see. He's a young Patroon."

"And you're full of shit. How do you get along with his kid?"

"Susan? She thinks I'm a cow. I am a cow."
Bobbie looked up.

"So? Knock off the martinis. Get a waist. You can do it. Look at this . . ."

She stood suddenly and whipped open her robe. She was displayed: bony pelvis, no breasts, wispy turf, thin arms and legs. She was a female boy.

"Remember?" she said softly.

"Yes," Julie said, going back to her solitaire.

---

**4**

---

South of the Vanderhorst mansion was a strip of lawn, some sand, a screen of trees. Then more sand, a narrow lawn, and the summer home of Dr. Benjamin Todd.

He lay on a plastic-covered couch in the living room,

wearing a cotton T-shirt and Bermuda shorts in a Black Watch tartan. His hairy legs and feet were bare. There was a bottle of California port on the cocktail table and a half-filled glass. He was reading an account of the mutiny aboard the British brig *Briarley*, in "Naval Trials of the Eighteenth Century" by Sir Wm. C. B. Everest-Brixton. It was a good read, and he was enjoying it.

When Susan came in, he turned his head and took off his glasses. She was wearing blue baby-doll pajamas. There was a Band-Aid on her left knee.

"My God," he said, "aren't you asleep?"

"What's she like?"

"Very thin. Elegant. Silver hair combed short. Very sure of herself. You'll meet her tomorrow."

"I like her records."

"I know."

"What's *he* like?"

"The piano player?" He shrugged. "There's something wrong there."

"What?"

"I don't know. His eyes . . . Something . . ."

She would be eighteen in another month. She wasn't beautiful, but her face was open and pleasing. She had a splendid sun-browned body; bleached fuzz on her arms, legs and the small of her back glinted in the sun.

"I got a letter from mother today," she told him.

"How is she?"

"Okay. She says to say hello to you."

"Hello."

"I think she'd like to come back."

"Mmm." He nodded, going back to the mutiny on the British brig *Briarley*.

"Don't you want her back?"

He closed the book, sat up and looked at her. "No. Do you, Susan?"

"No. I want it like this. Just you and me."

She vibrated. He blinked his eyes at the sun-burned radiance.

---

# 5

Mrs. Rebecca Drinkwater was wearing a nightgown made from an unbleached muslin sheet that had worn thin. It was really a poncho with a hole cut for her head. A strip of hem served as a loose belt. She was squatting on her haunches in the center of her bedroom. The door was locked; a dim bedside lamp tinted the room.

Her mouth was moving, and a rhythmic hum came out of her. In both hands she shook a buckskin bag with a drawstring top. Her knees were spread wide. She was not a young woman but felt no strain on the muscles of her thighs. She crouched comfortably on her hams, droning and shaking the skin bag.

She opened the string, spilled the chicken bones onto the bare floor. There they lay: leg bones, wing bones, a breast, all old and whitened. There was one black stone among them and one chipped shell. She stared at the pattern they made, poked the pile of bones with her finger. Then suddenly she swept them rattling away to the dark corners of the room.

# 6

Samuel Lees crouched in the screen of trees between the Vanderhorst and Todd homes. Surplus army field glasses were pressed tightly against his eyes.

He watched the bedroom window of Susan Todd. She went into the bathroom to undress, and he mumbled. When she came out, she was wearing blue baby-doll pajamas. She went downstairs. A few moments later she came up to her bedroom and turned off the light.

Lees urinated against the base of a Chinese ginkgo tree.

# 7

Hapgood Graves woke suddenly. His lids flicked open, eyes on that big fan hanging from the ceiling. He hadn't covered himself during the night; quilt and comforter were still on the floor. He went over to the window. White mist steamed off the sea, and the sun was a blur in a muslin sky. Fog was curling around trees, painting the house with bubbles.

Another day, he smiled. I made it again.

He pulled on a robe and straw slippers. He took his toilet case, went shuffling down to the bathroom at the south end of the hall. The bathroom was all right, old-fashioned but all right. To flush the toilet, you pulled a brass chain hanging from a tank on the wall.

He brushed his teeth, showered and shaved. He drank a glass of water. It was flat, with a taste of sulfur.

Back in his room he pulled on a pair of new white jeans. He had to take off the price tag and size tag. He wore no underwear. When he pulled up the pants, he got his hair caught in the zipper for an agonized moment. He said, "Come *on.*"

He laced a pair of soiled sneakers over bare feet and buttoned into a short-sleeved white shirt, letting the tails hang outside. The fog was in the room, and his skin was damp.

He went padding down through the quiet house, though once he heard a brief snore coming from somewhere. He found the kitchen. There was a sturdy woman in there, working at the stove. She turned slowly when he came in and looked at him.

I'm never going to lie to her, he thought suddenly. Because she'll know.

"Good morning," he said with a tight smile. "My name is Hapgood Graves. I came with Bobbie last night. You're . . . ?"

"Mrs. Rebecca Drinkwater. Breakfast in an hour. Coffee now?"

"Yes. Please."

She sat him at one end of the big wooden worktable and poured coffee from a blue enameled pot. It poured like tar.

He tasted it and knew it had been boiled. He waved away cream and sugar. The coffee was adrenaline; his eyes bulged.

"Best coffee I ever tasted," he said bravely.

She didn't answer. She was dipping slices of bread in beaten egg.

He saw her in profile: a hawk cast in bronze. She would swoop down on him, pick up his soft white body in her talons. Then she would fly away with him to a mountaintop. She would look at him for a while. Then she would peck at him.

"Thank you for the coffee," he said.

She nodded and he noticed her marvelous legs.

He wandered around the lazy first floor: dining room, sitting room, living room, library. That's where the piano was—in the library. It was a Steinway, 1890.

"Jesus," he said aloud, and didn't try it.

He went back through the hallway, out the door and down the steps on the land side. He circled the house. Off to the left was a tool hut. Rippled steel plates were painted green. It was a neat shed, surrounded by potted geraniums.

In front, seated on a wooden crate, was Tom Drinkwater. He was naked to the waist, his faded blue jeans were ripped off above the knees. His feet were bare. Sleek black hair fell to his shoulders. He had a cold face, a hard, dark body.

God, I'll bet he's hung, Graves thought enviously.

The boy was working with a jackknife on a cylindrical log, bark encrusted, about one foot long, six inches in diameter. He was hollowing it out, working slowly. He was cutting away, making a tube.

"Morning," Graves said.

The boy looked up. "Good morning, sir."

Sir, Graves thought. Next is Pop.

He watched the boy whittle. Flakes of the seasoned wood fell to the cropped lawn.

He could resist no longer: "What's that going to be?"

"A drum."

"You're going to hollow it through?"

"Yes."

"Couldn't you use an electric drill?"

The Indian boy paused but didn't glance up.

"I could buy a drum."

Graves wanted to laugh but couldn't.

"What about the skins?" he asked.

"I've got a couple of rabbits curing," the boy said.

"For both ends?"

"One till I hear how it sounds. Then maybe both ends."

"How did you learn to do this?"

"I read it in a book," Tom Drinkwater said, slowly carving away. "In the county historical society they got books on the Ikantos. How they lived and the things they made. This is how they made their drums. They used sharp stones until the white man came. Then they used iron knives. The drums that were covered with skin on one end were called *ipi*. The ones that had skin on both ends were called *tani*."

"The *tani* had a deeper tone. A booming tone."

"Yes," the boy said wonderingly. "How did you know?"

"I'm a musician."

"Oh, sure. I forgot."

"How are you going to fasten the skins to the ends?"

"Hi, Geronimo," a girl sang. "Let's swim."

She was skimmed with that pearly morning fog. Once the bikini had been brown. Now it was faded and she was naked. She burst, poking. Everything about her was ripe.

The Indian boy leaped to his feet. Log, knife, shavings spilled to the lawn.

"Hi, Susan," he said. Love and longing. "Sure. Swim."

She turned slowly to look at Graves.

How am I going to do it? he wondered. I am going to do it, but how am I going to do it?

"Hi." She smiled. "I'm Susan. I belong to Doctor Todd. You must be Hapgood Graves."

"That's right." He nodded. "I belong to Bobbie Vander."

They laughed. The Indian boy looked away.

"I love her singing. I have all her albums. Do you write her songs?"

"Not all of them. Some of them."

"They're very good."

"Damned right." He nodded.

She laughed again. "Listen. Tom and I are going swimming. Want to come?"

"Want to but can't. I didn't bring any trunks."

"I'd offer you a pair of Dad's, but you'd fall right through. You're a skinny one."

He liked sassy young girls.

"Dad's driving in after breakfast. I can ask him to pick you up a pair at Baumgartner's. That's our local Macy's. What size do you wear?"

"Thirty-two, or small."

"What color would you like? Polka dots?"

"Dollar signs on a light-green background."

They both laughed again. Tom Drinkwater started down toward the sea. She followed after him.

"See you," she called, turning to flip a hand at him.

He watched that ass go away from him. It was tanned and solid. How am I going to do it?

By the time he got to the shore they were both in the sea, stroking strongly. They were almost lost in the mist. He turned, trudged up the beach, cursing his body. Had he ever been young?

Pieter Vanderhorst and Samuel Lees sat at opposite ends

of the long worktable in the kitchen. Both were sipping coffee. Lees cradled his cup in two hands. Vanderhorst held his in his steady right hand.

Mrs. Drinkwater moved easily back and forth between stove and sink. She was barefoot. Her big brown feet splatted down on the worn linoleum.

"I'm going to cut them roses back," Lees said. "If it's all right with the missus. They're gone for the year. That rain yesterday finished them."

"Cut them back," Vanderhorst ordered.

"You know where the driveway comes in from the road? That culvert there is caving. Now is that ours or is that the county's?"

Vanderhorst lowered his head. He wasn't going, but since his stroke it took him a while to marshal his mind. He had to drive it.

"That's the county's," he said finally. "But no use waiting for them. It'll never get done this year."

Samuel Lees nodded. "It'll never get done," he agreed. "Now I can clean it out and put a brace in there to hold it over the winter. If you say so, Patroon."

"Yes. I say so. By next spring maybe I can get the county to replace it. All along there. My place and Todd's and the Breckinridge home and the Semanskis'. All along. The whole thing must be caving."

"That's right, Patroon. You get them to do something. Now, God damn it, we pay our taxes."

He rose and wiped a palm across his bristly chops.

"Now I'll get going," he said. "Mrs. Becky, I'll be up for breakfast. I'll have it in here and then I'll run out again."

She was silent, moving steadily.

When he had gone she came over with the coffee pot, poured the Patroon another full cup. She stood alongside him, on his right side.

He let his good arm dangle. He grasped her hard, rounded calf and stroked. She made a noise. He moved his hand up under the skirt of her thin cotton dress. His hand was warm from his coffee cup. He looked up at her, and she looked down at him. She moved her legs apart slightly. He clutched her and could feel her heat, her wet.

She began to quiver—a stroked horse.

"Soon," he said. "Today. Tomorrow."

They were like that when Grace Vanderhorst came in. She saw but she did not see.

"*Good* morning, all," she sang brightly. "What a beautiful, beautiful day! This haze will burn off by noon. You mark my words. And then it will be sunshiny. Mrs. Rebecca, have you seen my sewing box?"

"In the sewing room," Mrs. Drinkwater said. She moved slowly to the stove.

"Of course." Grace smiled. She opened the door of the big refrigerator, popped a strawberry into her mouth. "Oh, my! Isn't that nice. Did you sleep well, dear? Roberta and Julie are still beddy-bye, but I knocked on their door. Now what must I do to help? Let me see . . . Oh, everything is ready. Well, then. I'll just set the table."

"It's set," Mrs. Drinkwater said.

"Oh. Well, then. I'll just see how the flowers came through the rain. Perhaps a few forsythia branches in the cut-glass vase. Wouldn't that be nice, dear?"

"Yes."

She came over to kiss his right cheek.

"Did you sleep well?" she asked again, then swept out without waiting for an answer.

He looked at the empty doorway. Mrs. Drinkwater said nothing.

Susan Todd and Tom Drinkwater came plunging out of the surf. They were young seals, streaming, gasping and coughing. They staggered up to dry sand, threw themselves down on their backs. Sand stuck to them, but they didn't care. They lay there sneezing, sand getting in their long hair. They drummed their heels and squirmed their buttocks. They spread arms and legs to the molten sun, getting comfortable, laughing.

"Listen," Tom Drinkwater said. "You like him?"

She punched his ribs with a hard fist. "He's pale and funny and skinny."

He flopped over on his stomach, moved close to her. He took dry sand between his fingers: a little pile of sand. He drifted it down into her navel. When her navel was filled with dry, hot sand, he smoothed it over with a gentle finger.

"Do you love him?"

Her head moved. Faded blue eyes stared at him gravely.

"Tom, you're such a child."

"I'm sixteen."

"And I'm eighteen. Practically. Women mature much faster than men. That's well known. To me, you're a child."

"I love you," he cried hopelessly.

She stopped looking at him. She stared at the sky. It was beginning to shine: hard glaze. She closed her eyes. "Idiot."

He propped himself on his elbow, looked down at her, touched her hair. It was lank with sun, sand, sea. Around the edges of her shrunken bikini the tanned skin was white, a narrow trim of white. Salt was drying on her in patches of stain. Golden fuzz on arms and legs glinted, and heat came from her. He could feel it.

"Do you watch me at night?" she asked suddenly, eyes still closed. "Do you hide in the trees and watch my bedroom window late at night? When I undress?"

"No."

"Someone does. There's someone down there in the trees. I've seen flashes. Someone's there."

"Who?"

"I don't know."

"Sam Lees?"

"I don't know."

"You want me to catch him?"

"Yes. If you can. It makes me feel . . . I don't know. See if you can catch him."

"All right."

He lay back, spread arms and legs wide. When she turned her head to look at him, she saw a bird profile against a blueing sky. It was a rusted profile, etched on air.

She tilted her head far back, looked up toward the house. No one was watching. The deserted beach glimmered.

She moved her hand. Her knuckles touched the wet jeans stretched over his hard thigh. She rubbed softly with intent. His mouth opened.

She watched, fascinated. The mound rose as she rubbed his thigh.

"Susan," he gasped.

"Geronimo." She laughed and leaped to her feet. "Let's go. Breakfast. Race you to the house."

She began to run. Knowing he couldn't.


"There!" Grace Vanderhorst said, and stepping back she admired the crystal vase of forsythia. "Very nice. Now the Patroon will sit there and I'll sit at the other end. Roberta on the Patroon's right. Then Mister Graves next to Roberta so he won't feel like a stranger. Julie over there on the Patroon's left. And then Tom. With a place for Mrs. Rebecca if she wants to eat with us. And if Susan Todd runs over, why we'll just set a place for her next to Tom. Now we'll start with the melon. A half of lime for each. Then the French toast and pork sausages. I must make certain the syrup is heated. Plenty of hot coffee. Perhaps Mister Graves would like jam or marmalade with his French toast instead of syrup. I'll tell Mrs. Rebecca. We have orange and wild blackberry. A nice pot of tea for yours truly and anyone else who desires it. And then we'll finish with the cold strawberries which have been soaking in wine and brandy all night and should be just right."

She looked about the room, smiling and poking at her frizzy pink wig.

But there was no one there.

"Or plum," she said vaguely. "I do think we have some plum jam."

## 8

They wandered into the library after breakfast, mocked by the mildewed books. Hapgood Graves slid onto the piano bench, ran his fingers over fleshed wood. He opened the lid, stared at yellowed teeth.

"What do you think?" Bobbie Vander said.

"No matter what I play, it'll come out Stephen Foster."

He played a few bars of "Jeanie with the Light Brown Hair."

"See?" he said. "I told—"

He stopped suddenly. He stared at the piano. He played more Foster, went into Cole Porter. He tried some Chopin, a thing of his own. He looked up at her.

"Hear it?"

"What?"

He banged away, going up and down the keyboard. He played flashes of this and that. But mostly he tested tone, pitch, keys, chords. He stopped.

"The sound," he said. "Halfway between a harpsichord and a rinky-tink piano. Or maybe a glass harmonica. Not the kind you blow but the antique kind you stroked. I've never heard anything like it."

"Do you like it, Hap?"

"Like it? Mom, we've got to have it. That sound. We've got to ship this monster to New York or record up here. Jesus, baby, listen to it . . ."

He played a thing of his own, a song she had recorded that had made them a lot of money. It was called "Do You Know Him, Have You Seen Him?" The sound came out of the old piano, tinny and touching.

"I'll be damned," she said wonderingly.

"Oh, yes." He nodded.

He sat there a moment, caressing the worn wood.

"We've got to have it," he told her. "That's the sound. Tear your fucking heart out. Will the Patroon let us ship it to New York?"

"If he wants to."

"No." He worried. "It might not work. It's this funky room. The salt air. We'll have to record up here."

"Can they do it?"

"Sure. The engineers can do anything. But I don't want them fingering around with this. Leave in the noise of the sea and those crazy gulls. Oh, God, is this going to be good. Take a look."

He opened his folder, handed her a sheet.

"Read it out loud," he commanded.

It was called "The Fool's Love Song." She glanced at it briefly.

"No chorus?"

"Just read it out loud."

She began:

> "All the love whirls a lover;
> Does your bush burn for me?
> And I swear to have none over
> Light a candle on my tree.
>
> That wick I dipped at even side
> Returns to hunt my midnight dreams.
> No shims are left for me to hide,
> For clothes are never what they seams.
>
> I dived into your pearly tones
> And downed myself within the ink;
> I bate the fish that has no bones
> And brake the chain that has no link."

It went on for three more verses: a song of love garbled, of love corrupted and love betrayed. It hardly made sense: a gibber of innocence lost. But its endless punning and wry wit amused and touched: a child's prayer. The song said that hope was insane, but hope was.

She read the final line—"But does your bush still burn for me?"—and looked at Graves.

"What for Jesus' sake does that mean?"

"You don't have to know. Try it again. Slower. You haven't got the pace."

"Hap, can we get away with this?"

"Mom, you can get away with anything—and you know it. Try it again."

He made her read it through six more times. He was patient. He told her where the stresses were to fall. He gave her a feel for the rhythm.

She stalked up and down, reading aloud. She was as patient as he. She knew his worth. They kept at it. The words began to come alive.

She was on the fourth reading when Susan Todd came padding in, barefoot and bare-legged. She was wearing a brief pair of corduroy shorts that whistled between her hard thighs. There was a top of shrunken terrycloth and a brown skin gap between top and shorts. Her navel grinned at them.

Hapgood Graves didn't look at her.

Susan sat on the polished floor, out of the way. She folded down cross-legged, making not a sound.

Bobbie kept at it and didn't look around when her sister entered. Julie was wearing a caftan that hid her from neck to ankles. Her long, strong feet were strapped in sandals. She carried a deck of cards and sat at a small table near the French doors, in the brightening sunlight. She began to lay out a game of solitaire, listening to Bobbie recite . . . "But does your bush still burn for me?"

"All right," Graves said. "Now here's what we've got."

He propped up his work sheets, played it through. He glanced at Bobbie.

"Again," she said.

He played it through again.

"That's not my kind of stuff," she told him.

"It wasn't last year. It is this."

"Who the hell are you—Béla Bartók?"

"Listen again. And *listen*, for God's sake."

He played it through again.

"I'll never make it."

"You'll make it. If you have to whisper it."

"I'll never make it, Hap. It's freaky."

He drove her through it. She sang it: once, twice, three times.

"It's shit," she told him.

"That's right." He grinned evilly.

"I like it," Susan Todd said suddenly, her voice loud. They didn't even look at her.

"Again," he commanded.

She was a quick study. She had the words now. She paced

about the room, eyes half-closed, playing with her hair. She sang.

It was a small voice. Helen Morgan. Greta Keller. Marlene Dietrich. Billie Holiday. But it was your first screw and the first time you saw someone dead. You wanted to hit her because no one should get inside you like that.

Then she did it once more and it all came together. Everyone in the room knew it. It was all the poor sad fools in the world sniggled by their love.

Hapgood Graves closed the piano lid softly and gathered up his papers.

"Close," he said, "but no cigar. Enough for now, mom. We'll hit it again this afternoon. Go dunk yourself in the ocean."

Bobbie nodded. "Come on, Julie. Let's dunk."

Julie left her solitaire hand on the table, followed Bobbie out the French doors.

"You're wonderful," Susan Todd said to Graves. "You're a genius."

"Of course." He smiled.

"Play something for me."

"Not me, babe. I only play for money."

"Is that all it means to you?"

"That's absolutely all," he assured her.

She was still seated cross-legged on the floor. Her whippy arms drifted up slowly until they were wings. Then she floated to her feet, unfolding, using only the muscles of hips, thighs, calves.

He watched, fascinated. That meat tensing under tanned skin. He could not have done that in a million years. She stood before him, taller than he, challenging.

He held out his right hand, fingers spread. No trembling there. He selected the middle finger.

He reached out. He touched the naked gap between her

shrunken top and tight shorts. Touched her with his middle finger. She did not move. He started at her left hip, drew his finger lightly across the tight skin, feeling the youth.

His finger returned to that grinning navel. It probed, prying into it, turning. The finger was gentle, searching. It felt grains of sand, the heat. She stared at him gravely.

The next day was Sunday. They all went to church, sang "Praise God from Whom All Blessing Flow," and listened to a sermon exhorting them to be humble.

## 9

The seacoast of Maine, at that place, formed a wide cove. And within that arc was a series of smaller coves, a rhythm of curves. There was a stretch of beach and then, within each smaller cove, gray stone shoved down into black water.

When the sea was high, the tide frantic, it smashed itself into, onto, across, upon those points of sand and cliff. Always, even at low tide, there were currents and crosscurrents. There was turmoil, and beneath the surface a boiling.

Even a strong and expert swimmer found himself gripped. He was tugged, pulled at, flung. He drifted: out, in, sideways. Down. His strength went against the bubbling.

Farther out, beyond the embrace of the large cove, the sea was sea, a steady god.

Pieter Vanderhorst's favorite cove was between the Breckinridge home and the Semanskis, south of his property. A wedge of stone had been sliced from a wheel of cliff. Here was a narrow opening. (In came the sea, leaping and laughing!) Then it spread to a dark curve. It was sunless there. Green things sprouted from wet stone. It was a small piece of sand, a place for secret love.

He dragged himself along the beach. He stopped and looked back. There was his track in the wet sand: one good footprint, one endless scuffed line where his left foot dragged, punched holes where the cane went in. He laughed silently at this crippled code.

He lighted a dry Dutch cigar. He knew each deep draft might be the last: smoke stopping in his dead throat, coiling grayly in there while his sightless eyes searched the moon.

Vanderhorst found the secret place, wading through surf to get into that narrow opening. His canvas shoes and white cotton socks were soaked and sloshing. He gained the small beach, went far back against the stone.

He leaned, smoked his cigar. He listened to the crash, smelled rank life. His dead left hand scrabbled at the wet green stuff. Could he feel it? He thought so. Perhaps sensation was returning there. He willed it.

"Hello, moon," he said aloud, looking up. "Hello, stars. I, Pieter Vanderhorst, am here. And I live."

He shoved his cane deep into the sand so that it stood upright. Stone pressed against his back. He waited patiently.

Finally she came, wearing that curious sheet-poncho. She waded steadily through rising surf. She came up close to him.

"Rebecca," he said.

She took the cigar from his fingers and kissed the tip. He smiled. She puffed deeply. Smoke disappeared somewhere inside her. It didn't come out.

Then she kissed him, put her face into him.

"Patroon," she said, and slumped.

He held her with his good right arm. He bent close to breathe the feral smell of her: hair, face, neck, armpits. Her odor stuck into him and twisted. He gripped her tight.

They posed there a moment, carved. Then she pulled away. She held up the cigar, looked at him. He shook his head. She tossed it into the sea. There was a hiss.

"How is the boy?" he asked eagerly.

She opened the top two buttons of his shirt, peered at the mat of gray hair, the wire.

"It is the girl," she told him. "Susan Todd."

"I know." He nodded. "That is not good." Always, when he was with her, he spoke in her rhythm. "He will be hurt. What do the bones say?" He was serious.

She shook her head angrily.

"What may I do? Money?"

No.

"A trip somewhere? Send him to your uncle?"

No.

"Shall I talk to him about this?"

No.

"I am proud of him," he said. She gripped him tighter.

The black shiny hair was tied back with a shoelace. She whipped it off. Wind blew her hair around, lashed his face. He tried to bite it, take it into his mouth.

She felt him.

"Can you?" she asked.

"It will be the last thing that dies," old Vanderhorst told her.

She untied the strip of cloth at her waist, and the poncho floated away. She was naked there and gleaming, oiled by moonlight. Great melon breasts with long purple nipples stabbed at him. Her skin was vellum.

"Yes," he said.

She took his arms, turned him around gently. She held him strongly as she put her naked back against wet stone. She spread her legs, pulled him so his weight was against her.

"My love," he said.

She said something he did not understand.

She was with the stone, part of the cliff. She put him into her, threading him through her heavy thatch.

"All right?" he asked.

Her eyes widened and rolled up. She stared at stars. He forced closer.

"Patroon."

He laughed with joy. He was Pieter Vanderhorst and he was alive.

Sounds came out of her: a drone, a chant, in her language. She grasped his buttocks and pulled him tight. Her bare heels sank deeper in wet sand, and her legs spread wider. He felt the tremble of her skin, the shake beginning. Her pleasure was bliss to know. He squeezed with his right hand and dreamed heat and bones, everything that lived. He looked down at his limp left hand. It moved slowly toward the glow. Perhaps . . .

It was a glory. It was everything he loved: sea and stone, and this steaming woman. He knew the grease of her, sweet stench, lurch and gasp. They fluttered together.

The tide was turning. It came in and lapped their feet. White froth was curling. Still he pinned her to wet stone. She made no move to escape.

The old man leaned forward, bit the skin of her left shoulder. He bit until he tasted blood. Still she did not move or cry. He tasted her blood on his tongue.

"My love," he said again.

# ——————10——————

The boy in 3-B died at 4:16 P.M. In the movies he would have been golden-haired and smiling bravely. Actually he was mean and whining, with acne. But still: leukemia and nine years old. Mostly Dr. Benjamin Todd hated death: the bastard.

He drove home fast. He strode into the living room, poured a warm whiskey, and stared out the big window at the sea. It was still there. Well . . . what the hell. He gulped his drink.

Susan came in and looked at him.

"A bad day?"

He nodded.

"The Ferguson boy?"

He was crying. He tried to wipe the wet away so she wouldn't see. She came over, stood by him.

"You want me to stay?"

He shook his head, turned away from her.

"Tom and I are going into town to see a movie. We'll take the car. Okay? We'll be back before midnight. I made the salad and the chicken. Everything is in there. Okay? I got those little cherry tomatoes you like. And there's a nice honeydew the man said was just right. Okay?"

Suddenly he turned and grabbed her.

"Son of a bitch," he yelled.

She held him.

"Father," she said.

He wrenched away from her.

"Oh," he said. "I'm so stupid. I'll never learn."

She was wearing something blue and thin. She was bare arms, bare legs, bare love.

"You take care."

He nodded again.

She went away, looking back. He sat down and stopped shivering. The whiskey helped.

Once, a life ago, he had been a lieutenant-surgeon in a forward tent hospital under fire. Sleep had disappeared. The bastard had taken over.

They were waiting for the next seeping ambulance. He and the captain-surgeon went out for a smoke: two butchers in decorated aprons. They sat on either side of a tree. The top had been shot off, the trunk still standing. They sat there smoking, backs against the tree. Nearby was a pit with arms, legs, and dead things.

They heard a scream, a whine, a whir. They didn't move.

The tree trunk shuddered and jolted them. They peered around curiously, staring at each other before they looked at the wood. It was there, half-embedded in the tree trunk, right there between them, sticking out: this steel thing.

The captain-surgeon started giggling and never stopped for as long as he lived. It was only two days.

Benjamin Todd thought he had been spared for something important; something significant would happen to him.

He thought it happened when he married. Her name was Anita. She was as graceful as he was clumpy. When she went off the high board, she drifted in space. And when she came up dripping and grinning, well. . . .

Their first child was a son, Robert, who died at the age of two months from a rare respiratory disorder. Is it right that a physician's son should die? Their second child was Susan, who flourished. All seemed well.

Their marriage didn't die; it simply eroded. She wanted—what? He wanted—what? They couldn't remember. So it all went away. The ending was not significant. It was just an end.

But it scorched his ego. Small failure: small death. He was left with Susan. He worked hard at the hospital and read old books.

He was dark, square, and heavy, a thick man who trundled. And he was hairy. Black wool sprang from throat, chest, shoulders, arms, back. He didn't like it. He wore a cotton T-shirt when he swam.

Hair curled from every joint of his fingers. They were not a surgeon's hands. They were compact, dense. Still, he could stick two fingers into a small matchbox and tie a knot in silk surgical thread. He demonstrated this trick for interns, and they sighed.

He swam as much as he could. He went into the sea, far out beyond the arms of the big cove. Sometimes he just drifted. In the pool at the South Canaan Country Club, he did his one-breath-to-four-strokes, back and forth, twenty lengths. Since his divorce he masturbated once a week, on Friday night.

After Susan left, he poured another small whiskey and carried it into his ground-floor bedroom. He undressed swiftly, hanging his clothes away neatly, and sliding wooden trees into his shoes. He took a quick shower and inspected a pimple on the inside of his left thigh. He dried, staring at his squat, bristling image in the mirror on the bathroom door. He rubbed his jaw, decided he could get by without shaving. But he patted powder to lighten the dark cast.

He pulled on knitted briefs, not loose undershorts. He had developed intermittent twinges in his left testicle, and knitted briefs gave support. He guessed the condition was caused by the sudden end of fucking after twenty years of married life, two or three times a week. All those hours of passion, moments of intimacy. . . .

He stepped into lightweight gray flannel slacks and pulled on a dark-blue velour shirt, zipped up to the chin, with long sleeves. And he buckled on stained sandals. His wife had bought them in Mexico when they . . .

He inspected the refrigerator. There was not one, but two quartered chickens, fried in olive oil and oregano. The salad was immense, and he picked out a cherry tomato to munch. The honeydew melon knocked right, with a soft tip.

Julie Vanderhorst would want a dry Beefeater martini, on the rocks with lemon peel.

"Make it mild," she would say.

"Julie"—he would laugh—"there is no such thing as a 'mild martini.' A martini is a martini is a martini. Period. Asking for a 'mild martini' is like asking for 'a little garlic.'"

She would say that and he would say that.

He took a handsome crystal pitcher from the cupboard. He had bought that for his wife when . . .

He stirred the martinis conscientiously. He fished out the ice, put the pitcher in the refrigerator to chill. He turned away, then came back, poured himself a small martini and tried it. He paused, smiling. Right on. Then his smile congealed: The kid was nine years old, with acne.

Their living room was L-shaped, the short leg a dining alcove. Susan had set the pine table with cherry-patterned covering and napkins (of paper), German stainless steel, candles in etched hurricane lamps.

He wondered about wine. His liquor cabinet was really a book shelf. There was no white, but there was a half-gallon of raw Sicilian red with one of those ceramic stoppers with a little rubber gasket about it. If Julie wanted wine . . . If Julie wanted . . . If Julie . . .

"Hi?" a throaty voice called. "Anyone home?"

The door to the redwood porch slammed open. In pranced Roberta Vanderhorst: bare-armed, bare-legged, wearing a dress that seemed to have been crocheted from grocery store string. There were hard nipples there, he was certain. And white bikini panties showing faint through the spider's web.

She waved a bottle of wine. "Greeks bearing gifts!"

Julie followed, wearing one of those caftans she had adopted since she became plump. She was smiling, carrying a deck of cards.

"Ben! This nut insisted on coming along. Have you enough food?"

"Plenty," he assured them. He kissed Julie on the cheek. "Susan made two chickens and a giant salad."

Bobbie handed him the wine, turned up her face. So he kissed her on the cheek.

"And this completes it. I thank you. We'll eat and drink ourselves sick."

"And then the doctor will take over," Bobbie said.

"Martini?" he asked Julie.

"Make it mild."

"Julie, there's no such thing as a 'mild martini.' A martini is a martini is a martini. Period. Asking for a 'mild martini' is like asking for 'a little garlic.' Roberta?"

"Bobbie."

"Bobbie?"

"A slam of Scotch."

"How? Rocks? Water? What?"

"Oh . . . I don't know. Water, I guess. Some ice. Got any music?"

"Sure. The player's over there."

When he came back with the drinks, Julie was laying out a hand of solitaire on the cocktail table. Bobbie was shuffling albums.

"Look at all my stuff!" she exulted.

"Susan's a fan of yours."

She whirled to look at him.

"You're not?"

"Of course. I like it, too."

She laughed. "Oh, that Susan! You better make her wear a tent or buy yourself a shotgun. God, what a body. That Indian kid and the old geezer, Sam what's-his-name, they look at her like she's an all-day sucker. I think even Hap is getting ideas."

"You mean she—"

"Aw, come on," she mocked. She came over to shake his arm. "It isn't the kid's fault. She's just her. A sweet piece. She can't help it. I'm complaining because she makes me feel one year younger than God. She's so juicy."

"Yes," he nodded. "She is."

She put on an album of show tunes. They were instrumentals. She turned the volume down. She wasn't listening, but she needed the music there.

She went over, sat beside Julie on the couch. She swept the solitaire game into a messed pile.

"Forget the cards, kiddo," she said. "Drink your mild martini and live a little."

The sisters laughed and hugged each other. One with her boy's body flashing through the lattice of knitted string. She so thin and live with bud nipples poking, muscled legs.

The other as monumental as her father, as solid. She was blushed with sun, soft flesh secret within that cloak of wildly printed cotton. Her brown feet were bound in sandals. Dr. Benjamin Todd saw her smooth fingers clamped about . . .

It all went well. They ate, drank. They laughed. Candles were lighted. The night glowed. Bobbie Vander made it. She gobbled her food, but not tasting. She just stoked the furnace and related outrageous gossip about show business personalities, their sexual proclivities.

She smiled continuously at her sister. Then, as she came to the punchline of each anecdote, she would lean forward, look into Julie's eyes. She would put a hand on her sister's. Her sister would laugh.

A moment later Todd would laugh.

"Where is Hapgood Graves?" he asked once. "Why didn't you bring him along?"

"Working," Bobbie said promptly. "I told him to come over for a free feed, but he's got another three or four things to do. He likes to work. He told me once that writing poetry was 'a continuous orgasm.' That's not bad, is it, doc? 'A continuous orgasm'?"

"Not bad," Todd acknowledged. "Fatiguing perhaps."

"'Fatiguing perhaps.'" Bobbie mimicked him. She looked at her sister, patted her hand.

They returned the remnants of the salad to the refrigerator, dumped chicken bones into the pail, rinsed glasses. Stained paper cloth and napkins were crumpled up and discarded: a fast cleanup job.

Todd carried a bottle of brandy and three small balloon glasses; Bobbie brought cigarettes for all; Julie balanced one of the lighted candles in its hurricane lamp. And down to the beach they all went, kicking off their sandals. The moon was still there, quartering now. Stars were a zillion holes punched in a black sky.

They sat on the sand and listened to the sea.

"Wow," Bobbie Vander said. "This is it."

They lay back, spread arms and legs, opened their bodies to it. All three were stretched wide, free to the music.

"Jesus," someone said.

There was Benjamin Todd, then Julie Vanderhorst in the middle, then Bobbie Vander. Maybe they sipped a brandy. Maybe they plumed cigarette smoke into the swaying sky. They muttered, laughed. The candle guttered.

Todd's hand wandered, found Julie's hand and clasped. Those rosebud nipples showing through the patterned knit of Bobbie's silly dress. It wasn't Friday night.

And Bobbie's hand searched. It found and clasped.

The tide was going out. They heard crash and suck. There were sprinkles of light on the sea. The three of them sang a song. What was it? They were linked, hand to hand.

An age passed, but they were silent. It seemed right for that time. Thin shims of clouds passed before the sheen of the moon. It was a haunted night. It was cool. It was warm.

"I—," Todd said. Then stopped.

Julie's bare toes moved against his bare shin, smoothing. They slid up and down. A skim of sweat was on the palm of the hand he held. Far off, far up, an airliner hummed in the great circle to England.

Bobbie Vander was humming, too. She was muttering, drumming her heels.

Todd moved the back of his hand atop Julie's soft thigh. Naked heat came through thin cloth. He stared at whirling stars and wondered.

Bobbie sat up, propped. She looked down at the two of them, peering.

"Let's go for a swim," she yelled. Her laughter was harsh. "Let's go skinny-dipping!"

"Oh, Bobbie," Julie murmured.

"Don't," Todd said. "Tide's changing. It's a bitch out there. I've tried it."

"Are you coming with me or aren't you?"

They sat up and looked at her in shock. There was destruction in her voice.

"Please," Julie said. "You don't know. You don't swim that well. It's dark. Cold water. Splash if you want but don't—"

"Shit," Bobbie Vander said disgustedly.

It seemed to Benjamin Todd the black night suddenly exploded into pinwheels of action. There were flashes and glares, cries and shouts, tears and the gripping of fear.

Insane sequence . . . Bobbie bounced to her feet, bent over, crossed arms, grabbed the hem of her knitted shopping bag, straightened up, flipping it off. She stood there, a titless ghost.

They stared at her in astonishment: the waxen thing wavering in candlelight.

Bobbie turned, ran away from them, down to the gulping sea. It was an awkward run, her feet shoving out spills of sand. They saw her bones: ribs, spine, pelvis, bleached by the moon.

Julie stood up.

"Go get her. Please, Ben. Don't let her go in. She . . . Please."

Gathering momentum. Out of control. The night was.

"Bobbie," Julie called in a quaver.

Todd took off shirt and pants, flung them to wet sand. Julie bit her knuckle. He touched the back of her neck. He floundered down to the sea. The stupid . . . Something significant?

He was in to his knees, couldn't see her. He heard the start of a laugh out there. It ended in gargle and cough. Oh God. He waded deeper, searching. He was hardly to his thighs, but he felt that dreadful pull underneath on knees and calves. It pulled him sweetly: come, come.

The sea was sweeping north. There was roiling, sneeze of surf, a chop like hammer blows. He heard a bubbling wail. He thought he saw an arm raised. He cursed and plunged. He let it take him, not fighting it. He swirled, keeping his head high, staring through drenched eyes. He didn't want to start diving; not yet.

He heard a pained retching. A strained hand came out of the sea to clutch for a star. He dug toward it, getting heavy back and shoulder muscles into mad strokes.

She was an eel, greased by the sea. He couldn't hold. Finally he got an arm between her legs, an arm under her neck. He tried to hold her head up. His chunky legs drove. He went with the tide, cutting in, cutting in. He shoved her ahead of him.

He let his legs drop but couldn't touch. Then came more pumping, more stretching. He tried again. His toes touched. He dug in, pushing. He lurched toward the beach. Something sour was coming out his mouth.

His hands were under her shaved armpits, dragging her. His great chest was laboring. He flopped to his knees. He let her fall onto the sand.

A light came staggering down the beach, wavering: Julie with the candle still flickering in the hurricane lamp. She was weeping, echoing his anguished breaths.

He dragged to his feet, straddled Bobbie. He picked her up by the waist, face down. He bounced her, tipping her forward. She was a feather, floating in his harsh grasp.

Water streamed from her, from eyes, nose, ears, throat. It poured out. Then she puked: whooping, coughing, jerking. He kept pumping up and down, not caring how much he hurt her. Julie wept.

Bobbie moaned. She pushed at his coarse hands. He

flipped her, let her drop to the sand. She lay there, head turned to one side. Now spittle was coming out of her, dribbling down chin and neck.

Todd sat down heavily, pulled up his knees. He clasped them and rested his head, face down. He could feel diminishing strain on his lungs: the wheezing, a sob, catch and snort. Muscles in his arms and shoulders clinched in a sudden shudder, then smoothed out.

Julie Vanderhorst sat beside her sister on the sand, put an arm beneath her head, raised her slowly to a sitting position. Bobbie was coughing, spitting, something still gurgling in her throat.

"Hey, doc," she rasped with a crooked grin, "that's some crazy ocean. Right, doc?"

He raised his heavy head and looked at her. He reached out and slapped her across the face as hard as he could, wanting to tear her head off.

Her head whipped to the side. Julie wailed. A thin spill of blood came from Bobbie's lower lip. Her head moved back slowly. She stared at him with wonder.

He climbed slowly to his feet. "Get her home," he commanded Julie. "Blankets. Aspirin and brandy. I'll look in tomorrow morning."

He trudged off down the beach. He was still trembling, and not from cold. He had a big whiskey and then stood under a hot shower, his hair wet and streaming, eyes closed. After a while he thawed, and the knots loosened. He shouldn't have slapped her.

He was surprised to see how early it was. Susan wasn't due back for another hour. He pulled on a cotton robe and poured another whiskey. God, what an evening. Back to *Pickwick Papers*. The Fat Boy had just been awakened to serve the picnic lunch. Dr. Benjamin Todd began to smile. He read . . .

There was a faint tap at the porch door. He looked up and took off his glasses. Julie Vanderhorst was peering in. He rose, tugged his robe closed. When he opened the door, she came into his arms, weeping.

"Ben," she said.

"What's wrong? Anything wrong with Bobbie?"

"No. She's all right. She wouldn't drink brandy, but she took a sleeping pill. Is that okay?"

"One?"

"Yes. I gave it to her and hid the bottle. Is that okay?"

"I guess. Why are you crying?"

"I'm so ashamed. I'm so sick I want to vomit."

He got her inside, got her sipping a glass of port. Her tanned face glistened and she sniffed. But she calmed. He had forgotten what beautiful eyes she had. They glowed deep.

"I'm sorry," she said. "I'm so proud of you. Thank you. I should have done more. Bobbie thanks you, too. I might have stopped her. She'll thank you tomorrow. I hate it. Just hate it."

"Hate what?"

"People who do what they want to do and just don't care what it does to other people. She thought it was clever and crazy and she wanted to do it so she did it."

"She doesn't know the sea."

"It's not that. She doesn't care. She lives . . . oh, I don't know. These people who say do what you want to do, every minute. Live life up to the hair. Never resist temptation. Just do. Well, these people . . . you can laugh at them and maybe admire them. But when you suddenly realize they're living that way at the expense of someone else. Someone else is suffering for their freedom. Ben, I want to live, too."

"Sure."

"But I've never been able to do that. Just not care. I envy her. Oh, God. Ben, those pills you gave the Patroon. What are they for?"

"He may have another stroke. If he can get one of those spansules into him it might keep him going until I or someone else can get to him."

"How will we know if he has another—another one."

"You'll know. He'll probably fall down. Just cave in. Heavy breathing. Choking. Chest heaving. Tongue hanging out. Maybe a hand clenched into a claw. Oh, you'll know."

"How much time will we have?"

"Not much. Get the pill into him and then call me. If you can't get me, get Emergency at the hospital. Tell them what it is."

"He's not carrying the pills with him. I found that little plastic container on the library table."

"God damn it!" He slammed a palm against his thigh. "The son of a bitch just won't take orders! I'm sorry, Julie."

"That's all right. What should I do?"

"I'll read him the riot act tomorrow. He's got to have those slugs with him wherever he goes. They're no guarantee, understand, but they just might keep him going. Christ, what a man."

He flopped down on the couch. He pulled his robe closed over bare knees, raised the neckline to hide that snarl of black hair. She sat on the couch alongside him and curled her bare feet under.

"Julie, I'm sorry I slapped her. I shouldn't have done that. I'll apologize tomorrow."

"I'm sorry you did, too. But I understand. You thought she was hysterical."

He looked at her.

"Oh, no. I was furious with her. I wanted to hurt her."
She was confused.

"How do you two get along?"

"Bobbie and me? I love her as a sister and hate her as a
person. She loves me as a person and hates me as a sister."

"What does that mean?"

"I'm not sure." She laughed. "But you must admit it
sounds very profound."

He laughed too and lifted her hand. Everything about her
was soft . . .

. . . and warm. She was better than *Pickwick Papers*.
She was pulsing warm. The darkness was outside, beyond
the closed doors and windows. That whining kid with acne
was out there.

"I'm lonely," he said suddenly.

"What? What did you say, Ben? I didn't hear."

"Nothing."

"You said something."

"Nothing important." He smiled. "Just complaining."

He put an arm about her, pulled her close. She sagged
willingly, a quilted comforter against him. He admired that
helmet of burnished hair, flawless skin, all of her puffed
with health. She was burning.

Her unseamed face was bland except for those swimming
eyes. They looked at, into, through him.

"Julie." He beamed. He was suddenly happy.

She pulled the zipper down the front of her caftan. There
was a soft zzzzzz, and then there were naked breasts, a
gleaming sausage of flesh about her waist.

He stared at that tanned leather, sick with lust.

"How in God's name . . . ?"

"There's a little—oh, I guess it's a kind of porch. Not a

widow's walk. I have to go through Mrs. Rebecca's room and out one of her windows. It's the highest flat surface on the house. I sun-bathe in the nude up there. A beach towel over the tar. No one can see me. I'm like this all over."

"Jesus," he breathed. "You're something."

"I take a pitcher of martinis." She giggled. "I stay out there for hours. I'm all . . . it's just that . . . no one can . . . I just roll around."

He looked at her with wonderment, seeing that soft body rolling in the sun. He heard her groaning, raped by light. She would open her brown thighs to the heat. She was high up and alone. She would feel the steam of her own flesh.

He bent suddenly and tried to cram one of her sloping breasts into his mouth. She threw her head back and screamed with delight.

He moved a hand into the split caftan, around that plump waist, gently pinching. Her eyes grew wider and wider. There was a tide in her eyes, rising.

He could not feel her bones. She had no bones. But solid flesh pressed out everywhere, heated from within. His hands went onto her back, shoulders. He was touching, feeling. Oh.

Unaccountably he began singing. And she joined him. "Bringing in the sheaves. Bringing in the sheaves. We will come rejoicing, bringing in the sheaves." Their eyes locked, trembling lips almost touching.

They sang it, over and over, his hands grasping. She began to pant, the tide in her eyes turbid.

He stopped singing. He bent close to smell her. It was the sun. Up close, her skin blazed. He tasted her. She was sweet life.

"Bringing in the sheaves," she murmured softly.

He tasted, tasted, his tongue tingling. He stuck a nipple

in his ear. He licked an armpit, laughing. He searched for her hidden navel and finally found it.

He forgot what was outside the house. But then he heard the car coming up the driveway: Susan and Tom Drinkwater returning from town.

## 11

Summer moved along, oh . . .

The morning sun struck a match; blue sky flared. And there was perky Grace Vanderhorst, humming a gay little tune. She wore a poke bonnet and gingham ruffles. The raffia basket that hung from her wrinkled arm was lined with toilet paper.

"Good morning, Mrs. Vanderhorst." Hapgood Graves smiled. "Lovely morning."

"Good morning, sir," she sang delightedly, and touched him. "Yes, it is a lovely morning. Although, as I said to Mister Vanderhorst, I do fear the day will not be hot as there was red about the moon last night. You know what sailors say."

He did not, but nodded.

"Now, sir," the coquette said, "you must come for a walk with me along the beach. I am gathering shells."

"What—"

"The Ladies' Club at the church. We collect shells and paste them onto cards and baskets and make little animals from them. Have you written any nice poems lately? Oh, elephants and funny things. Then we sell them at our rummage sale. You must eat more; you are so thin. Now I

have an ashtray—a large shell with tiny shells glued around
the rim. So pretty. We use clear shellac so the shells won't
chip or lose their color. You must have that ashtray. I will
save it for you."

"You are very kind. But I don't smoke."

"Oh, how wise! Mister Vanderhorst, you know, smokes
cigars. Great smelly things. Dreadful. Oh, what a lovely
morning. I do believe I shall skip."

And so she did: skipping down the beach. Incredibly, he
found himself skipping along with her. Down the beach
they went, her basket swinging.

She stopped suddenly, put a hand to her heart. She
laughed up at him.

"Oh, my!" she said. "Wasn't that fun?"

He couldn't understand it. Why wasn't he bored?

She swooped suddenly.

"Look, look, look!" she caroled. "How lovely!"

She thrust a tiny shell under his nose. He looked. It was
pink and swirly. It smelled of fish.

"Very nice," he nodded.

"Are your parents alive?"

Graves was startled. "No, ma'am. They're both dead."

"Not dead, sir, not dead. But in another form. Oh, see,
another one!"

So they went, wandering down the beach. He searched
assiduously as she. The basket slowly filled.

"Now when I get them home," she said. "We're having
frankfurters and baked beans and sauerkraut for lunch. Isn't
that nice? I'll wash them and scrub them with a little brush I
have and then put them in the sun to dry. And blueberries
for dessert. Mister Vanderhorst simply dotes on blueberries."

He wanted to . . . to what? Kiss her, at least.

She was a crinkled little apple, sweet-smelling and clean.

Her light-blue eyes were as innocent as water: a ginghamed wraith. She should have been gift-wrapped with ribbons.

"Mister Graves, you must write a poem just for me. Will you do that?"

"Yes, I—"

"Oh, I do like poetry. 'Under a spreading chestnut tree . . .' I must remind Mister Vanderhorst to carry his pills. Doctor Todd insisted he must have his pills with him at all times. 'Where are the snows of yesteryear?' I do hope Mrs. Rebecca was able to buy frankfurter rolls. I love to eat frankfurters in rolls. With mustard, you know. 'The flowers that bloom in the Spring, tra-la . . .' A poem written just for me. Oh, my! It's like having an indoor picnic when you have frankfurters in rolls and baked beans and sauerkraut. I so enjoy a meal like that. I don't know what I'd do without that woman."

"How long has she been with you?"

"Who is that, sir?"

"Mrs. Rebecca. How long has she been with you?"

"Oh . . . a long time. A very long time. Now let me see . . . Yes. The girls were away at school. Mrs. Rebecca came to us, but she was a single woman then. And her name was . . . her name was . . . Drat. Now why can't I remember her name."

"It doesn't—"

"Oddfellow. Yes, that's what it was. 'Who touches a hair on yon grey head . . .' Oh, my, I do remember. Yes, she was Rebecca Oddfellow. A single woman. Indian, you know. And very pretty. She was with us, oh, perhaps two years. Then she went away. Just up and left. So sudden. And then we heard she had married Jimmy Drinkwater. He was an Indian and did . . . Everyone said he didn't have the right name because he didn't drink water at all. Do you understand my meaning, Mister Graves?"

"Yes. I understand your meaning."

"Oh, my, he had a bad reputation. Although I must say he was always a perfect gentleman with me. Look! Look at this cunning little shell. Isn't that sweet?"

"Very nice."

"And they said his head was lying a hundred yards away from his body. And when—"

"Whose head?"

"Jimmy Drinkwater's. Didn't I tell you? Oh, my, yes. He drank too much one night and fell asleep on the railroad track and a train came along. We had trains in those days. I suspect it was the night mail train from Boston, but please don't quote me on that."

"I won't, Mrs. Vanderhorst."

"You must call me Grace. That is my name—Grace."

"Grace in name and grace in spirit."

"Oh, oh, oh! What a sweet thing to say! I thank you, sir. 'Grace in name and grace in spirit.' Ketchup on the baked beans. And an onion and some salt pork in there. Perhaps you could call it 'To Grace.'"

"The poem I'm going to write for you? Yes, perhaps I could. But then what happened?"

"What happened? When, Mister Graves?"

"After Jimmy Drinkwater had his head cut off by the night mail train from Boston."

"How horrid! His head just lying there. In a little patch of pansies alongside the track. Well, then, Mrs. Rebecca came back to us, poor thing. And she had a son who is Tom Drinkwater. Such a handsome boy. Very quiet. But still water runs deep. Is that not so, Mister Graves?"

"If I am to call you Grace, you must call me Hap."

She giggled. A young girl cast down her eyes.

"Oh, I couldn't do that, sir. It is not seemly. People might . . . well, you know. Yes, that is what I believe: still water runs deep. Now in this little cove I have found some of my very, very prettiest shells."

He took her arm, helped her over the rocks. They gathered shells. It was cooler in the cove, and shadowed. Her basket was filled.

"I think I will just sit for a moment, Mister Graves. Just to rest a moment before the walk back."

Her face seemed suddenly pale. He spread his handkerchief on a slime-covered rock. He held her gently by the elbow and sat beside her. He looked at her anxiously.

Her head tilted forward, empty eyes hidden by the poke bonnet.

"Went away," she said. He could hardly hear. "Yes. Went away and suddenly married Jimmy Drinkwater. And came back with a son. Yes. That is how it happened."

They sat in silence. Sunlight sneaked into the cove. It reached for them, not touching.

"I do not understand," she said once.

Then she said: "Well, gracious, we must get back. 'It was an ancient mariner and he stoppeth one of three . . .' See? I do remember! Come, sir."

"Sure." He smiled. He took her basket, helped her to her feet. "Back to the frankfurters, baked beans, and sauerkraut."

"And indoor picnic!" she cried, and clapped her hands.

## 12

It was all with shouts, cries, and laughter ringing. The wedding-cake Vanderhorst home was sliced open to a summer world. Doors and windows called sun and salt wind. Billowing curtains stroked soft air.

There was that Saturday afternoon feeling: comings and goings, rushings, bumpings. Even Dr. Todd came home early, bringing the Vanderhorsts three cases of chilled Ram's Head, a local beer with a rampaging Pan on the label.

No table was set. But there were paper plates and napkins, plastic forks and spoons—and a great brown pot of simmering beans, frankfurters in endless strings, dripping kraut, the beer, a fragrant bouquet of scallions.

Everyone was everywhere, carrying food, bare feet smacking on warm floorboards; all wandering in and out. They called the Semanski twins up from the beach to join them. They insisted the bearded postman put down his leather bag to eat, drink, share the glee.

The Patroon was planted in his wheelchair, steadily gnawing a naked frankfurter with the good side of his mouth. His hooded eyes were alight.

Mrs. Grace Vanderhorst was an excited butterfly. "Do you have . . . ? Have more . . . But have you tried . . . ?"

Watchful, Tom Drinkwater squatted in a corner, black eyes following Susan. His upper lip was foamy with beer.

Julie swirled her caftan in and out. She carried a beer stein and a hotdog smothered in sauerkraut.

Benjamin Todd was seated on the dining-room table. Legs dangling, he hunched over, munching and swilling happily.

Bobbie Vander went whipping about, raucous and wicked.

Samuel Lees ate enormously, eyes swollen.

Susan Todd was in something thin, black, shiny, showing her mustard thighs and . . . and all.

Hapgood Graves sauntered quietly in his loose way, so disjointed. He flowed with a patient smile.

And Mrs. Rebecca Drinkwater.

"Play something for me," Susan demanded.

"I told you," Graves said, "I only play for money."

"But won't you do it for me?"

"What will you give me?"

"What do you want?"

He looked at her.

"Beer it up, baby." Bobbie Vander laughed. She perched on the arm of her sister's chair.

"Are you happy, Bobbie?"

"Oh, sure."

"You and Ben—it's all right?"

"Oh, sure, sure." She stroked Julie's hair. "We're great pals." She took Julie's free hand, held it in her lap. "He apologized and I apologized." She pressed. "Everything's fine."

"No more beer," Mrs. Rebecca said.

"One," Tom Drinkwater said. "Just one more."

"One more." His mother nodded. "One."

"Oh, Mister Vanderhorst," Grace said breathlessly, "I do so enjoy an indoor picnic. Did you see the shells I put out to dry? That nice Mister Graves helped me gather them. He is going to write a poem just for me."

"Yes."

"And he's going to call it 'To Grace.' Isn't that nice?"

"Yes, yes."

Bobbie Vander watched Graves down a stein of beer without stopping for breath.

"You'll sleep tonight," she told him.

"Will I, mom?"

"Let's go for a swim," Tom said.

"No," Susan said, her eyes wandering. "Not yet."

Mrs. Rebecca brought the Patroon a mug of black coffee. Their fingers touched.

"Frigging in the rigging," Samuel Lees muttered.

"Buddies?" Bobbie grinned at Benjamin Todd.

"Of course."

Julie hurried over, sat on the other side of him, touched him with her knee.

"Let's be friends, let's be buddies," Bobbie sang in a burlesque, reedy voice.

Hapgood Graves wandered into the library. He opened the old piano, lightly touched one key: flat.

A state squad car stopped by. Two troopers came in, grinning and were greeted. Hotdogs and beer for them. It was all right; there was plenty, plenty for all. Mrs. Drinkwater put another string of franks onto boil.

"Patroon," Sam Lees said.

"Yes?"

"You come with me a minute?"

Pieter Vanderhorst looked at him, then hauled himself to his feet. He lurched after Lees to the sea porch, followed the finger pointing to the south.

"The radio says small craft warnings in Portland. The radio says barometer dropping. Look at that."

A thin line of black was stroked with a marking pen across the blue sky. It seemed motionless. But as they watched, it oozed toward them.

"How long have you seen that?"

"Five, ten minutes. It's moving slow. Real slow. Now should we batten down?"

"Not yet."

"That's ozone you smell, Patroon."

"I know. But it's moving slow."

"You want me to put up the shutters?"

"I'll tell you when. There's time. Tell the Semanski twins to tell their paw. Send Tom to tell old man Breckinridge. I'll tell Todd. When this breaks up, then you batten down. Tom will help you. But wait. Wait till all this—all this"—he searched for the word—"all this jollity is over."

"We better button-up, Patroon."

"We will. It's coming. Ask Mrs. Vanderhorst where my telescope is. No. Ask Mrs. Rebecca. I want to look at that. It's gathering."

"Now, you're right, Patroon. I see it and I smell it. I'll do like you say."

"Yes," Pieter Vanderhorst repeated, searching the sky, "it's gathering."

"Oh, Mister Graves," Grace Vanderhorst breathed, "do play something for us."

He touched her wrinkled arm. It was velvet.

"No," he said, "but I'll play something for *you*. But we must hide in here and not let anyone else in."

"Oh, yes!" she cried delightedly, eyes bright as thimbles. "It will be our secret. Do you know 'Silver Threads Among the Gold'?"

"I can fake it," he said.

"Missy." Samuel Lees grinned, showing loose, stained teeth to Susan Todd. She turned away.

"I don't know," Julie said sorrowfully. "I think he cares. In some crazy way. But he's never said anything. I'm so fat."

Bobbie put a light hand on the back of her sister's bare neck. Fingertips under the hair scratched gently.

"I love you, baby," she said.

"It's him," Susan said. "I'm sure it's him. Filthy old man."

"I'll look out tonight," Tom Drinkwater promised. "You keep your light on till midnight. Move around up there. Pretend you're going to bed. You know! I'll be there."

"Promise?"

"I promise. If I catch him, I'll . . ."

"You'll what?"

"I don't know. Something."

"If he's not there, if no one's there, if it's all clear, throw some pebbles against my window and I'll know."

"All right."

She smiled at him and brushed against his arm.

Todd stood alongside the Patroon on the porch. They watched that black. It was no longer a line; a thick streak filled the southeastern sky. The Patroon was using his small brass telescope.

"When do you figure it will hit?" Todd asked.

Vanderhorst took the telescope from his eye.

"Look at those trees." He nodded toward the copse between house and beach. Tops were moving, bending and jerking. "I figure we'll get the wind by midnight. Glass is dropping fast."

"We heard it on the radio. The troopers got a call and took off. They're calling in everyone."

"Put your shutters up and move that furniture on the lawn around to the lee of the house."

"Yes, Patroon. I'll do that."

"I sent the Semanski twins home to help their paw. Tom went down to tell Breckinridge. You need a hand? I'll send Sam Lees over."

"No. Thanks. I can manage. You figure about midnight?"

The old man stuck his nose up into the air and sniffed. He stared at the churning sea, searched the darkening.

"About then. For the wind. High tides after that and rain. Maybe hail."

"Hail?"

"It comes from a sky like that. You have food in the house?"

"Enough for a couple of days."

"That's all right. If the highway floods, you come over here. We have a full freezer—if the power lasts."

"Thank you, Patroon. Maybe I should get to the hospital."

"Not yet. Right now your place is at home with your daughter."

Todd nodded. He went back inside and beckoned Susan. They trudged through the sand toward their home.

"'Darling, I am growing older . . .'" Mrs. Grace Vanderhorst sang softly in a clear, sweet voice.

Hapgood Graves placed his fingers lightly on the keys. His right hand was trembling.

Mrs. Rebecca Drinkwater neither looked at the sky nor listened to the radio. She knew. She opened windows top and bottom. She lowered wooden shutters. She went out to the steel shed, opened the door and back window so the wind could blow through.

The postman was long gone, hurrying. Sam Lees and Tom Drinkwater closed down the front of the house. They dragged porch furniture around to the land side. Suddenly it was night, at four in the afternoon. There was an acrid smell. They heard the whistle of wind.

"It's coming." Samuel Lees kept chuckling. "It's coming."

But it was slow in coming. They kept three radios going, listening to alerts. The storm was curling up the coast. It was lashing with gale-force winds. There were high tides, rain, possible hail.

The Patroon stumped about his territory, inspecting. His white hair was blown into a halo. He tested shutters, tipped over a concrete birdbath and put it on its side. He insisted the porch screens be removed and laid flat. The wind went into him. He gulped it, the darkling sky, and growing smash of sea. Mrs. Rebecca stood on the porch, hugging her elbows. She watched him as he stalked about, stabbing his cane into the land.

"'Silver threads among the gold,'" Grace Vanderhorst sang happily in the library.

Wind hissed.

Sam Lees filled kerosene lamps in case the power failed.

Suddenly they were in a tunnel. A growling howl out there. It was animal. Lights flickered.

"Wow!" Bobbie Vander cried. "Is this ever great!"

Old Vanderhorst looked at her. Many years ago he had been a seaman aboard a man-o'-war in the North Atlantic. The wind had come and bent a steel gun shield flat to the deck.

It grew and grew and grew. Bobbie stopped laughing. Now they felt it. It was throbbing. The old house trembled. It was alive out there. But it was inside them, too. Something was fluttering inside them.

Things bounced off the sides of the house. There were scrapings on the roof. Somewhere a window shattered. Lights went off, came on for an instant, went off completely. Kerosene lamps were set out. Flashlights and battery lanterns were passed around.

The world shook. Earth was jelly.

The shriek came earlier than Vanderhorst had predicted. About 11:00 P.M. Hapgood Graves, naked in his white room, clapped palms to his ears. He reached for his white powder, used it and stared out the window. White sea was coming for him. It was all he could make out: a black tunnel filled with boiling froth.

It went on, on, on . . . There were whinings, screams, straining of a giant throat. Then there was spitting, flinging phlegm. They huddled. They looked to the Patroon, sitting solidly in his wheelchair.

By midnight the worst had passed. The Patroon accepted his daughters' kisses and went up to bed. Lamps were turned off. Pale flashlights went drifting through the house. No one spoke. They heard only a derisive riflefire on walls and roof. They whispered prayers and slept. The storm hummed away.

Tom Drinkwater changed into a black turtleneck sweater, cotton and thin, and black jeans. He was barefoot. He used an official two-cell Boy Scout flashlight to inspect his collection, carefully arranged on the shelves of an unpainted pine bookcase.

Fishhooks. Steel trap. Arrowheads. Knife chipped from a single piece of stone. Photograph of Jimmy Drinkwater, in a tarnished brass frame. Stone ax, head attached to ash handle with rawhide thongs. A Valentine from Mrs. Grace Vanderhorst. A worn book: *The Ikantos: Their Life and Times* by Chief Jonathon Snow-Deer. Two rabbit skins, cured, tacked to boards, hair scraped away. Three goose feathers. A Bible: "Distributed by the Association for Indian Enlightenment." Hunting knife with a hollow in the handle for matches. Round brain coral from Florida. A pamphlet: *Karate Self-Taught.*

Hidden behind the bookcase was the stick from a chocolate Popsicle Susan Todd had sucked away. There was a yellowing magazine: *Bevy of Beauties.*

Tom picked up the stone ax, hefted it in his hand. Violence prickled his palm and spread like a fever. He burned with it. He put aside the lighted flashlight and dropped into a crouch. His left forearm was held out as a guard, ax gripped in raised right hand. The stone head made little circles.

Suddenly he struck, grunting, his body aflame. He whirled, going, "Ahhh" and "Heee." The ax flashed, flecks of mica in the stone glinting. The weapon rose and fell as he destroyed his enemies, ducking, lunging, stooping, striking, crushing skulls, and splintering bone.

He stopped as suddenly as he had started. He put the ax away, picked up the stone knife. He felt its sharp, rippled edge with his thumb.

He was a member of an Iroquois war party. They had captured a white man, white as Hapgood Graves. The prisoner was stripped naked and tied, arms stretched between two trees.

A skin-deep incision, an inch wide, was made high on the white man's chest. Then a strip of skin was pulled slowly downward and left dangling at the waist. The man began to scream.

Tom Drinkwater moved around him slowly, making cuts and pulling down torn strips of skin. Soon the white man was red raw to his waist. From the waist down a fringed skirt hung to his knees, dripping. His head had fallen forward but he was alive.

The boy looked at the stone knife in his palm. He slid it into the belt of his jeans and pulled his sweater down to conceal it.

He padded down the hall, down the back stairs. He unlocked the screen door, unhooked the heavy wooden door. Wind grabbed it eagerly, but he hung on. He searched a moment, found a piece of shell, closed the outside door, shoved the shell into the crack to stick it tight.

He took two steps and was soaked through. Thunder still grumbled, but the flashes of lightning had moved inland. Rain came from a spout, soaking hair, clothes, pressing him into soggy earth.

He loped lightly around the back of the house. Water came to his ankles. He bent swiftly, touched, tasted. It was salt; the sea was up that high. He moved through a rain ocean. Something hard was there; hail, a little. The night was mad. He went slowly through the trees, wiping his eyes with a soaked sleeve. He saw the Todd home, orange lights glimmering from Susan's room.

He hunkered, almost creeping. He drew the stone knife,

muttering something. He came up silently behind Samuel Lees. The old man had glasses clamped to his eyes. He was muttering something.

Tom Drinkwater pressed a hard arm across the old man's throat and pulled him backward, holding the sour smell against his chest. He jabbed the point of the stone knife into the softness under the loose jaw.

He leaned forward, whispered into Lees' ear: "You want to die?"

"No," Lees whispered back.

The boy nodded, released his grip. Samuel Lees dropped his binoculars. He plodded away, looking up at the curdled sky. His face was rasped with rain and tears.

Tom squatted in the cold wet. He picked up the glasses, wiped the lens on the inside of his sweater. He put them to his eyes, moved the knurled knob. There was Susan, still in that shiny black shift. It was a free skin.

He propped there, scrabbling about in the soaked clothing. He dug a handful of wet sand, pebbles, broken shells. He stood and tossed them against the lighted window. Nothing.

He scraped up another handful. Water ran through his fingers, leaving sand, stones, twigs, things. He threw with a hateful, wanting to break the window.

She came, looked down, peered, waved. She moved away.

He slid back under the trees. He wiped the glasses again, put them to straining eyes.

Did she know? Guess?

The black dress disappeared over her head. Black bikini panties came off. All tanned skin was there, blocked with pale triangles and a golden bosket. She moved back and forth before the window.

Chill and salt outside, and inside the burning. He could not move, rummaging her arching breasts. His aching eyes put shafts on her rubbing thighs. He probed. It was all hot. She pranced, posed.

"I. Love. You." he said aloud.

Windows went blind: darkness.

---

## 13

She was not stupid, but she was cursed with physical splendor that dazzled her. She came out of the sun, and every time she tried to think the heat melted her thoughts to mush.

She lay in bed, wondering who she was.

"Who are you?"

"I am Susan Todd."

Susan Todd: three Japanese syllables. But that wasn't who she was. Susan Todd was a label you sewed on camp clothes. It didn't say that youth caught in her throat and strangled.

When she was younger she *knew* she was not the daughter of her parents. She had been adopted and was, perhaps, a princess of royal blood, an orphan left on the doorstep in a snowstorm, the illegitimate daughter of a great ballet dancer who . . .

She was someone and something. Undeniably she existed. She could grip her own thighs or, by curling her legs behind her head while lying in bed, kiss her own breasts. She stirred men; she knew that. They remembered. Oh, she was there.

But inside that tight envelope of golden skin and . . .

Cut through the surging things to . . . Pry into everything pounding, ticking, pulsing, sweating, pumping, and there was . . . Susan Todd? Who? What?

She could do anything, be anyone: she *knew*. There was a time and a place for her. She had this—what? It was a passion, a tide of love for someone, for something. She could pour it out, just give. For whom? Where?

"And now, ladies and gentlemen, our prima ballerina in 'Swan Lake.' I give you . . . Susan Todd!"

"Darling, I need you. I cannot live without you. Every minute of the day and night I dream of . . ."

"I know I am dying, but it is a far, far better thing I do than . . ."

"Susan, marry me and the world . . ."

Ahh, what a silly maze. She was lost, rolling there on a damp sheet listening to a dying storm. What is life? That was the question: what *is* life? She could be . . . anything. The storm in her was not dying, tide not falling. Lightning flashes were still in her. She was charged.

"I love you." Who? *You!*

She baffled her. Boys put their hands on her and panted. "Ooh," they went, "ooh." But she pushed them off, rolled them off. There must be something . . .

Was Tom Drinkwater sitting in the sodden grass, watching her vacant window? Was Hapgood Graves dreaming of her grinning navel? Was Samuel Lees groaning and doing things to himself? The storm went out and out. Did it never fade?

Her life was all questions and no answers. She felt herself and loved herself, but it was not enough.

"Mr. President, I would like to present . . ."

She revolved, pillow to pillow, smelling her own bold body. If only she knew more, could ask someone . . .

# 14

The power came back early in the morning. The damage to the Vanderhorst home was slight. No food had spoiled in the freezer.

But all of Grace Vanderhorst's shells had been blown away. And the stinking carcass of a dead shark had been thrown up onto the lawn.

"We need a change of pace, mom," Hapgood Graves said. "A jingle. A patter song. Something with bounce."

"So?" Bobbie Vander said. "Write it."

He called it "Two-Ton Tessie from Ten-Ten-Tennessee."

"Let me play the tune for you," he said. He opened the old piano in the library. "It's not music; it's a tune. You'll do it with a steel banjo behind you. I know just the man."

She listened and laughed.

"That's funny," she said. "A kind of a folk song."

"Yes. A kind of one."

"Where's the lyrics?"

He handed them to her.

"I've got a gal who's five-foot-three,
Tattooed butterfly on her knee.
When she struts her stuff for me
That butterfly has got to flee!

She's . . . that . . . mind-boggle, horn-swoggle,
   eye-goggle, tit-joggle
Two-Ton Tessie from Ten-Ten-Tennessee!

The boys they come to have a spree,
To see that butterfly on her knee.
They give her dollars two and three,
To laugh with joy and shout with glee!

She's . . . that . . . mind-boggle, horn-swoggle,
   eye-goggle, tit-joggle
Two-Ton Tessie from Ten-Ten-Tennessee!

She serves the gents a golden tea
And shows the butterfly on her knee.
And when she gives them pleasure three
They graduate with their degree!"

She read it through to the end, giggling occasionally,
rolling her eyes, and once doing a burlesque grind-and-
bump. She caught the antique mood at once: Lillian Russell
in a whalebone corset. The song smelled of patchouli and
verbena, of a time when men wore diamonds and pregnant
women were in an "interesting way." It was so unlike her
own nakedness, and she loved it.

She finished and turned to Graves. "I'm with you. What
do you mean by 'pleasures three'?"

"Oh . . . you know."

"I guess. I think I better growl this one."

"I think you're right."

"Let's take it from the top."

He played and she sang. It came out right the first time.
They broke up. It was so silly.

"With a banjo you'll be great," he assured her. "This
one will be the single that makes it. You'll see."

"Yes." She nodded. "You're some nut, Hap."

She sat beside him on the bench. She put a hand under his loose shirt, scratched his bare back.

He had a sharp profile, honed by vice. They were alike in their whiteness, but his features were ice: a death mask cast after a long illness when human suet and wondering had drained away.

Having used his face so long as a disguise, it had become frozen and aboriginal. His smile was a grimace, and even in repose there was wooden mystery. It was a mold you wanted on your wall.

"Glad we came?" she asked him.

"Sure. Good food. Good swimming. Good sleeping."

"Good Susan Todd?"

"What are you talking about?"

"Don't con me, son. You're dying to push that."

He played something, fingers drifting lightly over nicotined keys. Once he had dreamed of . . . But that was in another life, and hope was dead.

"I see you looking at her," she said.

"Yes. I look at her."

"I don't blame you. She's a choice clip. But Hap . . ."

"What?"

"Don't make trouble."

He played some more, something gay and lilting. Then suddenly he crashed bass chords. The room filled with thunder. And as suddenly he stopped.

"Trouble?"

"You know."

"No, I don't know." He turned to stare into her eyes. "Unless you mean like you and your sister. And the doctor. That kind of trouble?"

She shivered a little and drew away from him. Finally she managed a bleak smile, held out a flat hand.

"Pals?"

"Sure."

They slapped palms.

"To each his own," Graves said.

They were so alike. They were twins with their wispy bodies and chicken bones. They were of such a size that sometimes, on the road, when she was too lazy to wash her lingerie, she wore his underpants or slept in his pajama tops.

They didn't have to talk. She would see a woman in a funny hat and nudge his arm. He would look and nod solemnly. Or they would be listening to another singer who would do something bogus. They would glance at each other and go through a little dumb show of vomiting.

Early in their relationship he expressed regret because she would not let him into her bed.

"That was our agreement," she reminded him. "You knew what you were getting into."

He looked at her with a warped smile that said, "I knew what I *wasn't* getting into." She understood, smiled secretly and touched him. Even then she knew his desire was a pose. His mistress was cocaine.

"Once more?" Graves asked.

She sang "Two-Ton Tessie from Ten-Ten-Tennessee," prancing about the library, playing it broad. She growled out the song, a soubrette in a Klondike saloon. Hapgood Graves lurched with laughter, bending over the stained keys.

"Oh oh," he gasped. "That's it. That is *it!*"

They strolled out onto the lawn, hand in hand. They sat at the umbrella table and watched little waves tumble toward them. Bubbling froth curled onto the sand. They saw Susan Todd go running down the beach, running frantically. She was alone.

"What's going to happen?" Bobbie Vander asked.

At the women's college she attended for two years she was envied for her musical talent. But she was feared. They said she was a woman who didn't care. Word spread . . .

A close friend took an overdose of sleeping pills. A roommate was withdrawn from school, placed in a sanitarium. The dean told her . . . She was found with . . . One night on the lawn she . . .

She sailed through it all with a hard smile. Nothing touched her except music. She had no taste for food or liquor, couldn't understand art, and never read for enjoyment. But bluesy ballads and love songs turned her inside out.

She worked hard at them, and the way she was living helped. She tried everything and walked away from it shrugging. Nothing caught her except the singing, which became increasingly professional. She was not born with that haunted, bittersweet voice; she earned it.

Her career followed a rusty pattern: smoky cellar clubs, flopping on the manager's cluttered desk to get the job. Then came a few benefits, afternoon TV shows. She had luck, and she began to catch on.

She was booked into a few good supper clubs. She fucked agents, managers, talent scouts, producers, vice-presidents; she paid her dues. Then she made a single 45 that took off. An album did even better. She was going.

Hapgood Graves made the difference. He knew music as she'd never know it. But what good was he without her?

"The world is full of guys who know music," she told him.

He nodded.

So they made their pact, and then there was no stopping them. They did Las Vegas, Miami Beach, the Waldorf, guest shots on prime-time TV, albums, university concerts.

They were always working; they were always improving. They tried some dicey things that came off. Critics cheered, and fan magazines slavered.

She had her style. That was part of the answer. It was her style, no one else's. It was not only the way she sang; it was the way she looked, dressed, moved. It was her.

She knew what she could do and what she could not, although Graves nagged her constantly to stretch her talent. She was willing to take a chance. She had gambled all her life, and she had the cool out and hot in of the professional gambler.

Some nights, on the road, alone in her hotel room, she wept softly. But not often. Usually she was chromium. A million young girls tried to imitate her. In Omaha, Bangor, and Phoenix there were ersatz Bobbie Vanders. She was a hairstyle, a skimpy shift, a bikini, a makeup kit.

But mostly she was a voice that could not be imitated. It came from her taints and lost dreams. Whatever she had been, was, would be, went into her love songs. The world listened, hearing an echo of its own ache.

"What's going to happen?" Graves repeated. "When? To whom?"

"'To whom,'" she mimicked. "Harvard creep. To us. How much time have we got?"

Graves shrugged. "Ella Fitzgerald's been around a long, long time."

"I'm no Ella and you know it. How much time?"

"Maybe another five years."

"And then?"

"Ask Sam Wartzenberg," he said crossly. "I'm not your manager. I'm not your financial adviser."

"What will you do?"

"Raise rabbits."

"*Schmuck,*" she said.

"How the hell should I know what I'll do? Something. A lot can happen in five years, mom."

"What are you sore about?"

"I'm not sore."

"You're yelling on me."

"Oh, Christ." He sighed and turned a shoulder to her. He tried to see Susan Todd, but she had disappeared down the smoky beach.

"What did you mean by that crack!" she demanded.

He knew at once what she meant.

"Did you ever notice how much Todd resembles the Patroon?" he asked her.

She looked at him strangely.

"You're the second one who's told me that. Julie thinks so too. You're both nuts. They don't look anything like each other."

"Of course they don't. But they're the same *type*. Big, wide men. Heavy through the chest and shoulders. And the way they move. They move ponderously. They put each foot down deliberately, as if they were planting it. As if they owned the goddamned world. I've known men like that. They don't like me. They're so fucking masculine. They're all Adams. They're always thinking, and who the hell knows what they're thinking about? They think all the time, and then they do something incredible like shooting a king or marrying a chorus girl."

"You think the Patroon and the doc are like that?"

"Sure. Men like that are sailors and doctors and sometimes painters. They usually make their living with their hands, one way or another. It does something to them. They turn in on themselves. The Patroon is like that: heavy and dark and brooding. I'll bet he's a stubborn son of a bitch."

"He is."

"The doctor's the same way."

"Let's you and me go to bed," she said.

But he knew her games.

"No. Thank you."

She told him what they might do. He heard her out patiently.

"Are you finished?" he asked.

"Yes."

"Then I'll go get us a lemonade."

"That's a good idea," she said happily.

──────────15──────────

Mrs. Grace Vanderhorst was wearing her summer "church dress," made from a pattern published many years ago in "The Delineator." It was flowered cotton with a ruffled collar, trimmed pockets, lace hem . . . and things.

She poked on her spectacles, snagged bows in her strawberry wig, and adjusted them on her pert nose. She peered at her list.

"Now then, Mister Vanderhorst," she said nervously. "Are you listening?"

"I am listening," he acknowledged.

He was dressed, seated on the edge of their bed. His hands were clasped on the head of his blackthorn cane, chin on hands. He attended her steadily.

"I am chairman of today's meeting of the Ladies' Club. Isn't it a lovely day? I am so glad it didn't rain. And I have made a list of things I must do so that I don't forget anything. Wasn't that wise of me, dear?"

"Very wise."

"I was up so late working on it. I didn't come to bed till almost eleven. I didn't wake you, did I?"

"No. I wasn't asleep."

"You should have said something. Then I would have kissed you good night. I wanted to, but I didn't want to wake you. But if I had known you were still awake, I would have kissed you good night."

"Thank you, Grace. That's all right."

"Now the first item says 'Doctor Ben—drive in—breakfast.' That means Doctor Todd will drive me in after breakfast. He promised he would. And after he leaves the hospital this evening he will pick me up at the church. That's very kind of him, don't you think?"

"Yes. Todd is a good neighbor."

"I am completely in charge today. 'Minutes last meeting.' That means I must call for the reading of what went on at our last meeting. Maggie Struthers is our secretary and she will then read the minutes. Do you understand that, dear?"

"Yes. I understand."

"Then I must say, 'Will anyone move that the minutes of the last meeting be adopted?' And then someone will say, 'I move the minutes of the last meeting be adopted.' I called Jean Gardner last night and she promised she would say that. Then I call for a vote, and everyone says yes, the minutes of the last meeting should be adopted. This is very official."

"I know."

"The next item says 'Knitting.' We are bringing our wool and needles and we are going to knit sweaters for the poor orphans of Nigeria. We have already—"

"Sweaters? Nigeria?"

"Yes, dear. Why? Is anything wrong?"

"Nigeria is in Africa. It is hot there. I do not think the orphans will need sweaters."

"Well, perhaps it's Eskimo orphans. I really can't remember. But we are going to knit. Sweaters and scarves and things. They will do good wherever they go, I am sure."

"That's true."

"Well, we will work until it's time for lunch. We are all bringing things. Mrs. Rebecca baked two apple pies for me yesterday and I am bringing those."

"I know. I smelled them yesterday."

"Well, she baked *three* apple pies, but one of them is for us. You must make certain you have a slice for lunch this afternoon, and Mrs. Rebecca says she has some sharp Cheddar cheese, so you can have your pie with cheese the way you like it. Now don't forget."

"I won't forget."

"Ask her to warm it up for you. You like warm apple pie with the juice coming out and cheese. Don't forget."

"I won't."

"The next item is our monthly book review. Miss Alice Bagley—she's the librarian, you know—she's doing a series of book reviews of great American classics, and today she is going to read her review of *The Last of the Mohicans*. That is by James Fenimore Cooper."

"Yes."

"Then after the book review, I will call for a general discussion of the book, and we will discuss it. We were all supposed to have read it since our last meeting, but to tell you the truth, dear, I have been so busy with my shells and things that I just haven't had a chance to get around to it. But I don't think that will hurt the general discussion, do you?"

"No. I don't think so."

"Then, after the general discussion of *The Last of the*

*Mohicans*, the Reverend Silas Abernathy is going to show us the slides he took on his trip to Hamburg, Germany, last year. I called him yesterday, and he believes his slides and lecture will occupy about two hours. Dear, would you like to come along? I am sure the slides and Doctor Abernathy's comments will be very interesting and educational. We frequently have gentlemen at our meetings, and if you'd care to attend, you'd be most welcome."

"I don't believe so. But I thank you."

"Well . . . perhaps some other time. Then, after the slides on Hamburg, Germany, Miss Agatha Forbes on the zither and Miss Abagail Forbes on the flute will deliver 'A Medley of Scotch and Irish Airs.' I am so looking forward to it. My, such talented girls! I was sure Mister Graves would be interested and I asked him if he would care to attend."

"And what did he say?"

"He said that ordinarily he would, but he's so busy writing the poems and music for Roberta's album that he just can't spare the time. But he did say that he felt the combination of zither and flute was very unusual and would undoubtedly result in memorable music."

"Yes."

"Did I tell you he is writing a poem just for me? He is going to call it 'To Grace.' "

"You told me."

"And then I must ask if anyone has any business they wish to bring up. I don't believe there will be any, but there *may* be. And if there is, then we must discuss it. And then someone says, 'I move this meeting of the South Canaan Ladies' Club be adjourned.' And someone seconds the motion. And I say, 'All in favor say aye.' And everyone says aye and we adjourn. Then Doctor Ben will pick me up and I will come home. Does that sound all right to you, Mister Vanderhorst?"

He looked at her tenderly, remembering something.

"It sounds just fine," he told her. "I think you have organized it remarkably well."

She blushed with pleasure, her eyes lowered.

"I do believe it will be a lovely afternoon," she said faintly.

After breakfast he stood on the land porch until Dr. Todd came to pick up his wife. He waved as they drove away. It was an occasion for her. She was alive with excitement.

Then he hauled his shattered body down to the sea. He leaned against an oak, as crippled as he, to tug off cotton socks and leather moccasins that Tom Drinkwater had made for him at Boy Scout meetings. He picked up a folding canvas chair from the lawn, dragged it after him.

He placed it in wet sand and sat down heavily. Warm sea came up to his bare ankles, laved his gnarled feet. A floppy canvas hat shaded his eyes. But still he squinted against the fire, staring out there.

*The sea. The sea! A man has not lived until he has known the sea. Felt the giant bounds the soul takes upward when the eyes look upon a world without limit, beauty without end. Always, everywhere, the sea rolls endlessly. Men come and go, and ships, and nations, and civilizations. But the sea! That rolls forever. It is life: constant and eternal.*

Pieter Vanderhorst, dreaming . . .

He had walked away from public school at the age of fourteen; said he was eighteen and shipped out as carpenter's helper on a wooden cargo ship harboring in Boston: the last son of a land family going to sea.

He never regretted it. He learned a trade and read the Bible, took knocks and gave them, killed a man in Dublin and loved a woman in Cairo, knew wars, storms, stars and peace. Always . . . there was the sea.

He came back to the land to open a carpenter shop in South Canaan, near the sea. It succeeded; he worked slowly but with craft and earned a reputation. Then he was in lumber, and his reputation grew. His virtues were his vices—fierce ambition, truculent honesty, frozen pride—and they saw him through. Men asked him to build for them. It was what he wanted; all his life he had been a builder. He assembled a staff of silent, cunning artisans.

But he would not work with brick, stucco, or cinder blocks. He would not touch plastic or aluminum sidings. Only the warm wood for him: smooth walnut, rough maple, solid oak, and veneers with the perfume of far-off jungles. Young architects came to him with strange plans for homes, beach houses, country clubs. He taught them what they might do and what they could not do with wood. They listened and trusted him, admiring the way he stroked seasoned pine.

And always he bought land, bought land, bought land: obeying an instinct once denied. He bought beach land, lakefront property, suburban lots, farms. He owned parts of the world.

Suddenly he was the Patroon. The original grant on his wall testified to the first Vanderhorst estate on the Hudson River. He sold off the shop, the lumberyard. He no longer built for others. He existed: the Patroon, complete man.

He was crumbling now, but with enough presence to awe. There was a swirl of thick white hair. Everything in his face was big: eyes, nose, mouth. His tremendous torso sagged back into the land. Those spatulate feet gripped the land. Those thick hands gripped everything, took it up and never once let go.

In the spot he was sitting now, slumped in his canvas chair, he had been sitting two years ago. He was drinking beer in the darkness with Dr. Todd. It was almost midnight. They talked of curious things. The doctor told a story:

"I was on night duty about six months ago. We got a call

from the bartender of the Pleasure Inn. That's a beer joint out on Route 9-A6. The owner is Peter Hranski, who is a pig. Foulmouthed and big-bellied. Loud. The bartender said that Hranski had been standing at the bar, drinking with his customers.

"Suddenly his face got red. Said there was a vise around his chest. Couldn't breathe. But he held onto the bar and didn't fall. The bartender said someone was driving him in. It sounded like a coronary, and it was. We got that great hulk bedded down and did what we could. God, he smelled. Well, we got him through three days, and I went in to tell him he had to stay in the hospital for a month. We settled for two weeks if he'd stay in bed at home another month. 'Doc,' he said, 'how soon can I fuck?' I told him, if he didn't want to kill himself, it would be three months. 'How about jacking-off?' he asked me. 'Still three months,' I told him. 'The heart doesn't know the difference.'"

It was that—"The heart doesn't know the difference"—that rooted Pieter Vanderhorst's mind. It puzzled him. Not in the sense Dr. Todd meant it. But its meaning seemed to go on and on.

Did it mean the heart couldn't distinguish between pleasures, as long as it was pleasure? Did it mean the heart didn't care who you loved, as long as you loved? Did it mean . . . What did it mean? "The heart doesn't know the difference."

He shook his great head and closed his eyes. He dozed.

He slept for perhaps ten minutes. Then laughter, shouts opened his eyes to see Susan Todd come staggering from the surf. She was all gleaming, water streaming from hair and flesh.

After her came Tom Drinkwater pelting her with handfuls of wet sand. For a brief moment they grappled, roaring their joy. Then she pulled free, dashed up the beach with long, loping strides. Young Tom went running after, reaching.

The Patroon watched from hooded eyes, hearing them after they were lost in the ground fog. "Su-*sann!*" he heard Tom call. Vanderhorst looked up, hoping. There it was—a single gull keening through an azure sky.

He rose slowly to his feet, plodded back to the house.

In 1957 Vanderhorst had broken through the west wall of the kitchen of his summer home to enlarge the dining room. He had then built a new kitchen of one story, butting on the enlarged dining room.

Each of its three sides had two windows. They were screened but not glassed, covered with interior shutters of wood. These were raised and lowered by ropes on pulleys, not unlike port coverings on a wooden cargo ship.

As the sun dragged out of the sea and drifted around to the rear of the house, a soft-edged beam came through each of the six windows in turn. Theodore, the fat, altered-male house cat, moved with the sun. He slept in the first rectangle of heat. When it faded, he rose, arched his back, yawned, strolled to the next, lay on his side, slept.

The varnished wood in this raftered room glowed with light. It was all airy, floating—a quiet aquarium. Crazy motes danced in salt sunlight. An iron rack hung over the burnished worktable. There were copper and steel pots, a giant colander, pans: dazzling. On the wall was a scabbard of knives and shiny kitchen tools.

The colors! A rope of red onions was there, and a long, bronzed Polish sausage, a wooden bowl of fruit: Concord grapes, peaches, plums. There was a straw box of blueberries, a ripening Spanish melon: hungry colors shivering in the light. From far off, in the library, came muted music. Somewhere was the sea. A breathy shout sounded from the beach. A fly buzzed. There was sting of morning heat and suddenly a kiss of breeze.

Old Vanderhorst sat at the head of the table. He forked away at a wedge of warm apple pie covered with a slab of Cheddar. He moved his eyes onto her.

She sat on the chair at his right, skirt pulled above her brown knees. She was leaning forward, hunched over, an aluminum pot between her feet. She was shelling peas, slitting the pod with a sharp thumbnail, flipping the peas down: plonk, plonk, plonk. She dropped the empty pods onto a spread newspaper.

He ate the pie, watched her work.

"Where is Lees?" he asked.

"It is Wednesday," Mrs. Rebecca Drinkwater said.

"Wednesday?"

She said nothing. Slowly it came to him that it was Lees' day off.

"Julie?"

"Up. On the roof."

With her thermos of drink. He knew them all.

They sat quietly. There was a caw of laughter from the library. Mrs. Rebecca finished the peas. She ran water into the pan, put it aside, gathered up pods in the newspaper, dumped it all into the high garbage pail outside the back door. She took his empty plate away, slid it noiselessly into the sink. She took the blue coffee pot off the low flame, poured them each a cup and hiked her chair closer to his.

"Susan Todd will not be going away to college," he told her. "She wants to wait a year. Her father agreed."

She nodded.

"I think the boy should go away," he said. "It is something I feel. He must spend time on his school work. He will not do it if she is here."

"Yes, Patroon. Where shall he go?"

"You are willing to send him away for a year?"

"Yes."

"I will ask. A prep school or military academy."

"They will laugh at him."

"Because he is an Indian? Let him be hurt. He must learn to live with it. Better than what will happen to him here. She is bored. She is playing with him."

"He is a boy."

"A handsome boy."

She burned with delight whenever he paid the lad a compliment. Her features thawed, eyes glowing. Lips parted. Her great breasts rose. Pride fizzed through her.

"Handsome!"

They went to one of the vacant bedrooms on the third floor. They bolted the door behind them and were swallowed by heat. They opened the window but the curtain did not stir. Air hung, dripping. There was an odor of ageless things.

She moved to help him but he shook her off. He sat on the edge of the bare mattress, undressing himself with one hand: unbuttoning, unbelting, standing to step out of his clothes. She watched anxiously.

Then he lay back on the rough tick. She stood smiling. She picked up his blackthorn cane, kissed the smooth, rounded head, rubbing it along her lips. She looked at him.

"Woman." He laughed.

Her skin was hot but dry. Did she ever sweat? He thought not.

She was more gentle with him than he would have liked, but he said nothing. Her hands grazed over him, and she spread him wide. He wanted to cry out. He grabbed a handful of her long, oily hair, stuffed it in his mouth, bit down on it.

Her hands memorized him, moving over the wounded

geography of his flesh. It was cut and rutted. There were trenches there and scars, flawed muscles and slack line.

How she roused him! My God. Now he owned the world.

He crushed her close with his good arm. He rolled over atop her, took her hair away so that he might kiss her open eyes. Her smooth legs linked behind his back, and he swam into her, groaning.

She pressed, pressed, wanting his weight, his sweet weight.

"Love," she said once.

They spent together, both swimming now, rolling in the warm sea. Their arms and legs bobbed about . . . somewhere.

Their rhythm died slowly . . . pulsing. She would not release him but held him close. He lived again on her breast, breathing her warmth.

They rubbed cheeks, felt, did young things.

"Love," he said once.

Parting from her was as painful as waking. He rolled aside. But still, arm to arm, leg to leg, they were linked in heat. He propped the naked pillow behind his head and looked down upon her. She was sprawled in satisfaction: a soft smear of brown-red-bruised flesh.

Eyes closed. "Do you love me?"

"I love you."

"Do I do good for you?"

"You do good for me."

Who said what?

It was a litany. She touched him softly.

Two blue-green dragonflies came skimming into the room, coupling. He watched them happily, those wild wonders waltzing. Then they were gone. An hour droned away, a summer hour.

"I wish," he said.

She stroked his cheek, kissed one of his twisted nipples. Her finger traced a great vein that wandered across his pale groin, down a heavy thigh, pumping.

"I don't know," he said. "I thought I did. Until the hospital. Now there is Julie. Up there with her drink. Wanting a skin like yours."

"What?" she said. "Tell me what."

"I thought I knew," he said. He was puzzled. "People act from greed. From lust, hunger, thirst, love, anger, fear, loneliness."

"Yes."

"But now I think: why fear? why greed? why love? When you plane a good piece of mahogany, softly, gently, the curls of wood flow away. You must not hurt the wood. Not gouge. Not scar. You float the wood away. With respect."

"Oh, yes. It is good."

"And as you plane, a new grain appears. The closer you get to the heart, the finer the grain. I think it may be the same with men and women. I am talking now of motive. Why people do what they do. Fear, love, greed, lust. I am now seeing they are wide words. Outer grain. Below them are other motives. Finer. More complex. Rebecca, Julie has a body much like yours."

"Taller."

"Oh, yes. Taller. But your breasts. Your fullness. Her legs are not as good, but her skin is yours. Her hair is shorter. But she is . . . sturdy, too. And she bakes her flesh to get your color. Now why is that?"

"Sun-tan. All white women want to be darker."

"Maybe. Maybe that's all it is. But now I wonder. Why people do what they do. Why does Hapgood Graves follow Roberta about? Why does Susan Todd show her body to men? Now, for the first time in my life, I would like to get down to the fine grain and understand."

"It is difficult to know what people think. They say one thing but they think another. I do not believe it is possible to know always what is in their hearts."

"I know: white man speaks with forked tongue."

She giggled and hugged him.

"Still," she said, "it is true for all of us."

"I suppose so. But . . . Here is what I wonder. Within the way we live are many layers of motives and reasons. Just like that piece of mahogany. And the top layer may be greed, let us say. Plane it away, and beneath is the reason for the greed. Gently plane that away, and there is the reason for the reason for the greed. Rebecca?"

"Yes. I understand. Down and down."

"Exactly. I knew you would know. Down and down. To the essence of the wood. But does the person know? Or is he simply greedy without knowing? Or loving without knowing why? Or fearful? Or whatever. Perhaps the heart doesn't know the difference."

"The heart knows only the top layer? The greed? The love?"

"I have been wondering."

"Patroon, I love you. Many, many layers deep. With your plane or sharp knife you can trim my heart to a pebble. And that pebble will love you. As small as you make it. And when the pebble is thrown into the sea, the love will stay. My spirit will love. Only you."

"You think we will live in another world?"

"You and I?" She was astonished. "Of course. Can you doubt it? Together."

He tried to enter into her again but he did not succeed.

# 16

The sun burned up the days. It came blooming out of the sea, a molten promise. It was, everyone said, the best summer in years: hot noons, cool midnights. The morning fog burned away and there was an infant world.

Old man Breckinridge had the tallest flagpole on the beach. It was steel planted in concrete. Each morning he stumped out and ran up Old Glory. Sunshine, rain, fog, storm—he didn't care; he put it up there. He took it down at sunset and folded it into a careful triangle.

Every year he wrote out a check to the South Canaan Fire Department. It was five hundred dollars for a fireworks display from his beachfront on the Fourth of July. It was understood that three hundred dollars went for rockets and two hundred dollars for beer, clams, and sausages for the firemen.

Property owners on the beach let everyone come in. The access road was crowded with cars. But even from South Canaan you could see the bursts over the sea, in the night sky. There were shouts. People sang.

Hapgood Graves took it into himself, laughing. He wandered down to watch solemn, helmeted firemen set up wooden chutes. They touched a rocket and dashed away.

*Pow!* In the sky was an explosion of color. Things went out in a frizzle of light: blue, green, red, yellow.

Clutching his cold bottle of Ram's Head he returned to the Vanderhorst beach. He sat down in the screen of trees, crossed his ankles. He watched the sky crack, hummed "Two-Ton Tessie from Ten-Ten-Tennessee."

"Hello there," Susan Todd said. She folded down beside him with her bottle of beer.

Night split down the seams. She watched a rocket burst, her eyes stuttering. Her mouth blinked. There was a smell of hell in the air: Lucifer. Something was burning.

"Hello there," she said again.

He turned slowly to smile. He had her. She was bored.

"I love this," he said. "It's beautiful."

"Will you write a poem about it?"

"Why not?"

She leaned against his tree. Their warm arms touched.

How black it all was. There was a dead moon, then nothing seared with brilliance. They saw . . . and heard: falling stars, fountain of noise.

"Boom," he said.

"Bang." She laughed. "I'm going for another beer. Want one?"

"Mmm. Bring some so we—"

He stopped suddenly. She drifted away. A great red streak thrust upward. "Oooh! Aaah!" He could hear dimly. It exploded in a splatter of light that fell, fell . . .

"Don't fall in love," he murmured. "Rise to love."

She folded beside him again. She placed four opened bottles of beer carefully upright in the sand.

"Mrs. Rebecca gave me these."

"May her tribe increase."

"Want to play a game?"

He slanted her a lazy glance. "What kind of a game?"

There was a little one over the water: sprinkle of sparkles, dark sea alive with dancing lights.

"Now this is called the Truth Game," she explained. "I ask you a question and then you ask me a question. But you must swear to tell the truth and nothing but the truth. Do you swear?"

"I swear."

"Cross your heart and hope to die?"

"Cross my heart and I hope to die."

"Okay. Now we start out by asking silly questions like 'What is your name?' and 'Where do you live?' But then the questions get harder and harder. You understand?"

"Yes."

"And then the questions get—well, you know—real personal. The first one to refuse to answer a question, that's the loser. Have you played this game before?"

"I've been playing it all my life," he said.

"What?"

"What does the loser and what does the winner win?"

"Oh, there's no prize or anything like that. It's just to see which of us is the most honest. You know, the loser is the one who refuses to answer first. It's a stupid game but it's fun. We used to play it all the time at school."

There was a hiss in the night sky, trailing dribbles of light. A flash made day. He turned quickly to see her. What was . . . He wanted to touch.

"Okay?" she asked.

"Who goes first?"

"I do because I'm a woman."

Now they were in secret darkness.

"And what is your first question?"

"What is your name?"

"My name is Hapgood Graves. Now I go?"

"That's right."

"What is your name?"

"My name is Susan Todd. Where do you live?"

"I keep a small apartment on the west side of Manhattan, but mostly I travel around the country with Bobbie Vander. How old are you?"

"I am eighteen—or will be in a week or so. How old are you?"

"I am thirty-six—twice your age. Isn't that nice?"

"Yes, that's nice. Where were you born?"

"Hey, wait a minute. I didn't get to ask my question."

Giggling: "You said, 'Isn't that nice?' That was a question and I answered it honestly and it counts. So now it's my turn."

A big rocket went up and smaller splashes sprayed: red, white, blue. Cold beer tingled tongues. The tree trunk was hard against their backs. Soft arms pressed. The velvet night would last forever.

"Well . . . all right. I was born in Wichita, Kansas. Why don't you want to go to college next year?"

"Someone's been talking. Because I don't know where I want to go—even if I can get in. I'm not even sure I want to go to college at all. Where did you go to college and for how long?"

"That's two questions. Do I get credit?"

"Oh, come on. Don't be such a grunch."

"I went to Harvard for one year. Do you miss your mother?"

"Yes, I miss my mother. Why did you leave Harvard after one year?"

"I got kicked out for peeing on a dean's door. Do you like living with your father?"

"Yes. Are you in love with Bobbie Vander?"

"Yes. How big are your breasts?" He stroked her with words.

"I'm thirty-nine C cup. But I'm not really that big. It's

just that I have a wide back. That's how they measure, you know. All the way around."

"I know. Are you in love with your father?"

"It's my turn. Are you a homo?"

There was a necklace in the sky, the jeweled sky: spangles and sequins, all glinting, pearls dripping from strings. His face was green in the sapphire glow.

"Not now," he said. "Are you in love with your father?"

"Yes. Do—"

She stopped suddenly, punched. They were shaken. Firecrackers went off down the beach: bombs, no light but thumps of sound. They felt it: thumps inside.

"Do you smoke marijuana?" she asked.

"No. Are you a virgin?"

Her face came close to his. Then came a blue rocket; he saw the twisted mouth open, heard the gasp.

"Have I won?" he asked gently.

"No. Yes, I am a virgin. Do you use any other drugs?"

"Yes. I sniff cocaine. Do you want me to fuck you?"

"Yes. Do you?"

"Yes."

In that glare clash they were so close. They touched only with lips, arms and legs hanging limp, all of them slack. Their eyes closed against brilliance shattering the sky. Their bodies were dead. Only their lips lived. It was a butterfly's kiss. It was a silken brush, back, forth. Their mouths trembled, toying and teasing, then wet and now sliding.

"Oooh! Aaah!" They heard the shout from down the beach. Light flared behind their closed lids: whirls and pinwheels. They waited for darkness, urged closer. They were sucking souls. They leaned toward each other, living on each other, wet mouths wanting as the sky cracked open with light.

She pulled away from him fast and looked at him with horror.

"I have a question coming," he said in a coarse voice. "Do you love me?"

Sound came out of her. At once she was standing, looking down at him. He saw: swell of thigh, bulge of breast, chin, nose.

"You win," she said, and ran away from him down the beach. She suddenly halted, came back, reached down a hand for him. He grasped it and was hauled to his feet.

"It's the end!" she said excitedly.

So it was: the Grand Finale, everything going off at once. The world shattered with blaze: grumbling and thunderings, screaming, explosions without end, light upon light, streamers going out, snapping candles, and red-blue-yellow-white blowing, fading, up, on: the world cracked open.

They stood, hand in hand, looking up. Their faces were red-blue-yellow-white. Their mouths stared at the crazy splendor. Their life split. Bang!

"When?" she asked breathlessly.

"Soon," he told her. "It's always ten minutes to never."

She pulled free, went running down the beach. He stared after her.

He trudged up to his room, smiling. He undressed, laughing.

He flipped lights out and took his powder. Then he rose again, turned on the lights, went over to the wicker desk where he kept his work sheets. He scribbled:

> "Don't fall in love, don't fall in love,
> Take wings and soar to find it.
> Fly high above, to pledge your love,
> And give a kiss to bind it."

He flopped onto the damp sheet, lights out. "And give a kiss to bind it."

Just before he soared he muttered, "Come live with me and be my love," and saw the cat who had written that: knifed to death in a tavern brawl. So be it.

"Don't fall in love . . ."

——————————17——————————

*Then wiggling like that. Waggling. Where the hell was they when he . . . Was it right a man should be born fifty years too soon? . . . on the bus. When he scrunched down he could see right up. Now blue they was with little flowers. Surprised she was wearing anything a-tall. No bra-zeer on her. Oh. Those loose titties. That Injun kid had no right. And the one in the park. She knew he was looking. She knew! "Hello, kiddie, my name is Samuel Lees. What's your name?" Smooth brown legs on her. Twisting. He'd give . . . Well, the young whores had no shame. Naked in public. Sometimes on that Susan you could see golden hairs. Hairs! Ah Jesus and hot crotch. He'd get the kid for that. Fix him right. Son, you don't fool with Sam Lees. Oh, the whores.*

He kept pint bottles of warm muscatel in the bottom of a brass-bound sea chest. Beneath faded overalls and blue work shirts was a neat row of soldiers. Emptied, the bottles were buried in soft, sucky ground across the access road. Ten years of empties were buried there. Last week he had dug to bury, and there was a dead soldier already there. He was paving that swamp with empties.

*The Patroon didn't know. Did he? That one in the*

*drugstore where he bought Ex-Lax and powder to make his dentures stick. "Good morning, Mr. Lees! The usual?" A shirt of that black flimsy stuff and underneath a white brazeer and what was in them. Bulging like that. The smell on her. Where was you when . . . Well, kiddie, snow on the roof, fire in the furnace. I could . . . yes, you'd be surprised all right. I know all the tricks. I could make you crying for it, I could. I'll fix that Injun kid. When she comes running out of the water. Looking around. Anyone want what I've got? Yes.*

The wine was warm and sweet. It was the only thing he could keep down. But every morning there was retching, belching, sneezing. He smelled wine on the scraggly, stained mustache hanging around his sagging mouth. The odor of wine was in him. He could soak his teeth, take a bath, soap and all, and dry off; then smell his armpits: warm muscatel. It was coming out of him, oozing.

*No, kiddie, I ain't one to look back. The old life weren't that good. It was hard. Now you come and sit right here on my lap. That's it. Right here. Yes. Now you call me "Daddy" and I'll call you "Kiddie." You're a pretty thing. All soft and warm you are. Young. That blond one with the Semanski twins. Hair right down to her soft little bum. Stepping out like a good mare. I know the tricks. I could teach . . . You have to live to learn, kiddie. Anything you want, Sam Lees can deliver. No one ever said . . . Right down to her asshole. You could . . .*

It was steamy on his sheet. The curtain of fog and sweat soaked to white flesh. He was wasted: soft breasts, blank nipples, scribble of gray hair. His old scrotum hung wrinkled, an empty wineskin. His body was shrinking in upon his bones: brittle. It was a windless night: thick air and him gasping. His legs were hairless. Two weeks ago he had sneezed and there was blood.

*Oh, kiddie, kiddie . . . Four years ago that one who said, "Pardon me, sir, could you tell me what time it is?" That wasn't what she wanted. He knew. Skirt up to her whoozis. Bare arms. She was naked under that dress. Not a stitch. Mother born. "Just sit right here on my lap and call me 'Daddy.' " Starting: "Ooh, daddy, I feel so funny." That's how . . . But just at first . . . Now was that one a blonde? The one who asked him the time. Where was that? Was that in Bangor? Portland? Well . . . Feel me, feel me. I'm here, I am.*

He had been steeped in hot water for seventy years. His body lay puckered. Flesh dissolved and skin shrunk in on coarse bones. His yellowed eyes glared angrily. Those corns and calluses, blue veins faintly flat, pierce of mothballs, slick sheen to his legs, stuff in his eyes when he awoke— what in Christ's name was happening to him?

*But that Susan! Yes, the best. Because she's so . . . I'll get that damned Injun kid. Oh, yes, I'll show him. That knife of his don't scare me a bit. Listen, son, Sam Lees has been up against knives before and I'm still here. Think about that, son. Hair! By God, you could see little hairs coming out of that hot crotch and the way the swimming suit sucked into her. Susan. I know you, kiddie. I know and I'm here for you. Now you just sit here on my lap. I'll call you "Kiddie" and you call me "Daddy." Oh, you're so warm and heavy. You smell nice. That's what your daddy has for you. Just saving it for you. For you, kiddie . . .*

The bottle was empty. His weak tongue licked softly around the glass mouth. Oh, kiddie . . .

# 18

It was a rock-torn land, twisty. Everything was gnarled: hard knots and crabbed burls. The Patroon belonged, for wood smelled tart and people were cross-grained.

He bought the big house in 1940. It was on a hilltop with gentle slopes, meadowland, a wood. A small stream wandered, and there was an orchard of stunted apple trees. The hard, green fruit was blushed on one side, with a tangy, puckering flavor.

The house was a century old, built by a mad sea captain. Five miles from the ocean with a widow's walk! There were cupolas and curlicues, seven bartizans, turrets and a wide verandah. Over that door, in stained glass, was a fierce American eagle with a flowing ribbon: "In God We Trust. All Others Pay Cash."

From his hilltop, in 1940, the Patroon could see gleam of sea and the lazy life of South Canaan. Slow traffic moved along Route 9-A6. It was all hazy in crackled sunlight, shimmery and far.

Suddenly he was surrounded. The town of South Canaan, no longer an incorporated village, poured up to his rail fences: jerry-built homes of stucco, gas stations and a shopping center, a complex of three-story apartment houses.

He would not sell. The stream dried to cracked mud. Small boys demolished his apple trees and played baseball in his meadow. The air was hazy with smoke and smelled of sulfur. But the crazy house still stood on the hilltop. He would not sell.

A few years after the war—the air still sweet—Grace Vanderhorst made summer sandwiches for herself and two young daughters. The three of them went plunging down the gentle slope to meadow and wood, swinging baskets, laughing, singing, waltzing through that Wyeth world.

They went running down. Running. Down. Oh, the dandelions! Put under the chin and "Do you like butter?" They skittered about, three children: one dotty, one all sensual and soft, one all nerve, and hard.

It was fair meadowland and creamy sun and two young girls. Julie was about eleven. Roberta was about nine. Everything was about to be—their fresh, crisp bodies in something cotton.

They ran and skipped and laughed, mother gasping with delight and holding her heart. There was soft grass and buttercups. They swung and called, saw seared bliss and a blood-orange sun. Round and round they went, screaming.

What a world! They danced through it all. It was sunburned, glimmering. It was a passion, and they lived, lived, lived.

And under the trees, in hot shade, they had their picnic: slices of chilled cucumber with lettuce and mayonnaise on limp white bread, cold chicken wings, white radishes, things that bit, a funny jar of lemonade. They kicked their heels!

The moment caught, held. There was peace and rum-

bling, love and sunshine. They were swimming in it. Good-
bye. Good-bye.

Grace smiled in violet shadow, nodding over her tatting.
The two girls went whooping into the dark wood. They
were lost in there, tripping. They fell yelping. So alone.

The Patroon had built a tree house for his daughters.
"Pirates Den" was burned into the wood. Up into the oak
they went, the little animals. There they were: so secret. It
was their own place. They giggled and rolled on the rough.

Roberta kissed her older sister.

"See?" she said.

Julie's eyes widened, flamed.

"And sometimes they want to stick their tongues in your
mouth," Roberta explained. "Like this."

"And lick your lips. Like this."

"And lick your tongue. Like this."

"And make their tongues go in and out. Like this."

Julie, shuddering faintly: "Don't."

But she lay quiescent upon her back. Sunlight came
blazing through cracks in the sloped roof. Bees were
droning somewhere. Julie wondered and was pleased, a
knuckle clamped between her teeth. She closed her eyes to
feel more.

Cool things were on her, in her. She heard Roberta's soft
chuckle and gasp. There was a strange scent, a wet warmth
suffused and flooded. She floated away.

"And now you must do it to me," Roberta said definitely.

A torch went to that day. It softened, sagged, melted. All
colors went running; sunshine and flesh were puddled.
Their bodies were steamed and raw.

"Up a little," Roberta commanded. "Higher. Yes, right
*there*. Yes."

"Pirates Den." It was their secret place above the world.
They did everything there, and flowed off smiling.

"Not with your teeth, silly," Roberta said.

In the big house, and later in the beach house, Julie and Roberta shared a bedroom. They continued to explore each other. They were greatly pleased, licking like puppies.

Older, their pleasures slowed, became more thoughtful. They had separate friends and separate dates. But they reserved for themselves certain moments . . . ritual and devotion.

If it was not love, it was passion in a mask. There was stiff mouth, rouged cheeks, painted eyes. But beneath the *papier-mâché*, lips were wrenched with lust. Then came a spitting gasp, anguish umbridled . . . ecstasy.

Julie, her mother's daughter, grew into a warm melon of a woman, all bursting and hairy. She was indolent, a taste for pleasure in her like melting chocolate. A touch could make her moan.

Roberta, her father's son, was the white shaft gleaming. She was a sword that slashed, a dirk that pierced. Hard bones bumped her thin skin. Her searching hunger never stopped: more, more, devouring. Where was it? Here it is. Take it. And she forced herself through life, elbowing.

They were graduated in the same class from South Canaan High School: Julie so slow, fast Roberta. There is a photograph of the two girls in their white dresses.

The photograph has yellowed. A corner has been folded. The emulsion has cracked and peeled there. They stand, holding hands. They exist. They stare bravely into the glass eye.

This photograph, framed, stands on the Patroon's bedside table in the big house. He has never solved its mysteries. He knows they are now women. They are sisters. They are daughters. They are his daughters.

But he cannot comprehend their images. A breeze moves their white dresses. Their smiles seem to move, fleeting, but caught by the camera . . . in what? He told his wife, once, that the photograph frightened him. She did not understand.

Finally the Patroon—he was God; he saw everything— sent the girls away to different schools. They obeyed, Julie waiting for what might happen, Roberta eager to make it happen.

It was their last night together in the big house. Their trunks were packed. In the morning they would take their separate ways. But now: sweet sadness, black night of gusty winds, tatters of rain against streaming windows.

"We'll see each other on holidays," Julie said. "And visits. And you must promise to write. Once a week at the very least."

Roberta smiled.

That night was a corrupt ceremony in a whirlwind. Flashes of green lightning corroded their swollen bodies. Their tongues murmured. Julie would remember with her flesh; Roberta would forget.

"Do you, Julie, take this man, Roberta, to be your Lawfully Wedded Husband? To Have and to Hold? To Love and to Cherish? In Sickness and in Health? As long as ye both may live?"

"I do."

"Say it."

"Do you, Roberta, take this woman, Julie, to be your Lawfully Wedded Wife? To Have and to Hold? To Love and to Cherish? In Sickness and in Health? As long as ye both may live?"

"I do."

Gorged nipples.

"What God has brought together let no man put asunder."

". . . put asunder."

"No man."

"No man."

Damp wind painted them sleek. They tasted loss, clutched to hold what had been. But their skin was bitter, mouths tainted with fear.

In a moment, frantic with parting, they were clamped, sliding. Their tongues were dill and their hair was straw. They flogged themselves to a sobbing climax. The pageant that began in the "Pirates Den" came to a weepy end.

In one sour orgasm all the youth seeped out of them. They were now women, knowing.

———————19———————

"It will be a slate day," Pieter Vanderhorst pronounced.

So it was. The smutty sky was a sidewalk of cracked tiles. Somewhere was the sun, lost. But mostly mist drifted sideways, a steel mesh that imprisoned: chain mail flung over the earth.

Driving toward the sea from South Canaan, natives took Route 9-A6. They turned left at the E-Z-Buy Supermarket onto Staunton Road. This paved two-laner ended at the access road that paralleled the beach. There were white summer homes, a gas station, grocery and hardware stores, an antique shoppe. Open sand lapped the road that went past Vanderhorst, Todd, Breckinridge, Semanski, and on south.

To the left was the sea. To the right was a marsh. In there were screeching birds and small delving animals. Once a fox was seen. A club of wild dogs trotted shoulder to shoulder, forlorn. Sometimes, at night, a crash was heard.

Between the Breckinridge and Semanski properties another road struck inland through the swamp. Eventually it joined Route 9-A6. It was a raised roadbed, a graveled one-laner. It darted straight as an arrow. This short stretch of stone was called Indian Road and so marked on local maps.

Bordering Indian Road on both sides, at exact intervals of twenty feet, grew Lombardy poplars, tall and stern. Hard trunks pointed with close, secret foliage. The funeral road was a dark corridor, tapering.

On this slate day, gravel had been painted wet and silent, stones gleaming. Mist sifted down and muffled the marsh. No bird calls there, no barks. It was an endless dream stretching into sleep, a gray world shrinking to a gone horizon.

Dwindling down that ghost road went Mrs. Rebecca Drinkwater and son Tom. Her shoulders shriveled beneath the blur. About her was a scrap of blanket. In his hand was a milk bottle, half-filled with water. It held a sweet nosegay of bright things: daisies, pansies, a rose, mimosa, a tulip.

The leaden sky pressed them to dwarfs.

Just before the junction with 9-A6 was the Indian graveyard. It was raised land and drained. No swamp was there, no trees; only a bald knob of earth, a fallen fence of rusted wire, strong weeds. Mist hung close, fitting the raw ground like a rug.

There were burned planks. There were stones chewed by three hundred years of wind bite. They leaned crazily, melting into black. The names were gone now. The stones were blind.

Here was a jar, a bottle of shriven blooms, a broken dish of meal. There was a skeleton of a rotted rabbit, there a silver spoon glinting. Two brave lances plunged into earth, garlanded with feathers faded and limp.

Torn paper was nailed to lath—". . . he . . ."—rain-

streaked. There was a dim tintype in a brass frame, eyes
blazing. A crossbar supported a wire hanger with a
shredded leather jacket, fringe muddied.

Here was a message sealed inside an empty pint bottle of
Old Overholt. There was the body of a cat, mouth open,
eyes mad . . . ooze of blood. Five old radio tubes were
thrust into mold in a careful pattern. There were parcels
wrapped in newspaper, tied with twine. Three new . . .
Mist sifted down and slickened chicken bones, stones,
shells.

They went to a place no different from any other and
squatted. Rebecca pulled at weeds. Tom set the milk bottle
firmly into the ground. His mother began to chant. He
looked at her curiously, then raised his face to the wisping
sky.

"Here?" he asked. "Is he *here?*"

She pointed to a greened wedding band fitted to a dead
twig.

His eyes dropped to that thing. Again she chanted. Now
he chanted with her. Their bare feet were planted, knees to
their chins. She peeled petals from the rose and gave him
half. Alternately they made a pattern on the damp, the circle
closing in upon itself, a perfumed spiral.

"You must go away," she told him suddenly.

"Go away? When? Where?"

"When the summer has ended. To another school. Away
from here."

"You want me to go away?"

"It is best."

"For who is it best?"

"For you. For everyone."

"Where will I go?"

"The Patroon will find a place."

"The Patroon. Always the Patroon."

"Maybe you will wear a uniform."

"The Patroon . . . This was his thought?"

"It was my thought."

"I do not believe that. I will not go. If this angers the Patroon, then I will move from his house. I will take no more money or food from him."

"Stupid!"

"How am I stupid!"

"You think the girl will marry you? Is that what you dream?"

"What do you say?"

"You know. You know. She plays with you. She touches you. I have seen. It is a game with her. Nice little Indian boy."

"Stop it."

"Brown doll for her to play with on summer days. That is all it means to her."

"You do not know."

"I know. I see everything and I know everything. Already she is tired of you. Now she is playing with the Anglo. The white one who makes music. Now she is touching him. Now you are thrown aside, forgotten. She is a whore woman."

Knuckles hit—no, pressed against her jaw. She rocked back on her heels, looking at him sadly. He bent his head. Long hair made a black tent over his face.

"I am sorry."

"If it will make you happy to beat me, then beat me. I swear to you on this grave I will do anything to make you happy and keep you well. In my mind it is best you go away. This is what the bones say."

"I do not believe in the bones."

"So? But you are not white. You do not believe in the bones and you do not believe what the Anglos believe."

"They believe nothing."

"Oh, yes. Oh, yes. But not for us." She swept an arm over the rubbled graveyard: shards, crushed things. "This is what we believe. You are different from this white girl. What you dream can never be. Go away. You will find a life."

"Not without her."

"Little boy. Become a man. Stand straight and try to think. The Patroon has been good to us. We have a roof."

"You work hard for it."

"To work is to live. I will work until I die. We have food and some money. This is no small thing. The Patroon wishes us well. Do you want us in the Home? Weaving baskets?"

"I will take care of you."

"Will you? By making one Ikantos drum a year and selling it? Think! What can you do? Before all, you need to learn. You must go away. As I say and as the Patroon says. You must forget this naked woman. You must learn how to make a life for yourself."

"A life? I will kill myself before I go away. I swear you that."

He straightened and stalked away from her. She made one meek sound. When she came onto the Indian Road he was twenty yards ahead. He was striding heavily on the gravel without pain, planting bare feet on the stones, not feeling them.

She plodded after him, her head down. The sodden blanket was clutched about her shoulders. At once, far off in the marsh, a loon made a single cry: piercing. It entered into her. At that moment, then, she wanted the Patroon inside her.

# 20

Hapgood Graves, at the age of fourteen, wrote a poem published in his school newspaper. It included the lines: "I shall breakfast every morning on scrambled scruples/And curse the day I was born."

At sixteen, while climbing a church steeple in Olathe, Kansas, at midnight, his feet slipped from a tile. He hung suspended from his grip on a coping. He looked down. Fear started in his dangling feet and oozed upward. Fear passed through his body, out his numbed fingers, and was gone. He was free. He hauled himself up and completed his climb. He perched on the topmost point, took off his clothes, stood naked and howled at the moon.

At seventeen, having finished a pint of sloe gin laced with grain alcohol, he drove a convertible off the road and into trees at high speed. He was thrown clear. His passenger, a boy he had been physically intimate with only an hour before, went through the windshield and was decapitated.

When he was nineteen, he appeared on the green at an Ohio college wearing a white linen suit, creamy slouch fedora, and carrying a rattan cane. He was set upon by hooting classmates. The suit was ripped to shreds, hat flung into the trees, cane splintered. He was tossed into a fishpond. The next day he appeared on campus in an identical outfit. Again he was roughed up, his costume destroyed. On the third day he appeared in similar garb. His classmates laughed and clapped him on the back.

The first song he wrote was called "Oogie-Woogie-Woo." It was ersatz Cole Porter. But he achieved small fame by playing and singing it at local parties.

He escaped military service when he claimed to be a homosexual and had an arrest record in New Orleans to prove it.

He went to Europe with the vague idea of visiting all the places mentioned in *Tender Is the Night*. In the south of France he got a job as "houseboy" in the villa of an elderly English widow. Her leathern skin was completely shaved and oiled. One night he stole a stuffed purse and ran off with a chambermaid. Four days later, *she* stole the purse and ran off with a garage mechanic. Graves then became the companion of a Greek industrialist. This lasted two months. When the Greek sailed back to his island, he provided Graves first-class passage to Mobile, Alabama, on one of his freighters, and gave him five hundred dollars in counterfeit U.S. five-dollar bills.

In Mobile, after his funny money was gone, he slept around. Sometimes he begged. Once he ate half a rotted melon he found in a garbage can. But he was writing—poems and music. He thought he was getting better. Never once did he fear what might happen.

A blind woman gave him money, and he got his union card. Soon after, he took a job in a small Pensacola nightclub that catered to junior naval officers. Graves' duties were to play "cocktail hour music" from 5:00 to 7:00 P.M., and again after midnight when the featured performers finished their sets.

The girl singer was Bobbie Vander.

"Would you like?" Susan Todd asked. "Would you like?"

Hapgood Graves: "Would I like *what?*"

"A picnic," she gasped, her face burning.

"A picnic." He nodded. "The Land of Noble Picnics. Sounds good. How are you going to handle it? Going to tell your father you've invited me to a picnic?"

"On Wednesday." She was breathless to get it out. "Mrs. Vanderhorst and Julie are going in to the Ladies' Club meeting. I'll tell Dad I want the car so I can go shopping. He'll say okay. I'll drive him to the hospital and I'll drop the Vanderhorsts off at the church. Then I'll drive back here. And you'll be walking on the road past the Breckinridge place. And I'll stop—you know, like accident—and I'll pick you up."

"Should I wear a false beard and dark glasses?"

"What?"

He wanted to hug her but settled for gripping her warm arms. She pulled away angrily.

"You're laughing at me. If you don't want to go, you don't have to."

He became solemn. "My dear, we must be discreet."

"Discreet." The word tasted adult to her. It was sophisticated. "Yes . . . discreet. That's what I'm trying to be."

"First of all, Susan."

He stopped suddenly. She had caught her breath, teeth on lip, biting. It was the first time he had said her name. She wanted to die. He saw it.

"First of all, where is this picnic to be?"

"There's a place about ten miles south of here. It's called the Highlands. It's like a cliff that hangs out over the sea. Nobody has a house there because it's all stone. The county put in some wooden picnic tables and benches and two outdoor grills. People usually go there on Saturday and Sunday but usually on weekdays there's no one there."

"All right. Now here's what we'll do. You tell your father you're inviting Bobbie Vander and me to go on a picnic to the Highlands."

"But—"

"Shut up and listen. Then you ask Bobbie, and ask her to invite me. Understand?"

"Yes."

"She will accept. Tell your father. At the last minute Bobbie will have a migraine headache, and just the two of us will go on the picnic."

"Are you sure she'll have a headache?"

"I'm sure. Pick me up here at the house. What about food?"

"I'll make some sandwiches."

"No tuna fish salad, for Chrissakes. I'll bring some beer. Why won't you look at me?"

"I am looking at you."

"You're not looking in my eyes."

"There. Is that all right?"

"Don't be frightened, Susan."

"I'm not frightened. I'm not."

"Are you chewing gum?"

"Of course not. I never chew gum."

"That's good," he smiled and touched her.

"Dad," she said.

"Mmm." He didn't look up from the pamphlet he was reading. It was called "The Battle of Gettisburgh as Seen by A Maine Volunteer." It had been published in 1879. Dr. Todd had found it in the dust of a South Canaan junk shop.

"Mrs. Vanderhorst and Julie are going into town for the Ladies' Club meeting on Wednesday. They'll want you to drive them. But I want to ask Bobbie Vander and Hapgood Graves to go on a picnic with me to the Highlands. So I thought if I drove—Dad, are you listening to me?"

"I'm listening. Picnic at the Highlands."

"Yes. Well, I thought I'd drive you to the hospital or your office on Wednesday and drop the Vanderhorst women at the church. Then I'll come back and pick up Bobbie Vander and Mister Graves, and we'll go for a picnic lunch at the Highlands. I'll make sandwiches. We'll be back in plenty of time so I can pick you up at the hospital or your office and also pick up the Vanderhorsts at the church. Okay, Dad?"

"What? Oh sure. Whatever you say."


"Hey, mom," Graves said to Bobbie Vander. "Susan Todd is going to ask you and me to go on a picnic Wednesday afternoon. Your mother and Julie are going to the Ladies' Club meeting at the church. Susan will drive them and the doctor into town, then come back for us."

"So?"

"So you're going to get a migraine headache at the last minute. You won't be able to make the picnic. But Susan and I will."

She looked at him.

"You're something, you are."

"That's right." He nodded. "I'm something."

"And what the hell am I supposed to do all afternoon, cooped up with those two pesky redskins and the old guy who farts?"

"You might practice 'Don't Fall in Love.' It's a pretty little ballad. Do it with an ache. Can you ache?"

"Sure. I can ache."

"Dot's nize."

"And you're going to ache when Doctor Todd cuts your cock off and jams it down your throat."

"At last!" he cried thankfully.

She laughed.

"I'm sorry you're not feeling well," Susan Todd called. "Take some aspirin or something."

"Oh, sure," Bobbie Vander smiled, on the porch.

Rebecca Drinkwater was peering from a kitchen window. Tom Drinkwater, whittling away at the Ikantos drum, raised his head as the car moved down the driveway. He stared at them. At the access road, Samuel Lees, working on the culvert, straightened slowly. His thin eyes followed the car as it turned south.

"That was discreet," Hapgood Graves said. "No one saw us."

Susan Todd giggled. "Do you want to drive?"

"I don't drive. Well, I drive, but I don't have a license. You drive and I'll look at your tits."

"Oh, you."

She was wearing a tennis dress: knitted tank top with narrow straps across tanned shoulders, hugging her. Then a short, pleated skirt, all white. It was whipped cream on chocolate pudding.

She drove well. He put his head back against the seat top and closed his eyes.

"I thought you were going to look at my tits," she said accusingly.

Corrupt them with words. Say tits. "Tits." Say prick. "Prick." Say fuck. "Fuck." Say love. "Love." And the deed is done.

"Later," he murmured.

The six-pack of Ram's Head was ice on his lap. He let it press into him, chilling and hard. He opened his eyes when they turned into a gouged road, climbing.

"Here we are," she said. "The Highlands."

It wasn't all rock. There were dauntless clumps of green,

insisting through stone. A broken cypress was there, and moss soft as flesh. There was bramble and one white toadstool.

He marched to the edge. He stood with toes hanging over nothing, hands on his hips. Behind him she made a sound. Far below, rock teeth grinned up at him: green-eaten stumps. Sea clogged there, saliva licking around.

He raised his eyes to the wine-dark sea. The froth was dappled with glints, heaving. And a crescent moon! Sailing through that blue-day sky.

"Please," she said. "Don't stand so close."

It was sharp as ether: sun-warmed, wind-chilled. There was a glory on everything. He wanted to be naked and skin-raped. It was a carved day, precise and lucid.

He turned slowly to look at her. She blazed in light. A halo scorched around her, distending, contracting. He closed his eyes, trying to . . . He heard the roaring down there, waiting.

She gripped his arm, drew him back.

"I'm afraid."

They sat across from each other at one of the slatted picnic tables. They sipped cold beer from cans, chewed warm sandwiches. She began speaking. He wondered if she had rehearsed it.

"I have no one to talk to," she complained. "Dad's a sweetie and he tries, but he really doesn't understand. I couldn't even talk to Mother when she was here. Now she's gone. I've got no one to talk to."

"What do you want to talk about?"

"Me. I want to talk about me. Do you think I'm conceited?"

He stared, squinting against the knifing sun. She quivered in pure light, laid open. She was all tender with soft petals peeled back. There was the gaping heart.

"No. I don't think you're conceited."

She caught a strand of hair, curled it on her finger. She put it in her mouth. She pulled it under her nose and stroked it like a mustache, looking at him.

"About me . . ."

Her voice was birdsong. Young longing washed over him in a golden flood. Hairs on her bare arms caught the sun and burned. Mint air bit his lungs.

He said something obscene.

She faltered, then went on.

He reached under the table, touched her bare knee: soft suede. She cut her eyes to him, mouth pouting. She leaned sideways, unbuckled a sandal, kicked it off. She put a naked foot onto him. He adjusted it, stroking a sugary calf.

What is it all about? She wanted to know. Why do people act the way they do? Why did her mother and father part when she thought they were so happy together? What was going to happen to her? How do you know when you are *really* in love? Did it hurt to die? Who was she? Was suicide so awful? Why do people hurt each other? That night on the beach, when they played the Truth Game . . .

She wanted nothing from life. Except everything.

"Isn't this elegant?" he asked. "A bare foot pressing my balls and us eating bologna sandwiches and drinking beer. How elegant can you get?"

"You're awful," she said.

"Oh, yes," he agreed. "I am awful. Everyone says so."

She dug fingers into her soft hair, combed it away from her neck. He watched, gripping her silky calf.

"I'm so vague." She sighed. "I know I'm vague."

"You're not vague. You exist."

She smiled sweetly, pressed her foot softly. Her eyes locked with his.

"I told the truth that night on the beach. I want to. Do you want to?"

"Yes. I want to."

Both murmuring. The shining day was a faint. Crystals of sweat on her upper lip were licked away.

"I'm so hot."

"Yes."

"When?" she asked.

His fingertips drifted from calf to the satin behind her knee.

"My tongue," he said.

"What?"

"Nothing."

"Well . . . when?"

"Are you frightened?"

"Yes."

"We must figure out how we can be alone. That is the problem. Logistics. Where can we go? We must be . . . discreet, again."

"Oh, yes." She nodded.

"We could leave notes in the hollow of an old oak tree."

"Must you make jokes about it?"

"Yes. I must."

"Dad's away all day. Sometimes he's called away at night."

"Not good enough. It can't be in your house. Or at the Vanderhorsts'. We'll have to find a place. Somewhere. Maybe outside. An outside place."

"Yes. All right."

"Think about it."

"That's all I've been thinking about. You're getting me so dizzy."

"Am I?"

"Maybe the station wagon?"

"Maybe?"

Her hand lay flat on the tattered wood, a strong brown squid. He put his hand alongside, palm down. His skin was white and hairless, grainy with pores.

"Look at me," he said. " 'The Mummy's Curse,' " he said hollowly.

"What?"

That carved sky—what was it? Sunlight crashed off the sea. Was it that razor day? Something was slicing into him. She was coming alive, no longer a thing. He saw bold nose, solid thrust of jaw, eyes that didn't float: woman to be.

"I was a faggot," he told her.

"When I asked you, you said, 'Not now.' "

"That's right. Not now."

"I don't care. I don't care what you were. Ever. Or what you did."

"You want us to start new?"

"Oh, yes!" She laughed with joy. "That's what I want us to do. Start new."

"It's too late."

"*We* can do it."

"Can we? I'm a fool. I've always been a fool. I will always be a fool. I do foolish things, and say I'll never do them again. But then I do. I do things I *know* are stupid."

She leaned forward suddenly. She kissed the back of his white hand. He stared at that bent, submissive head.

"I'm death for you." His voice was shriveled.

"Death?" she asked, looking up.

He was silent.

"Do you really sniff cocaine?"

"Yes."

"Can you stop?"

"I don't know. Maybe. But I don't want to."

"What's it like?"

"For me? Dreams of glory."

"I want to try it."

"Do you?"

"Will I become—you know—addicted?"

"Probably."

"Are you?"

"Yes. I am addicted."

"I want to try it."

In an instant she was gaunt; juicy body leached by that searing sun. She was condensed, the girl gone. Take your seats, ladies and gentlemen, curtain going . . .

"Oh, God," he said. "Oh, my God."

"What? What is it?"

He did not speak. She said, "I love you," looked up at him and waited. "Do you love me?" she asked finally.

"Hey there," he sang, "you with the scars on your thighs."

"I don't have scars on my thighs."

"Jesus." He sighed. "You're too much."

"Well, *do* you? Do you love me?"

"Love corrupts, and absolute love corrupts absolutely."

"What does that mean?"

"Does everything have to have meaning?" he shouted at her. "Some of the most important things in the world don't have meaning."

"Like what?"

He would not answer.

She sat miserably. He took his hand from her leg. He turned, looked out to sea.

"You love me?" he asked.

"Yes."

"Walk to the edge of the cliff with me. We will stand there, our toes over the edge. We will look up at the sky. Then out at the sea. Then down at the rocks."

Her eyes yawned. "I can't do it." She gasped.

"Do you want to try cocaine?"

"Yes."

"Then you must do this first."

"I can't."

"For me."

"I just can't."

He shrugged.

She began to cry, tears staining dark tracks.

"If you love me," he said.

She shook her head, hair in flashing swirl. He rose to his feet, started back toward the car.

"Hap," she called.

He stopped, not turning.

"Will you hold my hand?"

He turned then, gave her a hideous smile. He held out his hand.

He led her toward the edge, softly.

"You must open your eyes," he said.

She stretched her eyes to the sear. She took a step. A step. Step.

"Now stop here," he said. "Feel with your toes. When there is nothing, shuffle up and just stand. I am holding you."

Her head was tilted back, face dead. Her body rolled with terror. She shuffled forward. He stood alongside. Their wrists were coiled, hot hands linked.

"Sky," he said. "Up at the sky."

She saw immortal blue. It went to the stars, that baked glaze of sun. Her wide eyes swept, seeing it for the first time. It was original.

"Sea," he said. "Out at the sea."

Blue lead heaved in endless churn. She was in the sea. The sea was in her. It was all new. She had never seen the texture and form. How the world moved! It was hypnotizing as fire.

"Rocks," he said. "Down at the rocks."

Her head lowered like a wilting flower. He opened his fingers. Their hands parted. She stood alone. Teeth grinned up at her, below, far below. Everything shaved down to small and cruel. Fear crawled from her rock-cramped feet. She leaned forward and stared at death, vomit close.

"Are you going to push me?" she whispered.

"No," he said seriously, "I am not going to push you. Sit down now. Here. At the edge. I will sit alongside you. Dangle your feet over the edge. We will hold hands again."

So they did, thighs pressing. She looked down between her bare knees. Something was moving in her.

He touched her cheek. When she didn't move her head, he pulled around to kiss her mouth, gulping youth.

"Ah," she said. "Ah."

He smiled sadly.

They sat silently. She kicked her one sandal loose and watched it float away. It bounced off the cliff, drifted out, turned, twisted. It flipped off the green teeth into the sea and was gone.

"How do you feel?" he asked finally.

She was incandescent.

"Like I've been born. Like everything is starting."

He pushed up her skirt, put a white hand on her seasoned thigh. He nipped soft flesh with fingernails, but she did not wince.

"Soon," he said.

When he moved his hand upward, she clamped it tight. "Oh, don't. I've wet my pants."

# 21

Julie Vanderhorst was not a mindless woman; she was lazy. That fruity body luxuriated in heat and softness, melted in sunlight and pleasure. She touched herself and smiled.

She was forever starting vague projects: buying books, taking correspondence courses, attending lectures. Once she bought art supplies and once she considered becoming a tree surgeon. Everything ended in a game of solitaire.

Her summer sleep was dreamless. But during the day her fantasies were a clotted jungle filled with grotesque sins. Once she saw a large dog she . . .

Since Dr. Todd's divorce, most of her reveries involved him. She believed they should be married. It would be a happy union, filled with loud laughter and good meals. His blunt fingers excited her—and the hair on his body when it was wet, when he came surging out of the sea.

She saw them late in the evening. He would be reading one of his books. She would be playing solitaire. Then she would put away her cards and go into the bedroom. After a few minutes he would turn out the lights. He would come to her.

Then the dream became chaotic, a flash of hot images:

The door was locked, shades were drawn; God could not see. She groaned with content, sweat on her smooth flanks.

She was dimly aware of time passing: another summer. Addled by yellow sun and white gin she floated happily and waited. She was certain the game would come out.

The day began in glory. Waves heaved a crimson sun out of the sea into a blushing sky. Far out three stubby fishing boats nodded into the swell, bones in their teeth, jouncing and braving.

But the air was stuffed, the barometer slipping.

Julie slept late and woke suddenly. She looked across to the other bed, saw Bobbie had already gone down to breakfast. She threw the damp sheet aside, swung feet to the floor. She yawned, knuckled her scalp, yawned again.

She padded to the window and looked up: hazy, but the sun was there. She went into the bathroom and used the toilet, brushed her teeth, washed hands, face, armpits. She yawned again.

She came back into the bedroom and sat naked before the maple and bamboo dresser. She began brushing her hair: a hundred strokes back, a hundred strokes forward, counting aloud.

Then she looked at the brush anxiously, panting. There were only a few burnished hairs. She brushed the helmet smooth.

Carefully she did not look at the image of her plump body in the hinged pier glass. She pulled on cotton panties, stepped into a patterned caftan and zipped it up. She went barefoot down to the kitchen.

"Morning, Rebecca. I'm late again."

"Morning, Julie." Mrs. Rebecca smiled.

They were the likely sisters.

"Everyone's ate. Now I saved a waffle for you I can heat up. And some bacon. Coffee is hot."

"Feel," Julie said, putting the other woman's hand on the cloth bulging over her belly. "I'm starting a diet right this minute. Black coffee and nothing else."

She sat at the long worktable and watched the Indian woman move silently about the kitchen.

"Was everyone down?"

"Oh, yes. Roberta and Mister Graves are in the library. I expect they are practicing their music. Your father is out on the access road. He's looking at that culvert with Sam Lees. Tom is working on his drum. Your mother has gone down the beach to gather shells."

Julie sipped her coffee, watching.

"I wish I had legs like yours, Rebecca."

"Your legs are just nice."

"But your ankles are so slender. I have thick ankles. Thick ass, thick stomach, thick everything. Thick brain, I expect."

Julie rose. She wandered casually over to the refrigerator, opened the door.

"My stomach is rumbling. I need a nibble. Rebecca! A cherry pie!"

"That one is chilling. I got another cooling in the cupboard. We got some vanilla ice cream."

"I shouldn't. I *shouldn't!*"

She sat hunched over the plate, her strong teeth chonking into the bloody meat. Cherry juice and melted ice cream dripped from the corners of her mouth.

"Oh, God," she moaned.

She used a soup spoon for the red syrup, tasted the bite and sweet. Cold ice cream and warm pie slid down into her. She closed her eyes.

"You will get sun today," Rebecca said. "For a time. Then it will cloud. The Patroon says rain tonight."

Julie lighted a cigarette.

"Ooh, that was good. I think I'll take my cards and go up on your roof."

The blue sky was crackly. But to the south it turned pewter-pale. The fishing boats were lost ghosts. There was a soft taste of rain.

Julie climbed through the window in Rebecca's room out onto the tiny tarred roof and dropped towel and baby oil. She spread the blanket, unzipped her caftan, moved panties down and off. She was the highest person on all the baked beach.

She thumped down and sat cross-legged. She opened her thermos and poured the first drink of the day. She flipped cards lazily, her spine to the sun, feeling that channel melt and run. Heat came into her. She purred.

The furry air muffled her. She looked between her legs and saw pearls. Sweat popped. She was bedewed, dripping with rivulets and stain. Her skin panted, flesh gasping. There was pleasure there.

Roberta Vanderhorst stepped through the open window. "Jesus! What a beast!"

A floppy hat shielded Bobbie's face. She was wearing a man's shirt (was it Graves'?), sleeves rolled up on her colorless arms. Tight pants seemed painted on. She was a skinny-marink with sharp teeth, ice on a stick.

Sheep-clouds grazed overhead, scattered. But gray vertical plumes rose in the south: smoke pouring from a thousand chimneys.

Bobbie sat on the blanket, scratched her sister's sweated ribs. Julie's giggle went up like a startled bird.

"Lie down," Bobbie commanded.

"I'm so wet," Julie murmured, but stretched prone, pressed breasts bulging out.

Bobbie smoothed oil onto those beefed shoulders, that muscled back, those ruddy buttocks. One oiled finger explored the sunken spine thoughtfully, leaping over the bumps.

"Oh," Julie breathed. "Oh, oh, oh."

Bobbie oiled back of knees, rack of ribs, flare of hips. Her hard hand painted burning flesh, sliding, feeling, pressing there. Her fingers strolled about.

"Roll over," Bobbie ordered.

So Julie did, heaving over awkwardly. Her eyes were pressed to slits, her strained arms flung wide to embrace . . . what? Her swollen lips parted. There was a gleam of wet teeth, a smile to feel those tiptoeing fingers.

"I'm going out to dinner tonight," she said dreamily. "With Ben Todd. We're going to the Down East Inn. That's on Route Forty-two, near the Gresham turnoff. It's a nice place. They have good seafood. Lobsters and clams and things like that. We went there once before. It's very nice. Don't, Bobbie. Don't do that."

"Does it hurt?"

"Oh, no. They have this marvelous little bar with a big picture window overlooking the sea. You can look out for miles. The last time we went I had Long Island duckling. It was very juicy. Bobbie, I don't think you should. Please."

"He's such a lump."

"Who's a lump?"

"That Ben Todd. He's just *there*. He's so solid. Maybe you're right; maybe he's a younger Patroon."

"You don't like him because he hit you that night on the beach."

"Shit, kiddo, I deserved that. No, it's not that I don't like him; I just don't dig him. There's nothing light to him. He won't play with me."

"Play with you?"

"You know—the sex game. Grab-assing back and forth with words. Most guys I meet look at me and their eyes get a hard-on. He looks at me like he's guessing my blood pressure, or wondering if I have any blood at all. I mean, he looks right *in* me. You make it with him yet?"

"No."

"Why not?"

"Well, I—Bobbie, Bobbie, what are you doing to me?"

"You know what I'm doing to you."

"Well, it's just that we've never had a chance. People are always around. You know. Susan is there in his house. And. Maybe tonight."

"You *want* to ball with him?"

"Sure. I don't care. Yes. I guess so. I don't know. If he wants to."

"I don't think you should. It's your life, kiddo, but I don't think you'll be happy with him."

Julie's eyes opened wide to a sky that threatened.

"Why not?"

"Just a feeling I have. What's this scar here?"

"Don't you remember? We were climbing over that barbed wire fence outside the orchard."

"Oh, Jesus, yes. I remember. God, were you bleeding. But you didn't even cry. Sweet scar."

"Bobbie, I'm all oily and sweaty."

"Good. That's good. Yes. You taste salty and sweet."

Oil and sweat made stains on the white shirt.

"I wish," Julie said. "Don't. They'll. Someone."

She pushed gently at Roberta's head. Strong lips pulled off slowly, clinging. Until only a tongue's tip . . . Then Bobbie sat upright, shivering.

"No more sun today. It's all over."

Thin clouds jostled now. They watched as the sun drew away. A steel scrim of rain rattled down. With it came a cool wind.

They both stood. Julie bent to pull on her panties. Bobbie reached to touch her.

"I'll wait up for you. Tonight."


Benjamin Wilson Todd believed his name should be spelled *Todt*.

His lawyer father shot to death by a crazed client . . .

His mother dead of cancer at forty-four . . .

His young sister dead in an automobile accident at the age of eighteen . . .

His best friend a suicide in medical school . . .

Two wars with the red butchery of field hospitals . . .

Too many early morning hours in Emergency . . .

Patients coughing, groaning, wailing, spitting, vomiting, staring, swearing, screaming, gripping his hand until . . .

The bastard Death: it rode his back. He could not shake it off.

He should have been something else, not a physician. He should have been a surveyor, a farmer, a house painter: a day something, not a night something.

"I'm getting dark," he told his wife. "I mean inside. I feel it. It's heavy. I have to drive myself. Now everything is a weight. I'm lifting all the time."

"I don't understand," she said. "Is it your work? The hospital?"

"Partly that. But something else. It's a gloom. I want to stay in bed for the rest of my life. I can't see any reason."

"I don't understand," she said.

Soon after they were divorced.

It bothered him that he didn't need people. He had a taste for solitude. It had a thin, acrid flavor, like iced tea.

He wanted a warm ease, something to melt him. He wanted to throw open a window. In comes a soft wind, salt-tanged. Curtains billowing inside him. Sun shaft and laugh of sea.

Once, lying awake at three in the morning, staring at the black, he said aloud, "I will marry Julie Vanderhorst."

But in the morning he recognized it as a three o'clock thought.

Her animalism excited him. She would, he knew, crawl naked across the floor on her hands and knees. She would bend naked over the dining-room table. She would press heavy thighs gladly about his hips and stuff him into her flesh.

And then?

Next year he would be half a century old: two-thirds of his life gone. He wanted to die for something grand. He took fishbones from the throats of gasping children.

Trees met overhead. They went hurtling down that long, dark corridor. Rain was clean sweetness, dripping and glittering the road. It was a docile dew in headlight glare.

Through half-open windows came wet wind, spraying a skim. They were inside outside. They were safe in their steel cocoon but knew the night.

Todd turned to smile at Julie. "I like your perfume."

"I'm not wearing any!"

He bent briefly to sniff a bare shoulder. "You're right. Soap, suntan oil, sunburn, and you. Marvelous."

Something moved in her throat. She pressed her thigh softly against his, placed a hand on his knee. She put a hand at the back of his neck, pulled gently at wiry hair.

"This is nice. Don't go so fast."

"Aren't you hungry?"

"I'm always hungry."

He slowed, lowered a hand over the hand on his knee. They were alone on the road, alone everywhere. Her smell warmed him.

"I'm beginning to loosen," he said.

"Loosen?"

"I had a bad day. Every day is bad, but today was worse. I got all knotted. All tied-up. Ever feel like that?"

"No."

"Well, anyway, I'm happy to be with you now. I'm spreading out in a blur. Feels good. I may just let go of the wheel and let the car take us. Okay?"

"Sure." She laughed. "Okay."

He punched a button on the radio. A Portland station was playing "Red Sails in the Sunset."

"My God," he said. "I was about eighteen years old." He sniffed her skin again. "Oh," he said.

The road turned. They were running along the coast. Clouds parted, the wind shut off. There was a thin slice of moon, a fingernail. It was there a moment, then darkness again.

Because the windows of the tavern were misted over, they sat at an inside table, near a fireplace where small flames flickered in smoke from damp wood.

They had blood-rare beef and baked potatoes, bitter salad and pears in port, coffee and cognac. They ate in silence. He watched admiringly as she tucked away: precision of knife and fork, sharp teeth, rhythm of swallows, mysterious smile.

When he paid the bill at the cashier's desk, he saw a pyramid of candy boxes. He bought a pound of assorted chocolates and handed the package to her.

"Oh, boy," she said.

Beef-stuffed, brandy-warmed, he drove slowly home. Once she belched: a small belch. He loved her for it.

" 'Red sails in the sunset,' " he sang.

" 'Red sails in the sunset,' " she sang after him. But she didn't know any more of the words.

He pulled into his driveway. "Come in? Another brandy?"

"Is Susan home?"

"Yes."

"Not right now. Can we sit here a minute? Maybe in a while."

"Sure."

He cut the engine. Windshield wipers snicked to a stop. They watched rain make crazy rivulets down the glass. The radio was giving the population of Jordan. He flicked it off.

"Well," he said.

They heard a soft susurrus. Rain was all about them: on the roof, against the windows. But in the steel cave they were dry and warm. They were animal mates.

Their burrow filled with her stirring scent, wrinkling his nose, prickling his hair. Her feral heat filled the car. He turned sideways on the seat. He saw for the first time what she was wearing: a linen shift, wilted now, billowing in places. But it pulled tight over breasts and hips.

"Very nice," he said, touching a shoulder strap.

"May I open my candy?"

"Of course."

In the dim glow of the dash he saw boneless fingers ripping string and paper. They were soft fingers, smooth fingers. He had a sudden, shaking vision of tanned legs making a giant capital M. What was yawning there for him? A red mouth, bearded.

"Yummy," she said, inspecting the neat rows. "Creams and caramels and chocolate-covered cherries. Now this one's a fruit. A marshmallow here. Nougat. Wow. Want one?"

"Not right now. You go ahead."

She selected. Her teeth crunched. "Chocolate cream." Her eyes closed. A limp stele poked from her lips. Pink licked around. A crumb of chocolate stuck to her chin. He picked it off, popped it into his mouth.

"I think this one's a caramel."

She put it halfway between her lips, bit gently, and nodded. She looked at him, suddenly poked her face to him. He leaned forward, took the protruding part of the chocolate in his mouth, bit gently. Their lips touched, turned this way and that. They pulled slowly apart, caramel stretching, thinning to a string, parting. A hair of candy floated down upon their chins.

Their eyes fastened.

"Good." He nodded. "Bittersweet."

She picked out a little brown breast and held it up for him to see. "Cherry."

She slid it into her mouth. She closed her lips and waited. He kissed her then: he open, she open. She poked the warm sweet forward with her tongue. They bit together, juice running. They were smeared, lapping.

"Something else," she said faintly. "You start."

He picked out a chocolate-covered butternut. He held it between his teeth, lips drawn back. She was close to him now, pressing. Their teeth snapped down: crunch.

Mouths mingled. They tasted a warm mush of sweet saliva, bitter nut, sweet chocolate. Flavors raced back and forth. Tongues raced back and forth. They took little swallows, gave little groans. His hand was beneath her skirt.

"Marshmallow," she said dreamily.

They moved their heads in tiny circles, sugary lips sticking. They had one mouth, all tongues and gulps. Hands clenched. Hands clenched. Their breath was twice-breathed.

"Ben."

They stopped, trembling. Their faces were smeared, eyes strained.

"Ben."

He laughed, feeling warm ease, seeing a window opened on the world. "Julie, I want to love you."

She grabbed his hands to her breasts.

"In the back," he said. "I think there's a beach towel and a blanket back there. And a life preserver."

They dashed out their doors to find the back doors locked. They stood in rain to pull up lock buttons. Then they went flopping in, slamming doors, folding seatbacks down, panting, spreading towel and blanket, gasping, arranging the kapok life preserver as a pillow.

"Wicked!" Ben roared. "Very wicked!"

They lay on their backs, heads touching. He would giggle. She would giggle. She struggled up, rescued her candy box from the front seat.

"Umm," she said. "Umm?" she asked. But he waved her away.

She was a shade. He peered. Something was there. "Enough," she said, and put the candy to one side. She was so tanned she was invisible in the darkness. But there was a glowing dress, uninhabited.

"Are you on the pill?"

"No."

"I don't have a condom. Will you douche?"

"Oh, sure."

"Liar. Well, I have a shingle."

"A shingle?"

He touched her helmet of hair. It was polished, scented with salt and rain. He breathed her. Had he ever known another woman who smelled so . . . warm? She had an infant fragrance.

"Dast we?" she asked. "Susan won't come out?"

"No. Susan won't come out."

"Then let's . . ."

Flicks of rain went plinking across the steel roof. She sat up, turned her back to him.

"What?"

"The zipper," she explained.

He touched that channeled spine.

"No bra?"

"No."

He moved straps aside. She shrugged, pulled her arms free. Cloth fell to her waist. His hands spread.

"Oh," he breathed.

"Oh," she answered.

"Satin."

He closed his eyes, billowing.

"Don't move. For a while."

"All right."

His clumpy hands went dreaming. She shivered.

"I'm," she said.

"I," he said.

"I'm getting," she said.

"I am," he said.

"I'm getting so," she said.

"I am beginning," he said.

"I'm getting so I don't," she said.

"I am beginning to know," he said.

Then they were unable to care. They were bedlamites tearing at their clothes.

"Cold?"

"Burning."

She stretched far above her head, arms spread wide, slick hands clamped to door handles. He bent to see the giant M. He touched the bearded mouth. Her body heaved.

"Am I too heavy on you?"

She made a noise. Her arms came down. Her fingers threaded through the thicket on his back, gripping him down.

"More. Oh, more."

He held her breasts. He put his open mouth to neck, to shoulder, to cheek, to lips, to ear, to lips, to cheek, to shoulder, to neck, to shoulder . . .

He was in a warm sea, stroking. His legs kicked. Her strength shocked him. He was borne on waves. He felt the undulating lift and fall, crest and swoop. She was fearful as the sea. He swam frantically.

From her came a love song: rumble, sigh of wind, hiss of spume: sea sounds. All was in the rhythm of a deep tide rolling. It carried him up.

On he went, through the dark. She was leading, pulling him along. "Come. Come." Their flesh was rippling. They clung desperately, hearing a clangor now, a chime of pleasure so sharp it set them jangling.

And.

"You got laid," Bobbie Vander said. "I can smell it. Go wash that stink off. And swab yourself."

Obediently Julie headed for the bathroom, with a puffed smile.

Bobbie was in bed, a wrinkled sheet to her waist. Her button breasts were bared. She was smoking a cigarette, reading a two-week-old copy of *Variety*. Her square spectacles had wire frames.

She read the same paragraph three times, then tossed the paper aside. She slammed her cigarette to dust, swung out of bed, naked. She leaned against the bathroom door and watched Julie.

"Have a good time?"

"Oh, yes! Wonderful. We had roast beef and baked potatoes. And pears in port. A brandy afterward. And Ben bought me a box of chocolates."

"Where is it?"

"Where? Oh. I guess we finished it."

"That's the way to lose weight, kiddo. Where did you get jabbed?"

"What? Oh. In his car."

"Uncomfortable, isn't it? All those levers and pedals and the steering wheel."

"It's a station wagon. We were in the back. It's very roomy back there."

"Why didn't you get on the roof? In the luggage rack."

"The roof? Bobbie, it was raining. It still is."

She looked at her sister. "Fat idiot." She went back to her bed, pulled up the sheet, lighted another cigarette.

Julie came out in a robe. She sat at the dresser, began brushing her hair.

"How was it?"

"I told you. We had roast beef and—"

"Not the food, monster. The sex. How was it?"

"Mmm."

"Is he hung?"

"Oh, sure. He was very—you know—loving. He said he loved me."

"He did? What did he say? Exactly."

"He said, 'Julie, I want to love you.'"

"Great. That's a proposal of marriage right there."

"Well, he meant it."

"He sure did. He meant, 'Julie, I want to fuck you.'"

"It wasn't only that. I know it wasn't. He really does love me. I feel it."

"Don't con me, kiddo. I know what you feel. The old twitch."

Julie put the brush aside, took off the robe, climbed into her own bed. She stretched for one of Bobbie's cigarettes, lighted it, lay back. They stared at each other; sisters under the sheets.

"Do you love him?"

"I guess so. Yes. I know so. He'd make a very good husband for me. We'd be very happy together."

"Shit. He'll never ask you. All he wants to do is get between your legs."

"Bobbie, you're so wrong. If that's all he wanted he could have done that years ago."

"He was married then. Getting it regular. Now he's hard-up."

"You're awful. You think that's all men want. You think everyone is selfish. What's so impossible about him loving me and wanting to marry me? Am I so ugly?"

"You're beautiful, baby."

"Well then?"

"Can I come into your bed?"

"No."

The silence was harsh.

Roberta switched off the bedside lamp. There was no sound. The rain was seeping now. There was a faint night glow.

"Are you going to see him again?"

"Of course. If he asks me."

"He will. He just got a slice tonight."

"Bobbie, please. Don't talk like that."

"I don't want you to make a mistake. This man isn't for you."

"You don't want me to have any man. You're jealous."

"Oh, Christ. What's so wonderful about a man? Even if he's got a baby's arm with an apple in its fist. Big deal."

"I want a home of my own and a husband and children."

"Jesus. I got the brain and you got the tush."

"What's tush?"

"Ass."

"What kind of talk is that?"

"Forget it. What did you do?"

"When?"

"In the back of the station wagon. Tell me what you did."

"No. I don't want to talk about it."

"Did you come?"

"I don't want to talk about it."

"I hope he wore an overcoat. Or you spritzed yourself. Julie?"

"Yes. I did."

"Let me come into your bed."

"No."

"God damn it, I want to."

"No."

"He's probably stabbing every nurse in the hospital."

"Must you be so nasty?"

"It's the truth. Face it, kiddo. Married for twenty years. Flopping his wife whenever he feels like it. Then suddenly he gets cut off. He's tom-catting around. You better know it."

"It's not true."

"Shit. If I went over there right now and spread my legs, he'd be in like Flynn."

"You're so filthy. And it's not true."

"They're all alike. Shag 'em and forget 'em."

"Not my Ben. He's different. He's so—so thoughtful."

"'My Ben.' Oh, God."

They thought it was thunder at first. But it was an airliner, unexpectedly low. The drone faded and was gone.

Roberta tossed her sheet aside, slid out, sat on the edge of Julie's bed.

"Don't reject me. I can't stand that."

"I don't want to."

"You mean you don't want to right now or you don't want to ever again?"

There was a crash from the swamp. A rotted tree, roots loosened by the rain, went toppling into the muck.

"Ever again."

"What?"

"Ever again. I don't want to ever again. Bobbie, I don't want you to touch me."

"Why not?"

"I just don't."

"What the hell kind of an answer is that: 'I just don't.' Well, I do."

She slammed a claw under the sheet, grabbing. Julie pushed away, rolling. Bobbie ducked her head, fell onto the bed, yanking. Her bare feet pedaled the floor.

"Stop it!"

"You think you? You think I?"

"Stop it!"

"We can't just."

Julie wailed. Her hand sailed in a wide arc, fingers clenched to palm. She struck Roberta high on the left cheekbone, drove her head back with a snap of neck. They both gasped. Silence then.

"He hit me," Roberta said at last. "Now you hit me. Bobbie Vander, the human punching bag."

"I'm sorry, I'm sorry, I'm sorry. Please forgive me. I'm really sorry."

"You will be, fatso." Roberta nodded, climbing back into her bed.

"Bobbie," Julie sobbed.

There was no answer. Soon Julie slept sweetly.

# 22

Roberta Vanderhorst, naked saber, was her father's heir, the son her mother never whelped. She was the Patroon and would have her way. Obstinacy polluted her.

She had whetted a small voice into a weapon: pitch imperfect, phrasing unique. Her sound slid in like a knife, and turned slowly. She left a trail of bloodied critics from Manhattan to L.A.

She was a hard woman, in a hard business, in a hard world. She reached and took, obeying the Patroon's edict: "Grab life by the throat and shake it." So she did, and she got. No one had a right to be happier than she.

She was haunted only by time, by the swift course of time. "Where is the summer going? My God, was it a year ago we were in Denver? The day's gone fast, hasn't it, Hap?"

It was all going, rolling downhill. She stared at her image in the mirror; chisel nose, pointy chin, sharp lips. She decided she was not aging. There were no sleep wrinkles, no etchings of mirth, no blotchings of sin.

Still . . . a freezing was there. She could see it, congealing. Everything was setting in her face: molten steel cooling. Perhaps she should have a face-lift. But there was nothing to lift. It was tight. And beneath, showing, dry bones.

She had a boy's body. No, not that softness. A critic wrote, ". . . her Auschwitz voice . . ." He meant that dread sorrow. But also he was seeing her in a cellophane-thin dress of something blank, joints jutting. And it reminded . . .

She stood in glare, holding a "prick mike" in both hands, the knob close to her lips. She did not move so much as urge, inside the thin dress, a bit, offering the ridged and bristle.

Blue sound came out of her in a cry. There was contempt in her artlessness. "Here I am and fuck you." No tricks for her. There was no moaning, weeping, sighing, whispering falsetto and closed eyes. She gave straight. Pain flowed.

Once, years ago, she cut a man. They had bedded twice. Then he wanted and she didn't. He swung her around, laughing. She grabbed up a nailfile and slashed for his heart. He turned in time to have his arm ripped open.

It seemed monstrous that people should defy her. Worse, that they should put their hands upon her without her acquiescence. Or *touch* her, inside. She didn't want to be touched. She wanted control.

She fermented with longing. For what? She was successful, vengeful, and steaming with deceit. She had strength; not physical strength, but resolve. She had a rancid wit that might appeal to a bookish man. She was almost whole.

Hapgood Graves said, "This one is called 'Love Is Good Enough for Me.' Here's how it goes."

He began to sing in an emaciated voice:

"You can go through life with your fingers crossed,
Or search for a four-leaf clover.
You can hope for the wit of an Oxford don,

A personal loan from the Aga Khan,
A thick veal cutlet Parmesan,
Or . . . oh damn!
Love is good enough for me.
Yes . . .

Love is good enough for me.
It's the *ne plus ultra* of my content,
A private hell that is heaven-sent,
The goal of a gal who's pleasure-bent.
Love is good enough for me."

The song continued for another verse and chorus, then
went into a long, rapid patter of rhymed couplets listing
desirable possessions—"A lizard bag from a guy named
Gucci/A wild silk print from the house of Pucci"—and
ended with another chorus.

Graves was playing with words, piling them up like
children's blocks. It was an amusing song, facile and clever,
but long before the end he heard its empty echoes, and his
voice began to falter. His final line—"Love is good enough
for me"—whispered to its death.

Heat scummed the library. There was a gray film on
leather, ivory, wood. It hung in the viscid air, grabbing at
lungs, painting skin.

"What do you think?" Hapgood Graves asked.

Silence.

"Well?"

"Noel Coward you ain't," Bobbie Vander said. "I can
resist it."

"You *are* in a mood."

"It's a clinker."

"*Maybe* it's a clinker. I promised Jackson I'd deliver

fifteen songs. He'll cut three. I want him to cut the right ones. This *may* be one of them. It's psychology, mom."

"Oh, it's not that bad, Hap. You're right. It's just that I'm in such a lousy mood."

"You're entitled. Want to work?"

"No. Let's get out of this sweat-box and talk."

"Sure. Want to walk or swim?"

"No."

"Go out to that umbrella table and I'll get us some iced coffee and join you."

"You're a sweetheart."

"Damned right. If there ever was one."

A dry sun was sucking up the morning mist. The sky was colored with crayons. 1, 2, 3, 4, 5: fill them in with pink, blue, yellow, red, green. It was sweet and postcardy, wax over everything.

"Instant coffee," Bobbie Vander said, tasting.

"Don't complain. It's cold and wet."

The umbrella, sprouting from the center of a painted metal table, was yellow on the outside, with a frizzled fringe. Beneath were faded daisies. The canvas was sun-scorched, rain-beaten.

Shade was hot, but the sun was working; water was going out of the air. A sea breeze was born; trees moved lazily. The air cleared, and they could see forever. They lifted naked feet onto the table, sipped their cold, wet coffee and breathed.

"Instant people," she said.

"What?"

"Just add water, chill and serve."

He gave her the smile of a rug seller.

"Now let's see . . . what brought this on? No argument with Grace or the Patroon. You couldn't care less about the Indians. Obviously not Sam Lees. That leaves Julie."

"You should have been a detective."

"I am a detective. I detect you. Something about Julie. Something that's got your balls in an uproar. Want me to guess?"

"No."

"She kicked you out of bed."

Bobbie Vander laughed. "You son of a bitch."

"Am I right?"

She looked at him, reached out to touch his hand.

"We should have been lovers," she said.

"We'd have made miserable lovers. We know each other too well."

She moved her head back, out of the umbrella shade. White light sheened white face. Eyes were closed, the tight mask gleaming.

"Hap, remember that night in Vegas? When you were so high?"

"I remember everything. My curse."

"We almost made it then."

"Yes."

"Why didn't we?"

"It would have spoiled it."

"Oh? You know everything, don't you?"

"Yes."

"So tell me—what should I do?"

"About what?"

"You know. You know everything."

"What's so special about her?"

"Julie? She's a gorgeous animal. She's my sister."

"What else?"

"What?"

"What else? There's something more. I know you."

"You're right. She kicked me out of bed. There's that. And also she wants to marry Todd. Julie and him.

Married. A kid. All solid. Square. The family bit. You know? I couldn't stand that. It eats at me. She's so stupid. And she's got . . . And she'd have . . . And I would . . ."

He stared at her a long moment, eyes seeming to fall back into his skull and darken. "You're full of shit," he said finally.

"How so, *effendi?*"

"Wheels within wheels. Tell me about the Patroon."

"What about the Patroon?"

"When you were growing up. What kind of a father was he?"

She came alive.

"Good," she said promptly. "A good father. I was the son he never had."

"Mmm," he said wisely.

"Julie was mother's little girl, and I was the Patroon's son. I mean I was wild. You know, climbing trees, getting into fights with boys—all that. I think he loved it."

One side of the basement of the big house had been fitted out as a small carpenter shop. The Patroon had a heavy workbench, electric saw table, lathe, sander, grinder, drills, a pegboard of neatly racked hand tools. He did household repairs and made furniture as a hobby—simple cottage cabinets—most of which he gave away or contributed to charities and rummage sales.

Overhead was a bright light softened by a pyramidal green shade. Beyond this cone of gleam was quiet darkness, and there Roberta perched on a high stool and watched her father work.

The room smelled comfortably of linseed oil, fresh sawdust, and the perfume of exotic woods seasoning in an overhead rack. It seemed to the child a magician's den.

Wood shavings curled away with a life of their own; sparks went flinging from the grinder as a tool took an edge.

When the electric tools were shut off, when her father was working slowly, patiently, with his hands, he talked to her. He spoke about his voyages, the personalities of various woods, the perplexing ways in which people act, and how best to manage them.

(Later, when she was engulfed by the noisy complexities of her own career, she was to remember this workroom as a haven, and long for it. She could close her eyes and see her father's haired hands moving, hear rasp of plane and gentle tap of mallet, smell pierce of glue and warm scent of good wax.)

She asked questions, and never once did he fake or fob her off. He answered when he could. When he could not, he would say, "I do not know the answer to that."

She told him about things she was doing: dating boys, running the 100-yard dash for the girls' track team, taking voice lessons, reading a book of love poetry. His eyes were on his work, but he listened carefully to what she said. He never offered advice unless she asked for it.

Even when she was in college, home on holiday, she would seek out that high stool in the workroom and talk to the Patroon. He was still the most handsome man she had ever seen, but now she felt something else in him.

He was complete. He knew who he was and could live with it. Accustomed to young men continually seeking their identity, a life-style to which they could surrender, she found his monolithic dignity reassuring. In a mad world only he was sane.

Eventually, she came to know her presence there was important to him. Without a son, married to a chitchat woman, he had only this fierce, coltish daughter to come close to. He told her how necessary it was to make the right mistakes.

He was father, teacher, priest, friend . . . and something more. Once he carved a two-link chain from a single piece of pine. The two loops of wood could be twisted and turned, yanked and tugged, but never separated until they were smashed.

"He said I could marry him when I grew up," she told Hapgood Graves.

"He was already married. To your mother."

"Oh, for Christ's sake, Hap. It was just a joke. A joke he made for a skinny brat with long arms and legs."

"Round and round we go, and where it stops, nobody knows. So how come you left home when you were so hooked on daddy?"

"He wanted me to. He told me to."

"You were filling out."

"Well . . . sure. Whatever the hell that's got to do with it. He wanted me to *do* something. He knew Julie never would. He really wanted me to be someone."

"You're someone all right. You're a freak."

"So are you."

"I am. I know it. But, mom, do *you* know it?"

"The something of my discontent."

"What?"

"It's a quotation. I can't remember. Something of my discontent."

"'Now is the winter of our discontent.' Willie wrote it. From one of the king plays, I think."

"Intellectual freak. Harvard freak. Now is the summer of our discontent."

"Something like that."

"Hap, what am I going to *do?*"

"Do? Do you have to do anything?"

"Oh, yes. I can't just let things happen to me. I've got to make them happen."

"Poor bitch."

There was a glaze on everything: sky, sea, sun—all bloodless. She in her white dress. He in his white shirt and jeans. They were frail ghosts, rushing through an enameled world.

"I may marry Doctor Todd," she said dreamily.

"Oh, sure. To prove? To show? To punish?"

"You think I can't do it?"

It was his turn to touch.

"You're as far down as I am," he said.

"Did you scoop her in?" she asked. "Yet?"

"No. Not yet."

"You're going to?"

"Yes. I think so."

"What for?"

"You don't understand."

"That's right. Tell me."

"She's young."

"I know. So?"

"She's a virgin. She wants. It's there for me. Untouched by human hands."

"You're not so great in the sex department."

"Mom, I know it. But this isn't sex."

"No? What is it?"

"What is it? It's something out of a cocoon. She's all yearning. Tender. I've got to eat that. Swallow her down. Teach her what it's all about. If I don't, someone else will."

"Tell me, piano player: what's it all about?"

"I'm going to kill you some day."

"Probably. What's it all about?"

He looked at her.

He said: "When you've got cancer, you want everyone else to have cancer."

She bent her head. Possibly there were a few warm tears: small ones.

He peered out from under the shade. It was a sickening sky, all pukey pinks, lemon yellows, washed-out blues. There was nothing strong there. It was a stale watercolor.

"At least—" he said.

"At least—" she said.

Both at the same time; the plotters laughed.

"But that night in Vegas," she said. "If things—"

"Oh, Christ. *That* again?"

"If things had been different, just a little different, you and I might have been—"

"The greatest lovers the world has ever known?" He delivered a thin grin.

"Something like that."

"No. It wouldn't have happened. It couldn't have happened. We're half-people, you and I. Together we'd make one sick soul."

"You think we're sick?"

"Slug," he said.

"What?"

"A slug. It's like a snail outside its shell. But it's bigger. Smooth white and wet. A loathsome thing. I was going to a school in Ohio—this was before I went to Harvard—and I—"

"You never told me you went to a school in Ohio. How come you left?"

"I forget. I must have buggered *someone*. Anyway, I was pledged to this fraternity. The showers were in the basement. I stepped into this shower stall, and here was this big, white, wet, loathsome thing on the floor."

"And?"

"And? There is no and. I saw this slug in the shower of an Ohio fraternity. I just happened to think of it, that's all."

She nodded, understanding.

When she sang a love song, or called blues, her voice had a quality that terrified him. But it was her fine, vicious intelligence he loved. He wanted to think as she did: not in his usual visual images but with a pure logic he visualized as hard light.

He saw her intelligence as something trained at a ballet bar: long, sinuous, and capable of incredible and oddly exciting contortions.

Her brain, the way she thought, aroused him physically. It seemed absurd—was it mad?—to be so stimulated by a woman's intelligence. But Bobbie's was everything he admired: cool, lucid, and as devoid of fakery as a human mind can become.

Small head with long hair drawn back and pinned up; no makeup, tendoned neck; and finally one ripe muscle of a body that could twang into free air and suddenly freeze, hold, and exist suspended in space: that was how he saw her intelligence.

That it was inhuman he was willing to admit. Her logic would not embrace emotion, gut heat or all the irrational whims by which men and women are moved. She knew these things existed, and she used them, but she would not acknowledge their existence in herself.

There was a fascination in her intelligence; she was a new being and thought in a new way: A is equal to B, and B is equal to C, and therefore X is equal to Y. His mind could not make that leap, but hers could.

Part of his fascination was the horror felt at watching a high tightrope walker working without a net. We breathe a wheeze of relief when he reaches the other platform with quick little steps. But we are vaguely disappointed; it is not a satisfying end to the act. The logical end is death.

When Graves said to Susan Todd, "Love corrupts, and

absolute love corrupts absolutely," he had, in truth, been quoting Bobbie Vander. One night, on a flight to their first engagement in London, they had been high on pills, and they wandered into a discussion of why love songs are universally popular, and have been since the Song of Solomon. Why not songs of greed, songs of deceit, songs of grossness and brutality?

"Because," Graves explained, "love songs are 'nice' songs. They're dream songs. Pot-of-gold-at-the-end-of-the-rainbow songs. Love is what everyone wants and no one finds."

That was when Bobbie Vander said somberly, "No, Hap. People find it. But love corrupts, and absolute love corrupts absolutely. Parents and children, husbands and wives, and especially lovers: love corrupts them all. Because you have an image of the loved one. And the loved one, sometimes unloving, still attempts to adapt to your image. But then you find the image is a sad substitute of what you first saw in the loved one. We change to accommodate love. And by changing, we destroy it. That first insanity cools. By changing what we are to answer the lover's demands. And by answering them, we kill the heat. Nothing more? That's what the lover asks then. Nothing more? Is that all there is? If there's everything, there's nothing. There has to be something more."

"What?" he asked.

"Mystery," she said.

Now there was no coffee left in his glass. He took ice into his mouth and munched soft shreds. They bit his tongue.

"But why should Susan Todd have hope?" he asked Bobbie Vander.

"You have hope."

"Not really, mom. Sometimes I have dreams. But when I stop dreaming, I stop hoping."

"What do you dream about?"

"You. Mostly."

"You dream about screwing me?"

"No. I dream I *am* you."

"Well, that's a hopeful dream, isn't it?"

"No. That's just a manifestation of a death wish."

"You sure know how to say pretty things to a girl."

"I say pretty things to Susan. She's in love with me."

"I think you're in love with her."

"I love what she is. But I don't love her. There's a difference. Small, but it's there."

"Then why do you want to change what she is?"

"Why?"

"Yes. Why?"

He stared at her. "It's very complex."

"Cop-out!"

"All right. I don't know why. I just know I must do it."

"Why must you do it?"

"Because it—it will—it will *nourish* me."

"Nourish you?"

"Yes. I need her. Why are you going to louse-up Julie's life?"

"Because. Because I don't like people hitting me and rejecting me. Like I'm a nothing. I'm a something. People don't do that to me. I do that to people."

He laughed. "Oh, we're something all right. Both of us. The Bobbsey Twins at the Beach."

"I hate this day," she said, looking up. "It's like a crappy painting."

"One of those pictures you see on a religious calendar."

"Yes. Like that."

Sugary colors were running into one another, seeping, fading. Wine changed to water to milk to ink to blood. Overall was a glaze of soft wax. Colors crawled, melting.

"How are you going to do it?" she asked him.

"Love will find a way."

"Now you're beginning to talk in song titles. Where?"

"That's the problem."

"Not in our home? Not in Todd's home?"

"No. Not there."

"How about the back of the station wagon?"

"It's under consideration."

"I'll give you a dime if you'll let me watch."

"Want to take movies?"

"No. I'll help."

"How?"

"By applauding at the right moments."

"Mom, you're beautiful."

"I love you, too. We're two of a kind, aren't we?"

"Yes."

"Are you going to tell her about the cocaine?"

"I already have."

"What did she say?"

"She's fascinated. She wants to try it."

"Are you going to let her?"

"Sure. She's a big girl now."

"Her father will kill you."

"We'll be long gone before he finds out."

"He'll find you."

He shrugged.

"You just don't care. Do you?"

"No. I just don't care."

"He's a hard man," she said.

He looked at her strangely. "I know." He nodded. "A young Patroon."

"Thank you, Doctor Freud. Sometimes I'd like to jam an umbrella up your ass and press the button. For your information, my very own sweet, there was never, ever, anything between the Patroon and me. It was just the innocent love of a daughter for her father."

"Whee!"

"You're a filth."

"And how are you going to get Todd into the sack?"

"I'm going to sing him into it."

He looked at her curiously. "That should be interesting."

She shaded her eyes. She squinted far out to sea where two pallid sailboats, seemingly linked together with a cable, were running before the wind.

"Life can be beautiful," she offered.

"And fun," he added.

## 23

Tom Drinkwater, an ancient boy, woke instantly, alert, dry-eyed, and looked about for enemies. The world menaced: white walls, white furniture, white light. His nightmare had been a white blackness.

He rubbed water on his face; there was no need to shave. He pulled on faded, shredded shorts: hacked-off jeans. He had not bathed for three days. He had bathed in the sea but not soaped in the bathroom. His body had a faint cedar scent, and his young flesh was glabrous and pure.

He went directly to the sea, belly-flopped into the first big wave. He churned steadily to deep water, brown arms sunglinted. He surface-dived, grabbed bottom sand, rubbed it on his skin. Then he drifted in . . . dreaming.

In the kitchen he made coffee, a handful of grounds like

bottom sand tossed into boiling water. He made enough for himself and his mother. While his cup cooled he took the garbage can to the access road.

Lifting the heavy can tautened him and put a finish to his sweet body. He existed in space, crisp and concluded.

Tom Drinkwater, foreigner in his native land, returned to his coffee. He owned the deserted morning. It was his hour. He heard a single gull screech.

His mother came in, went directly to the saucepan of hot coffee. They sat across from each other at the worktable.

"Did you brush your teeth?" she asked.

He could not lie to her, and she sighed.

"Bigelow will deliver the clams and lobsters before noon. I want you to open the clams when it is time."

"The Patroon always opens the cold clams."

"I want you to open the cold clams."

"The old man has no strength in his hands?"

She looked at him. "The old man has strength."

He was a good boy; he helped his mother. He broke eggs into the pan, cut neat slices from the Polish ham, set the table in the dining room. Silently he obeyed her commands, but moving in his own rhythm.

When they all came down for breakfast, pattering, chattering, he went outside. Samuel Lees was setting up the long table on the front porch. He was wrestling heavy planks across two sawhorses. Then he would thumb-tack shelving paper to the planks and place chairs around, all facing the sea. They were to have a clambake.

Tom Drinkwater did not offer to help. He went to the toolshed and took up his soon-to-be-tube of wood, the knife embedded. He sat cross-legged on the stubbled grass, began to whittle, carve, cut away. He was close to the final hollow.

A tumid sun bounced out of the sea, orange and

gleaming. The sky sparkled. It would be a Tiffany day, blinding and rare.

He pried with the knife tip, feeling. Finally there was a thin film, a diaphragm. Then he was into it gently, and out of.

He held the log up to his eye. Light came through. He probed with the knife point, turning. The opening enlarged. There was a succulent smell.

He shook shavings from the short tube, put it to his eye again and searched through. It was a thick telescope, spiked with scapes of wood. He searched the white world.

There, through that tiny, scabby hole, were Susan Todd and Hapgood Graves, walking along the beach. Through his wood Ikantos telescope he watched, the secret sharer. So they strolled, laughing, touching, dashing, wading. A joke! They floated through life on a pillow of white dust.

Ancient boy Tom Drinkwater: contained in a completion of tanned hide. A line was around his body, a line around his soul. An eye glittered through his wooden telescope, his drum. It stared at a crank world.

Violence fevered him; an erection was there. He seemed so denied. Sometimes he stood before his little mirror and moved. He stretched his mouth, widened his eyes, grinned, yawned, laughed, frowned. He poked a finger at the mirror and the mirror poked a finger back. He was not invisible.

Now, staring through that splintered hole as the flesh he loved and the flesh he hated frolicked in the sea, he felt his own existence and knew himself. The rough tube at his eye enlarged and engorged, not only the injustice but his own flame.

Dreams whirled fiercely: mad montage of suffering and death. And through all a chill blade of Ikantos pride remained serene. It came unscorched through fire, unchipped by blows, unstained by blood.

So his morning went. The sun, crystal now, floated in alcohol air. Tom Drinkwater, fashioning his Ikantos drum, knew he would triumph: primitive son.

For hundreds of years—according to records of the first settlers—the crinkled coast near South Canaan had been blessed by a special form of sea lettuce. This plant, resembling a giant chicory, came in on the tide from late July to early October.

When the Patroon first arrived in South Canaan, the seaweed was used in soups, stews, salads and, after drying and boiling, as a medicine said to have great curative powers for catarrh.

More importantly, the bright green weed was used in the preparation of outdoor clambakes. After the clams and lobsters were laid to rest in the hot stone-lined pit, a thick blanket of wet sea lettuce was tucked tenderly around and over.

The steam that arose tickled the nose, excited the palate. It was a perfume of such salty delight that persons suffering from asthma frequently thrust their faces over the steaming pit to inhale deeply, swearing that nothing else in the world gave such relief.

About five years previously the crisp feathery plant began to go bad. The Patroon and other South Canaan residents blamed pollution from a new paper mill five miles north of the town.

Whatever the cause, the lettuce became brown, limp, discolored with blotches. It became evil to smell, evil to taste. It was no longer eaten or used as a medicine. Nor was it used as a cover for a clambake pit.

Mrs. Grace Vanderhorst had dried and pressed a frond of the original sea lettuce between two sheets of clear plastic. The Patroon made a simple frame of oiled walnut. This now hung in the library. The Patroon went in and looked at it occasionally.

Now, when a clam and lobster feast was planned, Mrs. Rebecca Drinkwater used an enormous two-section aluminum pot that covered two flames on the gas range. Lobsters were boiled in the lower section while clams were steamed in the colander top. This giant pot was frequently loaned to neighbors, churches, and civic organizations. It was dented. The bottom was almost burned through.

Mr. Joshua Bigelow did not have the best clams and lobsters in those parts, but the Patroon had been buying from him for thirty years and saw no reason to change. Bigelow's prices were fair, and he delivered when he said he would. Also, each Christmas he sent his customers a clamming knife with "Joshua Bigelow" branded into the wood handle.

Since the Patroon kept his tools and cutlery sharp and treated them well, he now had nineteen Joshua Bigelow clamming knives in his workroom in the big house.

Mr. Bigelow himself was pushing eighty. He looked remarkably like Popeye—an appearance enhanced by a corncob pipe cocked in the corner of his mouth. He was an expert on ancient reels and jigs, and was in great demand as a caller. Two years previously he had been interviewed on a Portland TV show during which he had danced a five-minute jig without removing his lighted pipe.

Ordinarily, deliveries were made by his fifty-year-old son, Aaron. But Joshua always delivered to the Patroon himself. The two men discussed the weather.

When Joshua and his Portuguese helper brought the moving bushel baskets (covered with squares of wet burlap) into Mrs. Drinkwater's kitchen—just when he promised he would have them there—Julie Vanderhorst was on hand and asked Mr. Bigelow if he would do her a favor.

Mr. Bigelow, who thought Julie was a fine figure of a woman, agreed instantly. The entire party was assembled on the front porch so that Mr. Bigelow could take their photograph.

They posed behind the sawhorse table, now covered with shelving paper. On it were plates, cutlery, bowls of green salad, tomato sauce, white horseradish sauce, celery and red radishes on ice, sea biscuits, loaves of rye and crusty white, and, to one side, a tub of ice water in which cans of Ram's Head and three bottles of California white wine were floating.

Pieter Vanderhorst sat in the center behind the table. Grace was on his right, Roberta on his left. Then, moving outward, were Julie, Susan Todd, and Rebecca Drinkwater, all seated. Hapgood Graves and Tom Drinkwater stood at the left, and Benjamin Todd and Samuel Lees stood on the right.

They laughed and joked, arranging themselves. Dr. Todd slid his hand into his shirt front, like Napoleon. Hapgood Graves refused to take off his sunglasses. Grace Vanderhorst clasped her husband's hand on the tabletop. Tom stared stonily at the camera. Sam Lees grinned. Julie leaned forward to glance at Dr. Todd. Rebecca's eyes were closed. The Patroon was a plinth.

Mr. Joshua Bigelow backed up on the lawn until he could get them all in. He snapped the shutter. This was the photograph that later appeared on page 32 of the New York *Times*.

The photograph itself has a curiously ancient quality, almost as old as the man who took it. There they all are: squinting, grinning, frowning, gawking. They are washed in sunshine. Behind them stream black shadows. There is a rough rhythm to the grouping, rising from the Patroon and seated women to the standing men. They resemble a

Victorian garden party, a meeting of a St. Petersburg revolutionary committee, the poet and friends at an outdoor lunch on the shore of Lake Como in 1912; dead and gone.

Search this document for clues. There are none. It is closed up. They are all frozen, armor on and visors down. They are hidden behind their faces, waiting for the heralds.

Hapgood Graves had never seen a live lobster, never in his life. Rebecca Drinkwater uncovered the first basket. He stared, clutched by the sight. There were the blue gray green metal beasts, writhing, scraping upon each other.

"You put them in boiling water?" he asked her.

"Yes."

"Does it hurt them?"

She nodded. "They scream."

He laughed. He had not suspected her of humor. "Won't they pinch you?"

"They are pegged. See?"

He leaned over the basket. He saw the little wood wedges plugged into the claws. He moved a finger cautiously closer. A feeler stroked him. Claws moved languidly. Encrusted things intertwined. They wriggled, striving to climb free.

He wrapped on a carapace with his knuckle. The tail curled under.

"Charles!" he said delightedly. "I never would have known you. You're looking well."

Mrs. Drinkwater smiled. "You know him?"

"Old friends. Went to school together."

She stooped swiftly, grabbed up Charles. Holding him by the body, behind the claws, she thrust the straining beast into Graves' face. He drew back, looking up at her.

"You want him? You want Charles?"

"What for?"

"A pet. You can have fun with him."

"Fun?"

"You can put a leash on him. You can lead him around on a leash. You can play with him. You can pet him. You can tease him."

"No. No thanks."

"Then into the pot?"

"Yes," he said. "Into the pot."

She nodded. "Into the pot."

She turned to the stove. Again he noticed her fine legs: slender ankles and calves bulging smoothly like a dancer's.

He watched as she put six lobsters into the pot. She lifted on the top section, dumped in clams.

"Half we steam, half we eat cold. Whichever way you like. You like them hot or cold?"

"Cold," he said. "I like everything cold."

Mrs. Grace Vanderhorst came drifting through the door.

"How divine," she said sniffing. "Mister Graves, have you written my poem yet?"

"Not completed, ma'am," he said, jerking to his feet. "But working on it."

"Butter and lemon," Grace sang. She hustled to the refrigerator. "We must have butter and lemon. How are the lobsters coming, Mrs. Rebecca?"

"All right."

"Don't show me. I don't want to look. It's so cruel. Dropping those living things in boiling water."

"They scream," Hapgood Graves said.

"Oh, I know, I know." She set a ceramic pot of butter and three lemons on the worktable. Then she hurried from the kitchen, hands clamped over her ears. "I don't want to hear them. I don't want to hear them."

They looked after her.

"They do scream," Mrs. Drinkwater said.

"Lobsters?"

"Yes. When you drop them in hot water. But you can't hear them. The sound is so high. But they scream. Boiled alive."

A few minutes later he wandered out to the porch. The sun was there.

They had platters of steaming lobsters, a zillion clams, green salad, chunks of tomato and cucumber, crunchy biscuits, and whiskered ears of shoe peg white corn from New Jersey, roasted in the husk, the tiny kernels with a subtle, lingering flavor, doused in butter and dusted with salt and fresh-ground pepper.

The Patroon nodded with pleasure, listening to the laughter. There was food and talk, cold beer and chilled wine, clear sky and hot sun. It was easy to feel hopeful.

Nothing was passed. They moved about the table, helping themselves and returning to their own chairs or taking others'. Tom Drinkwater sat on the porch steps, cracking a lobster claw in his strong jaws. Bobbie Vander wandered. Sam Lees plucked hot radishes from ice water and popped them into his mouth, grinning and munching.

Ben Todd surgeoned a loaf of rye. Julie dripped buttered clams into her mouth, eyes rolling. Grace Vanderhorst daintily dug for lobster meat with a tiny fork. Hapgood Graves played an ear of corn like a harmonica. Susan Todd, unexpectedly, helped Rebecca. The two hustled between kitchen and porch.

Graves looked up from his corn. He saw ripe, bare-armed women flashing down dishes of food, their skin aglow, panting, laughing, their faces flushed. He had a vision of the three . . . dancing.

"Brueghel," he said aloud. And him prancing in a cordovan codpiece from Abercrombie & Fitch!

Food slowed them all—that and the prying sun, the flaming sky. They slurped strawberries, dunked in wine.

They dug into sweet melon, poked at thin slices of cheesecake.

Pieter Vanderhorst rose, grunting. He smiled around and stumped his way down onto the beach. He saw Dr. Todd busy filling wineglasses. The Patroon lighted one of his baked Dutch cigars, belching. He blew smoke at the searching sun.

It was all good: good day, good company, good food, good life. Worry wizened. Far out the sea flashed. Behind him he heard young laughter.

And then. Suddenly. Darkness. Then. Sky slowly wheeling. Turning. Flopping over. As ankles melted. And knees. Hips. All loose. He went down slowly. Flowing. Cane balanced a moment. Then toppling. Cigar still clutched in his hand.

"I would like to say something," he said aloud.

He was on his back, going out . . . but still . . . He fumbled for a spansule, fumbled to breathe deeply. Toad death had a come-along clamped around his skull, chain tightening. He would not cry out.

From somewhere came a wild shout. He felt pounding feet: not heard but felt. The chain about his brain tightened. He grinned with pain. He would not cry out.

"Bastard!" Dr. Todd screamed.

His cigar was plucked, flung away. Fingers plucked at his pockets. His mouth was plucked open. Something was shoved down his gullet. He swallowed convulsively to keep from vomiting.

His eyes stuck shut. But he heard the sea, felt a wash of pain. His body tried to leap from hot sand but a weight pressed down. He heard a voice: "Tom! The big umbrella!"

Sharp pain slackened, dulled. There were pierces. His gummed eyes fluttered.

"I see," he said.

He looked up at the ring of masks about him. Faces, wide-eyed, nodded, a bouquet of dying flowers. Above, high through the circle, a fire.

Then there was shade and fading daisies. People were running. Sam Lees was dragging a wide plank from the table, dumping a trail of lobster shells and broken wine-glasses. Grace Vanderhorst was folded onto the sand, wailing. Others hopped, mouths open.

Pieter Vanderhorst looked at Roberta's wet face.

"Not this time," he said.

"You can't!" she cried. "Marry me!"

The Patroon's eyes moved to find his son. The boy was standing stolidly, arms crossed on naked chest. His long black hair fell to his shoulders. His glittering eyes stared down. The strong brown body was a totem against the sky.

Afterward, Hapgood Graves said to Bobbie Vander: "He came close to dying. You know. Death. The whole bit."

The lurid summer withdrew. But not at a constant rate. It was child's time, a balky beast: now hurtling, now stopping, hobbling, darting. Some days passed in a hot breath. Some lingered in cool tranquillity.

Later, people spoke of it as a vintage year. "Best summer since fifty-eight." Even in its worst moods it was comforting. Storms dwarfed man's greatest cataclysms. There was solace in that.

When days came beautiful into a new world—mystery and wonder. The sky was aflame. Europe was burning across the sea. There were flickers, nimble lights. And always, there was salt sea and mash of surf, a million darts when spray pounded into the air, went drifting on the wind. People laughed.

There were good fish that year, from all over: swordfish, salmon, flounder, cod, perch. The Patroon tried frozen trout from Japan. He pondered how *Japanese* they looked: delicate, frail, sketched with a brush. They were porcelain trout, glazed, waiting to be framed.

Also, that summer, fruit was swollen and sweet: the melons: cantaloupe and honeydews, casabas, Persians; berries: straw, blue, huckle; grapes, pears, peaches, and plums of sugar: all chilled and dripping; the oranges.

The Patroon sat out beneath the faded umbrella, sipping a glass of sherry. He looked about with new eyes, born again. All was beginning. He nodded to see a gull swoop and rise, something wet flopping in its beak.

Sunrise defeated sunset. He woke each morning in triumph, anxious to devour a little more, discover a little more. It was all fruit, juice on the tongue.

The tang of it! All was as it should be.

## 24

Susan Todd had drawn a neat map. She explained it to Hapgood Graves. She was intent, biting her lip.

"Now this is the access road." She pointed. "Here's where we are. Now you walk south until you come to the Indian Road. That's here. You turn right and walk up the Indian Road. It leads to the old graveyard. But before you get there you'll see a tree with a blaze on it. It's on your left."

"A blaze?"

"A big bare place on the trunk where someone cut the bark away. You can't miss it."

"I'm sure."

"Well, right next to that tree with the blaze is a path that goes south. I drew it right here. See?"

"I love your finger. I want to suck your finger."

"Stop it. Now you follow that path. It's all overgrown and you can hardly see it."

"That's nice."

"But even if you can't see it you'll be able to feel it. I mean it's hard ground. If you get off the path you'll be up to your ankles in squish. Maybe deeper. That's how you'll know you're off the path."

"Beautiful. But I mustn't struggle. Right?"

"What?"

"So I'm on the path. I'm heading . . . let's see . . . I'm heading south?"

"Sort of. South and toward the Route. Anyway you keep on that path for, oh, maybe five or ten minutes. It wanders a lot."

"Good. I hate straight paths."

"And then you come out on—"

"Don't tell me. I know. Boston Common."

"Why won't you be serious?"

"Because you won't let me suck your finger. Your sweet little tan little strong little finger. All right, I'll be serious. I follow this wandering path for five or ten minutes. I don't step in the muck. I keep on solid ground. And I come out— where?"

"In Our Place," she said breathlessly, staring at him with shocked eyes. "Oh, my God."

They were in the greened cove where Mrs. Grace Vanderhorst found her very best shells. They sat on a dry patch of sand, backs against the cliff, shoulders touching.

"What is 'Our Place'?"

"Tom Drinkwater took me there once. It was—I guess it

was two summers ago. He had a trap line out there and caught rabbits and things. But he never goes there anymore. I asked him. And it's like this raised place where a little hill of ground comes up through the swamp. And it's covered with green moss. Some grass, but it's mostly moss. And it's hidden all around by trees and creepers and bushes and things. And you'd never find it or even *see* it in a million years unless you knew how to get there by following that path. When I went there with Tom—I only went that once— well, he had a rabbit caught and hit its head in with a stone thing he had even though I asked . . . And once when I was at the Patroon's for dinner, we had fried rabbit. I couldn't even taste it because when you see it skinned it looks like a baby. A little naked baby lying there. All wet. I just burst into tears and ran home. And besides, Tom says there are no more rabbits in the swamp and he doesn't set out trap lines anymore, so that's why it'll be okay to go there. Did you ever eat rabbit?"

She was trembling, chewing on a knuckle. He looked at her and touched a bare shoulder with a fingernail.

"On the beach and July Fourth and up at the Highlands," she said, "and we still haven't *done* anything."

"Anticipation." He nodded. "It's best. No," he said, "I have never eaten rabbit."

Fog billowed in before dawn, clotting the beach and seeping through windows. There was angel hair on trees and bushes. Wisps swirled. Thin air caught in the throat.

When a smoky sun pulled out of the sea, fog moved inland. It huddled down in the swamp between the access road and Route 9-A6. It filled the marsh to treetop level, swirling, a gassy silence rolling.

Susan Todd woke to see shreds of cloud floating about her room. Wet lay on her skin. Her flesh was red-wrinkled. This was the day. She was sick with dread and an awful delight.

She heard nothing but the sea. It was before seven. Her

father was not stirring. She pulled on the faded bikini, went down through the damp house, out to masked land. She was alone on a blanked beach.

The surf was shivery. Combers reared up, came smashing down. Froth ran deep, with eddies, currents, undertows. Drift logs and planks slashed onto the sand. She was ready to give up.

She choked a breath of that airless air. She stripped off bra and panties, threw them back. She plunged into the curdled maelstrom, swearing aloud and screaming.

She dived low into the first deep wave. She came up fighting, swimming strongly to get beyond the crests. Cold water slammed her, but she stroked, stroked, trying to glide. Seaweed clutched her foot. She kicked free.

Suddenly she was beyond the break and towering up, swooping down as great waves moved under her. She felt them between her legs, surging.

Up she went, and down, pumping, struggling to keep from being pulled sideways along the coast. The strength of it! She felt pressure, tons of wet cold. She was caught up and tumbled.

Hair streamed out behind her. She felt her body: hard breasts, brittle ribs, taut buttocks. Her thigh muscles fluttered. She wet in the sea: brief warmth. She hugged her shoulders, laughed, and let the monster heave her, up and down.

Then, quickly brave, she surface dived, white ass flashing. She came up to spout saltwater at the murky sun. She took it all and flouted the beast.

She came staggering, stumbling, out of the grip of the growling animal. She buckled, trembling, to her knees. Her head went down to damp sand, hair hanging in dripping strands. Looking back between her legs she saw shiny whisks. Her joy was heat.

Hapgood Graves had purchased a wide-brimmed straw hat. Styled like a Western Stetson, it was white with a stitched brim of sky-blue. It cast a watery shadow on his face down to his thin lips.

He strolled south on the access road and turned right onto Indian Road as directed. Murk huddled about him. He moved to the left to search for the blazed tree.

He wore a long-sleeved dress shirt, cuffs turned up to the elbows of his hairless arms. He wore no underwear beneath rough duck pants. They stirred him. He liked it, walking with a curious cross-toed step.

He peered at each trunk looming. There was a square of blankness, bark cut away. The flesh of the tree was wet and gleaming. He looked down, moved cautiously to his left, wading through puddles of thick fog.

It came to his knees, hips, throat, and muffled him. He moved his arms like a swimmer, trying to push it all back. There were swirls and billows; he floated.

He scuffed his feet to keep on firm ground. He stepped slowly. Suddenly ooze was over his sneakers. He retreated hastily to hard earth.

"For years I followed a twisting path," he said aloud.

It didn't taste right. He tried again. "For years I followed a twisty path." That was better. "And never found a home," he added. He put it together:

> "For years I followed a twisty path
> And never found a home."

He began to hear it.

A hooded world enveloped him. He knew it would go on forever. Forever would he stumble along the twisty path and never find a home: south to Boston, New York, Philadelphia, fog hiding it all, Baltimore, Washington, Miami, and across to L.A.

Fog hid the world, and the path turning, snarling. He would shuffle on to Mexico, and down, down, down. He would limp through South America, through jungle fog and big city fog, searching for the hidden path and humming. He would fall to the tip, the very end.

"You found it!" Susan Todd cried with a shrill laugh, peering at him over a brambled wall. Her mouth was strained.

Suddenly, seeing her flaming eyes, he smelled the swamp, sweet and cloying. He would put tongue to her. He would taste rank earth, rot and dying things, dead fern and . . .

"Hello!" he caroled. "So this is where you live."

Like the Indian cemetery the hidden hillock thrust up through marsh. But this was a green breast, covered with tight moss sprinkled with bright red flowers: clots of blood upon a lawn.

Around were brambles, ivy, shrubs, tangle of vines and stunted trees, framing that steamy amphitheater. Beneath the moss: coarse decay, studded with broken shells and beach pebbles.

The vaporish day wrapped this secluded place in heat, swaddled it with bandages of cloud. They lay on their sides, facing each other. Liquor popped from her skin. He drew a finger down her bare arm and tasted it: salt.

She was wearing remnants of a shirt much like his. Sleeves were torn away at the shoulders; long tails were knotted about her waist. There was a gap of skin between shirt and plaid Bermuda shorts.

"I went swimming this morning," she told him eagerly. "Early. I've never been in a sea like that. The waves were a mile high."

"Were you frightened?"

"For a minute. Then it was glorious."

"You see? If you hadn't stepped to the edge of the cliff, you wouldn't have gone into that sea."

"Yes," she said wonderingly. "That's true."

"Are you frightened now? Here? With me?"

"Oh . . ." She looked away. "Maybe. A little."

"Look at me."

So she did.

He unbuttoned her shirt. He untied the knot at the waist. He flicked it open. She was bare. But his eyes held to hers.

"Did you bring it?" she asked breathlessly.

"Bring what?"

"You know."

"Say it."

"Well . . . cocaine. Did you bring some cocaine?"

"Yes. I brought it. Do you want to try it?"

"Yes."

"Say it. Say, 'I want to sniff cocaine.' "

"I want to sniff cocaine."

Still staring into her eyes, he reached. He bent his first two fingers, took a tender nipple between the two second joints, began to squeeze. Her eyes closed.

"How does it work?" she whispered. "I mean, what will happen to me?"

"Usually it excites."

"Excites?"

"Yes."

"I don't understand. You mean I'll get excited?"

"Whatever excites you normally will be heightened. Music, words, colors, sex, swimming, eating . . . whatever. With cocaine it will excite you more. What excites you?"

His knuckles tightened. Her face showed no pain.

"You," she said. "You excite me."

"Then I will excite you more."

She opened her eyes. His hand began to turn slowly.

"You're just making all this up."

"That's right." He nodded. "I'm making it all up."

He took his hand away. He lay back, arms stretched above him. He stared at livid smoke drifting across a sultry sky.

She leaned over him and looked. Then she lay down upon him, bare chest against him. She grasped his arms. Her hips and legs curved away. Her head, turned to one side, rested on his shoulder.

"Tell me something awful you've done."

He laughed. "I'm not a villain, you know."

"I don't mean something awful you've done to someone. I mean something you did *with* someone. You know. Like once you were drunk or had some cocaine and the two of you . . ."

"You mean something different?"

"Yes. Like that."

"You mean something *evil?*"

"Well. Yes. I guess that's what I mean."

"All right. I'll tell you something. I was being kept by a woman. This was in Europe. She was an elderly woman but she had a good body. Very strong. She was all tanned. I mean tanned all over. Much deeper than your tan. She was a meerschaum pipe. Her body was all rope. Muscles and tendons and veins and things bulging under her skin. She was shaved all over and kept her skin oiled. Well, I had this apartment right next to hers. I had a closet and she had a closet. And there was just a thin partition between our closets. And she insisted that I drill a hole through the thin wall between our closets. And this hole was to—"

"I don't want to hear any more."

"Sure you do. This hole I drilled was about as big around as a silver dollar. And every night—"

"Please, Hap."

"What I remember most about that closet was the smell. There was an old fur coat in there, and rubber boots, and some old dresses with feathers. Everything musty and ancient. And there I was with my—"

"Hap."

"You asked me to tell you something different I've done."

"I'll never ask again. I swear."

"That's good. Never ask again."

He put her gently onto her back. Her mouth was wide, eyes wide, crisp nostrils peering at the heat. He felt nothing. But she stirred, her thighs scraping.

"Was this your father's shirt?"

"Yes."

He pushed it out to her upper arms. He unbuttoned, unzipped the plaid shorts and pulled them off. She lifted her hips to help.

"Jesus," he said.

She was white and tan, quivering, bubbling with slick. A soft pulse flickered under her left breast.

"Now please," she said. "Please now."

He took the silver filagree box from his pocket, slowly, watching her. He flipped the lid open, laughing.

"See? Hot dog number one top grade you bet, *memsahib*. Zo."

He took a small pinch between thumb and forefinger and pried it into his right nostril. He snuffed deeply, eyes bitten.

"The key," he sang. "The key to the lock to the door to the house."

"Now me."

"Just a tiny pinch. A wee pinch." He shoved it into her right nostril. "Sniff it in deep and go with God."

She obeyed, her eyes closed.

"I don't feel anything."

"Wait. Wait."

They waited, the center of a fog puff. Heat pressed but they went lifting off the spongy turf.

"Things are turning," she said. "Can there be that many shades of white?"

"Oh, yes." He nodded. "Shades."

She moved to him, smiling. She was lying on her side, breasts slowly swelling down, melting. Her chin was propped on a palm, eyes glittering. He poked at her.

"Tell me about that closet," she said. "You know. What you did through that hole in the fur coat."

"You really want to hear?"

"Oh, yes."

Once again he began to recite the novel he had been writing all his life:

"There was a blare of trumpets, a flourish of banners, and the Marine honor guard snapped to attention. 'Gentlemen,' Humphrey Bogart called out. 'And ladies,' he added in his slight lisp. 'The Emperor'?"

"Mmmnnmm-mmmnnmmm-mmmnnmm," she went, satisfied with his story.

"The curtain parted and Mary Garden strode in, looking neither to the right nor to the left. He was wearing his usual costume—double-breasted pin-stripe from Brooks Brothers—and his hand was in its customary position, tucked into his lapels where, Horatio Hornblower knew, he clutched the butt of a Smith and Wesson Salad Oil 'Silent Appeaser.'"

"If I could be a soldier," she mused. "Not to kill. I do not wish to kill anyone. But I mean like in a parade. A march on this big parade ground. Millions and millions of soldiers all dressed alike. Everyone alike. And I'd be right in the middle. Marching along."

He toyed with her, pushing her this way, and that, rolling her over, and back. He played a new song along her spine, his fingers twinkling on the keys. He swayed happily on the bench. Her eyes yawned. She did not cease smiling.

" 'A strange man,' Lady Godiva murmured to me. 'But fascinating.' I nodded, hardly listening to her words. I had been hired to guard the wedding gifts, and that's all I was interested in. They were lined up on a W. & J. Sloane refectory table—fabulous stuff like Cellini silver, Morris silver, Swedish glass, Max Glass, a cupie doll from Coney Island, and a bowling ball with holes for six fingers. Worth a queen's ransom. 'My lord,' Disraeli said, stepping forward. 'May I present my niece for your lordship's pleasure?' "

"So hairy," she said. "I saw him once. And when mother was there I could hear them through the walls. 'Must you?' she kept saying. I thought she was saying, 'Mustard. Mustard.' And I thought they were having franks and I wondered why they didn't give me one. But she was saying, 'Must you. Must you.' Then she screamed. It was."

He dabbled. He couldn't touch enough of her. But he could feel, nip, pinch, twist, pound, stroke, flick. He could learn that cream, sweet cream, and that rotted fern . . .

"Do that again," she commanded.

"All right."

"Again."

"All right."

"Again."

"Now you do it to yourself."

"All right."

"I hadn't seen Marilyn Monroe in years," he went on. "A lively thing who made her debut at Will's Globe. I remember her famous speech, saying, 'Chollie, I coulda been a contendah.' Tear your fucking heart out. Then the band started up—the Beatles singing, 'Sweet Little Yellow Bird' with Eddie Duchin on piano. I've got a tin ear—I really smoke too much—but the music got to me. Lillian Russell grabbed my arm and gave me a look, and I *knew*.''

"Look. This is where I shaved my armpits, and I cut myself here. I used my father's styptic pencil and it stopped. Should I shave all over—like that woman in Europe? Should I be totally, completely, absolutely, finally naked, nude and bare? I mean except for the hair on my head. But should I take all my other hair off? Every hair? Every single hair? Would you like that?"

"It was one of those nights you'll remember for at least a week. Beautiful women. Handsome men. Music. Gaiety. Pastrami from the Gaiety Delicatessen. Tempest Storm from the Gaiety Burlesque. And anything you wanted to drink— Bisodol, champagne, Dr. Pepper, LSD on the rocks: they had it all, served in the best Woolworth glasses and chilled with Freon spray cans from DuPont. 'It blows the mind,' Descartes whispered to me, caressing the bare shoulder of Rasputin.''

"Oh, I love me." She nodded happily. "I use two pillows and bend my body up and backwards until my toes touch the wall. Then I can. I love me. Love me. No one knows that. With my tongue. Can I marry me? Is that legal?"

He kept his shirt and jeans unstained. His body did not touch her body. But his hands . . . chords and harmonies. He laughed her into positions. She twisted gladly. He tried to think of lines to follow ". . . and never found a home."

"Oh," she said once.

"'All right, Louie, drop the gun,' I laughed to Louis Hayward. He smiled in return, took out his handkerchief, and flapped it in my face. 'The finest swordsman in all of

France,' he sang out. And there were Bela Lugosi and Peter Lorre, exchanging bites. 'And who is your friend?' Winston Churchill asked me. 'General Tom Thumb,' I replied. 'The woman with whom I am intimate.' And he said, 'It is better to have loved and lusts than gathers no moss'!"

Juice of her! Fresh juice! It dribbled onto the green and fertilized the world. He swabbed her with a little patch of moss, sniffed it, tucked it into his pocket. Immortality was there.

She moaned. He laughed at the way she was folded up, nibbling her own knees. Then she thawed straight and slept. He stood, stalked steadily about his hidden kingdom: five steps across, five steps back.

"Where has love gone?" he declaimed. "It's gone for all of us. Love has gone away. Except for Uncle Gus."

After a while she awoke and dressed. She kissed his cheek. She went first. He waited ten minutes, then stepped his way back along the path. He turned left onto the road. He wanted to see the Indian Graveyard.

She was fragmented. She led her burst body home. She was splintered. Come along now, she told herself sternly: one moment drifting, on her toes, on her knees.

Her memory flapped, raw-edged rags ripped from a larger banner. Or a worn sheet? When she turned into the access road, the day swayed, hesitated, then renewed its flight.

Tom Drinkwater was raking the beach in front of the Vanderhorst home. He waved. She waved back. He motioned toward the sea. She shook her head, raced into the house. He stared a moment where the glow had been.

She lay on the floor of her bedroom, certain the bed's softness would suffocate her. Her arms and legs spread wide of their own volition; she did not will it. She touched herself gently. Hello there. What had happened?

Petals had been stripped away. Not all but some. Yet the flower was stronger for it. The heart of the flower was closer to the sun. Until she was revealed. Her.

---

## 25

Everything went sailing that night: clouds, moon, stars: all sweeping. The horizon healed, no line between black below and black above; a sparkling sphere.

Dr. Benjamin Todd, a book open on his lap, sipped warm whiskey on his porch. Slouched in a beach chair, he looked about and sipped the world. He was the center; it all revolved around him.

It did revolve as he looked up: stars winding their courses, moon on track, clouds playing out their changing patterns. Life moved cool: above, below, about.

Fog was gone. Now the air was full, washed. There was a hint of something sere, a crispness, a new season waiting. It all turned around, year after year. And it was pleasing.

Susan had gone to her bed, pale and tired. Her period, she told him. He prescribed an aspirin, a glass of port, a kiss. Away she went with a glance of pure love.

It was a good time, a holy night: murmur of sea and murmur of sky. The moon sounded, thin and whispering. Beyond all this—sky, sea, moon, stars, surf, clouds—the world had a tone. Life had music. He could hear it, deep and full, a diapason. He could feel it. Something was trembling deep.

A daemon drifted to him from the Vanderhorst home. Across the lawn it came, through the trees, floating silvery and free.

"Did you ever see a dream walking?" Bobbie Vander asked him.

He laughed and dragged to his feet. "Did you ever hear a dream talking?"

"Well, I did," she finished, standing in front of him. Her silk tent draped. There was not enough wind to move it.

He looked at her eggshell smoothness. She seemed all surface. Her composure daunted him. She commanded, and he was an intruder in his own home.

"What are you doing?" she asked.

"Oh . . . trying to read."

"Did you find what you're looking for?" she said offhandedly, and he became aware of her cat's wisdom.

"Can I get you a drink?"

"What are you having?"

"Whiskey. Bourbon."

"Have any wine?"

"A glass of red wine?"

"A bottle of red wine, please."

When he came back with the full bottle and glass, she was slumped in his chair. Bare legs were shoved out, clay in the moonlight. He sat across from her.

"Do you want a light out here?"

"No. The sky's enough. I've never seen the ocean so calm."

"It happens once or twice a summer. The wind dies. The tide hesitates before it changes. Then it's a pond."

They looked out. The sea heaved gently. There was surf, and far away as many colors as an oil slick making patterns, reds and blues moving, greens and yellows shimmering.

"Thank you," she said, and peered through the glass of wine at a crinkled moon.

"I checked the Patroon yesterday. He's coming out of it fine. A very strong man. Good heart."

"Yes."

"Just make sure he carries those spansules with him, wherever he goes."

"I'll nudge him. But you know the Patroon. He'll do what he wants to do. Mother was a handful for a few days, but now she's back to what we laughingly call normal."

"I don't think there's much point in my trying anything there. Your mother is a happy woman. Or content anyway."

"Oh, sure."

He laughed suddenly and slid down in his chair. He tapped the rim of his whiskey glass against his teeth.

"A few winters ago your mother had a bad cold. She came to me and I wanted to give her a shot. In the ass, you know. My nurse was in the office. But your mother wouldn't take down her bloomers. She said it wasn't seemly. She was back the next day wearing an old, worn pair of drawers. With fingernail scissors she had cut a little hole in the seat. About a half-inch square. All I could see was a square half-inch of skin. So I gave her the shot right there. She's a marvel, she is."

"Yes." Pause. "You haven't asked about Julie."

"And how is Julie?"

"Okay. She's snoring right now. Drinks in the sun, eats and sleeps. It's a good life."

"Sure. Wouldn't mind that myself."

It was cool, lazy talk. They went sailing with the polished night, voices low, movements slow. Their heads were tilted back, faces painted, legs poked out. They drifted.

She looked at him. His eyes were closed.

"Sleepy?"

"No. Just relaxed."

"Want me to go?"

"No."

"I couldn't sleep so I thought I'd take me a walk on the beach. Then I saw your light and invited myself in."

"Glad you did."

She couldn't get a handle on him. He was withdrawn from her. There was no leverage there.

"Know what I'd like to do?" she asked him.

He opened his eyes and looked at her. She saw then what a solid man he was.

His ugly face had a hard, cruel majesty. He was a boxer; not the prizefighter but the dog: jowls, dark beard, expression of ferocious alert.

Bottomless eyes, crooked mouth, lined cheeks . . . it was the first time she had seen him. He troubled her. He was stone. How do you sing to stone?

"What would you like to do?" he asked. "A night swim again?"

"Oh, no," she said. "I've learned my lesson. No. What I'd like to do . . . What I wondered . . . If we . . . "

(To herself: "Kiddo, you're blathering.")

*"What,* for God's sake?"

"Well, I thought. We could sit down on the beach. In the sand. Near the water. Maybe a little bonfire. You could make a little fire in the sand. Some wood?"

Silence.

"All right," he said finally. "You go on down. Take your wine and my drink. I'll get some wood. Some of it's tarcoated. Now that should burn just fine."

She was standing there, hugging herself, watching the sky go by, when he came trundling down with a canvas carrier of wood, some newspapers, chips. She watched him heel out a shallow pit, crumble newspaper, lean on chips, add tarstained wood, put a kitchen match to it.

"Banzai!" she cried, flame pinking her.

It flared up, died down, then settled. It began to glow and crackle with blue-red-yellow-green flame.

He sat cross-legged, peering into the heat. Still she stood, washed in that island of flickering light and warmth.

"Nice," she murmured. "Now that's nice."

All around was the dark, out there.

She stalked about the fire holding her elbows. She thought she saw flames dancing on the slow sea. Once she touched him, just let her fingers touch his hair. He didn't respond. He was tending their greedy little fire, feeding it. It hardly smoked at all.

"Should I sing?" she asked him.

"Sure."

"You want me to sing?"

"Sure. Yes."

"My hysterical fans." She sighed.

In her Central Park West apartment she had a collection of old 78's—*old* ones. The oldest record she owned was a Perfect label. It was recorded by Cliff Edwards, also known as Ukelele Ike. He sang "It Had to Be You," playing the ukelele. On the other side was "California, Here I Come."

She had purchased this thick, brown record in a junk shop in Detroit. It was all scratched up. She had played it a hundred times. Now the scratch was so bad she had to turn the volume up to full and treble down to nothing. But it still got to her.

This man, whose voice wasn't all that great, plunked his ukelele and sang "It Had to Be You." Every time she listened she wept. She had never recorded it, but she had tried the song at concerts. No one caught it. Maybe it was just her. Hapgood Graves told her to forget it.

But she couldn't forget it. "It Had to Be You." So now she sang it again, wandering around their little bonfire, squeezing her arms. The stone man stared into flames.

She couldn't manage the scratch, but she could handle the longing, the wail. Her small, thin voice split the night, knifed it and went out over the water. "It Had to Be You."

She wasn't self-conscious about her singing. She wasn't embarrassed when people asked her to sing at parties, with no accompaniment. "Sure." She hit clinkers, went off-pitch, but it never bothered her. She just opened up and let the sound come out. "It Had to Be You."

"Sing it again," he said, not looking up. "Please."

Got him.

She walked down to the water and threw it out over the sea. She stood with eyes closed, hands on hips, and sobbed it out. The darkness took it all. But he heard it.

She came back to the fire and poured herself another glass of wine. "How about that?" She laughed. "Does that get you where you live?"

"Yes. Where I live. Sing something else."

She tilted her head back, looked up and around that dark, ringing vault. She had planned the concert but not the auditorium.

There was a puddle of flame, of warmth, and beyond were far reaches, stretching to unimagined pain. Light flickered, died, bloomed. Burning wood snapped.

"And now," she announced formally, "I would like to sing 'Down in the Depths on the Ninetieth Floor.'"

She stood with her back to him, facing the sea. Her sound pierced out. He couldn't hear all the words. Many of those he heard he didn't understand. But the voice . . .

The voice: in the center a tiny hot bonfire, crackling and snapping, all-colored heat in a little pit in the earth. Beyond, on the fringes, was a cool, endless sphere. He heard the heat and saw the cool. He was fevered, shivering.

She sang him a concert. She stalked about him, moving into shadows until he could not make her out, coming back to stand in flame.

She sang old blues: Bessie Smith, Helen Morgan, Billie Holiday, some of Hapgood Graves' things. They went into him, down into him, turning. He had not, he knew, in his lifetime, jelled. The word amused him: "jelled." But it was true—he hadn't. Now, as she sang, he . . .

She drifted in and out of fire, black to red, the thin throat corded, mouth wide, eyes pressed. Once he saw her silhouetted: naked boy's body beneath the silk.

"'But God bless the child . . . ,'" she sang.

The voice was part of the night's music. It was screech and weep, moan and wail. It floated on the jigsaw sea and soared to the chandeliers, prying at him.

They were love songs: love asked, love given, love rejected, love spurned and grabbed.

And love lost, corrupted and killed.

"'He's just my—,'" she started, then stopped suddenly. "Enough," she said. "Always leave them laughing when you say good-bye."

"Not yet. Please."

She didn't answer. She folded down alongside him, staring at fire. She sipped her wine.

"I need another drink," he said hoarsely. "Will you be here when I get back?"

"Yes."

"Can I offer you some food? Cheese and crackers? Anything?"

"No. Thanks. The wine is fine."

In the kitchen, mixing a new drink, he paused, chin down.

"What's happening?" he asked aloud.

She was lying neatly on the sand, wineglass held on her bony chest. She was dreaming at the vast.

"Isn't the beach cold and damp?"

She nodded.

He sat near her. He placed tarred sticks on the slumbering fire, drew back from a sudden flare. He pushed sand close, added more wood, poked chars. The caved male performed his task.

"About a year ago," he said, "I was going through this antique shop on Main Street. Just browsing. I had bought some old books there and some antique jewelry for my—for my ex-wife. I found this filthy painting in a corner. I mean it was encrusted with dirt and dust and cobwebs. I'm going to tell you right now it wasn't a long-lost Rembrandt or anything like that. It isn't worth a fortune. Anyway, I had old Simon Barnes dust it off. Even after he wiped it you could hardly see what it was supposed to be. The colors were very dark and the cheap gilt frame was almost black. Anyway, I turned it over, and there were no stretchers or backing. The damned thing had been painted on wood. I thought maybe it was a hundred years old. It was a landscape. There was this river running by what seemed to be a castle. Lots of trees and shrubbery. In the foreground was this meadow where a shepherd and shepherdess were tending their flock. It made you laugh. You understand? But it was a professional job of painting. Lousy but professional. Months later I showed it to Bob McCready. He used to teach History of Art at the university, and he said I was exactly right. He thought it had been painted about a hundred years ago in Germany or Austria when art factories were turning out this stuff in gilt frames for middle-class families that wanted a genuine handpainted painting to show how cultured they were. These days they buy French posters. Well, anyway, I bought that silly painting and took it home. I mean my winter home on Gervase Street. I decided I'd clean it myself, so I went to Miss Burnett's Art Shoppe on High Street. She sells knitted coasters and sequin kits and cocktail napkins with Scotties on them and little plastic plaques that say, 'Jesus Saves.' Once I thought that would make a marvelous advertising slogan for a bank: 'Jesus Saves—Why Don't You?' Well, Miss Burnett had a liquid that's made to clean oil paintings. She told me to work very slowly and carefully, dipping Q-Tips in this liquid and cleaning just a little bit of the painting at a time. Okay. So that's what I did. Now as I started cleaning the dirt and grime off this old painting, it began to come alive. I mean, originally it was painted dark with lots of browns and ochers and golds and deep greens. But with the dirt and dust of a century on it, I mean you could hardly *see* it. But as I dabbed away with my little Q-Tip in this stuff I bought at the Art Shoppe, it began to come alive. It was like creating a world. I knew it was a crappy painting, but the foliage wasn't done badly at all. A tree looked like a tree. And it began to come green. And the iridescent lake. And the tower of this castle silhouetted against the sky. I wiped the dirt of a hundred years away, and it all began to come through. Oh, hell, it wasn't great art. It was shitty art. So sentimental. But it was like a forgotten dream. I wiped all the grease and grime away, and there it was. Not shining exactly because it had been painted murky to begin with. But now you could see it. That crazy dream.''

She waited, but he had finished.

"And?" she asked.

"And what?"

"What happened then?"

"Happened? Nothing happened."

"What's the point of this story?"

"There is no point," he said. "I bought a cheap old painting and cleaned it. I'm sorry. I've bored you."

"No, you haven't."

"Well . . . You provided the music. I provided the words."

"Hapgood Graves does that for me."

"Graves. Is he laughing at me? Does he think I'm funny?"

"Hap? No. That's his way. He laughs at everyone. Mostly he laughs at himself."

"What does he do?"

"Do?"

"I know he's your accompanist and writes poems and love songs. But does he have any ambition?"

She sat up and hugged her knees. She looked at him coldly.

"I think Hap's only ambition is to write poems and love songs."

He took a deep breath. "I'm sorry. Forgive me. What a stupid thing to say. Ambition? Jesus! Poems and love songs are enough. I'm ashamed."

She took off silver sandals, held bare feet to the shaking flame. Her toenails were silver, too, on uncorned toes. She had thin feet, boned, strange things that could grasp.

"That's all right," she said with a little shrug, a little laugh. "What's so great about love songs? What happened to it?"

"To what?"

"That painting you were telling me about."

"Oh, that. It's in the waiting room of my office. Patients like it. I think it soothes them. They keep telling me it's a great masterpiece and very beautiful. But you were talking about love songs."

"Was I? Love songs. Well . . . Song writers. You should see the things they send me. Cries in the dark. The poor shits. And their lives? So cruddy. A hot pastrami at the Stage; that's dinner. Then a quick bang on Eighth. Such children. Love? What do they know about love? I'll tell you: it rhymes with above. That's what they know. Moon rhymes with June and love rhymes with above. Or maybe dove. Then home to a Times Square hotel. Where they write 'Once You Fall in Love.' And wake up belching and retching from cheap booze. Fat little guys covered with food stains. Cigars and ballpoint pens in their breast pockets. Yids and Smokes and Wops with all that gravy on them. So sordid.''

"And all they write about is love?"

"Love. What the hell is that? Will you tell me? A four-letter word. What is it? The bastards have conned us. Love. What *is* it? Just tell me what it is. I'm not knocking it, you understand. It's my living. That's all I sing about. So that makes me just about as good as they are. Right? Me with the cheap cigars and gravy stains. Because that's how I make my living. They write 'em and I sing 'em. But what *is* it?"

Behind them on the access road a wild car roared. They heard drunken screams and laughter. A young voice shouted, "Most!" Then sound droned away into the silent night.

"I think," he said slowly, "love is a kind of sacrifice. Sacrifice . . . Yes. That's as close as I can come to it."

But she didn't hear him.

"What's so awful," she said, plunging on, "is that out of these poor, sad shits—out of their gonads, I guess—they're all lousy lays—right out of their balls comes a song. Now and then. I mean they don't *live* it. They don't *know* it. Their lives aren't romantic, and love to them is a fast blow-job in a phone booth. But occasionally—just *occasionally*—you'll get music. It will mean something and everyone will be singing it. And you'll remember it for the rest of your life. I just don't understand it. They're so cheap, and what they do is so expensive. Believe me, I know them and I've never figured it out. Roses blooming out of a dung heap. Something like that."

"Hapgood Graves isn't like that. Is he?"

"He's got it in him. They've all got it. Hustlers. The lot of them. I don't care if the guy writes great Broadway musicals or if he writes jerk-off music for skin flicks. If he's writing love songs he's a hustler and con man. But people seem to want it. I guess they need it. So I keep singing it. And coining dough. What does that make me?"

He waved it away.

"Love," she said scornfully.

The night sky grew weightier. Dark compressed. The brave fire flickered, a pinpoint in all the nothing. "I Can Dream, Can't I?" Drums there, and a soft guitar. He heard it, though she was not singing.

He let the fire die. They watched it pale down: tongues, licks of warmth, blackness closing in.

"Listen. That story I told you about the painting. It did have a point."

"Did it?"

"Dirt accumulates. Grime. Until you can hardly see what is underneath. Whether it's good or bad isn't important. But you clean the dust away, and then you can see what's down there."

"Are you talking about my singing?"

He was grateful. He looked at her admiringly.

"Yes. That's why I told you that story. Your voice—those songs you sang—love songs—began to clean some of the grime away. On me."

"Written by Times Square pimps and sung by a Times Square whore."

"I'll take it. Will you sing for me again?"

"Maybe."

She held palms to buds of blue that blinked, went dead.

Like the Patroon, he did not think it unmanly to say what he felt, and she let it touch her. She lived with no values but herself: her talent, her drive, her spiteful intelligence. Doubt was an alien, and confession a weakness.

But she was attracted by his sure masculinity, and menaced. If he was right, then she was wrong. Was it possible she needed? It seemed shameful, and her victory was tainted.

"Let's take a little walk down the beach," she said. "Just a short one. Then we'll come back and I'll go home. I can sleep now."

He kicked sand onto the embers, stamped them flat. They strolled south. She hummed something.

"What's that?"

"Something Hap told me about this afternoon. He's working on it. He just started it. So far he only has two lines: 'For years I followed a twisty path, and never found a home!' "

"I like that."

"It's got a nice bite. Here's how it goes . . ."

She sang the two lines. Then sang them again. He felt the familiar knife, scraping inside. He reached for her hand. She let him take it.

They wandered down to the Breckinridge place, to the pipe flagpole planted in concrete. They stood a moment, looking out.

The dark was complete now, sky inked, moon scratched out. Luminosity was gone from the sea. The tide had changed; a driving wind crisped the waves.

He held her hand. He knew she was there, something in the darkness. But the flesh he felt was soft, cool, unsubstantial. He had a moment's horror of holding nothing but a disembodied hand. Comparative Anatomy 3-4.

He felt up. He held limp fingers with one hand, and with the other he felt the flat wrist, round muscle of arm, bone of elbow, gristle of shoulder beneath the silken sleeve.

He tugged. She came into his arms, looming out of the black. She was against him, pressed. He did not kiss but in this ghost embrace shoved his face close. She floated there, somewhere off.

He held a fluid. She flowed around him, wind-whipped. Dimly their eyes . . . He held a tone, something vibrating, a throb. He gripped nothing, but strained to see. His locked knees shook.

"Let's run back," she said strongly. "Let's run along the beach just as fast as we can."

"All right."

"Let's take our clothes off."

"Don't be absurd," he said.

But they did run.

## 26

In Pieter Vanderhorst's home it was made clear that each—family and friends—saw to his own: made his bed, cleaned his mess, kept tidy.

Once a week, early on Tuesday morning, an elderly Ikantos lady, Mrs. Thomas Nofire, and her two middle-aged daughters, arrived to vacuum, dust, empty waste baskets, clean the general rooms downstairs.

First, Mrs. Rebecca Drinkwater served coffee in the kitchen. Then the Indian ladies bound their coarse hair with cheerful bandannas and swarmed through the house. Most of the cleaning was sweeping up sifted sand. But they also took down, washed and rehung curtains, oiled furniture, mopped toilets and bathroom floors.

They finished before noon. At this time the Patroon would invite them into the library. He gave Mrs. Nofire ten dollars and served her and the daughters each a glass of port wine.

He invariably asked after the health of Thomas Nofire, bedridden for eighteen years since he fell from the mast of a fishing boat. Mrs. Nofire would say he was as well as could be expected.

Mrs. Nofire and her daughters did not touch the kitchen. This was acknowledged to be the responsibility of Mrs. Rebecca Drinkwater. It was her domain. It was also the center of life in the Vanderhorst home. Family and guests came here for a drink of water, conversation, a cookie, a look in the refrigerator, a slice of cheese, or just to sniff at steaming pots.

This room belonged to Theodore, the cat, as much as it did to Mrs. Drinkwater. He dwelt there. When necessary he strolled to the back screen door. Here he would wait patiently (it opened inward), making small sounds until someone opened it.

Then, with a king's dignity, he stalked to bushes along the access road. There he pissed or shit, as required. He then walked back, pushed the door open with his nose, and coiled down into a square of sunlight. It was a good life.

Only once, in recent years, had he invaded other parts of the house. On this occasion, slamming open the door, he darted in frantically. He raced into the library where the Patroon sat reading a two-year-old copy of *Science & Mechanics*.

At the Patroon's feet Theodore deposited the dead body of a field mouse, spine neatly broken. Vanderhorst looked down at this unexpected gift. Then he looked at Theodore. He bent to touch the cat's head. "Good boy," he said.

In that tangled summer, flocky days were without start, without finish. Rooms were sprinkled with liquid sunlight, the kitchen doused in it.

Mrs. Drinkwater's favorite knife was a half-inch wide on the top edge and dwindled down to razor. The Patroon kept it so with a whetstone.

The steel of this knife had been purchased from a small company in Birmingham, England. In thirty years the Patroon had purchased four knife steels from them. Each year they sent him Christmas greetings.

The Patroon, who had worked with tools all his life, insisting on buying "blanks"—handleless cutting, sawing and gouging instruments. He would then fit the handle himself, suited to the person using the tool.

His hands were broad and heavy. Handles of his personal tools were made to fit his hand: big, rugged. Mrs. Drinkwater's hands were slender, with tapering fingers. Samuel Lees' hands were unexpectedly dainty.

The Patroon believed a good tool was simply an extension of the hand. If the handle was made for the person who used the tool, fatigue was less. The tool truly became an extension of back, shoulder, arm, elbow, wrist, hand, fingers. So he bought the steel and turned the wood handles himself, attaching them with bolts or hammered rivets.

Now, on this Tuesday morning, after the departure of Mrs. Nofire and her daughters, he sat at the worktable in the kitchen. He drank black coffee from a mug and watched with pleasure as Mrs. Drinkwater prepared to cut slices from a clove of garlic. Her favorite knife was at hand.

"Big knife for small chores," he said. She smiled, not looking at him.

From a straw basket she selected a crown of garlic,

ridged, with little whiskers sticking from the butt. She held
it up to the light, then sniffed at it.

With a fingernail she slit the paper skin and pried out a fat
clove. She placed it on a slicing board the Patroon had
made: cubes of hardwood glued in a haphazard cross-
grained pattern.

She took off the tiny tip and tiny heel of the clove, letting
the heavy knife do the work. Vanderhorst watched her
strong, brown fingers moving surely, gripping, turning,
fingernails peeling away the film.

Naked clove on wood, the gleaming blade sliced down:
pungency sprayed. Thin slices—light coming through
them—fell away into a neat pile. *Chunk* went the knife
edge, biting board. The clove dwindled to the final cut.
Pearly meat spread out. Perfume of pure garlic spangled the
air.

The Patroon looked about the kitchen. Deck the Halls
with . . . or was it Vermeer? Warm wood and red onions,
drowsing cat and straw basket, sunlight bubbling: this
room, this Dutch painting, had a life of its own, a swelling
pulse.

Was he seeing everything for the last time? If he felt it, it
must be so. Rebecca Drinkwater cast her stones and shells.
Isaiah Todhunter, the banker, wore a copper bracelet
because it reduced the pain of his arthritis. If you believed,
it was so.

The Patroon reached across the table for Rebecca's hand.
She gave it to him gladly. It was smooth brown, hairless
soft. He lifted fingertips to his nose, sniffed with delight.
That racy odor pricked his appetite.

He hauled himself to his feet. With his stick he went
limping heavily about the kitchen, smiling at it all.
Vermeer. Definitely, it was Vermeer. He remembered now.

A good Dutchman. He might have Vermeer's blood in his veins. It was possible.

He sat down again, suddenly weary, feeling worn. Muscles were losing temper, flesh losing tone: all going slack. But he, himself, was young, strong, hard as ever, inside. Gristle might soften but blood didn't cool. Breath might falter but hope ran hot.

It pleased him to watch the woman he loved at work. Her bare, sun-sheened hands and arms—so *live*. He followed the push-pull, hold-twist: chicory ripped apart, watercress plucked, tossed into the garlic-rubbed bowl.

Cukes were scrubbed clean of wax and sliced, tomatoes were wedged, onions shaved, crisp bacon crumbled, radishes quartered. Her strong hands were in everything, folding, turning—a song of doing.

She added olive oil and wine vinegar, using a walnut spoon and fork carved by the bedridden Thomas Nofire. The wood of the salad bowl darkened, soaked and aromatic.

The Patroon smelled it deep, this luxury of scents, this symphony. He leaned forward to inhale fresh, gleaming things, to draw it all into himself. She laughed to see him happy, paused to touch his cheek. He turned to kiss her cool fingers.

Peasant Rebecca. Sturdy Rebecca. Pieter Vanderhorst once tried to imagine this body made for sweet work put into the ground, flesh becoming rich soil, bones becoming fine dust. But there would remain something he could not see.

She was neither short nor tall, fair nor dark, slender nor plump. She was as you saw her, depending upon your mood and need. Withal, she was a closed and secret woman. Her eyes pierced the world. Her serenity could not be fretted by the inevitable.

The thing in her so deep he could not find was mystery, as

dreadful and alluring. There was no end to her, no limit. She went on and on, into the dwindling distance, infinite.

He knew the perfume of her lips, taste of her skin—the beloved. He knew the heat of her haired embrace. Flash of eyes, lightning smile, sudden surge of ruddy breasts, push of thigh—he knew, he knew.

But beyond all this the dark mystery beckoned: come away, follow, the search is all.

Fathomless woman. Disturbing woman. He could not rid himself of the notion that, somehow, she had conceived and brought forth his son as a deliberate act of allegiance, a duty of fidelity. The wide-eyed cat raced across the floor to deposit at his feet its precious gift. So she, knowing his want, took gladly his heavy penetration, welcomed that joyous ejaculation and . . .

"I want," Tom Drinkwater said at the outside door. He stopped, seeing the Patroon. Through the open door a single cloud ball rode high in the blue. Shrill of gulls made a vinegar cut in the oiled air.

"Come in, come in," the Patroon said. He held out his hand. "Let me see."

Tom handed him the hollowed log. Vanderhorst inspected it. He felt inside, his blunt fingers, hand and wrist going through.

"You must sharpen your knife. Here, in the middle you are beginning to gouge. One place, here, you are close to the surface. Smaller cuts now. Slow. Sam Lees will tell you where the stone is. In the shed. Sharpen your knife first. Then make smaller cuts. Then file and sand."

His voice was curt, commanding. Tom Drinkwater took back his drum log. He stood at the other side of the table, staring at the old man. His mother brought him a cup of black coffee. Steam came off the quivering surface.

Tom said stoutly: "That is not the way the Ikantos made a

drum. They had no file and no sandpaper. They carved it out. Only with a knife."

Pieter Vanderhorst looked up at him with slitted eyes. He, too, might have Vermeer's blood. It was possible. The Patroon once believed that each stood alone in this world: a post. But perhaps we are all entangled: a slither?

"Do as you wish," he said to the boy.

"I wish to speak to you."

"I am here. I will listen."

Tom sat down across from him. He put the log drum on the table between them. He looked at the Patroon steadily.

"My mother tells me to go away to school after Labor Day. She tells me to leave your house and South Canaan. She says you agree with this."

Vanderhorst turned slowly to look at Rebecca. She stood in the middle of the floor, not slumping. Her arms were folded, her hewn face hickory. Only her eyes lived. He swung back to the boy.

"She speaks the truth. I want you to go away."

"Why?"

"Your grades have not been as good as they should be. You are capable of better. There are too many distractions here. You must learn to make your own way, to live and work with other boys your own age. You must get away from your mother and from me. It is best for you."

"Who are you to tell me what is best for me? *I* know what is best for me."

The Patroon rose unsteadily to his feet, leaning heavily on his cane. He thrust his sprained face across the table, eyes slicing.

"You are a fool," he spat at the boy. "A fool! You dream a dream that can never be. Use your brain. Do you have a brain? Then use it! You need an education, the best you can get. You must work at it. You must work hard and sacrifice and make your mother and your people proud of you."

Tom Drinkwater stood also. He leaned forward. He stared defiantly, face only inches from the Patroon's.

"I will make them proud," he shouted, his spittle in Vanderhorst's face. "I am an Ikantos. I don't belong to you. I am not your slave. I do what I wish to do."

The Patroon's chest grew. Heavy cords pressed in his throat. The wrenched face darkened with blood.

"You an Ikantos?" The words were thick, bubbling like phlegm. "Do you know what the Ikantos call a brave who slinks after women? Who carries for women? Who sits with the women and laughs at their gossip? Who is not a man? That is the kind of Ikantos you are."

"You cannot—"

"I know you. I see you trailing after the Todd woman like a whipped cur. That is all you can think of. That is all you dream. Do not talk to me of making your mother and your people proud. You only want to smell—"

The boy caught up the heavy knife from the table. He held it pointed at the Patroon's chest. The blade wavered. His knuckles were turned down. He held the knife as a key. Vanderhorst looked at the shaking steel.

"Oh-ho," he boomed. "See the Ikantos brave on the warpath. Here I am, Ikantos brave." He straightened, threw his stick from him. "Here I am, warrior. You see, I have no weapon. Stab me now. Plunge in the knife. I will respect you for it. Go ahead. Kill me if you must. Do it now."

Rebecca Drinkwater took one small shuffling step, then stopped. The three stood, caught. Outside, the creak of gulls; inside, Theodore stretched his mouth in a pink yawn.

"Hello, hello, hello," sang Mrs. Grace Vanderhorst, popping through the inside door. She was all frills and frizz, her blue wig tipped rakishly toward one ear. "Oh, what a lovely day it's going to be! Mrs. Rebecca, may I have a cup of tea? Please say I may. I would dearly love a nice cup of tea."

Tom Drinkwater made a sound. He flung the knife to the floor, turned, rushed from the room.

"Oh, my," Grace Vanderhorst said. "Is he feeling poorly? Calomel-and-rhubarb is very good."

Gripping the edge of the table with one hand the Patroon bent slowly, carefully, and picked up his cane. He straightened, looking at neither of the women. He took the log drum under his arm, stumped from the room. They watched him go.

He climbed the stairs, stopping at each landing to gulp at air. He stood before the door to Tom Drinkwater's room until breathing eased, fever cooled. He knocked. No answer.

He turned the knob and entered. The boy had ripped off his shirt, was lying on his back on the chenille bedspread. One brown arm was across his eyes.

He heard the Patroon enter, close the door. He took his arm down. Dark, glittering eyes watched warily as Vanderhorst set the drum atop the bookcase.

"Let us talk without shouts and without threats. I will explain what I want, and you explain what you want. Then we will come to an agreement."

The boy did not answer. The old man pulled the straightback chair up to the bed and sat down heavily. He clasped his stick tightly with both hands.

"First of all, you must know that my home is your home. I do not want you to leave my roof. Even if you go away—"

Tom started to speak. The Patroon held up a hand. "Let me finish. Then you may speak as long as you wish. Even if you go away, I want you to return to my home. I wish you well. You must know that. I want your life to be long, profitable, and happy. I do not send you away to punish you. I think that by going away you will get a better education. I say this because you will be away from Susan

Todd. I know you think you love her. But at your age you cannot speak of love. When you are older, when you have an education, when you have a job, then you can speak to her of love and marriage. If she should then say yes, I would be happy for you and give you my blessing. But now it is foolishness. That is why I wish you to go away. Your mother wishes it also. We understand how you feel. But we want what is best for you. Now you may speak."

Tom Drinkwater sat up, swung his bare feet to the floor. He sat with his back to the Patroon. His voice was low and flutey, breaking.

"It is not a foolishness. It is my life. I believe you speak the truth when you say you want what is best for me. That is what you *think*. But she is what is best for me. That is what I *feel*. I know what you have done for my mother and for me. It is no small thing. But if I did as you wish and went away and could not see her or hear her voice, then something bad would happen to me. And I would blame you and my mother for causing it."

Silence.

"You could visit," the Patroon said faintly. "You will come home on holidays and during the summer. You can write to her."

Tom shook his head, long black hair swinging.

"She would find other men," he said miserably. "She would forget me."

"You know her."

"Yes." Despair. "I know her."

The Patroon sucked in breath. He clamped teeth on his slack lip to keep from weeping. Hopeless love. Was his any better?

He looked around the room through bleared eyes. Indian relics. Souvenirs of a lost people. A boy trying to remember who he was. Victim . . .

"It is not necessary we decide at this time," he said to Tom's back. "I ask only that you think of what I have said and what your mother has said. I ask you to think about it. Will you do that?"

Nod.

"Think about it, and we will talk again on Labor Day. Use your brain as well as your heart. I know you have a good mind. I know you can think. On Labor Day you will give me your decision. I will then agree to whatever you say and will argue no further. Is that satisfactory?"

"Yes. Satisfactory."

"Meanwhile, this is your home. Please do not leave it. Were you going to leave it?"

"I was."

The Patroon nodded and climbed to his feet. He stumbled toward the door. He had stepped into the hall when the lad called, "Patroon." He turned back. Tom was standing, facing him. His handsome features were pulled.

Vanderhorst stared at his son through squinted eyes. The boy loomed dark against tatters of shine. He stood tall, straight. The Patroon wanted to blurt, "Listen! You are my son." But he kept his silence, his promise.

The boy was him. He was born again. That vital body was his when he ran away to sea. He was created anew. It was his blood, his flesh banded with sunlight there, glowing.

A world was waiting, life waiting to be raped. He would see to it. He would teach the boy, tell him the ways, the secrets. Keep him from hurt and smooth the . . .

"Patroon," Tom Drinkwater repeated.

"What? What is it?"

"Would you have let me kill you with the knife?"

"Yes."

# 27

How the years whirled around for Mrs. Grace Vanderhorst! All love and party dresses. Mama had said to her, "Dear, as you go through life, always remember that if you act like a lady, people will treat you like a lady." And so it was. Everything gold and shiny, like the hair on that doll Papa had brought her from Philadelphia. When was that? Oh, years ago. Years and years ago. "My baby," he called her. Papa. What fun they had in the big house. Mama and Papa and Grace and Henry who didn't want to be called Hank. He went away to war and never . . . Todhunter. That was her name. She remembered. Grace Todhunter. There were many, many Todhunters in South Canaan. Mr. Todhunter at the bank was a cousin. Not a first cousin because his mother and Grace's mother had been . . . well, it was very complicated. Hide-and-seek. All through the big house on rainy days. And the picnics! The dances! Church socials and train trips to Portland where they ate at that hotel. What was the name? Never mind. "Don't you worry," Papa had said. "You just do your best in school and stay as sweet as you are." The girls in the graduating class danced around the May Pole. Her pink dress and white lace stockings. When did Papa go? Well, Mama went first. Yes, that's right.

Then Papa went, and she was all alone in the big house. Except for Abigail and Florrie, and cousins and uncles and aunts always coming to visit. And then Mr. Vanderhorst. "Grace, may I present a very good friend of mine, a newcomer to our town, Mr. Pieter Vanderhorst." So handsome, so strong. Just like Papa. No, it couldn't have been the pink dress when she danced around the May Pole. Perhaps the blue chiffon with the ribbons threaded through the bodice. "Jimmy crack corn, and I don't care." How Mr. Vanderhorst laughed when she tried to sing "Ramona" and got the tune all mixed up with "Juanita." Now the weather this summer would give even sinners second thoughts, for it was truly made in heaven. "I hear the mission bells above." The years, the years. How many scarves and sweaters had she knitted for the poor and afflicted? During the war she had been a Grey Lady and visited the wounded boys in the hospital, and she said to this one boy, "Please, tell me what I can do for you." And he said, "How about a" and then he said that word. Marian Englehardt told her what it meant. Such a funny word. She never heard it again. "A married lady never lets her husband see her totally unclothed," Mama had told her. "Therefore, pull on your nightgown, dear, before removing the garments next to your skin." So much laughter. Papa did like a good laugh and was always reading funny little things from the Boston *Globe* which was delivered to him every morning so he could read it at the breakfast table. Trumble. That was the name she had been trying to remember for so many weeks. David Trumble had tried to kiss her at Mary Landers' tenth birthday party, and she had slapped his face. David Trumble. See how it all comes back? He was gone now. Was there some scandal? Oh, so many were gone. Marvin Peckinpaugh and Alicia Powalski and Robert DeVries and . . . well, so many others. Mama and Papa, of course. She must ask Doctor Ben to drive her to the cemetery and she'd take them a nice little bouquet. Mimosa, perhaps, and some forget-me-nots. Did the Patroon have his pills? She would ask him again the very next time she saw him. She would just nag, nag, nag because men are so forgetful. Like that nice Mister Graves. She would remind him again about that poem he was going to write just for her. When she got it she would paste it in her memory book with her report cards and Valentines and Henry's last letter home. "Dearest Sister, I want to tell you something I have never said before, and that is I love you and Mama and Papa." But she would think about the nice things, the happy things, because there had been so many nice, happy things in her life. She had so much to be thankful for, she knew, and those poor children in Europe and Africa and China who don't have enough to eat. Christmas! That was one of them. They always had a big baked ham for Christmas dinner, and Papa would stand there ready to carve and say, "Now who wants the drumsticks?" How they laughed! There always seemed to be a golden haze and bells softly ringing. Years that glowed. "Oh, Grace, Grace," Miss Forsythe said, "can't you understand that one-quarter is not larger than one-third even if four is larger than three? Dear, dear, what's going to become of you? Well, you must try very hard to stay just as pretty as you are right now." That's what Miss Forsythe said to her. Yes. "Down by the Old Mill Stream." They sang that after Papa bought his first car. No. That's not right. It was a song that had the name of the automobile in it. Now she must try to remember what that song was. She would not ask Mister Graves. She would remember it all by herself. And then, after her marriage, they sold Papa's big house and moved into Mister Vanderhorst's big house because they certainly didn't need *two* big houses. Still . . . Then things seemed to speed up. Days, weeks, months, seasons, years just spinning along. Goodness, a mother with two grown daughters! When they ran down that hill, down to the meadow, and had their picnics at the edge of the wood. And the girls would wander off to pick wildflowers and play games and she would take a little nap. Time going by like a film at the Bijou that sometimes speeded up and . . . Norma Shearer was so beautiful in . . . What was that movie? Now that was something else she would remember with no help from anyone, thank you. Then Rebecca came to cook for them. But she went away for a while, and then she . . . Now Roberta was back and they were all together again and having good times and laughing. Everyone was so kind and laughing. She would make certain the Patroon took care of himself and carried his pills with him on all occasions. It was such a *pretty* summer! They would have more parties, and perhaps Mister Graves would play some of the old love songs for them, and they would all sing. Nice, happy things.

Mrs. Grace Vanderhorst, seated at her pine worktable in the sewing room, was busily making little birds and animals out of pipe cleaners. Margaret Buncombe had asked her to serve on the Place Card Committee for the first church supper after Labor Day, and of course Grace agreed at once.

It was decided the place cards were to be pipecleaner birds and animals, painted with watercolors, glued to stand upright on file cards. Each member of the committee pledged to make twenty-five of them.

Grace had asked Mister Vanderhorst for names of birds and animals she could make. He had willingly written out a list of forty, beginning with aardvark and ending with zebra. He had also found a book in the library with illustrations of what most of these creatures looked like. Mrs. Vanderhorst was working with the book open before her. She was having trouble with the anteater. It seemed to resemble the collie she had already made.

Outside, a squall was sweeping over. Rain came down in endless dotted lines. But the darkness wouldn't last. Far over the sea the sky had cleared. Waves out there were freckled with light.

From the room below, the library, came the tinkle of the old piano. Mrs. Vanderhorst paused at her work to listen, head bent, nodding happily as Roberta's voice soared through the house.

When she looked up, Julie was in the room, smiling down at her, swathed in a bright red caftan. Julie was carrying a pack of cards and a stoppered thermos with a water glass inverted over the neck.

"That's nice, isn't it, mother?"

"Oh, my, yes, dear. It sounds like such a . . . such a happy song."

"May I sit here a while? I won't bother you."

"What a question! Of course, you may. What are you drinking dear—a lemonade?"

"Something like that. Would you like a cup of tea?"

"Oh, no. Nothing for me now, thank you. I must finish two more today. Look—this is my poodle. Do you like it?"

"It's funny."

"Funny? Well, of course it will look more like a poodle when I color it. I think I'll make it a black poodle."

"That would be nice, mother."

Julie thumped to the floor and sat cross-legged. She poured herself a drink from the thermos and began to lay out a hand of solitaire.

"Mother, did Roberta say how long they were going to stay?"

"Now let me think, dear. I do believe she said until after

Labor Day. Yes, that's right. She and Mister Graves are going back to New York right after Labor Day. Isn't it a shame they can't stay a little longer?"

"Yes."

"But it's the theater, dear. The show must go on, you know."

"Roberta isn't in the theater."

"Well . . . practically. It's really the same thing. My, she is so talented. I don't know where she gets it. Or spotted. There are spotted poodles, are there not?"

"I wish I had a talent. For something. Anything."

"Now, Julie, we can't all be singers or writers or painters. You are a dear, sweet girl and very lovely, and you must count your blessings. Just as I do."

"I saw an ad in a magazine the other day that said you could become a professional photographer and have a good-paying career. Maybe I'll send for the booklet."

"Would you like to be a photographer, dear?"

"I don't know. I guess so. Why not?"

"Well, of course I don't want to discourage you, and I don't want you to think I disapprove of what Roberta is doing, but I do feel marriage, a home, and children are the best career for a young lady."

"But you can't do it by yourself, mother. You have to wait for a man to ask you."

"Yes, that's very true. There. That is my anteater. Now I will do my gorilla."

"How did you get father to propose?"

"Oh, my, that was so romantic. The church was having a hay ride and I invited Mister Vanderhorst, and he said he'd be delighted. Well, after the ride—I remember we sang 'Love's Old Sweet Song'—we came back to the church for a buffet supper in the basement. I made the German potato salad. Then later, when Mister Vanderhorst was walking me home, he proposed. I told him later it was the German potato salad that made him ask for my hand, and he said yes, that was so. But of course, he was only joshing."

"How did he say it?"

"Say what, dear?"

"How did he propose?"

"Why, he said, 'Miss Todhunter, will you marry me?' And I said, 'Yes, I will. Mister Vanderhorst.'"

"And then he kissed you?"

"Yes, he did. On the cheek. Your father is a gentleman."

Julie nodded. She was seated solidly on the floor, back straight, draped in crimson. Only the stem of her neck and her plump face were bared. She was a Chinese doll with a bell of lacquered hair: nodding, nodding, nodding.

"Maybe I'll ask Doctor Ben to take me to the church supper."

"Julie, the book says the gorilla sometimes stands upright on his back legs and beats his chest with his fists, making a hollow, booming sound. My goodness. But he usually walks and runs on all fours, with his front knuckles on the ground. Now do you think I should make my gorilla standing up or running?"

"I think he should be standing up. Most of your other animals are on four legs. This will be different."

"That's true. Very well, I will make him standing up, beating his chest. Oh, how hairy he is. Doctor Ben, did you say? That would be nice. And Susan, too, of course."

"Well, I wasn't thinking of inviting Susan. Just Ben."

"Do you think that's wise, dear? After all, Julie, he *is* a divorced man, and you know how some people talk."

"Oh, mother. You'll be there, and father too, probably. Besides, what's wrong with being seen at a church supper with a divorced man?"

"There's nothing exactly *wrong* with it. But it doesn't look nice. Couldn't you find a young man your own age?"

"Who, for instance?"

"What about that nice Mister Foyle? Even if he is a Roman Catholic."

"Terry? No thanks. All he talks about is soccer. Besides, Doctor Ben isn't that old. Ten years older than I am, or maybe a little more."

"But divorced, dear."

"Mother, you're so old-fashioned. Lots of people are divorced these days. They haven't committed any crime. The marriage just didn't work out, that's all."

"Because they were too selfish, that's why. And didn't do their duty."

"Their duty?"

"To love and to cherish until death do them part. You swear to it, and that is your duty."

Julie swept a hand across her cards. "It's not going to come out. I just know it." She lay back on the floor, water glass of martinis held on her stomach.

"Duty, duty, duty," Mrs. Vanderhorst sang serenely. "All is duty."

"I feel so useless," Julie said, closing her eyes slowly.

"You are *not* useless. I never want to hear you say that again. That is blasphemy. We are all put on this earth for a purpose. I love you, the Patroon loves you, Roberta loves you. Many, many people love you."

"Nothing ever happens to me."

"It will, it will. You'll see. You'll get married and have children and live happily ever after. I just feel it."

"I wish I did."

"I know what I'll do!" She clapped her hands together. "I know just what you need. Oh, why didn't I think of it before? It's just the thing."

"What's that?"

"I'll make you a little sachet of dried lavender. In a muslin bag. And you must wear it on a string around your neck so it hangs down between your bosoms. Yes. That's just what you need. I was wearing one exactly like it the evening Mister Vanderhorst said he liked my German potato salad. I'll get to work on it as soon as I finish my gorilla."

"Thank you, mother."

There was no mockery in her voice. The sachet would be an amulet. Julie believed in luck. She believed in astrology, the good of even numbers and the evil of odd, the need to toss spilled salt and knock on wood.

Below, in the library, they soaked in silence. Through a veil of white curtains sunlight stabbed glinting off the sea. Patterns went dancing across the ceiling, vibrating stars of light.

Hapgood Graves sat slumped on the bench, one arm atop the piano. Head down, he touched yellowed keys lightly, not sounding them. His fingertips drifted, pausing, kissing smooth ivory.

Bobbie Vander slouched in the leather swivel chair behind the desk, swinging softly side to side. Head back, her eyes followed the movement of those glimmering stars on the ceiling. Her shirt was unbuttoned to the waist.

Susan Todd was seated on the floor, back propped against the bookcase. Her knees were bent, brown thighs yawning. Her elbows were on her knees, hands dangling. She watched Graves' wandering fingers.

"Let's—" Susan started, then stopped. Her voice was unexpectedly loud: a stone into that pond of quiet. Ripples spread. "—go for a swim. Hap? The water will be warm. It's a beautiful day."

Bobbie lowered her eyes slowly to stare at Susan. "A beautiful fucking day. Do you know how sick I am of beautiful days? One after another. What's so great about sunshine, kiddo? Or blue sky or fresh air or that damned ocean that never stops? The great outdoors. Biggest drag in the world. It's so sweet and sickening. Screw it. You want to swim, Hap?"

"What? Oh. No, I don't want to swim. We've got more work to do."

"Besides, I look like a swizzle stick in a bathing suit," Bobbie grumbled. "If I had tits and a tush like yours, baby, you'd never get me out of a bikini. But I'm an inside, nighttime woman."

"Good title," Graves murmured. "Oh, inside, nighttime woman/why don't the sun never shine on you?"

Susan unfolded to her feet, clutching a book shelf to drag herself upright. She stretched, reaching up to clench at air, ribs pressing, legs hard. Her chin strained in a shuddering yawn.

"Come over here," Bobbie commanded.

Susan moved to stand in front of the desk.

"Around here," Bobbie said, swinging in her chair. She twirled right around twice and stopped to face toward the side. Susan stood before her.

Bobbie bent to feel Susan's plush calves, knees, thighs. She reached up to pulp her breasts. Susan drew back, grinning foolishly. Hapgood Graves began sounding soft chords.

Bobbie put her hands on Susan's waist, hips. She reached around to feel, grip.

"Christ, what a carcass," she muttered. "Kiddo, if I had a body like yours, I'd spend the rest of my life on my back. Can you sing?"

"What?"

"Sing. You know—like songs. Can you carry a tune?"

"Well . . . I've never studied or anything like that."

"What songs do you know?"

"Oh, I don't know any songs. I mean all the way through."

"You must know *some* songs."

"Well, I know most of 'Love Is Here to Stay.'"

"Hap, you know that?"

"Sure."

"Start singing it. Hap will come in on your key and give you a little help."

Susan Todd, quavering, started singing "Love Is Here to Stay." She sang one verse, voice breaking, Graves vamping softly behind her.

"Okay," Bobbie Vander said loudly. "That's enough. I've heard worse but I don't remember when. Can you move?"

"Move?"

"Like dancing. Did you ever have the radio on or a record and take off your clothes in front of a mirror in time to the music?"

"Well—uh—I—"

"Hap, play 'A Pretty Girl Is Like a Melody.'"

"Sure, mom."

"Now move, baby. Just strut back and forth. Stick out the lungs and come down hard on your heels so everything bounces."

Susan moved awkwardly across the room. Bobbie Vander nodded solemnly. Hap turned sideways on the bench to watch.

The young girl pranced anxiously. Her chin was high, breasts jogging under the thin T-shirt. She kicked her feet out, striding, arms flopping.

"Faster, Hap," Bobbie called with a wolfish grin. "Swing your arms, kiddo. Back and forth."

The tempo quickened. Susan rushed to keep up with it.

Arms flung. Sweat glistened across forehead and upper lip. Darkened patches glued the shirt to her heaving torso.

"Faster, Hap," Bobbie Vander yelled.

Susan Todd was almost running. She threw arms and legs about frantically, berserk puppet, a marionette with broken strings. Her mouth was open, gulping. Her eyes began to bulge, dazed.

"Kill it!" Bobbie shouted above the piano pound. Graves ended with a crashing chord. Susan took two more tottering steps and stopped, swaying. Her wet breasts were shaking, leg muscles fluttering.

"What do you think, Hap?"

"She'll do. She's got all the equipment. Learn some tricks, and she could be great."

"Maybe flashlights on the tits?"

"A glow-in-the-dark G-string?"

"Or a little feather duster."

"Or a mirror."

"The ass is just fine."

"She can swing it."

"We could help Kupferman work up an act."

"Maybe on a couch."

"She starts on her hands and knees. Bare tush sticking out."

"Right. Then flops over, her legs waving in the air."

"What?" Susan Todd asked, still panting. "What are you talking about?"

"A career for you," Bobbie Vander said. "A great new dancing career. Maybe three hundred a week. Say good-bye to this turd-kicking town."

"The bright lights," Hapgood Graves said. "Broadway. The Great White Way."

"A star on your dressing-room door," Bobbie Vander said.

"Then Hollywood," Hapgood Graves said. "Television. The whole bit."

"I don't know," Susan said slowly, puzzled. "You're not . . . ?"

"You'd have to work at it," Bobbie Vander said. "Dance lessons. Gorgeous costumes. A routine designed just for you. But they're always looking for fresh meat, and you've got what it takes, kiddo. Right, Hap?"

"Right," he said.

"Gee, I don't know," Susan Todd said, biting at a thumbnail. "You mean in a theater? In a play? A musical? I'd be a dancer?"

"Something like that." Bobbie Vander nodded.

"I don't know. You think . . . ?"

"Of course."

"I'd have to talk to dad."

"Oh, no," Bobbie said quickly. "Don't do that. Think it over first. Decide what *you* want to do. Then tell me. If you decide you want to give it a try, I'll talk to your father."

"All right. I guess that would be best. You really think I . . . ?"

"No doubt about it," Graves assured her. "We've seen a lot of young girls who want to get on the stage. Most of them never make it. But you're a natural."

"Natural sense of rhythm," Bobbie nodded.

"Grace in motion," Graves said.

"Sexy but dignified," Bobbie nodded.

"Oh, boy." Susan Todd grinned. "Imagine me on the stage!"

"Think about it," Bobby Vander told her. "Look at yourself in the mirror and think about it. Now get out of here and get your swim. You smell like a hot horse."

They waited a few minutes after she left. Then they looked at each other. They collapsed into laughter, bending over, heaving, weeping with laughter.

"Did you see her?" Graves spluttered. "Did you see her?"

"I saw her," Bobbie said. She wiped streaming eyes with a knuckle. "I saw her. That was beautiful. 'Grace in motion.' You're too much! God, it's fun to be a prick."

"Well, we've had our kicks for the day. Come on now, let's do some work. We'll take it from the top again. And watch your phrasing on that second chorus. Sometimes you hit it and sometimes you slide right off."

"My God, Hap, she's innocent as a pint of cream."

"Before it sours. Yes. Let's go, mom."

She sat alongside him on the bench, one arm across his thin shoulders. She leaned forward to peer at the scrawled words on his work sheets . . .

For once he had suppressed his nervous need to play with words. He had written a compassionate love song for himself:

> "For years I followed a twisty path
> And never found a home."

He was writing of the wanderer, and in language mordant but tender he told about the search . . .

> "Until I came upon a heart
> As bleak and cold as mine . . ."

Scorning a conventional chorus, the song was divided into three free-flowing verses: seeking, discovery, love. The last verse, hopeful but filled with a self-mocking rue, concluded . . .

> ". . . and so shall both
> Endure this life, and even death

Will bow in awe of timeless love
That lives beyond the final breath."

Bobbie Vander held the final note, then let it drift away. They sat in silence.

"Yes," Bobbie said finally, "I'll drink to that. Not the easiest song I've ever done, but it gets to me. It's good, Hap."

He smiled and turned. He slid a hand into her unbuttoned shirt, his palm against a bare pancake breast.

"The lines in the song," she said. "They're about us, aren't they?"

"The lines about undying love?"

"Don't be a *schmuck*. You know what I mean. 'Until I came upon a heart/As bleak and cold as mine.' *Those* lines. You were thinking of us, weren't you?"

"That's right. Lord and Lady Macbeth."

They huddled together, heads touching. The sun was gone from the room. Light had become flimsy.

"Will you be glad when we're gone from here?" he murmured, pressing close.

"Yes. You know what I miss most?"

"What?"

"Neon signs. If there was just one on the beach that said 'Bar-B-Q,' flashing red and blue, I'd feel better. And the smell of frying. Silly?"

"Not so, mom. It's the people that bug me. They're all right, I guess. Inoffensive, certainly. But they crowd me. I want to be on a plane with you. Just the two of us. Dopey with pills. Flying to the next gig and making up dirty stories about the other passengers. Silly?"

"Not so. Did you ever know Si Handler? A smoke."

"Bass man? Tried rock on a cello?"

"You're thinking of Sy Chandler. No, Handler, was tenor sax. He was with Bernie Primadora for a long time."

"I don't know him."

"Well, Si got onto the hard stuff and after a while he never did come down off the moon, so Bernie dumped him. I was with Bernie almost six months, you know. This was the year before I went single-O. This Si Handler was something. He really threw me. He was a liar. It was his bag."

"A liar?"

"He lied all the time. Deliberately. He enjoyed it. I mean he lied when he didn't have to. We'd be in the hotel, and I'd say, 'Si, how is it out?' And he'd say, 'Raining cats and dogs.' And of course the sun would be shining. Or he'd tell me, 'Lady, I overheard Bernie talking, and he's going to dump you on Saturday.' Or he'd say to the drummer, who was a great cocksman, 'Hey, man, there was a chick up here looking for you. Her pappy was with her, and he looked mean.' All lies. Or you'd ask him to give someone a message for you, and he'd get it ass-backwards. All on purpose, of course."

"Crazy. What for?"

"Like I said, he enjoyed it. I asked him once why he lied so much, for no reason. He said life was so fucked up naturally that if he went directly against the truth, he'd be setting it right."

"My God. A philosopher."

"Something like that."

"What made you think of him, mom?"

She shrugged. That flat little breast moved up and down on his palm. The arm across his shoulders hugged him closer.

"You haven't stabbed her yet, have you?" she whispered.

"No."

"And you're not going to, are you?"

"No."

"Not because you don't want to, but because you can't."

"That's right, mom."

"You could make it with me."

"I know."

"But you're not going to get the chance."

"I know that, too."

"We're a couple of shits, aren't we?"

"We are indeed."

"But you love me, don't you?"

"Somehow." He nodded.

"Why is that?"

"Like the song says. You're my mirrored ache. The missing half of me."

"I'm not much."

"You think I'm more?"

"Well, you're the only one I've got. I can tell you things."

"Like what you're going to do to Julie?"

"That's right. And to the good Doctor Todd."

"What are you going to do to him?"

"Ball him till his molars melt. Then I'm going to take that nutty little plane out of here and leave him with Mother Five-Fingers."

But her laugh splintered.

He looked at her, troubled. He pulled away, out from under her clasping arm. He began again to sound gentle chords.

"You're faking me, mom," he said. "For the first time."

Her head fell forward.

"Todd?" he asked.

"Yes. I think. I don't know. I hate that feeling—not knowing."

"What is it?"

"Just him."

"The young Patroon?"

"Is that what it is? Maybe."

He had thought of her as an ice sculpture: hard outline and shiny surface. But now he saw the corners dulling, water blemished as the thaw started. Uncertainty was fueling her.

"Is it bad, mom?" he asked her softly.

"For me it's bad. I don't need anyone. Never have."

"I liked you better that way."

She looked at him shrewdly. "Misery loves company."

"Thank you, Publilius Syrus."

"Who the hell is he?"

"The first guy to write 'Misery loves company'—or something like it."

"What do you think of him, Hap?"

"Publilius Syrus?"

"Idiot. Ben Todd."

He shrugged. "I told you. Not my type."

"He may be mine."

Graves played a few bars of the Wedding March.

"Oh, no," she said. "Not that. Definitely not that."

"Then *what?*"

"How the hell should I know? He may turn out to be a sorry fuck."

"Did I ever tell you my original Fractured French? Definition of *Les Miserables:* man with a short penis."

"I don't like dirty jokes; you know that. Julie says he's great. But what the hell does she know."

"No basis for comparison?"

"Just guys who keep their socks on. If he turns out to be as good as she says, I'm in real trouble."

"Oh," he said. "It *is* bad."

"I'll work it out."

Shadows came creeping, worming their way across the polished floor. The sun had moved away from them. The day was tarnished.

"Did you give her the stuff?" Bobbie Vander asked.

"Yes. She's on."

"She like it?"

"Sure."

"Well, what do you *do* with her?"

"Play her like a flute."

There were clouds now, and sickish light. The sea was rising, tide coming in. They heard the lick and gulp, the mad scream of gulls. Out there.

"Do you love me?" he asked.

"I need you. Or someone like you."

He nodded. His wise smile went quickly.

"She's something," Bobbie Vander said. "I touched her up."

"I know. I saw."

"God, she's something. A young Julie."

"Was Julie like that?"

"Greater. You wouldn't believe."

"Did you . . . ?"

"For years. When it started we didn't have any hair. This kid reminds me so much . . . Christ, is she ever young. It comes right out through her skin."

"I know."

"Hap, you're the brain. Why do we do it?"

He pounded out chopped bars of "Pomp and Circumstance," then stopped suddenly.

"Because we're romantics," he said solemnly. "Hopeless romantics."

They were seated close, noses almost touching. They

were staring at each other, eyes into eyes. The French door to the porch was flung open. Susan Todd stood framed, faded bikini dripping.

"Wow," she said. "Was that ever great!"

Skin glistened like wet pearl. Hair writhed about her shoulders. She was bulging, but sea-tautened. There was a nimbus around her clean body.

They looked at her. Looked. And looked.

"Am I interrupting something?" she asked anxiously.

"Nothing important," Bobbie Vander said.

## 28

A football moon spiraled through the darkling sky. There was a falling star. The Patroon, propped against the cliff in his favorite cove, marveled at what his eye could see of a heaven ablaze.

The luminous night stretched to ever. Flames leaped as he watched: silver, lemon, blood; streaks and clouds of light. He blew a feather of cigar smoke toward worlds unknown and said, "Hello."

Rebecca was late, but he cherished the solitude, the hugging solitude. The thick wind coming off the sea was salt, fish, and something deep, far down and rumbling.

How it all whirled! Was there a cycle he could not see—something monstrous and grand? Perhaps a great slow circle came around, came around—a huge clock. He could see seconds, occasionally glimpse minutes. But hours? He was a tick of time, no more than that and probably less. A doctor holds the babe up by the heels and spanks it into death.

Pieter Vanderhorst laughed at the insane wonder of it: so nothing and so something. He thought of death with calm, loving the snaggle of life. He was leaving a strong, handsome son to stare at those same stars and say, "Hello."

The Patroon thought "Invictus" had been written just for him and wondered that other men succumbed so easily. He knew his philosophy was rude and gawky, but he had built it himself of calamity and painful thought. He did not add the floor until the joists were true.

He was, he acknowledged, a peasant, and had earned a peasant's faith: merit and reward have nothing in common; there is quality in human beings; a man may be educated well and be a fool; when life ends, trouble ends; money is all.

Dr. Todd's enemy was death. He was a physician, and his hatred was understandable and admirable. The Patroon's enemy was life. That it was a quixotic struggle, sure to end in defeat, only, as he said, made the cheese more binding.

He had endured—what had he not endured! Buffets and blows, sorrows and disappointments: they had been hammer clangs that struck him tighter until he was condensed and hard, and could endure.

Slammed down, he arose. Crippled, he healed. It had always been so. He would not let hope wither. There was joy in stretching his muscles against life. And a son robbed the final loss of bitterness.

A woman in San Francisco—an educated woman who was not a fool—once said to him, "Pieter, you think with your body." She was right: he was not cerebral. He might consider choices, but his final act was never what he could do but what he must do. It was, he admitted, no choice at all.

He waited an hour, growing uneasy when Rebecca did not come wading to him through the surf, with teeth gleaming, loving eyes.

He pushed himself away from the stone. Leaning heavily on his cane, he went dragging back to the house, a darker shadow in the dark. He stopped once to search the sea. There was phosphorescence out there, glinting. And something else. What was it? As dark as his own moon shadow.

He made no effort to soften his clumping climb to the third floor. He would not sneak. He dragged down that somber tunnel to Rebecca's door and knocked, but the dim chant continued. He listened a moment, half of torn face sagging. He pushed open and stepped in, pulling the door tight behind him.

She was crouched on the bare floor, lost in a thin earthy shift cut down from one of Julie's worn caftans. Naked arms and legs streamed, catching guttering light from two red candles. Before her was a pile of bones, one dried lobster claw.

He went to the hard bed and sat down heavily, hands clasped on the knobbed head of his stick. He put his chin down, watched her gravely.

She crooned, crooned, poking at dead things, seeing how they rolled and fell. Her body bobbed slightly, back and forth. Slowly she genuflected, eyes slitted.

Animal shadows wavered on the blank wall, looming, shrinking. The room was a cave, with black corners, spurts of fire.

Her skin flamed as he watched: red, yellow, orange. He let her night beauty seep into him, feeling the mystery in the cave. His love for her was a primeval terror.

She looked up at him, not seeing.

"What do the bones say?" he asked gently.

Her eyes rose from the depths to stare at him. She shook her head.

"Something bad?"

She was silent. He saw horror.

"Is it death?"

She would not answer.

"My death?"

She lay full length upon the floor and began to crawl slowly. He watched her pull herself along on elbows and knees. Her straining fingers scrabbled at smooth boards. She came to him, put her face upon his feet.

He looked down on her: that twisted hair varnished with candle glow, sweet nape of neck. He leaned to touch her. There was warmth there. But she shivered.

"It is nothing," he said. "Nothing."

She writhed forward to clutch his legs. She put her head upon his knees. He stroked her hair, pulling fronds of that strange fern between his fingers. Live hair entwined him, holding his hand.

"Do the bones say when?"

She raised her head. Fluttering flames behind her put a black mask on her features. He saw only glimmering eyes, shiny as wet stones.

"Soon," she said.

He nodded, smiling and stroking her hair. He drew a finger across her wet cheek.

"Why do you weep? You said to me we will meet in another world where we may show our love."

"Yes. That is so."

"Come. Sit beside me so that I may hold you."

So she did, but she held him, strong arms pulling him close. He felt her heat swallowing him: an odor of want and blaze.

"I would like to prove my love," he said. "To enter into you. But tonight I am tired."

She took his hand. She raised fingertips to her lips, kissed his palm, held his hand against her throat. Then she leaned away, unbuttoned her thin dress, pulled it open.

She held her left breast and cupped it forward. She put

her other hand at the back of his neck and urged him to her gently. She bent to him.

That ruby eye glared as he moved closer. He took it into his broken mouth, lips pressing, and tongue, and easy teeth. He sucked her strength.

Animal shadows wavered into one two-backed beast, flickering on the wall. They hunched in their cave, painted with bronze light.

Her head went back, neck taut. Her pulse was purring. They sat linked as wax melted, light died. Until their shadows filled the room.

## ———29———

Dawn brought a yeasty moiling in the eastern sky. It unrolled slowly until all above was unmarked paper. The baby sun was a blur, shimmering bull's-eye in a target of vapor.

The wind from the south grew in strength. It was an odorless gas, a hot blast that fevered skin, withered leaves. Flowers bent before it. Grass dried, shriveled, died.

The marsh behind the access road fell silent. That furnace wind sent animals to holes, birds to shade. Only snakes baked on gravel and stone.

Old Sam Lees shambled from the kitchen door. The barren air shoved flannel down his throat; he gasped to breathe. Squinting up, hand cupped around his eyes, he saw that nacreous sky, the sun bubbling.

Head down, grunting, he plodded out to the road and turned left. He scuffed up to Indian Road. There he turned right, heading toward the cemetery. Heat of the gravel came right through the thick soles of his heavy work shoes.

Shoved deep in the side pockets of his faded overalls were two empty pint bottles of muscatel. He'd bury 'em in the swamp, then get back to the house quick. A man couldn't breathe that hot wind. There was no good to it.

Just before he got to the graveyard he turned off into the wood and bramble. Behind a poplar he dug his heel into earth. The top inch was dry, powdery. Below was damp ooze. He heeled out a hollow trench, dropped in the empties, kicked dirt over them, stamped it all flat.

He stepped back onto the road, headed home. He raised his eyes. Damn. There, in the distance, was the Todd girl. She was walking toward him, wading through a water mirage. Sam Lees rubbed his eyes. She was still there; no doubt about it. Wearing some kind of short thing with little straps across her shoulders. Arms were bare. That thing was so high up on her naked legs you could almost . . . When the wind blew . . .

His eyes bleared. He rubbed them again. When he looked she was gone. Now what the hell. Now what in the name of Christ was the girl doing walking into the swamp on a day like this?

Maybe to meet that Tom Drinkwater? Maybe to play some games with the Indian kid? Like "you show me and I'll show you." Maybe that's just exactly what she was out there for. Now if he could just get a look at them, catch the two of them together playing games, all accidental like . . . well, a word to Doc Todd or the Patroon would settle that ratty kid's hash. He never had given back the field glasses he stole that night. Well now . . .

Sam Lees walked faster. When he got to the place he figured she had turned off, he slowed down and zig-zagged from one side of Indian Road to the other. Damn if he didn't find a path leading away. A narrow twisty thing but a path all the same.

He stepped along, following all its turns and bends, grinning. He'd be very polite. "Oh, I beg your pardon. I didn't see you there." Or maybe: "Sorry. I didn't know you was out here. Now you just go on with what you're doing."

That crazy path went on and on. He heard voices and looked up. There was a circle of thicket ahead. The voices came from there. He moved slowly, slowly. No use scaring them. Up to the bush he went, then down on his knees. He crawled quietly. Closer. He could hear her talking now, just as plain. He parted the creepers a little and peered in.

Little Lord Jesus!

"Of course he loves me," Susan Todd was saying. "But he's such a *boy. Such* a boy."

"I'll bet he's hung like a man," Hapgood Graves said. "Ever make it with him?"

"Don't be a silly, silly. I told you on the beach I was a virgin."

"He's got the hots for you. It's in his eyes."

"Oh, I know. He follows me around like a little puppy dog. It's really a joke."

"Do you think he's laughing?"

"Well, what am I supposed to do about it?"

"You might stop touching him up."

"I don't."

"You do. I've seen you."

"Well . . . not since you and I . . . I mean, I hardly talk to him anymore."

"But you did before, didn't you? Before I made the scene."

"Well . . . You know . . . I was so *bored.*"

"What did you do?"

"Oh . . . just things."

"What kind of things?"

"You really want to know?"

"No, I really don't want to know. That's why I asked."

"Don't be so sarcastic. You can really be obnoxious at times."

"What did you do to him?"

"Like we'd be swimming together, and we'd surface dive, and I'd let him kiss me. Little things like that."

"You let him feel you up?"

"Well, he wants to get his Red Cross certificate so I'd pretend I was drowning and he'd rescue me."

"And he'd tow you in by the tits?"

"You're awful, you know that? You're really awful. Let's take it now."

"In a little while."

"I want it now."

"Patience, patience. What else did you do to him?"

"I'm not going to tell you. If you won't do anything for me, then I won't do anything for you."

"A very sensible attitude. You're learning. Take off that demented nightgown or whatever the hell it is."

"Then will you give it to me?"

"Yes."

"Promise?"

"Sure."

"Okay . . . It's off. Now give it to me."

"No."

"But you promised!"

"I lied."

"Oh, you're such a shit. A *shit!*"

"First, tell me what else you did to him."

"Well, if you must know, sometimes I touched him."

"Where?"

"In the water. On the beach."

"Beautiful moron, wake unto me . . . I mean where on him did you touch him?"

"Oh. You know where."

"Show me. Touch me where you touched him."

"Well . . . there."

"More."

"Like this?"

"Yes. Just like that."

"Can I have it now?"

"All right. Can you do it yourself?"

"Of course, silly. I know how."

"Not so much. That stuff's expensive. Just a pinch."

"This much?"

"That's plenty. Sweet dreams."

"Aren't you going to take any?"

"Sure. And away we go."

"It's so good, so good. It works a lot faster now."

"I know. Come closer to me."

"Like this?"

"Fine. Your skin is dry and hot. I've never seen skin like yours. It's golden velvet with a matte finish. The only blemish—the only one I can find—is your appendicitis scar. It looks like a strip of Scotch tape with a thin red line running down the middle. But other than that, your skin is perfect. I think hundreds of small, timid animals were gassed to make your skin. These animals were killed and their tender little pelts shaved. Then the hides were pieced together with great cunning and invisible stitching on the inside. The only opening left was what looks like your appendicitis scar. Then you were crammed through that opening until you filled out your skin without a wrinkle. It's good material. It will probably wear well and last for years."

"Thanks a lot."

"Welcome. You like this?"

"Everything you do to me. Everything. Am I still a virgin?"

"Don't you know?"

"Not really. I don't remember everything."

"Don't worry about it."

"Ooh . . . That hurts."

"Really?"

"No. Not really. Do it again. Oh, my God."

"Don't you enjoy having a nice little Indian boy in love with you?"

"I told you, I was bored. It was just something to do."

"Didn't you *want* him to fuck you?"

"Of course not."

"Come on."

"Well . . . maybe. Once or twice. But we never did. I tell you everything and you never tell me anything."

"But I make you happy."

"Yes. You make me happy. I'm really finding myself."

It was a swelling thing to have a man twice her age listen to her, but sometimes she wondered if he disliked her. She was so young she had never met anyone who disliked her on sight; the possibility destroyed her.

He was undeniably handsome, in a still, austere fashion, but he was a foreigner. He was of another country, his obscenity a strange language. His astringent cynicism ate away at everything she thought was so.

In high school, to protect her virginity, she had devised a game she played with lecherous lads whose hot hands searched. She called it the "Why Game."

"Let's park here."

"Why?"

"We can look at the moon."

"Why do you want to look at the moon?"

"Well, we can talk."

"What do you want to talk about?"

"You. Let's talk about you."

"Why?"

"You're so beautiful."

"Why am I beautiful?"

"You just are. Let's—you know . . ."

"Why?"

And so on.

After one experience with her "Why Game" most teenaged Lotharios gave up and told friends she had sucked them. She never lacked for dates.

But she was undone by her own cleverness. The "Why Game" became less of a game, and more. She found herself continually asking, "Why? Why?" No one answered. The questions embarrassed and they thought her strange.

When she asked Hapgood Graves "Why?" he told her, in tones contemptuous of her stupidity. He had been everywhere, done everything, knew all. He was life beyond South Canaan—that "turd-kicking town."

When she sniffed cocaine, she was one with him, as cool and knowing. The drug anesthetized her doubts and made her sure. She was scarcely conscious of what he did to her. She traveled in his foreign land—a mature, sophisticated woman who could say, "discreet," "incredible," and "I'm really finding myself."

She ached for those moments in the swamp. Then she was not the child of Anita and Benjamin Todd; she was a royal foundling deposited on their doorstep by a faithful retainer to protect her from the machinations of a wicked prime minister. Her name was not Susan. It was Adelina. Or perhaps Camilla.

"Roll over," Hapgood Graves instructed.

"Do I have to?"

"Yes."

"You're mean. I know what you want to do."

"This?"

"Yes, that. Do you get pleasure out of that?"

"No, I hate it. It sickens me. That's why I do it."

"*Must* you be so nasty?"

"*Must* you ask such stupid questions? Your brains are in your ass."

"I don't care. At least I'm good for something."

"That you are. And here's something we haven't done before."

"Oh, Hap, Hap! That *does* hurt."

"Just relax, relax. There. Isn't that better?"

"Yes. Better. When you do that do you love me?"

"Of course."

"Say it."

"When I do that I love you."

"Am I a beautiful woman?"

"You are a beautiful woman."

"Am I the most beautiful woman you've ever known?"

"You are the most beautiful woman I've ever known. The catechism according to Saint Susan."

"What does that mean?"

"Nothing. Not a thing."

"Now I'm off. I'm really gone now."

"Where are you?"

"I'm the sun, Hap. I'm shining down on everyone."

"That's nice."

"Now I'm a gull. I'm swooping and soaring."

"Good on you."

"I'm going to shit down on you."

"Why would you want to do that?"

"It would be fun. Now I'm a cloud. A big white cloud. I'm just drifting."

"Sleepy?"

"Not yet. I feel so good. Now I think I'll do things to you. You're always doing things to me. Now I'll do things."

"Do you know how?"

"You tell me. Tell me how to make you happy."

"Is that what you want to do—make me happy?"

"Oh, yes. I want to make you so happy that you'll never want to leave me."

"All right. I'll show you how to do it. Here . . ."

"I've never done that before."

"You said you wanted to make me happy."

"All right. Yes. Oh. Yes. Like that?"

"Slowly. Shine like the sun. Soar like a gull. Drift like a cloud. Why, yes. Like that."

"Oh, Hap. I like it. I love it. I feel so close to you. Now you really love me, don't you?"

"Sure."

Later, Samuel Lees stumbled down the winding path. He gained the Indian Road, went half-trotting toward the access road and home. He was heat-choked, eyes stuffed. He put a hand across his heart, felt the faltering thump.

Images thronged, enough for a thousand dreams. He didn't . . . He couldn't . . . God! The sights he had seen that day! He wouldn't tell a soul, not a soul. But he would watch them, and follow, and return, and see . . .

Tom Drinkwater was sitting out in front of the toolshed. He was out there in that sun and heat, working away stolidly, fitting a wet rabbit hide to the top of his log drum. Well, kid, if you only knew . . .

# 30

Drawing on, drawing on: the magical summer of their lives. Now in the sky was a tilted sword of a moon, a verdigrised scimitar. Stars were rigid and piercing. The wind was rude, the sea too edged for night swimming.

They gathered, wearing sweaters and jackets. All were there, the last time they were to be together. They sat on the porch, on the lawn. French doors to the library were flung open. Quiet light flowed from that polished room.

Roberta had promised a "concert" for this night. Hapgood Graves was seated at the piano. He waited until they settled. Then he rose and announced: "Ladies and gentlemen, Miss Bobbie Vander."

They applauded politely. They peered into the library, waiting for Bobbie to make her appearance from the hallway door.

But suddenly they heard her voice behind them. She was in darkness, on the beach, singing, "Falling in Love Again." They laughed happily, clapped, turned to see.

She came toward them slowly out of the night. Her silver silk was wind-flicked, the scarf about her throat waving at the sky.

Graves, still standing, marveled at her professional guile. It was theater for an audience of eight: deception and hoke, surprise and expectation fulfilled. He sat then and played, picking up the tempo as she moved closer to the house.

She milked it: halting in half-light, knowing the picture she made. She was a white shadow against a black sea. Standing erect, feet together, hands clasped behind her, she was a little girl lost.

Her voice went with the wind. She didn't force it. She knew what she could do, and what she could not. "Falling in Love Again." It was her own, a private confession.

It was the sound that shook them. It was so naked. They knew she held nothing back. She made them share. She made them feel, things they had never felt before. They couldn't believe those things were in them.

Before they had time to recover, before they could wonder if they should applaud, she strolled into light. Hapgood Graves, consulting a scrawled program they had planned together—they were both professionals— slammed into "Two-Ton Tessie from Ten-Ten-Tennessee."

After that she sang "Love Me or Leave Me." Then "The Fool's Love Song." Then "I Can't Give You Anything but Love, Baby." Then "You're the Top." Then "Love Is Good Enough for Me."

She moved in and out amongst them, wandering around. She went into the library to touch Hap's shoulder. She came out again to pat the Patroon's cheek, to smile at Dr. Todd. She swooped suddenly to kiss her mother's wig without missing a note.

She threw a net about them. Heads turned as she moved, eyes probing her magic. Back and forth she stalked, gestures small and controlled. She gathered them all up until they belonged to her.

It was while she was singing "You're the Top" that Susan

Todd rose from the lawn where she had been sitting alongside her father's beach chair. She slipped into the library, sat on the piano bench next to Hapgood Graves.

He looked sideways at her. Then, as Bobbie sang, he leaned toward Susan. He whispered the words of the lewd parody—almost as famous as the original lyrics:

> "You're the torrid heat
> Of a bridal suite
> In use.
> You're the breasts of Venus,
> You're King Kong's penis,
> You're self-abuse."

Susan Todd shouted a single laugh, then clapped hand to mouth. A few heads turned. Tom Drinkwater was leaning against the oak, hidden in shadow. He saw the two in the lighted room, close.

Bobbie Vander sang: songs she had made famous, old songs they had forgotten, songs remembered. Then, feeling the strain, she got them all singing in a ragged chorus. Old favorites: "Oh, the moon was shining bright along the Wabash." "Come, Josephine, in my flying machine, going up, she goes!" "The sun shines bright on my old Kentucky home." It all came back. Even the Patroon was persuaded to sing two verses of "In the Baggage Coach Ahead."

Then it was over. There was applause and laughter. They all trooped into the kitchen where Mrs. Rebecca Drinkwater had prepared little sandwiches and cookies. There were pies and cakes, coffee and tea, whiskey and wine if desired.

It was welcome warm in there, shutters down and Theodore purring, rubbing against their shins. There were good smells and loud talk. All of them were together. The night was outside. Everyone told Roberta how wonderful she had been.

"I wish we had taped that, mom," Graves told her. "What an album that would make. 'Concert on the Beach.' With all the background noise."

"I was great, wasn't I?"

"The greatest," he assured her.

Sam Lees left, a slice of rhubarb pie balanced on his hand. Tom Drinkwater disappeared. The Patroon excused himself. Susan Todd slid away. A few minutes later Hapgood Graves was gone.

Benjamin Todd finally was alone with Bobbie, in a corner. She was bending down, scratching Theodore's ears.

"You were marvelous," he told her. "I loved every minute of it."

"Thanks."

"I was wondering . . . Could we—"

"Going, Ben?" Julie Vanderhorst asked. "I'll walk you home."

Then they were all gone, except for Rebecca Drinkwater. She looked about at smeared dishes, half-filled cups and glasses, spilled sugar, broken sandwiches, a red-tipped cigarette butt stuck into a piece of Boston cream pie.

Silence still quivered from shouts and happy laughter. But over all, hanging in the air, was stale smoke and something tainted.

As they were walking to the Todd home through damp and dark, the back of Julie's hand brushed his. Was it an accident? No accident? But he did not take it. They were together and apart. Who was this woman?

They stood awkwardly on his porch. Her pouty face turned up to him. She was not Roberta; he ached for solitude. Now he would walk her back to her home. She would walk him back to his. He would . . . All in silence that endless wandering. And he had to piss.

"Wasn't Bobbie wonderful?" "Yes, Ben." "I don't know when I've spent a more enjoyable evening." "Mmm." "That voice of hers! It goes right through you. A quality. Really something to hear." "I know." "And that business of walking up from the beach. Out of the dark. Wasn't that great?" "I guess so." "Julie, what's wrong?" "Nothing's wrong." "You seem so—I don't know. Quiet. Depressed maybe." "I guess I'm depressed." "Oh? About what?" "Everything." "That's worth being depressed about. Want to stop in for a nightcap?" "Yes. Please."

He motioned her toward a soft chair and hurried into the bathroom. Relief was almost sexual. He rinsed his hands, rubbed cold water on his face. He looked up suddenly and saw a reflection in the medicine cabinet mirror. Brief dislocation: a dense, brooding stranger with a sullen mouth. Then he recognized himself. But what was . . . Had something changed?

She was leaning back on the couch, looking about vaguely. She didn't know what to do with her hands. The bright overhead light was cruel, delineating puffy face, bags swelling beneath her eyes. She was soft and vulnerable. He switched on a table lamp. Light came through a rosy shade. He turned off the room light. Then she was a boss pear: tanned skin and juicy, lightly freckled and blushed.

"Want me to light a fire?" "No. I'm all right." "What would you like to drink?" "A martini, please, but—" "I know, I know. But make it mild. You're a wonder." " Am I, Ben?" "What's that supposed to mean?" "Mean? It doesn't mean anything. May I have that drink?" "Coming up." "Ben, the thing I'm depressed about—" "Wait'll I get the drinks. There are cigarettes in the box on the desk."

In the kitchen he poured a Scotch and drank it off in two gulps. Then he mixed another on ice with a little water. He stirred Julie's martini. He looked down into the pitcher and saw the swirl of silver silk as the wind tugged her dress, flipped her scarf to the sky.

It was a shattered night, episodic, with no continuity. He wanted to be alone to sort it out. It had a new logic. Meaning eluded him. Something was happening. He was on stage, lights in his face. Everyone knew the plot but him. What were his lines?"

"Here we are. On the rocks?" "Please." "Got everything? Want some music?" "No, I don't think so." "Okay. Now what are you depressed about? Besides everything." "The way I live, I guess. And you." "Me? I depress you?" "You and me, I mean. Tonight you hardly spoke to me. You kept watching Bobbie. That's all you've talked about. And after that one night in the car, you haven't asked me out. You haven't made love to me or showed in any way that I meant anything to you except a fast bang. I thought after that night we'd . . ."

"Falling in Love Again." He heard it and saw a white shadow against the black sea, that silver sliver of a woman. Images of her turned over in his mind like flipped diagrams on an anatomy chart: "Epidermis Front. Musculature Back. Circulatory System. Genito-Urinary. Digestive System. Lungs and—" He went deeper, deeper. The final chart: something? nothing? What was on the last chart? It had to be something, something significant.

He saw Julie's lips moving. He watched them, hearing but not listening. The words had no meaning. And it was not the right voice. The curtain was up. This was Act I. But he could not grasp the grand design. How could he speak his lines if he didn't know his role?

". . . so what am I to do? Ben? Do you hear me?" "Of course I hear you." "Well then, what am I to do?" "Do? At this moment I'd guess another drink would be in order."

"No, I don't want another drink." "Of course you do. I'll make it mild." "All right. But that one tasted funny. I think you put in too much vermouth. Or maybe it should have lemon peel."

When he came back with fresh drinks, she patted the cushion beside her and said, "Sit over here." "First, I'll put on some music." "If you want to. But nothing by Bobbie." "Maybe I better not play anything at all." "Ben, were you going to play something by Bobbie?" "Yes, I was." "Well, I don't want to hear it." "All right." "I don't want to hear anything more by her." "All *right*. I said all right." "I've had enough of her for one evening." "Julie, I won't . . ."

So it went. They talked at each other. He lost all sense of their involved litany: "Don't. I won't. She really. You wouldn't. I said. Why will. I can't. Please tell." Follow the bouncing ball. Angered, at himself as much as her, he went into the kitchen, brought back the bottle of Scotch and pitcher of martinis.

They drank, inspecting the ceiling. Then he felt a warm weight on his thigh. He looked down. Her hand spread out like a starfish. As he watched, fingertips curled, dug gently. The thing moved, coaxing. What a curious thing it was. Slice it into sections and new hands would grow. They would be perfect little hands, all coaxing, inching at him.

"Ben, you're angry with me." "I'm not angry." "Yes, you are. I can tell." "Julie, I am not angry." "I can tell you are." "Oh, Jesus." "What's wrong with me, Ben?" "Nothing's wrong with you." "Then why aren't you nice to me?" "I thought I was nice to you. I've tried to be." "Well, you're not. You're cold to me. You don't even know I'm alive." "Julie, for God's sake . . ." "Look at this," she screamed at him. "Look at it! I wore it just for you!"

She leaned to him, ripped down the zipper of her caftan.

There was a string around her neck. A little white bag hung from it, down between her grapy breasts.

"What?" he shouted, jerking back. "What is it? What the hell is it?"

"For you," she sobbed. "Just for you."

Her face was all rubbery, squeegeed, eyes squinched shut. Tears leaked, making wandering gray trails down her swollen cheeks. Her body was slack, without grace: instant age.

He felt the little bag. It crackled faintly. He leaned forward to sniff. Lavender. It was a sachet. She grabbed the back of his head, pulled his face into her damp breasts.

"Ohh," she groaned. "Ohh, Ben."

He knocked her hands aside and struggled to sit upright. He pulled away, stood shakily.

It happened about a year ago. Not his patient, but he had been called in. He could do nothing. This thirty-two-year-old man, married, with two children, and bleeding ulcers. Just before he died he looked around the room wonderingly. "What was that all about?" he asked.

Todd took quick steps to the porch door. He flung it wide and opened his mouth to gulp air.

"Perfect timing," Bobbie Vander said. "Got a drink for a soul in need?"

His mouth still gaped. She looked at him quizzically. She reached forward, put a finger under his chin, closed his mouth firmly.

"That's better," she said.

Unexpectedly, she put out her hand to him, arm straight. Startled, he shook her hand. It was dry and cool.

"What's up, doc?"

Todd was puzzled. "Come in, come in, come in." But he did not step aside. She pushed past him.

"Ah," she said. "Sister."

She slouched to the wicker chair, coiled into it, lighted a cigarette. All her movements were sinuous. She was a snake in a bread basket.

"What in Christ's name is that thing hanging around your neck?"

Julie zipped up her caftan. She finished her drink, poured another from the pitcher. Ben closed the door, came back into the room. His face ached with his smile.

"Well," he said.

There they were. A silent week went by.

"A drink!" he cried. "Bobbie, would you like a drink?"

"Yes, I'd like a drink. Wine, if you have it."

He took a bottle of Beaujolais from the shelf and stumbled into the kitchen. He broke a fingernail on the foil. The cork wouldn't budge. He put the bottle between his knees, heaved upward. The cork broke halfway down the neck. He stared at it. He found an icepick. He shoved it down into the cork. The pick pierced through; the cork remained lodged. He tried a knife blade. Slowly the cork moved down into the bottle. Then it shoved free. Red wine sprayed up into his face. He stood trembling. Now he knew: the play was a farce. "Places, everyone."

He poured a glass of wine. Little bits of cork floated on the surface. He picked them out with a paper towel. He wiped the rim of the glass. He lifted it. His hand shivered so badly wine slopped over the rim. He put it down, took three deep breaths, picked it up again. This time he got it out to Bobbie. Then he excused himself, went into the bedroom, changed his spotted shirt. He didn't bother with a tie. He didn't look at the stranger's reflection in the mirror.

He came into the living room. He finished his drink, poured another. Apparently they hadn't moved, hadn't spoken. He sat in the hard armchair primly, feet together. He looked down at the drink in his clumpy hands. One of the ice cubes had a fly frozen exactly in the center. Now how the hell had that happened?

Julie finished her drink in one tremendous swallow that spilled from the corners of her mouth. She let it drip. She poured herself another from the pitcher, not looking at them.

He stopped, stabbed by Bobbie's cold stare.

"Julie," he said, "I don't think you—"

"Let her do what she wants. Let everyone do what they want. Sell pot and poison and opium in Walgreen's. First come, first served. If she wants to be a drunk, let her. If people want to sniff cocaine, let them. If they want to kill themselves, that's okay, too. No one should interfere. We're all supposed to have brains. If we want to destroy ourselves, who's to say no? It's the individual's decision. No one's got a right to interfere. Nobody's business but our own. Right?"

"You don't really believe that," Todd said.

"I am not a drunk," Julie said.

Roberta smiled sweetly.

"What about children and idiots who don't know what they're doing? What about disturbed people who'd buy that stuff for murder? Are you saying—"

"Put on some music, for Chrissakes." She yawned. "Gerry Mulligan. I know you have it. I saw the album last month ten years ago."

He couldn't find the Mulligan. He played an album of Noel Coward and Gertrude Lawrence. They sang "Some Day I'll Find You" from *Private Lives*.

She looked at him. "Thanks," she said.

"I was telling Julie how much I enjoyed your singing tonight. It was very enjoyable. It was—"

"You told me."

"It's a lavender sachet," Julie said defiantly. "Mother made it for me."

"Don't you like Noel Coward? I thought you'd like this. It's so . . ."

She took a little bit of cork off her tongue. "You're a lousy bartender."

"Would you mix another pitcher, Ben? This is all water."

"I couldn't find the Mulligan."

"That beach was goddamn cold. My throat feels like sandpaper."

He gave up and trudged into the kitchen. He mixed another pitcher of martinis. He brought that in, plus the wine bottle and more ice cubes.

Now Bobbie was sitting on the couch alongside Julie. She reached up to stroke her hair.

"What's wrong, baby?"

"Don't touch me."

"What did you do to her?"

"I didn't do anything to her," he protested. "She's just depressed. She said so."

"What happened, Julie?"

"Nothing happened," he said angrily.

"Let her say it."

"Nothing happened," Julie said dully. "That's what happened. Nothing."

"Did he try to rape you?"

"Oh, good Lord!" He stood, paced around the room, looking at her and shaking his head.

"Well, she was all unzipped when I came in."

He stared at her disgustedly. "I assure you that—"

She went into chuffs of laughter, rocking back and forth. She pointed at him.

"Stiff, stiff, stiff." She laughed. "What a cube you are! I'm putting you on, for God's sake."

He tried to grin, but it didn't work.

"Doc, you want to rape her, go right ahead. Be my guest."

"Oh, shut up."

"Yes, shut up," Julie said.

Roberta was delighted. "Let's scream at each other."

"Why should we scream?"

"Because people scream when they get out of control. Then they say what they're really thinking. And I'm so fucking bored I could climb walls."

"You *are* a bitch, aren't you?"

"Ah, now we're getting somewhere."

"A real bitch." Julie nodded.

"Drink up, sister. Doc's not going to give you the beef injection tonight."

"Did she tell—"

"Tell me what?"

"I hate you," Julie muttered. "I've always hated you."

"Not always, baby. She's a solid piece, isn't she, doc?"

"You're disgusting. Maybe you both better go home."

"Not yet. It's just getting interesting. Are you going to marry her, doc?"

"Don't call me 'doc.'"

"Are you going to marry her, Doctor Todd?"

"This is neither the time nor the—"

"Frigging prig."

"Are you, Ben? Going to marry me?"

"Julie, for heaven's sake."

"I'm going to get drunk."

"You are drunk," Bobbie told her. "But you can get drunker. There's a whole pitcher there."

"Don't do that," Todd said furiously.

"Do what?"

"What you're doing."

"It's her decision. You're not going to marry her and she wants to drown her sorrow. What's so awful about that?"

"I didn't say I wasn't going to marry her."

"You didn't say you were."

He started to speak, then stopped. He glowered at her, a braced gladiator, trying to divine the role she was playing. She returned his look blandly, her face closed.

Why was she savaging him? It was more than bitchiness, more than the cruelty of a cunning woman with a venom-tipped tongue. This was bald hostility. She was assaulting him—and what had he done to her?

He had the sense that she was attacking because she felt threatened. Somehow he was a danger to her, and she meant to strike him down. He had met similar enmity in patients dying incurably or fated for a dodgy operation. Unable, or unwilling, to blame God, fate, or their own poor luck, they turned their rage onto the doctor, the messenger who had brought the bad news.

"You go to hell," he said slowly to Bobbie.

"Hey!" she sang delightedly. "Now we're getting somewhere. Now the clothes come off."

"I'm not going to take my clothes off," Julie said.

"Why not, baby? You don't have any secrets from us. Does she, doc?"

"Why don't you go? Just go."

"How come you got a divorce, doc? Couldn't cut the mustard?"

Her slashing attack bewildered him. She swarmed all over him, elbows and knees flailing. Repulsed at the throat, she punched at the groin. He could not counter that demonic fury.

"She was beautiful," Julie said. "Very slender. A blonde. A very good swimmer. Wasn't she, Ben?"

"Yes."

"And a diver. She was a wonderful diver. Wasn't she, Ben?"

"Yes."

Bobbie crossed bare legs. She linked bony fingers around a bony knee and rocked back and forth. "A wonderful diver," she repeated dreamily. "Every woman should be a wonderful diver."

"Why *did* you get a divorce, Ben?"

"I don't see where it's any concern of either of you."

"Couldn't cut the mustard."

"I liked her and she liked me," Julie mourned.

"Ever make it with her, baby?"

"Stop it," he said hoarsely.

"Stop what? Julie swings both ways. That's no secret. I do, too. What are you going to do—call the cops?"

"I don't understand."

"Sure you do, doc. You understand. But you won't admit it. Not even to yourself. Stiff upper lip and limp lower cock. Right?"

"My wife—my ex-wife never—"

"Sure? Are you sure?"

"She never did," Julie said vaguely. "I know she never did. It wasn't that."

"Then what was it? How come a slender blonde who's a great diver just walks away from a twenty-year marriage? So anxious to get away that she leaves the kid with you. What *was* it?"

"It wasn't anything. It just didn't work, that's all."

"After twenty years?"

"She was bored. You understand? Just like you. She was bored and I was bored. It didn't mean anything anymore. So we decided to part. Sorry. No scandal. No hidden vices. We just decided we'd be happier apart. That's all there was to it. Satisfied?"

"Nope. Drink up, baby. Take more. Not good enough, doc. I was ribbing you about cutting the mustard. Julie says you're a great lay, so it couldn't have been that. So it was her. Right? She hated it so you started sleeping around. Right?"

"Yes, goddamn it!" He jerked to his feet. Why was he screaming? "She hated it. Hated it! It was a duty and she did it. She looked out the window. That's what she did. She looked out the window. She never said anything. Why shouldn't I fool around? She was dead. The bastard. You think that's something? It was disgusting to her. I could tell. I was disgusting to her. My hands, my hair, my cock. Everything. She suffered me. You miserable bitch, she suffered me. There. Are you satisfied now? Are you satisfied?"

Bobbie lighted a cigarette, leaned back. She puffed and sighed with content. "That's more like it," she said.

He trembled, staring at her. Finally he put his hands on his hips. Something was catching in his throat.

"A wonderful diver." Julie nodded.

They looked. Her eyes were shiny agates. Flecks of white spittle had gathered in the corners of her mouth.

"She's a lush," Bobbie said. "We better get her home."

"She's not a lush," he cried angrily. "Don't call your sister a lush. She's got problems and she drinks more than is good for her. But she's not a lush."

"Have it your own way, doc. Let's get her home."

They lifted her between them. Her armpit was wet under his hand. She was walked, stumbling. They got her out the door, across lawn, through trees, onto the porch of the Vanderhorst home.

"I can manage now," Bobbie said. "You stay here."

She disappeared. He stood broken. Her voice, that feeling voice, had betrayed her. For her "You stay here" was not a command; it was an entreaty.

Suddenly he was backstage. He saw the propped scenery and machinery of the play. He saw the purposeful movement of the crew, the rush of players from the footlights as they hurried to change costumes and remove their masks. This farce was deadly serious. It was a business.

Bobbie loved him and wanted him. Either or both, and he thought, with wonder, both. Something was moving in her. It was a melt that frightened her. His instinct that she bullied because he threatened her was almost correct. He was not the true menace but her passion was.

He should have shouted out and clicked his heels, but he felt only sadness for her pain. He sensed the upheaval that must be racking her, even as the Patroon's stroke shattered him and left him weak and trembling.

This whole woman, this complete woman, *needed*. She would fight it and deny it. And as the need grew she would grasp her mask tighter, to keep it from slipping, and she would attack, attack, attack. Until finally, weary with the struggle, she would shrug and show her teeth.

He wanted to leave this doorway and walk the deserted beach alone and think and try to understand. But gradually, as he waited, his golden wisdom slipped off into the night. His sympathy was tucked away. He saw only the temper of her flesh. Fuddled by lust, he awaited her return.

Then she was there.

"Where's your car?" "Is she all right?" "Where's your car?" "My car?" "That's right, dummy. Your station wagon." "It's in the driveway. Behind my house. Why?" "Let's go." "Why the car? We could go to my place." "Isn't Susan there?" "No." "Where is she?" "I don't know." "Don't you care?" "Of course I care. But I trust Susan." "Do you? Let's get in the back. Fold the seat down." "You're going to get dirty." "How did you know?" "What? Oh. I meant you're going to get dirt on you." "Don't give it a second thought. Everything washes off. That's my religion. As you go through life, kiddo, always remember: everything washes off."

Silver silk came blossoming over her head and was tossed. She was naked, hairless. He had dreamed something infinitely smooth, polished. But she was ribby. She was metal-hard but spiny. Bones jutted; skin stretched tight: all of her pulled. He could not feel slack skin or loose flesh.

He peered close, staring in the darkness. There was an odor to her: something sharp. He put tongue to her neck. A tang there, sharp fruit that bit. She was all hard and crunchy. Her blood would be acid, smoking.

"Why are you all shaved? You look like you've been prepped for a hysterectomy." "I did it last night. I was shaving my legs and got carried away. I didn't have much anyway. Like it this way?" "You're like a young boy." "Ever make that scene?" "What scene?" "We're not communicating, baby. We're not having a meaningful dialogue. With a young boy. Did you ever fuck a young boy?" "Don't be silly." "Is that the way doctors talk— 'Don't be silly'? Well, did you or didn't you?" "I didn't." "I did. He was sweet but clumsy." "How old was he?" "Oh, about eleven or twelve. Around there." "Jesus Christ." "No, it wasn't. His name was Bob. He'll never forget that scene. As long as he lives. He wasn't circumcised. Are you circumcised?"

He lurched to kiss her, to shut her mouth. But her strong mouth gaped, hot, wet, and again the tang. She moved under him stealthily. She pushed him away. She held her tensed forefinger with her thumb and flicked him. Again.

"Hurt?" "Yes."

Something sounded in her throat, something exultant. He wanted to punish her, or himself; he didn't know. Her hands were at his shirt buttons: cool, dry fingers. He despaired. What was . . . She pushed his hands away.

"I'll do it. You *are* hairy. Oh, my God, you're so hairy." "Beauty and the beast." "And which am I? Jesus, look at you. You're an animal." "Yes." "I had a dog once." "You owned a dog?" "Goddammit, don't play cute with me. You know what I mean. A German shepherd." "I don't want to hear. I don't want to know." "All right. Kiss me here. And here. And here. Not with your teeth, silly."

Then she was a rage, a frenzy. She led to the edge and kept him tottering with a cadence he couldn't solve. He bit her to keep from crying out.

"There there," she said, laughing. "Cool it, doc."

Something in him wept for fullfillment. It was a birth. Something ached for birth. It came teased to life, straining to break free. It was meaning. It was the significance he sought: the secret throb of life. He shuddered with bliss.

"I know," he said suddenly. She didn't ask what he knew. Her shadowy mask floated above him. He grasped her tenuous body to link forever. He arched to be one. He wrenched his head side to side so ferociously that . . . And made an infant noise, at parturition. He hissed faintly. No louder than a soul escaping.

"Read any good books lately?" she gasped.

But she said, "Oh." "Oh," she said.

## 31

On the evening of August 29, Benvenuto D'Lorca, master of the fishing boat *Santa Lucia II*, reckoned his position as approximately 100 statute miles northeast of the island of Guadeloupe in the French West Indies. The sky was clear that night, but a long greasy swell was beginning to heave. D'Lorca's other two boats, *Maria* and *Mother of Mercy,* were well out to port and starboard, about a mile behind the leader.

At 5:00 A.M. the following morning, D'Lorca was shaken awake in his bunk by twelve-year-old Jesus D'Lorca, his brother's youngest son. It was the first time Jesus had been out of sight of land. He was awed and excited by the immensity of the sea.

D'Lorca had slept in stained tan pants and a torn singlet. He pulled on short sea boots and clumped up on deck. He went directly to the taffrail, kneeled and thanked God for allowing him to see another dawn. Then he stood, looked around at the horizon.

But there was no horizon. Nor sky. Nor sea. *Santa Lucia II* was suspended in the middle of a pearl-gray globe. Sea-colored sky merged with sky-colored sea. The heavy swell had deepened. D'Lorca could feel it under his feet, could hear the creaking of his boat as it slid down, came up, bit in again. To port and starboard the other two boats were phantoms: gone, there, gone.

The captain sent the boy below for coffee, then climbed to the bridge. The helmsman looked at him questioningly, but D'Lorca shook his head. He stayed near the wheel for almost three hours, drinking black coffee laced with sweet brandy. Shortly after 8:00 A.M. he saw a lightning in the east. Scraps of white-blue, high up. The gray fog was in motion, folding in upon itself.

Then there was a hole. Through it D'Lorca could see a world of still sky, not sun. And something curious. It was a huge round spiral of cloud, an inverted soup plate. Even as he watched it seemed to revolve. Then the fog closed; the bright world was lost.

"God *damn!*" D'Lorca said bitterly.

He jerked a thumb across his shoulder. The helmsman nodded and began to put over. At the same time D'Lorca started cranking the hand siren faster atop the wheelhouse. As *Santa Lucia II* came about, *Maria* and *Mother of Mercy* did the same, pulling in closer to the lead boat. D'Lorca wished he had a radio so he could tell people what he had seen, to warn them.

About the same time on that day, the ATS-3, a geostationary satellite over the Atlantic, began transmitting pictures of tropical cloud systems. Florida weather stations received their first alert shortly before noon. An international precautionary warning was then sounded.

A news announcer on a Miami station ended his 1:00 P.M. broadcast by stating: "What may prove to be the first tropical disturbance of the season appears to be shaping up in the area of the Leeward Islands. 'Hurricane Hunter' planes have been dispatched, and small craft warnings are now in effect from Puerto Rico to Grenada. It is still too early to predict the course and strength of the disturbance. Stay tuned to this station for further details as they become available."

Captain D'Lorca's little fleet rushed home to harbor. The master watched Jesus scurry to bring food and drink up to the men on deck. When he got a chance, he patted the boy's smooth cheek and smiled at him.

# 32

Sullenness in Tom Drinkwater was really young pride. He was not crabbed; he knew lively joy. Shimmering between youth and manhood, he listened to his body and heard it growing.

Not only the flesh bloomed but perception, understanding, awareness of the world about him and its tribe. But for each secret solved a dozen sprouted, mocking. People said but people felt: that was one of them.

Sea was sea; sky was sky. He knew sand, beach, shells; wood, iron, tools; flame and fire, animals in the swamp; dawns, sun and moon; muscle ache and dreamless sleep. These things were in him; he in them.

But mysteries grew infinite. What did a rainbow mean and why did his mother look at the Patroon so? Sounds brought tears; the smell of rain could make him laugh. Being an Ikantos swelled him but he ached to be as others.

Susan Todd: there was a word—love—and it must be that. It was something vibrating between lungs and loins, a breathless hunger. It was his brain steaming with such precise fantasies that his eyes could see, ears hear, fingers touch.

Compared to this, all he *knew* was a penny on his tongue.

For she went on forever, in a thousand guises, in a million reveries. Until all he knew revolved about this burning sun of woman, this life-giver. Man-ness, Indian-ness, be-ness: she cast them in long, strong shadows, or short and faint.

He lay spread-eagled upon the beach, black hair fanned, russet skin tight against a cool morning breeze. His eyes were lidded against early glare. His dreaming fingers stroked clotted sand. And they would have a boat . . .

A shade came between him and the sun. He opened his eyes. She was there: jigsawed blaze fitting the blue sky puzzle. She had a hand to her hair, pulled it away, let it move like flame on the wind.

"Geronimo," she said.

She folded onto the sand alongside him. Without word or cause she nuzzled his neck, kissed his shoulder. "Sweet . . ." she said. He turned onto his side, touched her hair timorously. ". . . boy," she said.

She lay away, staring wide-eyed at the still sky. Breath caught in him. He flopped, face on hand. He wondered at her whittled profile. There was a distinct line where lips ended, pored flesh began.

The marble troubled him.

"Susan."

Silence.

"I was going for a swim. Want to go? The water's cold, but if you swim hard it isn't bad. Tide's going to change in an hour. Right now it's set. We could swim down to the Semanski place, then back. Susan?"

She turned slowly, looked at him with curtained eyes. "What?"

"Swim. Do you want to swim?"

"Oh. No. You go ahead, Tom."

"What's wrong?"

"Nothing's wrong."

"You seem so . . ."

"Do I? Seem so?"

She was unbearably tender with him: a tenderness that cut, slashed; tenderness that bruised; punishing tenderness, hurting; tenderness that twisted, pounding. Her fingers stroked his cheek.

"I love you," he said. She smiled.

"I never see you anymore," he cried angrily. "We never swim together. Or run on the beach. Or anything."

She didn't reply.

"What's wrong? Something's wrong. Don't you remember? We went into the sea together. And what we did. I thought. Susan, why can't we? I want to see you and be with you. My drum is almost finished. You didn't even ask. And you're always busy. Yesterday morning was beautiful. But you. The Patroon. Listen, Susan. Oh, my God. Because I'm an Indian? Is that it?"

"What?"

Furious, he took her hand and pressed it against his testicles.

"There," he said.

"There?" she asked.

They lay in silence, limp hands clasped. He tried to glare life into her lifeless stare, prodding her to gladness or to grief. But her coated eyes looked at a coated world.

It was late now, the heat of summer waning. And something all about them not of autumn chill. The sun was shining, sky still blue, the sea cheerful and alive. But somewhere, far off, something dread was coming. Tom Drinkwater, who knew sea, sky, sand, beach, shells, wood, iron, tools, flame, fire, animals, dawns, sun and moon, muscle ache and dreamless sleep, knew this too: the something far away and coming.

"Let's swim," he said again.

When she didn't answer, he said quickly, while courage steamed, "I love you, Susan. I will never love anyone but you. They want to send me away so I won't be near you, but I won't go. We could go away. You and I. Yes. I love you. If you tell me to steal, I will steal. Or kill. And I will kill. Whatever I must do to be with you. Yes. I love you. I am older than you think. I know things. Did I tell you my drum is almost finished? You and I. Susan? Please. I love you."

Her apricot-blushed body had not changed, but her eyes had perished. He had once accompanied his mother to a funeral of an Indian. The aged Ikantos had been laid out on a plank table and bleached clamshells placed upon his eyes.

Tom Drinkwater lurched to his feet and went stumbling down to the water, into the cold sea. His skin constricted, scrotum wrinkling. He caught a breath and plunged, stroking out to the deep. He churned through a wave, pumping to get beyond the break.

The grip of it! Now he could laugh, muscles strained. The chill! His arms went lifting to glory, pulling the whole sea beneath him, kicking it back. To Europe and away with a lift and a shove, push and fling: Tom Drinkwater alive and laughing.

He knew the sea, *knew* it. He knew those drags below, the crash above, all its moods and angers, calms and sweet delights. The water slewed, caressing. He floated on his back. Wavelets lapped over and smacked his face with foam.

He went on until weariness came and he was dead. He thrust arms and legs, heaving himself out of the sea. He looked eastward, endless and beckoning. And they would own a boat . . .

He turned then, floated and paddled. He stopped to revolve in his own ocean, rotating his body around and around, spluttering. Then he gripped himself, shoulders, arms, legs: Tom Drinkwater in the world that spread everywhere. His world.

He came slowly to shore, smoothed and calmed. He waded dripping onto the sand, shaking himself like a wet dog. He tossed back his long black hair, looking.

But those phlegmy eyes were gone.

---

## 33

Twinkles of ferris wheel smearing an indigo sky. Lark! Bulbs of merry-go-round blurring over saddled swans. Red-green-blue neon on the Whirl-Away. Up and down she goes! Revolving Crack-the-Whip. Eyes red. Noses green. Bare shoulders blue. Step right up!

The Parkhouse Brothers Carnival: "A Stunning Phantasmagoria of Thrilling Delights!!!" In the meadow at the junction of Route 9-A6 and Staunton Road. "The wonder midway of a million exciting joys!!!" Bright splutters from the Saturn Rocket. Bright cries from the Dodgems. Bang! it all went.

Clanks, chinks, thuds, screams! From ticking Wheels of Fortune, Funny Money, Bingo, Bango, Bongo, Fish-for-Wealth, Toss-a-Ring, Pitch-a-Ball. Wow! Over all, "Love Makes the World Go 'Round," squealing from an electric organ. Jangle! Juke boxes spangling jazzy tunes. Noise crashed. Merged. Joy!

Smells? To clog! Popcorn, cotton candy, frozen custard, hot dogs, fried sausage, clams, hamburgers. Beer, beer,

beer. Swallow and gulp! Lips brimming. Laugh-spluttered into the neoned night, excitement-hot. Fevered eyes and voices that choked. "Naughty 'n' Nice!" Large tent where reflective women displayed their breasts (and sucked their teeth) as the moving climax to "An Exciting Panorama of Feminine Pulchritude Through the Ages!!!"

The carnival come to town! Wonders.

They drove over in Todd's station wagon, parked across the road near the E-Z-Buy Supermarket. The doctor, Susan, Roberta, Julie, Hapgood Graves, and Tom Drinkwater. Todd bought tickets for all. In they plunged! Giggling.

Shout! Shout! That grinning throng. Duck in pretended fear as cars of the Whirl-a-Gig zoomed overhead. Yelps! Hold me tight! Kiss me now! Round and round.

And then . . . Ooh . . . In the tents: Loony-Bin, House of Death, Lovers Lane, Hall of Mirrors, Fun Fantasy. Well . . . "You're awful! Just awful!" Sweet-smeared lips. Spilled. Dripping. Ahh, who cares? Throw a baseball. Toss a dart. Buy a potholder from the church booth.

"Love Makes the World Go 'Round."

Explode with the world! Suspend all but gladness. Freely gorge and freely spend. Night heated with human sweat and fried meat. Take it in. More. Live! Round the glitters went. Black night split by neoned day. Good-bye, death! Screams from the tinkling rides. "Hold me, doll." "I think I'm going to be sick."

The Hall of Mirrors. Oh. What a scare! Stained tent. Worn boards. A billion mirrors, full-length. Set at right angles and at crazy angles. A maze! There you were and there you were and there you were. Walk and bang into yourself. Dent your own nose? Fun! And you shrinking down but suddenly cut off. Where were you? Who are you? Let me out! A hundred yous threatening.

"Let's," Bobbie Vander sang. "Come on. Let's!"

So she and Julie and Benjamin Todd entered into the Hall of Mirrors. Laughing! Julie carrying the giant panda she had won at Toss-a-Ring. They separated. Wandering down reflecting corridors.

Cries. Merriment! Sobs? Calling, calling. Suddenly a stranger staring at you. Mouth open. But not. A hundred miles away, shrinking. All strangers wandering. Feeling. Air was glass. Who is that? Everyone floating! Friends and strangers. Floating on glass. Away.

Dreams. Glistening dreams! My face, my back, my face, my back. Endlessly. Julie, clutching her stuffed doll, went giggling down the glass tunnel to her little her. Looking at strange faces. Distorted forms. People she didn't know. Children. Dwarfs. Codgers. Cripples! All wavering and waving. Here we are! Where are you?

Crazy dream. Silver dream! Once removed. Or twice. Images intertwined. Kiss me. I am you! And then. Dream? Well.

Roberta and Ben Todd. Far away and dreaming. Reflection? Shimmering image. Embraced and kissing! His hands probing her back. Flicking her ass. Where were they? Julie turned. There they were again. In profile. Ben and Bobbie. Lips! Lips to lips. What? Julie turned. There they were again. Fingers! Mouths moving. Julie turned. There they were . . .

A rocket went up, cracked the sky. Oh! That was the signal: one hour before closing. "Please, ma, one more ride." And scurrying. Spinning they all went. Beer! Candied apples. And a lucky winner bending craftily over his set of plastic wineglasses.

"Love Makes the World Go 'Round" throbbed the organ. While weary children, weary adults dragged to the exit. Buying a homemade cake or pie from one of the booths set up by local charities. Absolution for joy.

The House of Death was open to the stars. Flappy walls painted with iridescent skeletons. Gorgons! Monsters and devils. Chimeras! Walkways heaved. Groans came from nowhere. Ghastly! Women huddled close. Quivering! Escorts laughed nervously. There there.

Into this canvas hell rushed Susan Todd and Hapgood Graves. In their wake came Tom Drinkwater. The three took a shaking walk. Flinched when goblins sprang at them! Wincing in The Cave of the Monsters. Lizards spat steam at them. Dragons waved with rubber paws! Shrieks and moans were all about.

Separated by the crowd. Weeping children! Laughing parents. We're in hell! Darkness and heat. Feeling fumbling stumbling. Don't be afraid. It's all in fun!

Then. Suddenly. Sputtering electric arc. Grinning Pan! Goat teeth gleaming. Slavering. Sweet, sweet stink of corruption. Lovely rot! Perfume? Incense? How did they do it? But a vision of . . .

Blue-white light. Flickering. Tom Drinkwater saw. There they were. Not embracing. Standing apart. A little. But her hands on him! Standing motionless. Pan's wet smile. Pan's sweet perfume. Looking. Looking! She felt.

All to an end. Music crashing. Shouts and drunken calls! Carnival closed down and darkened. Home, home. Everyone home. Cars pulled away. Yells! Organ limping to a dripping end. "Love Makes the Worrrr . . ."

Good night. Good night!

Lights in "Naughty 'n' Nice" flicked off. The sky seemed to drum.

# 34

"How could you be happy with him?" Roberta asked her sister. "Neither of you is strong enough to take."

Julie rolled under the blanket, turning her face to the wall. The stuffed panda was clasped in her arms. Its button eyes stared thoughtfully at the ceiling.

Bobbie sat swagging on a little maple stool before an electric heater. She was naked, thighs splayed wide to rosy glow. Face, neck, breast, torso, legs were painted with heat. But through the closed window behind her filtered thin moonlight. It was silvered and put hoarfrost on her pale skin: ice-needles shivering along her spine.

"You kissed him," Julie muttered. "I saw you."

"Oh, for God's sake. I *told* you. We were wandering through those insane mirrors and suddenly bumped into each other. He grabbed me and said, 'Hello, friend,' or something stupid like that, and then he kissed me. Big deal."

"*You* were kissing *him*. I saw you. Over and over."

"Okay. We were kissing. Over and over. So do me something."

Julie was silent a moment, puzzling what she might say next.

She slipped through life swaddled in feathers. Others could react instantly and instinctively with anger or despair. But in her, strong emotions were enfeebled by her placid good nature. There was a time lag. "I ought to be furious" came before "I am furious."

Julie whipped around and sat up. Blankets fell to her bare waist. The panda flopped to the floor, bounced, rolled once, and came to rest face down, stuffed arms and legs reaching.

"Why are you doing this to me?" Julie wailed. "You're going away in a few weeks. Ben doesn't mean anything to you. Why are you trying to take him away from me?"

"I don't have to try. He's doing all the work."

"You're hateful."

"I sure am, Juju."

"Juju? You haven't called me that in years."

"Haven't I? Forget him, baby. You're better off without him."

"I love him."

Roberta looked at her. The heater, tilted upward, put her eyes in red shadow.

"You're a pisser, you are. A month ago you didn't know. Maybe you did and maybe you didn't. You weren't sure. Now you love him and want to marry him."

"I do, I do!"

"Bullshit! You just want a man. Any man. A home of your own where you can slop martinis, eat chocolates, and play solitaire to your heart's content. And bang away like Jesus-be-damned. I'm telling you Todd isn't the guy for you. You need a truck driver to belt you around, pour your gin down the sink, and kick about thirty pounds of lard off your fat ass. You need Humphrey Bogart and you're looking for Ronald Colman."

"I've got to get away from here!" Julie screamed at her.

"Can't you understand that? I can't spend the rest of my life with momma. I've got a life to live. I've got—"

"Keep your voice down," Bobbie said calmly. "Unless you want the Patroon charging in here in his nightshirt."

In their early youth, with so few years between them, they competed in a spleeny war for their parents' kisses and the smiles of relatives and friends. Their love for each other, their physical love, began as a kind of shrewd armistice that brought an end to their squabbles.

Pleasure kept them docile until they learned manners, but by then it had become habit and had assumed a significance that they could not comprehend but could not deny.

As young girls, each had her braveries and cowardices. Yet they seemed to fit as key and lock, each existing for the other. It was this unnatural dependency that persuaded the Patroon to send them on to different schools rather than any definite knowledge of their incestuous tumblings.

Having driven an ax to split, he was content to let them hammer in the wedges. They grew apart, and their lives as young women veered, drew away, and finally separated until they were obverse and reverse of a thin coin that was now, if anything, memory.

Old soldiers dream of old battles because, with the sliding of years, memory of terror fades and what remains is the fond recollection of intensified life, of moments so electric, so bursting that everything after is thin porridge.

So old lovers, in time, forget the miseries and defeats, remembering only the winning and the splendor. So Roberta and Julie, with the memory, unconsciously sought a rejuvenation that could never be. They chose pain, as old roués must be whipped before they can experience once again the ecstasy that came so easily when the world was young.

Julie swung naked out of bed and sat there slumped,

shoulders collapsed, head hanging. Soft hair screened her face.

"You hate me," she said dully. "I know you do. For some reason you hate me. You don't want me to be happy."

"Don't be such a shithead."

"Then why are you doing this to me?"

"Doing what?"

"Taking Ben away from me?"

"I've got nothing to do with it. He's giving of his own free will. He's a grown man. He's doing what he has to do. And besides, I don't recall your being all that nice to me this summer. I wanted something from you, and you slammed me in the chops. That was nice."

"I'm sorry. I'm sorry I hit you, Roberta. But you really didn't want anything from me. You were just going through the motions. You were curious if I would want to if you wanted to."

Bobbie looked up in surprise. She was so used to her sister's plump affability, so used to her ignorance of ideas, that sometimes she forgot Julie's blood knowledge of her, Roberta's, mind's maze and heart's labyrinth.

"Oh, sure. You're sorry."

"Please forgive me."

"I'm the forgiving type. Everyone knows that."

Julie came up from the bed. She dragged across to Roberta, dropped clumsily on the floor alongside her. She put one arm on Bobbie's leg, rested her chin on Bobbie's knee.

"You're going to catch cold down there, kiddo."

"Bobbie."

"Now what?"

"If I . . ."

"If you what?"

"If we . . ."

"If we what?"

"Well, if you . . ."

"Jesus Christ, you're a great brain, you are. If you give me a munch tonight, will I lay off the doc? Is that what you're trying to say?"

"Bobbie?"

"I'll think about it."

"Please?"

It was too late. A month ago it might have worked; then Roberta was a woman who wanted everything that was coming to her. But her sense of Ben Todd was the first loosened chunk; the flood threatened to pour through. "The heart doesn't know the difference."

She looked down. Julie's puffed face turned up toward her, with eyes swollen, lips parted. And the flesh spread in dunes of tanned skin. She stroked Julie's hair, that waxed casque.

"I'm not a turd," she murmured. "Really I'm not, baby. But I've been shoved around so much. This fucking business I'm in. I sat down and planned it: after I made it—I knew I'd make it—I'd have my own way. No one would push me around then. Not anymore. Then I'd be a taker. I wouldn't be a giver. Julie, you're a giver."

"I guess so."

"I planned it, like I've planned everything. I mean I really thought it out. I'd be hard. Nothing would dent me. Because if I couldn't have my own way, what the hell was it all about? If I couldn't do that, then I blew it. You understand?"

"Sort of."

"This goddamn summer. That lousy sun. It scrambled my brains. Now I'm not *sure*. I don't *know*. I feel differently."

"About Ben Todd?"

"Ben Todd and you and the Patroon and Hap and everyone and everything. Jesus Christ, baby, what's happening to me?"

She began to cry. Her shoulders didn't shake and she didn't sway or wail. It was not grief. It was the sad weeping of the voyager, gripping the rail, watching the homeland fade below the horizon. Her spine was stiff, head high, and tears came through, slow at first, then a flow.

"Bobbie," Julie said, bewildered, "what . . . ?"

"Forget it," her sister said in a coarse voice. She made no effort to wipe the tears away. "Get your *tuchis* off the floor and under the covers. I'm going to unplug the heater and open the window just a bit."

The bed steamed with their heat. Bobbie threw one blanket to the floor, then rolled back. She clasped Julie's soft bulk, burrowing into her nuzzling.

"Jesus," she breathed. "This is something. You're air, you are. As soft. I could float on you. This is just what I need tonight. Just comfort."

"Bobbie, what you said—about me wanting any man. I guess you're right. But you don't know what it's like. My life, I mean. This is the first time you've been home in ages. I'm here all the time. I never go anywhere. Mother's a dear and I love her. But you know what she's like. The lavender sachet and all. The Patroon scares me. I wouldn't dare talk to him about—well, you know, about things. Sometimes I go out with men. But they're all . . . That's why Ben is so important to me. He really is my last chance."

"Don't talk crap."

"He is, Bobbie, he *is*. I feel it. I just feel it. I want something to happen to me. I want to *do* something. I know I drink too much. You think I'm a drunk. Well, I'm not a drunk—I mean I'm not an alcoholic or anything like that—but I do drink too much. I could stop whenever I want to, but what's the point? And I am too fat. I know all that. You don't have to tell me. But I need help. I can't do it all alone. I'm not as strong as you are.''

"My God, kiddo, you think I go through life grinning? I work at it. Every minute."

"Well . . . maybe you do. But I don't know how. I need someone. You don't but I do.''

"You don't think I need anyone?''

"No, I don't.''

Bobbie shook her head. "You're beautiful. Just beautiful. You don't have the slightest, do you? You haven't understood a word I've said.''

She shoved her body into that sweet glow, hiding. Julie was all around her. She was engulfed, taken in and swallowed. She curled up in a closet of flesh, spiced with bay.

"Sisters," Bobbie murmured. "It's got to be the goddamndest relationship in the world. Friends and enemies. Lovers and haters. Partners and rivals. One minute we're screaming at each other and the next minute we're crying on each other's shoulders. What keeps us together?''

"I don't know.''

"What keeps us apart? Do you love me?''

"Yes, I do, Roberta.''

She kissed Bobbie on the lips, clinging. That meadow behind the house. Running down. Running. Down. The tree house. Now you do it to me.

"Juju," Bobbie said.

"Why did you start calling me that again? It means magic.''

"I know.''

"Bobbie, are you . . .''

"Am I what?''

"Are you happy?''

"Christ, I never give it a second thought. There's no guarantee in this world, baby. Happy the way that would make you happy? No, I'm not. Happy the way that makes me happy? I thought so. Now I don't know."

"But are you right and I'm wrong?"

"There are lots of kinds of happiness, kiddo. Here's one of them . . ."

She scooched down to run her tongue lightly along Julie's padded ribs. She went flicking, licking the icing on the cake.

"Oh."

"Yes," Roberta said. "Oh. Remember that night after the prom when we . . ."

She pulled away and scrabbled on the bedside table for cigarettes. There was one left. She lit it, took a puff, leaned forward, locked lips, let smoke escape into Julie's mouth. That was how they smoked their final cigarette.

This act, this bittersweet echo, came closest to a renewal of the past. But it was words without music, evocative and empty as the printed lyrics of a love song. The melody was lost.

"You know what would make me happy?" Julie asked.

"What?"

"You'll laugh at me."

"I won't laugh at you. What would make you happy?"

"I'd like to be a barmaid," Julie said dreamily. "Or, you know, like a cocktail waitress in a nice place. The tips are very good and you meet a lot of people. I'd wear like a short frilly skirt and black net stockings. Like a French maid, you know. I bet I'd be very good at it and make a lot of money. You can laugh now."

"Julie, I'm not going to laugh. I don't think it's such a nutty idea. You *would* be good at it. Your legs are good and your lungs just don't end. I bet you'd bring in a lot of business to the right place. Sure, maybe the guys would pinch your ass and make a pass, but what the hell. You could mean a lot of dough to some smart owner."

"And I'd remember what the regulars drink and I'd say, 'The usual?' I like people, Bobbie, and I'm good at getting along with them. I could do it. I know I could."

"And the guys would buy you a round."

"That too. But mostly I like the kidding around. There's a place out on Route 9-A6 that's decorated like a colonial tavern. It's a nice clean place and everyone's so friendly. Terry Foyle took me there. He was in the men's room a long time and I got talking to the waitress. She said that some weeks during the summer she makes almost three hundred dollars. And most of it is tips so she doesn't pay taxes on it. And she was going to marry a fellow she met there. One of the customers."

"Sounds good, baby. Just one thing."

"What?"

"I don't know how the Patroon would take to this idea."

Julie stiffened. Slowly the dream leaked from her eyes.

Roberta stubbed out the cigarette. They lay in silence, away from each other. The room gradually chilled. Julie shivered once, and Bobbie retrieved the blanket from the floor and tossed it across their legs. Julie turned to look at her.

"Do you promise?" she asked. "Really promise?"

"Promise what?"

"You know. About Ben Todd. Will you give him back to me?"

"You're such a bunny. No, you're a panda. A stuffed panda. Kid, my thing with Todd will probably last about as long as a fart in a keg of nails. By the end of next week I'll be long gone. Then he's all yours. What the hell do I need him for? I've got Hap. I need a man with me to hold open doors and get the luggage off the plane and tip bellhops and make sure no ringside drunk starts pawing. Hap does all that for me. He's in love with me. Did you know that? Well, he is. The guy's a natural-born victim. So what do I need Ben Todd for? I don't need him. As long as I've got Hap, you can have Ben. Fair enough?''

"Thank you, Bobbie.''

In time, Julie's breathing throttled and she rolled onto her side, her back to Roberta.

"Bobbie,'' she said sleepily, "if you want to . . .''

"No. I don't want to.''

After a while Roberta crept from under the covers and went to her own bed. She straightened out the cigarette butt and got two puffs before it began to burn her fingers. She snuffed it out.

Julie was asleep, not snoring but making a moist, suffering, "Uhh, uhh, uhh.'' Once she moaned and turned over. Roberta heard this, and a bird screech from the swamp, and the endless thump of waves upon the beach.

What bothered her most about what was happening to her was that it might affect her voice. Her sound might become soft, warm, and fruity. Then she would flutter and coo. She would pad her bra and call people "Darling.''

It seemed a high price.

# 35

"Now officially named 'Hurricane Ava,' the first tropical storm of the season slammed into the island of Guadeloupe late last night, leaving a ten-mile path of death and destruction. Winds of more than a hundred miles an hour dumped four inches of rain in a period of one hour. Three fishing boats seeking the safety of the harbor capsized, and all aboard are feared lost. In addition, loss of life on the island is believed to be in the hundreds. Thousands are homeless, and it is estimated that property damage will . . ."

Exhibiting the inconstancy that was to characterize its violent fourteen-day life, Hurricane Ava spun northward after devastating Guadeloupe. Tracked by planes, satellites, and shore-based radar, it avoided Puerto Rico and the Dominican Republic. Yet, even at a distance, tides were several feet above normal and winds at gale force.

Making a ninety-degree turn, the storm swept across Cuba, destroying thirty percent of the sugar crop and causing heavy flooding in the lowlands. It was estimated that more than a thousand perished. All communications with the U.S. naval base at Guantanamo were severed for a period of eight hours.

The charted path of the storm indicated it was heading for the Gulf of Mexico and the coasts of Louisiana and Texas. But once again the behavior of Hurricane Ava proved unpredictable. It combed through the Florida keys, causing enormous destruction of shore installations and small boats. During this phase, the Finnish tanker *Klanga* broke in two and foundered with the loss of all hands. More than twelve hundred requests for assistance were received by U.S. Coast Guard stations in the area in a period of twelve hours. The cruise ship *Hispanic* lost its rudder and drifted for twenty-four hours before being taken in tow and brought safely into port.

Hurricane precautions were in effect from Miami north to Charleston. The storm made no direct strike against Miami, which suffered high tides, flooding of coastal highways and considerable wind damage to palm trees and beachfront luxury hotels. But Hurricane Ava "came ashore" at Fort Lauderdale, causing several deaths, and then went bouncing up the coast on an erratic course that caused heavy loss at Lake Worth, Cape Kennedy, and Daytona Beach.

Meteorologists described Hurricane Ava as "the worst in fifty years." Winds exceeding two hundred miles an hour were recorded at Kennedy. The area near Jacksonville Beach took almost six inches of rain in less than two hours. Along the coastal highway travelers were trapped and drowned in their cars. An eighty-five-foot yacht was carried two miles inland and beached on the lawn of a monastery.

Those who survived spoke of a "flat rain"—sheets of water carried horizontally by ferocious winds. At one mobile home park near Pontevedra, thirty-eight units were totally destroyed with an estimated loss of life of sixty-three. Curiously, the park's swimming pool was completely emptied by the high winds and was found dry and cracked when the storm passed.

Small craft warnings were now in effect as far north as Halifax. Ships at sea waited for the latest advisories before their masters decided to beat for harbor or head eastward for deep water. But all was chance. Hurricane Ava, capricious in its cruelty, skipped northward, the great stern eye glaring down at scows and oceanliners, at families huddled in cellars and at tourists drinking noisily at "hurricane parties" in the lounges of glass hotels. Hopefully it would turn eastward, spending its fury in the chopped seas off Newfoundland. But it taunted: turning away, then coming back to bloody the coast.

Charleston Harbor escaped serious damage. But a few miles northward the inlets leading up to Myrtle Beach were ravaged by enormous tides and winds of a strength beyond the memory of the oldest residents. To this day, on the lawn of a courthouse near Pawleys Island, a wooden telephone pole is displayed. The winds of Hurricane Ava drove fragile stalks of sea grass completely through the wood.

As estimates of deaths and destruction of property continued to mount, governors of several coastal states signed emergency decrees. In two states, already crushed by the storm, martial law was declared, and National Guard troops were mobilized to provide assistance and prevent looting. The President canceled a state visit to Brazil and remained in the White House, awaiting requests for federal aid.

Hurricane Ava turned eastward, and Virginia, Maryland, New Jersey and New York escaped the full force. It was hoped the final turn had taken place. But the storm once again veered inland, strength undiminished. It was estimated the eye would pass over Cape Cod and possibly come ashore at Gloucester.

By this time, all coastal areas as far north as St. John's in Newfoundland were battened down. This is a hard land, and the people are hard. No "hurricane parties" were held. Small boats were double-snagged, wooden shutters nailed tight, kerosene lamps made ready. Dusty stores of candles were brought up, emergency wards in hospitals made ready. Outdoor dogs were dragged in and chained. Last-minute shopping was mostly canned soups, bread, cheese, whiskey, and flashlight batteries.

Hurricane Ava touched at Newburyport in Massachusetts, then withdrew twenty miles off the coast to swirl its strength. Even offshore its awesome power was felt: pounding rain, an ululant wind that made people cover their ears to keep out the pain, tides that swept away carefully tended beaches and crunched at the pilings of beachfront homes.

That mocking eye stared down at boarded windows and families crouched in basements; at boats tipping crazily, steel ships whining at their hawsers. The eye saw it all, touching with wind, flicking with rain, probing, waiting. Huddled children pulled up blankets and laughed with excitement. Old men lighted their pipes and said, "Shit." Women ran fresh water into every pot and kettle available, filling the bathtub. You couldn't tell . . . It might . . .

# 36

Hapgood Graves listened to the wind. "It sounds like Spanish liturgical music of the fifteenth century."

He stood on the patch of lawn in the swamp, head cocked, hands on hips. He wore canvas shoes on bare feet, flannel bags, a long-sleeved V-neck tennis sweater. Thin hair whipped across his eyes.

He felt the sky's oppression and the wind's thrum. It was all moving now, a great swirling about him. The brass chain had been pulled, the toilet flushed. Caught in the vortex, he saw the cartoon caption: "Good-bye, cruel world."

"It's coming." He nodded. "You can feel it. The Patroon says late Saturday night or early Sunday morning."

Susan Todd, seated on the turf, reached up to take his hand. She looked at him with haggard, loving eyes. Flecks of rain marked her face with a few wild tears.

"We can't stay here," Graves said. "Too cold and too wet."

She made a sound and gripped his hand.

"Don't worry." He smiled knowingly. "I have some coke for you. Take it and go back. We better not meet here again until after the storm."

"Then? Hap, you promise?"

"Sure. Of course."

He went through life dispensing promises as others toss away dead matches. He did not consider them lies, just fees paid for instant gratification. Most people accepted the word for the deed. And he could always mitigate his reneging with another promise: leaving a trail of sand castles all over the world.

"But, Hap, you'll be going away."

"Not for another week. We'll have plenty of time."

"Take me with you. Please."

"Let's not go through that again. I told you I'll write as soon as I get settled in New York."

"Then you'll send for me?"

"We'll see what happens."

"Won't you call me? To talk to me?"

"What if I get your father?"

"Then I'll call you."

"I don't have a phone in my apartment. But I'll get one. As soon as I have the number, I'll write you and then you can call me. How's that?"

"All right. I guess. You *will* write?"

"I said I would."

"But sometimes you lie."

"True. But I'm not lying now. I'll write."

"I love you so much."

"I don't blame you," he said solemnly.

"Come sit down. Here. Beside me."

"No."

"Just for ten minutes."

"What for?"

"My God, Hap, must you be so nasty? Because I want to kiss you and hold you. Is that so awful?"

"Five minutes. Then we've got to get back. The rain is coming. And I have to work with Bobbie."

"Bobbie. I think you love her more than you do me."

"She's my meal ticket. If it wasn't for her, I'd be hustling my ass again. And I'm getting a little long in the tooth for that."

What he sought from danger and from drugs were brief moments of keen lucidity when he could shrug off his pose like a worn bathrobe. Then, naked, he saw himself in a blinding glare. Chilled champagne bubbled through his veins.

Then he knew: ambition leap-frogging talent, dated style, warped taste, shriveled will, an inability to sacrifice today's pleasure for tomorrow's happiness: he knew it all.

But strangely, in those charged moments when he saw himself clear, he was not dismayed. For there, in a way he could not understand for all his cleverness, was hope: a whitewashed wall against the sun.

"Will you please sit down?" Susan asked him. "There . . . That's not so bad, is it? Now put your arm around me."

"Yes, mom."

"Oh, darling, what am I going to do?"

"About what?"

"You. When you go away. I'll miss you so much I already miss you, and you haven't even gone yet."

"You mean the dust? Not to worry. I'll leave you some and tell you where to get more."

"You mean right here in South Canaan?"

He was amused. "Right here in this rustic paradise." He nodded. "You can get anything you want anywhere in this great land of ours. If you know where to look and have the dibs. You won't run short. Just take it easy and don't let daddikins see you when you're flying. Think you can remember that?"

"Of course I can. You treat me like I'm some kind of moron."

"You are. The juiciest moron I've ever met."

"That's better. Kiss me, Hap."

Her eagerness daunted him. He would have preferred sobs and a hopeless struggle. She was so young and unpracticed that she did not comprehend the game he was playing. She gave him the "Maja Desnuda" and what he really wanted was "September Morn."

"No," he said. "I don't want to kiss you."

"Why not?"

"I'm not in the mood."

"Well, I am!"

"Tough shit. You'll just have to suffer."

"Please. I'll be nice to you."

"How will you be nice to me?"

She told him.

"Not good enough. We've already done that. Can't you think of something we haven't done?"

"But, Hap, we've done everything."

"Not everything. I'll think of something. I'm very imaginative."

"Yes, you are. I never knew . . . Oh, Hap, it's been a wonderful summer. Just wonderful! The best summer of my life. The very best. I've changed. Don't you think I've changed?"

"No doubt about it."

"I've become a woman. I really believe that. When the summer started I was just a girl, but now I'm a woman. Aren't I a woman, Hap?"

"You're a woman."

"I've done so much this summer. I've learned so much. Now I know what life is all about."

"I can't take much more of this crap."

He bent to kiss her, to shut her mouth, and Samuel Lees, crouching painfully behind the bramble, wriggled with delight. About time. Now maybe that feller would take her clothes off and do those things to her again. They was a long time starting, but now they was starting.

Hapgood Graves pushed up her skirt. He touched the skin on the inside of her thigh, just above the knee.

"That's as soft as you are," he told her. "As tender. Tanned, with golden hairs. Warm. Now why should a little piece of skin like that mean so much? It's just skin. Everyone has skin. But your skin is enough to make me believe in God."

She straightened her leg. "Do you really think I can become a dancer?"

"What? Oh. Sure. I was young once. I had skin like that."

"Hap, you're not so old."

"Not much over three hundred. I wonder if that's why I do it?"

"Do what?"

Do what he did to her. Age punishing youth? It might be as simple as that. Experience seducing innocence? He dug deeper. It might be that hope came to her so easily while he had to suffer for it. Her easy hope offended him. He was an old, old cardinal who doubted the efficacy of prayer, and here this kid priest came along with cheerful babbling: "Now I lay me down to sleep . . ."

"I told Bobbie it's because when you have cancer you want everyone else to have cancer. That's closer to the knuckle."

"Hap, you don't have cancer, do you? Would you like daddy to examine you?"

"Oh, Christ. No, I would not like daddy to examine me. He'd never find it."

"He's a very good surgeon."

"If he cut into me the stench would blind him. No, moron, I do not have cancer. Do you believe in evil?"

"Evil?"

"E-v-i-l. Evil. 'Live' spelled backwards. It's an acquired taste. Like black olives and chocolate-covered halvah. But once tried, never denied."

"Hap, did you sniff before you met me?"

"No," he lied. "This is the real Hapgood Graves talking. The one and only. The original and nonpareil. Lecher, fornicator, thief, liar, seducer, cheat, sodomist, addict, fancyboy and all-around no-goodnick. Oh, God, if I could only feel guilt."

"About what?"

He looked at her. "Succubi your baby with a Dixie Malady," he sang. "And if I could only be as brainless as you. I have brains, but something else seems to be missing. What do you suppose it is?"

"I don't know."

He knew. The word was "soul," but it was so pretentious he could not utter it without grinning foolishly. He was a plastic man who had to teeter on the edge of a cliff before he could feel.

"You know what life is?" he demanded.

"What?"

"It's the fucking libretto of an Italian opera."

"Hap, you're funny."

"You have no idea how funny."

"You're shivering. Are you cold?"

"Someone's walking on my grave."

Suddenly, without warning, he pushed her over backwards onto the moss. He yanked up her skirt and buried his face in her satiny belly. She felt something on her skin. It might have been rain.

It ended as abruptly. He pulled away and tugged her skirt down. He stood shakily and brushed his knees. He reached a hand, hauled her to her feet.

So soon? Sam Lees groaned.

"Listen," she said breathlessly, "if the storm really does hit, daddy will have to go to the hospital. He'll probably sleep there. If it gets really bad, I'm supposed to go over to the Patroon's house. But I'll be alone for a while at least and you can come over. I'll tell daddy you came to keep me company because I was afraid. And we can be alone. You know? I mean in my bedroom. In my bed. It'll be the first time we've been in bed together. Hap? What do you think?"

"We'll see. We can't plan it. We'll just see what happens and play it by ear."

"All right. But won't it be wonderful? We'll get high and do all kinds of groovy things. It'll be a marvelous way to end a marvelous summer!"

## 37

A torn moon raced through a ragged sky. Wind wrapped the house in an endless sough. It came from high up, far out. Flashes tore the black reaches. Air hissed in that fused world.

Inside, closeted and warm, the Patroon listened to the crackle. But there was a stout roof overhead. The heater was glowing, all golden and rosy. Light pressed back the darkness. And he breathed sweet human odors, flowers and bedding, waxed floors.

His velvet wife worked away in her bentwood rocker, swaying gently and smiling. Her nimble fingers twirled long bone needles. And the purple scarf inched off her lap.

He gazed at that pert, vacant face with an affection so intense it was almost love. Steel spectacles were about to slip off her little nose. Her strawberry-hued wig was tipped askew. And there were those soft lips he once held between his teeth. Her young innocence radiated, and when he laughed with joy she looked up, poking her glasses back in place.

"Mister Vanderhorst?"

He had been pondering how to say it. To speak of death to this woman seemed to him as vicious as striking an infant or kicking a pup. He wanted her to be, always, a stranger to hurt, to know nothing but rainbows and dawns, to drink tea, gather shells, knit, and love God.

"Grace," he said gently, "I know it disturbs you to talk of such things, but it's sensible and it's necessary. So if I should die before you, you will know exactly what I have planned. Can we talk about it now?"

"I am sure you have done the right thing. You know how confused I get, dear. Do you have your pills with you? I really don't understand it all."

"The pills are on the bedside table. Grace, there is very little to understand. The bank and David Ballinger have their instructions. David has a copy of my will. Cousin Joseph has agreed to act as executor. All this is in a sealed envelope in the safety deposit box. The key is in the upper drawer of my desk in the big house. With a tag on it. Clearly marked."

"I do wish he didn't drink quite so much."

"Who is that?"

"Joseph. His Dorothy told our Rebecca that he sometimes has three cocktails before dinner."

"In all honesty, I do not believe that rules him out as executor of my estate. He is an honest man."

"He was a funny little boy. Such a tease. Once we went skating at the lake, and he sneaked back into the stove-house and tied everyone's shoelaces together in hard knots."

"Yes. Also in the safety deposit box you will find a short list of things I would like you to do in the event of my death."

She looked up, eyes glistening behind frail glasses.

"Grace, there is no need to cry. I am just trying to be prudent in case something should happen to me."

"Nothing is going to happen to you."

"I don't believe anything *will* happen. But if it should, I want to leave my affairs in order."

"It doesn't matter. I don't want to be in your will. You can take care of the girls and—and Rebecca. And Tom. But if anything happens to you, I don't want to go on living. I will kill myself."

"Grace, Grace." He pushed clumsily to his feet, stumped over to her chair. He put a hand lightly on her shoulder. "Dear Grace."

She turned her head to the side, rubbed a tender cheek against his knuckles. "I will, sir. I will kill myself. I don't want to go on living without you."

He grunted something and swung away. He dragged himself to the oak barometer on the wall, inspected it with blind eyes.

"I want the Bartholomew Brothers to handle things. I do not want to be buried by that smart aleck Jason Wolfe. Is that clear?"

She nodded dumbly.

"It's all in the letter I am leaving for you. In the safety deposit box. You will find complete instructions. Draw on your joint account for out-of-hand expenses until the will goes to probate. And I don't want to hear any more nonsense about your killing yourself. The girls will need you."

He went back to his armchair and fell into it heavily. He sat brooding, hands clasped on the head of his stick. He listened to wind sigh and hollow sea boom, threaded through with the comforting click of bone knitting needles.

"They won't need me," she said finally, faintly. "No one needs me. No one has ever needed me."

He was sick with the knowledge of the wrongs he had done her: infidelities and treacheries, some large, some shamefully petty. Did she know? Could she guess? He wondered dismally if a man can act—in anything, anywhere, at any time—without corroding faith.

"I have needed you," he said somberly. "Since the day we met. That is the truth, Grace, and you must know it. You have made a home for me. I don't mean just four walls and meals served on time. I mean a *home*. A warm place where I am safe. Where I know I am loved and exist. How else would I know I exist? If it wasn't for you. You are a very special kind of mirror for me."

Needles went tickling away in the cocoon. The purple scarf crawled to the floor. Her thin shoulders were bowed, sweetly submissive. Those dear hands were worn.

The wind began to gust. Windows rattled. The sea crunch was closer. Blue light slit the night. A few moments later thunder grumbled, cracked, grumbled again, went fading off.

"Grace, do you remember that time we went to Montreal? Four or five years after we were married."

"I do believe it was five years, Mister Vanderhorst. I was carrying Julie at the time."

"Yes. That is so. There was a man in the hotel dining room."

"A fat little man with a pointy mustache? And the waiter spilled soup over him?" She was smiling now. "Oh, yes! I do remember. And do you remember Abel Krudza's wedding reception when his father became tipsy and upset the punch bowl? Oh, my!"

"Yes," he said. He was smiling now. "And my birthday when you and the girls—"

Somewhere a window shattered. Broken glass tinkled down.

## 38

"How was *that?*" Benjamin Todd asked.

"What do you want—a medal? It was all right," Bobbie Vander said. "I've had better and I've had worse."

She got out of bed and padded naked to the window. She pulled the curtain aside, stared at the sea.

"Jesus, will you look at that. Those waves must be twenty feet high. They're coming up to the house."

"My God," he said. "You've got no ass at all."

"That right. I'm just one big crack. Listen, doc, you think the water might get up here?"

"Might. Five years ago the tide came all the way up, across the access road and flooded the marsh."

"What happened?"

"Nothing happened. A few trees got knocked down. Some windows were broken and some lawn furniture washed away. Then the water soaked in. Ruined the lawn. I had to resod."

"Well, I don't like it."

"Nothing you can do about it."

She came back to the bed. She sat on the edge and turned from the waist to stare at him.

"You're a fatalistic bastard—you know that? The next thing you'll be saying is 'What will be, will be.' Yes, there is something I can do about it. I can get out of this pisshole as fast as I can and never come back."

"You don't really mean that."

"Don't tell me what I mean or don't mean. Ben, you should have let me do it. I told you to let me do it. I like it better that way. I like to be in control. And I know tricks you haven't even dreamed of."

"I doubt that. I may not have done them, but I've dreamed of them."

"Well, I've done them. Christ, you're a hairy ape. Why don't you let me shave you?"

"No thanks."

Susan gone, somewhere, he had asked Bobbie over for a drink. She said she would come. She said she wouldn't. She would. She wouldn't. Her uncertainty stunned him. *This* woman?

The afternoon had been a cyclone: alternating spasms of malignant bitchery and loving warmth. He had never seen a woman so torn: the storm without, the storm within.

She gestured wildly. Her speech became increasingly profane. She seemed eager to disgust him. She pled for rejection. She acted the fool. She parted her thighs and mocked him. And when he tried to embrace her, she knocked his hands aside and then suddenly hurled herself on him, sobbing.

His love for her included so much fear it was almost a religion. He had never before loved such a force. She bewildered him. She made him feel that when he entered her, he came close to the mad heart of life. There was no victory, for either, but both knew a pristine sublimity.

She went back to the window again to gloom at the sea. She was a hairless sprite. There was nothing blooming about her body. She was all roots.

"I don't like it," she repeated.

"Why not?"

"I told you—I like to control things. It scares me."

"Scares you? You're the girl who went in swimming at midnight. Remember that?"

"I remember. The night you hit me."

"I thought you promised to forget that."

"I haven't."

"I told you I was sorry."

She shivered and let the curtain fall. "The Patroon figures it'll hit tomorrow night. He doesn't think it'll miss us."

"Even if it misses by fifty miles, we'll get plenty. In fact, sometimes it's better when you get the eye. That can be a calm. When you get the winds around the eye, you're in real trouble. Listen, Bobbie, I wanted to ask . . . I'll probably go to the hospital tonight or tomorrow morning. If things get bad, I'll sleep there over the weekend. Susan wants to stay here, but she promised to go over to your place if things get rough. Will you keep an eye on her?"

"'An eye on her'? Like the eye of the storm?"

"You know what I mean. Will you watch out for her?"

"No."

"No? Why not?"

"I don't want the responsibility. I'm not a den mother. Let the kid look out for herself. She's old enough."

"You're sweet, you are."

"That's right. Light me a cigarette, will you."

"That's the fifth you've had this afternoon. I didn't know you smoked so much."

"I don't. Usually. But that damned sea has got me nervy. I don't like the way it pounds and crashes out there. And that fucking wind has been wailing for three days. Just light me a cigarette and stop playing doctor."

She came over and lay down beside him. She took the lighted cigarette.

Her breast was still, but inside she felt all the functions of her body and heard their music: surge of lungs, slam of heart, gush of blood, and in her groin a hot ticking. She had never before been so alive, and she was awed.

The first time she had taken Dexedrine, she had been fragmented. Her mind split into a thousand jagged wedges, and she had more power than she could endure. Then she felt like a sheet of safety glass, hammered and starred, but held together by an invisible bond. She felt like that now.

She apologized. Not to Ben Todd but to herself, for her betrayal. She had "gone over," and had not been bribed nor tortured beyond withstanding. Something even now singing in her veins had been her undoing: a germ, a virus. And the first symptom was a sprouting perception that words were symbols of a myth that might explain her.

"Hold me," she said.

He took her in his arms. "Why you poor little dear," he quoted, laughing, "you're trembling, aren't you?"

"Go fuck yourself."

"An anatomical impossibility."

"That's what *you* think. I saw it done once in Mexico."

"You're joking."

"Sure. I'm joking. Just hold me and shut up."

"My God, you're thin."

"You want pork chops, go jump Julie. You want smoked turkey—you got it." She sang lightly: "Come live with me, my darling."

"What's that?"

"Hap's latest. The final song for our album. We're all finished."

"Sing it for me."

"I don't know it. We were supposed to rehearse it yesterday, but something was wrong with Hap. The fantods or the vapors. Something. Anyway, he didn't feel like working. We'll go over it next week. Nice tune."

"Please sing it."

"I told you I haven't got it. I'll give you all I remember of the first chorus. It's a folk-songy kind of thing. Goes like this:

> 'Come live with me, my darling,
> And find the land where wonders grow.
> A world of joy and sweet delight
> Da-*da*-da-*da*-special glow.'

That's all I remember."

"It's lovely. Very haunting. 'Come live with me, my darling.' All right. I'll come live with you."

"What the hell would I want you for?"

"You could shave me."

"No thanks."

Once more she got out of bed. She ground her cigarette to dust, went over to the window. She pulled the curtain aside again, stared at the sea.

Waves lurched up in frenzy, boiled over, hissed, and then came cracking down. She heard the boom, saw froth pillows and floating spume. Troughs were so deep that bottom showed. Then walls of black water shoved high. There were logs, dead fish, flotsam. The birds had gone.

"What's *with* you?" he asked.

"Ahh, screw it!" she said. "What can it do to me? Right?"

She sat up in bed alongside him, clutching her knees. He saw her raptorial profile, one eye searching. He leaned forward to kiss her muscled arm. She looked at him, then unexpectedly put a stiff thumb in his mouth.

"Suck," she said.

Gently he pulled her hand away. She wiped her wet thumb on his thigh.

"Bobbie, when are you going?"

"In a few minutes. Don't rush me. Oh, I know fellers like you. Fellers like you just want whatever they can get from a girl, and then fellers like you cast us away as if we were careless trifles. Oh, you fellers are all alike. You just want to work your evil way, and—"

"Will you just shut up for a minute? You know what I mean. When are you and Graves going back to New York?"

"Next week. Probably on Friday."

"Then what?"

"Then what *what?* We hole up in New York. More rehearsals. Lots of hard work. We do the album. Fights and screaming. Some interviews. Maybe some crap shows on TV. Then we go on circuit again. This year I think we start out on the Coast and work our way east. Concerts, nightclubs, one-night stands, college proms. Vegas for Christmas. Down to New Orleans for the Mardi Gras. Back to Chicago. The usual shit."

"What's going to happen?"

"I just told you."

"I mean to us."

"Oh. Us. Well . . . we're going to get married and live happily ever after."

"Can't you be serious?"

"No."

"Are you just going away? Going out of my life? Forget all about me?"

"That's right."

It was shameful to surrender gladly and kiss her chains. She could not in one lewd afternoon or one sensuous summer repudiate what she was and what she had vowed.

Nothing irrevocable had happened. She might still save herself. But the discipline she prized was benumbed. She was swimming for her life in a cold sea, and as much as she told herself to kick and strike out, she became leaden and overcome by an inscrutable languor. So the weary swimmer, strength hamstrung by terror, ends by thankfully seeking the deep, the unknown deep, the peaceful and enveloping deep.

He lay back. He turned onto his side, his broad back to her. "I thought it meant more to you than that," he muttered.

"You thought wrong."

"It meant more to me."

"Did it?"

He whirled around suddenly and sat up again. He stared at her hard eyes. "I don't believe it. Bobbie, I just don't believe it."

"You don't want to believe it."

"All right—I don't want to believe it. You mean I'm just a fast screw? Is that all I mean to you? Just someone handy you can go to bed with? Is that all?"

"That's all. Just like Julie was to you."

He wrenched out of bed. He pulled on his undershorts, stalked about the room, breathing deeply. He had the chest of a basso profundo. Finally he stopped and glared at her. "You're disgusting. Disgusting!"

She smirk-grinned at him. "What are you bitching about? You got your rocks off, didn't you?"

He took quick steps over to the bed. He grabbed for her with quivering hands. She made no move, just sitting there. Then she slowly straightened her legs, sat leaning against the headboard, arms folded.

"Go ahead," she said softly. "Touch me and I'll kill you. I don't know how I'll do it. Scissors, knife, gun. Somehow. But if you put a mean hand on me, I swear I'll do it. But before you die I'll cut your cock off and jam it down your throat."

He stood shocked at the curdling venom. He looked at her and didn't doubt. A steel shutter had rattled up. It was a whole new life, a world he never knew. He breathed a new gas. It was piercing, something that heightened awareness and tingled nerve ends.

"You would," he said.

"Yes." She nodded. "You better believe it."

And as suddenly the shutter was down, she was back, here and now, smiling. She relaxed, spreading her legs, shoving and scrunching down into the bed. She reached for him with pliant arms, fluttering her fingers.

"Take off those stupid bloomers and come hold me," she commanded. "I don't like the sound of that sea."

"There," she said later. "I told you it would be better if you let me do it."

But he wasn't listening. He was lost, gone somewhere. "Da-*da*-da-*da*-da-special glow." He was out of himself and tumbling, circling the eye of the storm in a tightening spiral. And suddenly he fell into that calm float, drifting, round and around, slowing.

"Did I hurt you?" she asked him.

"Yes. I don't know. I guess so. I know I ache."

"You'll get over it."

He opened sticky eyes. He saw her through a blur. She lay on her side, head propped on her hand. Turgid nipples stared at him.

"No. I won't get over it."

He reached to touch and noted coldly that his hand was trembling. His square fingertips traced bumps of ribs, soft indentation of waist, flare of hip, hard thigh.

He cleared his eyes on her, and the certitude grew in him that he was close to a cataclysmic change. No. Not change so much as revelation, followed by sudden budding and growth.

Now the significance he had sought all his life seemed tantalizingly close. It was there, on the tip of his heart, but his recognition of it was bridled by the hopelessness of his love.

Unless . . . unless the curb itself might be the clue. A love without hope was not a love without worth. Perhaps he had not been so far from the mark when he gave to Bobbie's question, "What is love?" the answer, "A kind of sacrifice."

It grew increasingly clear. He could put it into words now and extend its value: "A losing cause is better than no cause at all." He walked all around it, inspecting. It was sturdy, without frills, demanded work. It was his style and would give meaning to his life.

"If I ask you to marry me, to give up your career and marry me, will you do it?"

"No."

"If I ask you to marry me, and you can keep on singing, keep your career, travel wherever you want, but just let me see you occasionally—will you do that?"

"No."

"Will you let me travel with you? Just to be with you?"

"Forget it. You haven't a prayer."

"God, you're hard."

"That's right."

"I love you, Roberta."

"Why not? I'm a very lovable kid."

"I can't let you go. I *can't*. There must be some way . . ."

"There is no way. I told you, Hap does my fetching and carrying. And he's a hell of a musician. What do I need a private doc for? Besides, you'd never last."

"I swear, I—"

"You couldn't stand the pace. You've got no idea what it's like. You're too soft. Stay in South Canaan, doc. This shit-kicking town is your speed."

"Strange."

"What's strange?"

"I'm saying foolish things. I'm acting like a fool. I know I am. But I don't care. You're more important to me. If you said pack up and come, I'd do it. I'd leave everything and go with you. I'd walk away from everything and go with you. If you said the word."

"Don't worry. I'm not going to say the word."

"What am I going to do without you?"

"Beat your meat probably. Better yet, why don't you marry Julie? She's a sweet girl."

"I don't love Julie. I love you."

"Love? What the hell is love?"

"Don't you know?"

"Not me, kiddo. I just sing about it."

"You told me that, but I don't believe you. You want it. I know you do. Or you couldn't sing the way you do."

"Forget it. It's just a word. Use 'shit' instead of 'love' and after a while the songs sound just the same. 'Shit, your magic spell is everywhere.' 'I'm in the mood for shit.' 'I think I'm falling in shit.' I could sing love songs that way, and it'd tear your heart out. I told you it's a con game."

She was defeated by the oppression of words. She could not express, even to herself, her unfamiliar needs except in those sleazy phrases by which she earned her way. She was the undertaker, to whom sorrow is profit, suddenly faced with a death in his own family.

But the sterility of those phrases was also her defense. The words smelled to her of empty nightclubs and cold cigars. She would not sing her own love song to Ben. She could not.

"Oh, God," Todd brooded, "what am I going to do?"

"Go on, marry Julie. She's a good lay. Maybe a little lazy, but you won't have any trouble in bed. And she's a good cook. You know, plain stuff like steaks and roasts and meat loaf."

"No hope for me?"

"Not with me there isn't."

"I want to die."

"So die already. I got to get dressed and get back. First I think I'll wash some of your sweat off me. Jesus, you sweat like a horse. Did you ever notice that sex sweat smells different from regular sweat?"

She went to the bathroom. He heard the sound of the shower. She began to sing "It's De-Lovely." After a while he got out of bed, pulled on a robe. Just as he got to the bathroom door, she turned off the shower and pulled back the curtain.

She was slick steel, milled smooth in glistening planes and compound curves, all oiled with steam.

She looked at him without expression.

"I love you," she said.

# ────── 39 ──────

Hurricane Ava rushed toward the coast. The cruel eye glared down upon Portsmouth, Kittery Point, Kennebunkport. Winds flattened Portland, and great tides sank more than two hundred small boats off Chebeague Island and Boothbay Harbor. A state-wide emergency was declared; the National Guard was mobilized.

As the storm approached, swirling winds brought rain, and sometimes hail, of such fury that windows were shattered and metal roofs flattened. In some homes, doors were sucked outward, rugs and furniture moved toward the giant vacuum. The ripped sky filled with planks, shingles, shards of glass. Near Bath a highway patrolman was decapitated by a flying snow shovel.

Tides measured twenty feet above normal. Small boats not crushed at their moorings were plucked up and flung inland. Beachfront homes went down in splinters or buried beneath a flood of muck. Wells were poisoned by salt, and the path of the cataclysm could be followed by failing lights as local power stations blacked out, and radio and TV stations went off the air. Hospital corridors were jammed with dead and injured. As casualties continued to come in, schools and churches were used to shelter the wounded and homeless.

The agony lasted almost three hours. Then, suddenly, a calm descended, more frightening than pound of wind and tide. Weatherwise residents were not tempted to venture outside. For this was the pitiless eye of the storm, and as it passed over, the air was still, almost breathless. Rain dribbled away; the sea seethed. Then the eye slid away northeastward, and once again the rains came, winds howled, the sea proved its strength. Lightning ripped open the night; thunder cracks set dogs yelping, and farm animals stampeded in terror.

South Canaan, sheltered in curving horns of cliff, awaited the assault.

Wind began building up on Wednesday and by Saturday had reached gale force. With it came rain, first in lines, then sheets, then solid walls. Surprisingly warm at first, it cooled through that week until on Saturday afternoon it had the stab of sleet, the bludgeon of hail. The marsh behind the access road filled rapidly. Soon trees were poking from water stippled by the driving rain. Animals fled inland; motorists on Route 9-A6 slammed on brakes to avoid hitting rabbits, wild dogs, squirrels, raccoons, a frenzied doe; and crawling things sought branches and rocks above the rising waters.

The Indian cemetery was flooded. A single faded pennant tied to a lance ripped in the wind.

On Saturday morning the Patroon fought his way outside. He stood grasping a porch pillar. His white hair flung: Moses in a whirlwind. His marveling eyes searched the coast.

His God was not a kindly gaffer with chin whiskers. God was sea, sky, stars, and the sweet dirt. God was the coming around of seasons, bloom and blight, flood and drought, calm and storm, all the movements of this sounding earth and its echoes.

The sea slammed in with a complexity of currents, a puzzle of tides. He saw monstrous waves, crests unbroken, roll on to smash their weight against stone cliffs. He felt the ground tremble, earth shaken by this primitive collision. The ocean was halfway across his lawn. As he watched, brown spume came bubbling up to stain the white steps beneath his feet.

He had no fear for his home; he knew its strength. But he also knew the fantastic whims of a storm: a roof peeled off and flung aloft; shutters jerked down; sudden flooding; a ruffian wind that inserted steel prods into every chink, prying.

A hundred yards offshore, unaccountably, a bare-masted yawl snapped on the waves. He saw no one aboard. It yearned up, spanked down. As he watched, it broke up, shredding away to cracked planks. The Patroon turned, pulled himself back into the house. He closed and bolted the door.

Darkness came shortly before noon. It rolled in from the sea, billowing, greasy as smoke. It covered the land. Benjamin Todd, driving to the hospital, switched on his lights. He leaned forward to peer through the murk.

The funereal symphony grew. A shrill dirge of wind thrust through the sea rumble. The harsh lash of rain made a discordant chorus to solo bursts of thunder. Gun cracks were everywhere in the black sky, following daggers of green-white fire that stabbed sight and left an after-image that burned.

It was a demented world. Fear grew as order disappeared. Docile, familiar nature had turned raw beast. Men hunched their shoulders and spat. Women soothed the wails of scream-eyed children. Now the darkness was in them. Death came on the wind. Nothingness was all about.

It boiled on. There was a cavern out there, booming with madness. Torn screeches banged down lost corridors. It was the exultant howl of the brute. There was no end to it.

## ————40————

They were ruined in their dream, Hapgood Graves and Susan Todd. The wrinkled sheet was brassed with tarnished light and their own damp stains. Outside the world tore itself apart, biting. They were lost to it.

"In my novel . . ." he said. "The one I've been writing . . . it so happens . . . " He made a thin, epicene gesture, then lifted her hand, regarded it gravely, placed it upon his face. The hot palm was down, pressing his nose flat, muffling his mouth, fingers poking at his lidded eyes.

She offered a happy moan and brought her bare knees up tight to kiss them. The golden arms and legs barred his pale flesh. A rain bird beat heavy wings against window glass. Who knocked on the roof? She took her hand away to suck his bruised tongue.

He cried out with merriment and delight. They laughed together, lapping. His long prehensile toes pried into her and scratched. "Now that," she said, and shook her fist at God when thunder cracked, the house moved.

He slid through her fingers. They lurched. "Is this it?" he

asked. Light turned violet; they waited for denunciation. It fluttered in them. They were ruffled doves.

"I could," he said, and "I could," she said, but the dream escaped, blown inland to crush a home. Sea roar swaddled them as she dutifully repeated the blank verse he had taught. Lights flickered, went off, came on again. He whispered something but she did not hear.

"I am the storm," she said sternly. Wind, rain, tide plundered his body. Flaccid, mouth open, he let her rage. He was afraid to taste lest his tongue stick to chilled steel. He heard a song he had never heard.

The silver pillbox grinned on the table. He reached. Elegantly they sniffed again, the mad dandies. They soared to a shimmering calm, then heard a raucous sea.

He slid from the bed and bowed deeply. He pressed heel into arch. He held a hand to her and simpered. She stumbled to him, touched his fingers. The ballet began.

How they flew! They went twirling and scraping, dipping in each other's arms. There was a little kiss, a little theatrical laugh: "Ha-*hah!*" And away they went.

Sportive, they paused a moment to consider their smeared reflection in the black window. They loved to see their images move, what they did. Tendrils of outside rain streaked their sweated skin.

The baton whipped. Storm music climbed and engulfed them. They swam naked through the beat, whirling, twisting, grasping. They ended crumpled on the floor, throwing kisses madly to the tumult.

They lay slackly, biting gently, nibbling.

"I *am* a dancer." She gasped, and he said, "*Danseuse.*"

Mouths were open, arms and legs spread wide. Each time the thunder cracked they pumped up to meet it. They were plundered by the storm. It was a game. They wailed with the wind: "Oooh-weee-ahhh-uuu-reee." They mimicked the rain's susurrus: "Ssss-wsss-ssss." They grumbled with the tide.

"Not 'boom,'" she chided, "but 'ca*room*'!"

*Caroom,* he thought, but did not speak. Her flesh was not chilled steel. His tongue peeled away easily. She had a gloss.

"Do you love me?" she asked dreamily.

"Mom," he answered.

A vagrant draft shivered them. Night came into the room. They rolled together.

"I love you," she said, wondering at the sweetness. "*I* love *you.*"

"Yes."

"And that's who I am."

"Who?"

"Now I know."

"Who? Who are you?"

"The love. Don't you understand? The love. For you. That's who I am."

"You love me?"

"Oh, yes."

"Truly?"

"Truly."

"Would you die for me?"

"Yes. Happily. No. I don't want to die. I want to love you."

"Well . . . at least you would suffer?"

"Gladly."

"Tits wrenched off with hot pincers? All that?"

"If I can love you."

"It's the dust."

"No. Without the dust. I love you without the dust."

"Liar."

"You don't believe me?"

"I believe you. But you don't know the truth. You just *think* you love me."

"Isn't that truth?"

He pondered a moment. "I can't stand a wise-ass."

He climbed slowly to his feet. "Come along." He stretched a hand for her. They lolled back into bed, pulled up the sheet. They lay nose to nose, staring into each other's eyes, hands slowly busy. When it hurt too much, their eyelids fluttered, eyes closed, eyes opened again to stare . . . sleepily.

"This is very rare," he lectured, "and you must never forget it. You will never again be as close to another human being."

"I know," she said drowsily.

"Also, I talk too much."

"I know."

Finally, lacerated by pleasure, they lay gasping, sharing one monstrous breath. The whole house shook with their vapor. They heard the groan and creak, the shiver of wood.

"I want to be you," he murmured.

"Mmm."

"I want to love. Hope. Maybe there is something. No. But perhaps. Sometimes I think . . . You brainless idiot. How sweet not to think. Only to feel. That is what I want. To go on floating. Everything and all. How marvelous! There's the joy. If you have enough money, of course. That's why I write love songs. I thought I had . . . Your body is a honeycomb. Is there truth in beauty? How many Palmolive wrappers does it take to shingle a boxcar? Now you know who you are but who am I? Three months ago I knew. Have you corrupted me? Can innocence corrupt? A nice point, professor. So who won? Tell me that, oh, wise one. Have I made a fatal error or are you fatally correct?"

"What?"

He sat up in bed and yawned. He stretched wide his thin arms. He cocked his head, listened to the end of the world.

"And now, sweet moron, I suggest we bathe our juices away."

She was lying in the tub, jets from the shower splaying off her burnished skin. He stood naked, adding his stream to the hot spray. She laughed delightedly, jutting her body up, offered out to meet.

"There is much to be said for despair." Hapgood Graves nodded.

Samuel Lees stood knee-deep in a pudding of sand and sea. Oilskin turned the rain, but beneath seeped an old man's sweat: fear and longing. He embraced a tree, the hard young body in his arms, between his legs.

Above, the lighted square was calm: eye of his own storm. He had seen naked dancers jerking behind glass, rainstreaked and wriggling. Gone now; still he endured to stare. They might reappear. They might . . . If only he had his field glasses. God *damn* that Indian kid . . .

Lightning and thunder moved inland. The sea was still rising, wind on the prowl. It tempted with a sudden drop, then gusted to a banshee wail that bent his tree like a willow wand. His old muscles ached. He wanted to be dry, warm and safe.

He took a last look at that golden opening to Sweet Jesus. It was blank. They were in there. The vision corroded him: acid in his stomach, a mouth of bitter grit.

He pushed the tree away, turned to the Vanderhorst home. Wind grabbed for his sou'wester; only the chin strap saved it. He bent from the waist, dug into steaming gruel with shuffling steps. Eyes were pinched shut, hands outstretched.

Light chinked from kitchen shutters. When he turned the knob, wind plucked the door from his grasp, slammed it to the opposite wall. Theodore leaped to his feet, all arched back and squeal. Lees fought the door shut.

Mrs. Rebecca Drinkwater stood at the sink, methodically peeling potatoes with her heavy knife. She looked around as he stumbled through the room. She did not speak to him nor he to her.

The old house twanged to the storm, humming of strained timber. But as Sam Lees dragged himself to the third floor, along the corridor, he heard another sound, a drumming.

He stopped outside the bedroom door of Tom Drinkwater. It was coming from in there: a primitive rhythm, a steady thump with a crippled counterpoint. He flung open the door.

"You gimme my glasses," he shouted. "Now God damn it, you gimme. Them's my glasses. Bought and paid for."

Tom Drinkwater in faded jeans, meshed singlet, left off his drumming. He put the finished Ikantos drum carefully to one side. Glossy black hair hung lankly to his shoulders. His eyes blazed at the old man.

"There are your glasses." He motioned toward the bookcase. "Take them."

Lees scuttled across the room. He grabbed up the binoculars and retreated to the door, not turning his back on the boy.

"You think," he yelled. Breath grabbed in his throat, sticking hot. "You think. I could."

The Indian boy stared. Age defeated Sam. It wasn't fair. It wasn't right.

"The two of them," he screamed suddenly, spitting to get it out. "Yessir, the two of them! What do you think of that, boy? Right up there in her bedroom. Hey? All alone they is. Old man to the hospital. And them naked. *Naked* I tell you!

Susan and that Graves feller. Dancing naked. Bare-assed the two of them. Doing God knows what. But we know—don't we, boy? All alone and naked. Now you tell me what the two of them are doing. Hey? You just tell me. And I can tell you . . ."

His voice dribbled away, spittle on a bristly chin. As he watched, rheumy eyes rounding in terror, the boy stood. He stretched up tall, thin, dark and hard. Skin snagged tight on his skeleton. Cheekbones poked white. Ten fingers spread, pulled taut, trembling.

Tom Drinkwater moved slowly. His bare feet slapped on floorboards toward the door. As he passed the bookcase one arm floated up of its own will, free. Fingers grasped the handle of the stone ax: massive head attached to ash shaft with rawhide thongs.

Lees stumbled backward into the hall, one arm thrown up to ward off the blow. His shoulders hit the far wall. He slid . . . slowly . . . down to a crumpled heap of yellow oilskins. Old eyes were bleary with tears. But the boy stalked by and left him snuffling. Samuel Lees, choking, grabbed at the chin strap of his sou'wester. The button popped off, rolled away and was gone.

Tom Drinkwater slid in a dawdling dream, ax tapping gently against his thigh. He wafted down the stairs, around the entrance hall, into the kitchen. Each step was a reverie: pull of muscle in his leg . . . knee bending . . . foot rising . . . body sloping . . . sole touching floor.

His mother's head came up like a blossom softly blown. She turned slowly to look. Even the clatter of the knife as it fell from her hand lasted and lasted: tip of knife clinking to sink . . . blade clanging . . . handle thudding down. He heard it all, in all its separate parts: beads on an endless string.

Her left hand drifted to her breast. Her right hand floated out to him. Her lips twisted lazily and came apart. When she moved to stop him, she swam through bloated air, dress billowing like a summer cloud.

He glided uphill to the Todd house with torpid grace. Rain was a gentle drizzle, wind a kissing breeze. The sea unfolded quietly on the beach, each wave in soothing cadence. He strolled around the front . . . and up the steps . . . and onto the porch . . . and through the door . . . and up the stairs . . . and into the bedroom, lulled and soaring.

There. They. Were.

They lay side by side, frail white and warm gold. Eyes were closed. They were breathing faintly. Inside arms were crossed so they could hold each other in their undream.

Tom Drinkwater rowed through sweated air to stand at the bedside. Weaving gently, swaying, he saw Graves' pale skin was marked with veins: a tracing of blue ink, a map to nowhere. A tiny bubble was shining on his lips.

The ax was going up. Lightning flashed like a strobe light: up, up, up, with smears between. The Indian boy stretched high to one long muscle. Knuckles of both hands were sallow on the shaft. Up. Up. Flecks of mica glinted in the great stone head.

He was onto his toes, calves and thighs tight, quivering.

The ax started down, the slow voyage home, the fall, drifting downward. Again, seen through a stroboscope: down, down, down. Extension: stone to wood to flesh. His elbows were locked, arms corded. Down.

Quake. In stone, wood, and on through hands, arms, shoulders. The ax struck high on Hapgood Graves' brow, at the hairline. It crushed through skin, bone, gristle, into the gray mystery of the man. He did not move.

A bouquet of red flowers bloomed up. Crimson gouts spread in a slow crown. They sailed in graceful curves to strike walls, floor, face, and body of Tom Drinkwater.

Where each blossom struck, a clot appeared with tapering tentacles radiating. At the end of each was a dot of red like a period. Blood rained. It whispered down. The dead man's head, cracked open, showed its crawling secrets to the world.

Tom bent against a hot rain he smelled but could not see. He pressed to the other side of the bed. He pulled his eyes from her nakedness, fearing his strength would drain away and pride melt down to scalding tears.

She moved! Her body moved even as the ax floated upward to stretch his arms. He was heaving downward— stone tied from above, something holding it back—when her eyes opened slowly. She looked at him.

The blunt and bloody edge struck into that open right eye. It cleaved into, down, through cheek, lips, crumbled teeth, chin. A cool, unseeing left eye watched a fountain bubble up. No jet here, but a steady spring, thick gurgle that lifted, spread, fell back.

He looked down at his hands. He willed them to unclasp, but they would not. Ax embedded in jaw and throat, still his fingers were fastened tightly to the slippery handle. Until he bent forward to bite his own hands. Then his fingers flew wide. He was free.

There was a ruby haze. He could taste its rank sweetness. It was everywhere in the room. In him. He turned away, peering through the sifting fog.

He waded to the door, slipping once on  .  .  . He faded to his knees. He rose again to float away. But now he was moving faster. Clock hands came unstuck, time ticking to a normal rhythm.

He heard the hard crunch of waves, lament of wind, whip crack of rain and sleet. There was a far-off flicker of lightning, a cough of thunder. It was all coming close again. The storm raced. Time raced. Life hurried to be done.

He slammed the kitchen door and slumped, weary shoulders against wood. He looked to his mother. Had she moved since he had gone? One hand was to her breast, one flung out to stop him. Had he been gone? Or fancied . . .

But then she saw red designs on his face and clothes, his dripping hands. Her face decayed; he knew he had been gone. She slumped to her knees, fractured. He stalked without speaking. When the door to the entrance hall stopped swinging, she saw his track: sand, sea, rain, all tinted pink. Her wail began.

Samuel Lees had not moved. He sat on the floor of the upstairs corridor, his back against the wall, yellow oilskins spread wide. He was weeping noisily, coughing, snuffling, choking, spitting tears.

Tom Drinkwater stepped over him, into his room. He reached for his drum. Darkness. Power failed; all lights went off. Splits of cold lightning stabbed through shutter clefts.

Ring alarum and wild excursions! Cries from the girls' room. Pound of running feet. The Patroon's deep rumble. Then, from the black kitchen, a knife-edged shriek that scraped marrow from bones, scratched along shriveled spines.

Shouts. Spurts of lighted matches. Bobbing lanterns. Pale flashlight beams wavering. "Phones are dead!" Yells. Smash of glass. Curses, and somewhere on the roof an endless hammer.

Mrs. Grace Vanderhorst stood at the foot of the stairs. She lifted a lantern high, clutched a quilted robe. Wild eyes searched for meaning. Julie and Roberta found the kitchen with flashlights. The door banged wide to . . . They stepped with bare feet onto red-tinged tracks.

They rushed to their mother. Screams for Samuel Lees, for Hapgood Graves, for Tom Drinkwater, for the Patroon. Where were the men? Where was Rebecca? Bumpings and stumblings. Reflections of that shrill wail still bounced off walls, up stairs, down corridors. What?

Outside, the Patroon and Rebecca leaned into the torrent. He did not have his cane. His heavy arm lay across her shoulders. Her strong arm went about his waist. He carried a kerosene lantern. Its feeble light made a thin puddle around their feet, circling as the lantern swung. His nightshirt and her thin dress plastered against crawling skin. Hair was wet-tight against skulls.

Into the Todd house they went, calling the boy. Empty echoes. They wandered from room to room, staggering, those clinging twins. Then they dragged up the stairs, calling. Into the abattoir. Lantern held high, a rat's tail smoking from the wick. Calling.

They stood, looked, and knew it all: matter gray and coiling, splintered bone, shivers of teeth; his red-frothed smile; her open eye, calm and reflective; fresh-blood smell; the sheet wet and gleaming; crimson cordial on walls, floor, decking the room.

Their arms were still about each other. They turned to gaze at each other with eyes as black and dull as dry wells.

Without knowing why—never to know—they pressed cold, wet bodies together, pressed hot, seeking lips. It was a young kiss, lustful, full of promise and demand. They wrestled blunted tongues and gasped with live delight.

Still huddled, they fell away from that dread place. They went out to a cleaner rage, calling, calling. Their words were flicked away and shredded, or stamped to silence by sea roar.

They moved about aimlessly in widening circles, the swinging lantern raised high. Yellow flickered on the whirring rush of all things about them: cascade of surf, spray ripped away and dashed. Once again the inky night was streaked across with crackling arcs.

Rebecca's hand on the Patroon's arm stopped them. Beyond the brawl, below the brawl, they heard a man-made sound: the crippled cadence of a drum. They waded through gush. Boards were against their ankles, stones and shells underfoot, a tangle of weed and soft, slimy things that kissed and clung.

Tom Drinkwater stood waist-deep, braced, staring out to ever. The beloved Ikantos drum was in his arms. He heard their shouts and turned slowly. A stab of lightning touched him a blue-green wraith.

He flung the drum away, back, toward them. Then he waded down sturdily. They plunged after, weeping and calling, still with their arms about each other. They were endless twins. Their tears splattered far.

Until they could go no farther. They felt that awful pull. They stood deep, feet sinking into swirl. They were buffeted by the crash, foam bubbling faces and hair. They staggered in the sea smack, wiped their eyes and watched.

He waded out as far as he could go. Then he dived, came up, dived again, came up. Arms pumped strongly now, legs flashing. He was gone in darkness, then alive in lightning glare.

They strained forward as he dwindled. "Tom!" the Patroon shouted once, and "Son!" Hawk of defeat. The word came out harsh, jammed back into his twisted throat.

Until they saw only the wrangling sea. Still they

watched, waiting. But only the sea. And finally they turned, wearily, and pushed away. They trudged back to the home of Pieter Vanderhorst.

The front door yawned. In the glare of lanterns and flashlights the women waited in white. Grace came down into the filth-topped water. She took the Patroon by the other arm. She and Rebecca supported him. They pressed him into the house, into the dark house.

On the porch, Julie and Roberta aimed their flashlights into each other's wet faces.

"What?" Julie said. "I don't understand. What happened?"

"It's the Indian kid," said Roberta. "He pulled the Dutch act."

------------------------ **41** ------------------------

In the tar blackness before dawn the slickered police departed. They lifted their grisly burdens, swathed in rubber sheets, and whirred away with soft sirens. Coffee and answers had been served; reasons shunned for another day.

Another day? The Patroon thought it conceivable— logical, even—that the sun would not rise that morning anywhere. His life was dust; why not his god of dawn, seasons, and the cycle of years? Darkness was everywhere.

He came out onto his porch dragging a straight-backed kitchen chair. The brass telescope was clasped beneath his arm: officer of the deck of a foundered ship.

The littered beach was a dwarfs' battlefield. Lawn furniture was a jumble of twisted aluminum tubes, splintered wooden slats, torn canvas. The old oak lay on its side, hungry roots yearning to the lowery sky. Ocean garbage surrounded the house: rotting fish, weed, gummy planks, pitted boulders, and a piece of billboard that said ". . . when you . . ." in flaming red.

The Patroon sat stolidly through the false dawn, not moving. He heard the storm growl away to the northeast and watched far-off lightning flicker in the new sky like guttering candle flame.

The rearguard of summer had lost to winter's scouts. The sea had thickened, to quicksilver, and moved sullenly. The surface had tightened, the color frosted and turning the old sun's lemon light.

The after-storm sky was a swiftly unreeling curtain, spooling off a horizontal spindle. Moist gray went billowing and flapping, thin enough to show weak shadows racing. Rents in the curtain let through swift brushes of sunwash, then closed, and the world smelled of December.

He was on his feet, searching that desolate sea with his glass, focusing on each bobbing blot of flotsam, when the door opened behind him. Roberta brought him a mug of steaming coffee, laced with brandy. She was wearing jeans, a man's shirt, a sleeveless sweater that had belonged to Hapgood Graves.

When he took the telescope from his eye and sat heavily, she handed him the hot cup. Their fingers touched.

"Can you sleep?" she asked. "A little?"

"No."

"Ben is alone. I want to go over there."

He looked down at her. He stroked her cheek with his crippled hand, and it did not surprise him that he could move it.

"Yes," he said. "Do that."

"Patroon," she said, "I don't understand."

He was silent.

"Are there things that are unknowable?"

He smiled sweetly. "I fear so," he said.

He sipped his coffee slowly. After a moment she leaned to him and put her head against his knee.

"I thought life had spit me out," he said to no one. "As something bitter. Hard and old. It could not chew me and gave me up. But I was tricked. Made a fool of. It waited. Waited and laughed. I should have known."

"Don't blame—"

"Blame?" He caught her short. "What blame? There is no blame. No one is guilty. Each did what he had to do. Graves. Susan. Tom. We are all driven. Blame Theodore for breaking the spine of a field mouse?"

Their intimacy kept off the chill. They huddled, as they had in the workshop of the big house, when she was growing, when he led and she followed. They were warm together.

"Did you know he loved her so much?" she murmured.

"Tom? Yes. I knew."

He drained his coffee, set the empty cup aside. She took his hand. The fingers were still warm.

They stared at that leaden sea. It was all molten, waves heaving up but not cresting. Far out, above the horizon, a thin border of washed blue promised clearing. But the smell of salt and putrid things turned the air.

"Oh . . ." she said. "I don't know. I thought I did, but I don't. Patroon, do you remember when you told me that love corrupts?"

He nodded.

"You meant, didn't you, that the lover corrupts the loved

one? I mean, the loved one changes to fit the image—to fill out the image—the lover has. And by changing, becoming corrupted, the love is completed. Then it is no longer a mystery and it dies. Isn't that what you meant?"

He turned slowly and looked at her with a kind of horror.

"Roberta, Roberta. You have always thought me a more complicated man than I am. I was a sailor and a carpenter. You should have remembered."

"Then what *did* you mean?"

"Love corrupts. Simply that. It corrupts nothing, but love itself corrupts. As wood rots and iron rusts."

She was shocked. "But what corrupts love?"

He rose slowly to his feet. He raised the glass to his eye again and swept the lorn sea. He searched each bundle hurried in on the tide. Then, unaccountably, he reversed the glass and peered at a tiny world.

"Oh . . ." he said. "Time. And the weather."

He sat again with a codger's sigh of weariness. Her fingers touched deeper into his knee, and she turned her face to kiss the cloth. She saw bowed bulk, shoulders slumped, head hanging. That monument come crumbling down? His defeat was so unthinkable she sloughed it off.

"Patroon."

"Yes."

"Will you listen?"

"Yes."

"Something I must tell you. Ben Todd wants to go away with me. To marry me or travel with me. I said no. But Hap's death changes things."

He thought on that. "Perhaps Susan's death changed Todd. What he wants."

"Maybe. I don't think so. If anything, Susan's death cuts him free. Is that cruel?"

"Yes."

"Yes. But it's true. If he still wants to come, I want him."

"You love him?"

"Ahh." She shook her head disgustedly. "I don't know. I think so. I'm not sure. It's like learning a new language. I can speak it now, but I can't think in it. Yet."

A movement caught his eye. He pointed suddenly. The daisied lawn umbrella, beaten down in clotted sand, flapped its fringe. A horseshoe crab moved out, peered, scuttled down to wet. It dug, writhed in, and was gone.

"You know what that will do to your sister?"

"She'll get over it."

"Yes. She will. Will you?"

"Maybe. In a week, a month, a year. But maybe it'll take. No guarantee. You taught me to do, to follow what I felt, and do."

"Yes," he acknowledged sadly, "I taught you that."

"It'll be a can of worms, I know it. I'm the problem, not him. He knows exactly what he wants. Me. But I'm writing a love song. I don't know how it'll come out. Maybe it'll be the blues. You know? But maybe I can make it. Just maybe. What do you think, Patroon?"

He looked about at the churned beach, the stenched wreckage, all plowed up. The puzzle had been scrambled, pieces lying crazily, swollen, and never fitting quite the same again.

"I find it hard to think," he told her. "Of anything. I will just sit here and look through my telescope and try to find Tom."

He stood again, put the glass to his eye, began to sweep the sea slowly. He was a captain now, braced on the quarterdeck, and his loss had majesty.

"Your son?" she asked.

The telescope did not waver. He did not take it from his eye to look at her. She was not certain he had heard, and she repeated: "Your son?"

"I do not love you the less," he said steadily. "Or your mother. Or Julie."

"Patroon . . ."

"Go inside. The wind is sharp."

"I'll wait here with you."

"Thank you."

"There's no chance that he . . . ?"

"No. No chance. He is dead. I know that."

He sat again in his straight-backed chair, brooding at the sea. She moved closer so that her shoulder touched his knee. So they sat, and waited, and watched. A few birds came back.

## 42

Floodwaters drained away, leaving a gray scum upon the marsh. It dried to a thick crust and cracked. Edges of each segment curled up brown. The earth was a jigsaw of ill-fitting pieces.

Dross lay over the Indian cemetery. Stones, flags, banners, bottles, plaques: all encrusted and befouled. Only the plump grave of Tom Drinkwater showed turned earth. It was black and pungent, and it steamed in the pale sunlight.

Three days after the storm the broken body was tumbled

ashore near the Breckinridge place. The coroner, who examined the corpse, described it to Dr. Benjamin Todd as "a burlap sack of mush."

A quiet service was held in the Vanderhorst home. Members of the family and a few Indian friends attended. Afterward, mourners walked behind the slow-moving hearse to the graveyard. The Patroon also insisted on walking. His dead leg dragged, limp foot scuffing caked gravel.

At the graveside words were spoken. The pine coffin was lowered. Mourners departed, singly or by twos and threes, wandering down that lonely road between rows of trees savaged by the storm.

Only Mrs. Rebecca Drinkwater remained. She squatted, not caring that the hem of her best dress brushed the moist dirt. She patted smooth the mound over her son's grave. Then she cleaned away debris from her husband's grave and found again the brittle twig encircled by a greened wedding band.

From a paper shopping bag she took Tom Drinkwater's Ikantos drum. The heads of rabbit skin were pierced, but the tube itself was intact. She had tied it about with a wire of tiny glass beads of red and green and yellow and blue. She had tacked a single turkey feather to the wood.

She planted the drum upright, firm on her son's grave. She pressed it down into the soft loam where his heart might be. She bowed her head and wept dry tears.

Her education at the Indian mission had been one long sermon, preaching that pleasure must be paid for, and every happiness has its fee. All those skinny teachers with long faces and gaunt conscience . . . The dormitory smelled of mothballs.

But later, when she returned to the people of her tribe,

she learned the possibility of joy without guilt. There was much sin and laughter. Life was to be celebrated; weeping was for death.

The Patroon's love, and hers for him, opened her like a blossom spread to the sun. He was a deep man, and potent, and after love-making he spoke to her in a way that proved he cherished her presence and respected her worth.

She obeyed him, as an Ikantos squaw should. His demands were gentle, and if their love could not be public, it seemed a small thing. Their son was strong and handsome, a fitting reward for their unblemished passion.

And now his broken body lay beneath the earth, and she smelled mothballs once again. The bill for her happiness had been presented.

She began keening, head nodding to the monotonous rhythm of her lament. She had brought along a clean clam shell in the pocket of her dress. As she wailed she drew the ragged-sharp edge of the shell down the undersides of her lower arms. She made two long cuts on each arm, elbow to wrist.

Skin stretched open in shallow splits. Dark blood welled, slow at first, then faster. She let it gather, cover her hands, drip from her fingertips to soak into the steamy soil of the new grave.

A shelf of pewtered clouds drove swiftly across the sky, blanking the sun. A cool, damp wind huffed from the sea. The world was close, pressing in, and she was alone.

She crouched a long time, detailing the litany of her sorrow. Her wounds clotted; blood crusted on her arms.

Then she stood stiffly, looked about at the ruined Indian cemetery. All the memories were drowned and dried. But through the cracked earth came whispers.

She moved slowly to the gravel road and stopped. Birds

had returned to the swamp, and running, creeping, crawling animals. She heard barks, hoots, calls and whistles. There was a whir of wings and somewhere, high up, a squabble of gulls.

She looked to the left, toward the sea, to the house of Pieter Vanderhorst, home of the Patroon. She could see the surly ocean heaving in a crisscross pattern as the tide changed.

She turned her back to all of it. She moved to the right, bare feet scraping muddy gravel. She walked steadily, not looking back. Toward . . .

## 43

They twanged like stretched wires and sat peering into their raddled future. Misting rain spun a halo around the single streetlight, orange and dim. The gleaming pavement led into dark.

Bobbie Vander, dissolved deep in silver fur, slumped on the hardwood bench before the post office. Her hands were buried in pockets, her chin lost. Tiny pearls of drizzle were strung on her false eyelashes.

Beside her, hunched over, arms on knees, Dr. Benjamin Todd entwined his fingers in the children's game: "Here is the church; here is the steeple; open the door and see all the people."

On the wet sidewalk in front of them matched luggage was neatly stacked. And Todd's leather Gladstone.

He rose to pace nervously. He looked up the street for the bus to the airport.

"Sit down," she growled.

Obediently he sat on the bench next to her. He pulled up the collar of his raincoat.

"It's really coming down."

She turned to stare at him. "Did you expect it to go *up?*"

"I just meant—"

"I know what you just meant. Doc, let's get one thing straight from the start. You don't have to make conversation. Especially about the weather. You don't have to get the jits about waiting. You're going to spend half your life waiting. Just play it cool."

"Yes. Cool. All right. Are you hungry? We'll be able to get sandwiches at the airport."

"I know."

"We'll have to change in Boston."

"I know."

"We'll have forty minutes in Boston. Maybe we can get something to eat there."

They looked at each other. They were never, ever, going to hand-and-hand it into the sunset. It was going to be squabble-and-shout: some Cockney dish with more bone than meat, and more gristle than either.

She so nervy and alert: brittle; and he so solid and burly, loving. She was, he knew, a salt bitch. He was, she knew, a solemn clod. Their flicker had to be nursed and shielded from the wind.

She sighed. "Light me a cigarette." She took it from his shaking fingers. "Go on back, doc. It's not going to work."

"It *is* going to work," he said fiercely. "It's got to work. There's nothing here for me. Just with you. You're the only chance I've got."

She turned her eyes away, stirred by his nakedness. "Your funeral." She blew smoke up into the mist.

He wondered, acknowledging his hatred of death, if his love for her was not an admiration of her hard fearlessness. She had an impudent bravery; he could imagine that if told she was suffering from a fatal sickness, she might reply, "So?"

But there was more than that. There was his doctor's need to cure her pathology, simply to heal and make whole. In that sense she was his patient, and a challenge.

And there was her abiding sensuality that uncovered in him layers of fleshy delight he had never known existed, just as if a grown man suddenly discovered he had a gift for contrapuntal harmony or flying a kite.

He knew all this and he knew nothing. Except that he loved her. And he was unwilling to probe deeper, afraid that by endless peeling it might shrink, diminish, and come to naught. It was too precious, too fragile to expose to cold reason and the raw night air.

"What will we do?" he asked. "I mean after we check into the hotel."

"I'll call my manager. Tell him I'm back in town with the songs. We'll talk about finding a new accompanist. About rehearsals and taping. I'll have a meet with him and the agency people, and we'll go over the bookings. The tour. Plenty to do."

"For you. What about me?"

"You?" Laughing. "You can rinse out my undies."

He bent his back, clenched hands between his knees. "All right. I told you. Whatever you say."

She put a mild hand on his arm. "Take it easy, doc. I was ribbing you. Don't knot up. You'll sit in on everything. You'll be there. Just keep your mouth shut and follow my cues. Nod when I nod. Frown when I frown. Just follow me."

"Yes. I'll follow you."

They heard the mournful blast of the bus horn. Far up the street golden eyes winked, vanished, grew larger.

"This is it," he said.

"This is what?"

"It. What I've been waiting for. Needing."

She didn't answer.

She was a churn and thought it likely she might remain so for the rest of her life. She took both sides in an endless debate that seemed all rebuttal and no decision.

Caged so long by her own ego, she now sought to break out. But it was a new and threatening world. And just like the freed prisoner, she looked back with fondness at those dear, familiar bars, and she wondered.

Did she need? Could she give? Did she love? She was shedding her identity, and the new skin didn't yet fit. It rubbed and rasped her raw. She could appreciate her loss but barely glimpse what she might gain.

Worst of all was the loss of control, the handing over of her happiness to this hunched stranger who sat beside her in a black raincoat and cracked his knuckles. Who in Christ's name was he?

The Patroon had said we are all driven, and he may have been right. There was a stinging pleasure in that: willy-nilly doing what she had to do, denying her regret. My God, she was becoming as fatalistic as Ben!

Unless . . . unless the breaking out was a deliberate exercise of her own will, the need for something more, the soul's cry for nourishment even as a vitamin-starved body dictates a curious diet.

If that was so, then she was still master and no man's

creature. But then how account for the tenderness she felt, the obscene desire to sacrifice?

Her cigarette butt was burning her fingers. She flung it away angrily into the street. There was a brilliant shower of sparks. A glow blinked, then went out.

She was convinced their life together would be a special kind of hell. Change whirled her about and she hummed "The Fool's Love Song."

They sat without speaking. The airport bus rolled to a stop across the street. It was dappled with wet, the windows fogged. The door slammed open; the Negro driver stepped down and waited.

She stood. She opened her fur wide, then snugged it tightly about her.

"Bring the luggage," she ordered.

She walked quickly to the bus. Carrying the suitcases, he stumbled after her, and they went away.

---

# 44

Julie Vanderhorst wondered what it was like to awake with clean breath and a sweet tongue. She hoped for a morning without an ache that gripped her skull with an iron wig. She vowed each new day to postpone her first drink until noon.

But dawn brought dry heaves, biting gut, feverish eyes, a right hand that wavered uncontrollably. Nothing helped: pills, chalky pink liquids, early food, fruit juices—nothing. She could not sign her name before noon. So she did not wait.

She fought to keep that first swallow down. She took deep breaths, stalking about, hand on stomach, going, "Ooh. Aah." Another sip. "Ooh." Another sip. "Aah." The first drink disappeared like water, barely rinsing her mouth. The second brought a steady hand and scraped teeth.

The third made her normal. The fourth coined remorse. The fifth inspired philosophy: she had bad luck; that was the answer. And then came a slow game of solitaire. The cards were placed precisely, with little snaps.

Julie Vanderhorst, mummy in a soiled caftan, sat on the floor of her bedroom placing her pasteboards. She glanced at the window. Outside an angry fog writhed, but thinning. There would yet be sun, the washed-out sun of September. But it was a warm sun if you were naked and sheltered.

She had been eating less. After Rebecca left, family meals had been light. And since they were moving back to the big house on the weekend, no supplies were laid in. She nibbled celery and radishes, determinedly ate salads and lean meat. No more of Rebecca's cherry pies and brandy-soaked peaches.

But a thick bulge now fell onto her hipbones. Her waist was still good, but below and above . . . slack thighs and drooping breasts. Her flesh had lost elasticity. Poke with her finger and it remained poked for slow seconds before it filled out again. She was a lump.

Watery sunlight spilled across the floor. She grabbed up cards, oil, shaker, glass. She climbed to Rebecca's room and went out the window onto her tarred porch, her secret place. She was smiling.

There was cheesecloth across a flimsy blue sky. The sun was rimless, just glowing, a pale lemon swimming. But she could feel it, finally, muddling her.

The sixth drink brought forgiveness, the seventh forget-
fulness. All those to come made their own happy fantasies.
People and events dissolved in creamy clouds. Reality was
a deranged world where only lunacy was sane.

She touched herself, opening brown thighs to the hopeful
sun. Her skin crept to the cool breeze. But within was that
luxuriant fire to tingle and flick. Soft time stretched like
chocolate-covered caramel pulled between lips.

She drowsed away, swimming in the heat and swallowing
it. She was enjoying it all so much that the shock was
greater when fat tears spilled. Right down her cheeks they
rolled, seeking her open mouth and lapping tongue. Salt as
sea, those tears.

## 45

Thin tears squeezed from the eyes of Mrs. Grace Vanderhorst. She moved unsteadily about the white bedroom
that had been occupied by Hapgood Graves. She folded his
clothing, shuffled his papers and personal effects.

All were tucked away in his canvas suitcase and a carton
that had "H & L Peaches. With heavy syrup" printed on the
side. She had promised Roberta to ship everything to a
cousin of Graves in North Dakota. Roberta had taken only
the songs for the album and the empty silver filagree
pillbox, returned by the police.

Mrs. Vanderhorst sat heavily on the edge of the bed and
began to turn over papers. Her glasses slipped to the end of
her nose. She read slowly.

There were lines, verses, snatches of songs, unmailed letters, incomplete poems. There was a whole sheet of paper with but a single word on it: "finuish." Now what could that mean? There was a return airline ticket to New York, a five-dollar bill with a big red cross marked on each side in grease pencil. There was a funny little lapel button that said BE A GOOD GUY.

He had been such a talented young man. So artistic. Gifted. Yes, really gifted. God moved in mysterious ways. It was difficult to see how it all could be a blessing in disguise. As it undoubtedly was. But now who would bake apple pie for Mr. Vanderhorst just the way he liked it?

The church supper was only two days away and more place cards were needed. More twisted pipe cleaners. Perhaps she would make a laughing hyena. And moving back to the big house. So much to do now that Rebecca was gone. And the purple scarf to finish for the orphans in Ghana.

What was important was to take each task as it came. Not to doubt. Work hard and do one's duty. Be grateful for each day. Each hour. Life was a priceless gift and one must be thankful. There is a reason even if it is not granted to us to see it.

Now here was something strange: a folder of matches, and inside the cover Mr. Graves had written "Where are you?"

Directly below the room in which Mrs. Vanderhorst read and packed, sniffed and brooded, the Patroon lay awake in bed. His cane was alongside on the carpet, pills on the bedside table. He stared at the crackled ceiling, his mind as crazed.

All the dead. Mortal summer.

His mind slid away from the butchery. He recalled

Rebecca's shriek, power failure, stumble down the stairs and out into the wildness. Inside the Todd house, calling.

Then there was a lapse. He could not see, could not imagine. He was outside again with Rebecca, lantern swinging. The moiling sea, sound of drum. His blue-green son lifted high on a wave, dashed down and smashed. He remembered that.

Son dead. Rebecca gone. Susan Todd and Graves dead. Roberta gone with Todd. All, everything, dashed down and smashed. He could not believe this horror was the king's justice.

Wind still scoured the night sky. He heard the heavy sea punch endlessly at rock cliff and sand beach. There was a new moon, a ragged melon slice. All had the meaninglessness of the eternal.

But he was not eternal. Nor were those now dead and gone. Where was the import? He started over, hoping this time to find the clue. Rebecca's shriek. Power failure. Stumble down . . .

But perhaps it all began much sooner, years ago, in his youth or at his birth. Then he might accuse his parents, their parents, all who had come before. Then he might blame life itself, the condition of being human. But there was no blame.

He had always had a high sense of his own worth, but the violent events of the past week had diminished him, had diminished all men. Now he was one with those who had died in forgotten battles, for the glory of forgotten gods.

He would like to know one answer before he died. Not all answers, nor *the* answer, but one small answer. The question was "What is love?" But he was weary. He wasn't thinking straight.

Far inside his skull, in dim, wet reaches, something

began to sound, no louder at first than an Indian drum in a storm. It was a throb, thump, a pound that echoed the ocean's ancient measure.

Lucid, knowing what was happening to him again, he turned slightly. He reached toward the plastic bottle of pills on the bedside table. His hand stopped, hovered.

His son had committed base murder and paid for his infamy. Did he, Pieter Vanderhorst, have the courage to pay for his betrayal? Of wife, son, and the woman he loved. He could live, seek redemption through suffering. He could die, offer his life as atonement.

The blows were heavier now, and deeper. They racked his brain. They came faster. Soon, he knew, they would merge into one agonizing explosion of pain that would slam him into darkness. Even now the room was dimming, wavering. The drum was everywhere.

One trembling finger touched the plastic bottle, curled about it. He would . . .

"Mister Vanderhorst!" his wife cried. She came skipping into the room, laughing, weeping. Her wig was tilted; glasses slid down her nose. "He did it! I found it! He wrote it just as he promised he would! I found it in his things! Please listen to this, dear. It's called 'An Early American Valentine.' It says: 'Written by Mister Hapgood Graves and dedicated to Mrs. Grace Vanderhorst.' Now I'll read it to you:

'Come with me where roses nod
And sunbeams dance above.
Then I shall press thy hand in mine
And speak to thee of love.

Oh dearest, dare I hope to tell
All that thou meanst to me?

For thou hast won my heart to wear
For all the world to see.

Within that rustic bower, sweet,
I'll pledge my heart is thine;
And we shall dwell in Heaven if
Thou art My Valentine!'

Oh Mister Vanderhorst, isn't that the dearest, sweetest thing
you've ever heard?"
    But there was no answer.

# LAWRENCE SANDERS

## "America's Mr. Bestseller"

| | |
|---|---|
| __THE TIMOTHY FILES | 0-425-10924-0 — $4.95 |
| __CAPER | 0-425-10477-X — $4.50 |
| __THE EIGHTH COMMANDMENT | 0-425-10005-7 — $4.95 |
| __THE DREAM LOVER | 0-425-09473-1 — $3.95 |
| __THE PASSION OF MOLLY T. | 0-425-10139-8 — $4.50 |
| __THE FIRST DEADLY SIN | 0-425-10427-3 — $4.95 |
| __THE MARLOW CHRONICLES | 0-425-09963-6 — $4.50 |
| __THE PLEASURES OF HELEN | 0-425-10168-1 — $4.50 |
| __THE SECOND DEADLY SIN | 0-425-10428-1 — $4.95 |
| __THE SIXTH COMMANDMENT | 0-425-10430-3 — $4.95 |
| __THE TANGENT FACTOR | 0-425-10062-6 — $4.50 |
| __THE TANGENT OBJECTIVE | 0-425-10331-5 — $3.95 |
| __THE TENTH COMMANDMENT | 0-425-10431-1 — $4.95 |
| __THE TOMORROW FILE | 0-425-08179-6 — $4.95 |
| __THE THIRD DEADLY SIN | 0-425-10429-X — $4.95 |
| __THE ANDERSON TAPES | 0-425-10364-1 — $3.95 |
| __THE CASE OF LUCY BENDING | 0-425-10086-3 — $4.50 |
| __THE SEDUCTION OF PETER S. | 0-425-09314-X — $4.95 |
| __THE LOVES OF HARRY DANCER | 0-425-08473-6 — $4.50 |
| __THE FOURTH DEADLY SIN | 0-425-09078-7 — $4.95 |

Please send the titles I've checked above. Mail orders to:

**BERKLEY PUBLISHING GROUP**
390 Murray Hill Pkwy., Dept. B
East Rutherford, NJ 07073

NAME _____

ADDRESS _____

CITY _____

STATE _____ ZIP _____

Please allow 6 weeks for delivery.
Prices are subject to change without notice.

**POSTAGE & HANDLING:**
$1.00 for one book, $.25 for each
additional. Do not exceed $3.50.

| | |
|---|---|
| BOOK TOTAL | $_____ |
| SHIPPING & HANDLING | $_____ |
| APPLICABLE SALES TAX (CA, NJ, NY, PA) | $_____ |
| TOTAL AMOUNT DUE | $_____ |

PAYABLE IN US FUNDS.
(No cash orders accepted.)